THE BLACK HAT

Gabriola, BC Canada V0R 1X4

The Black Hat
ISBN 978-1-927755-90-7 (paperback)
ISBN 978-1-927755-91-4 (casebound)
ISBN 978-1-927755-92-1 (ebook)

Printed on acid-free paper that includes no fibre from endangered forests. Agio Publishing House is a socially responsible company, measuring success on a triple-bottom-line basis.

10 9 8 7 6 5 4 3 2 1

DEDICATED TO JUDY

THE BLACK HAT

BOOK ONE
of the
Noir Intelligence Series

A Novel

H.B. Dumont

CHAPTER 1

Alexandra Belliveau had forgotten how much she missed the serenity of the lowlands and the Ardennes. The swaying of the train and the cadence of the wheels on the tracks had lulled her to sleep as a child on those many trips she had taken with her mother, Maria, between Luxembourg City and Dieppe and other locations on the Normandy coast. There they had stayed for days, sometimes weeks. Something about the coach's warmth and movement also triggered memories of returning from trips to Montigny-lès-Metz, in the Moselle Valley, where they had stayed for several weeks.

As the train drew closer to Luxembourg, the signs announcing the stations – Namur, Libramont and Arlon – created context like an artist's preliminary brushstrokes on a blank canvas. The landmarks of the passing countryside and villages were becoming clearer as the ground mist retreated with the warmth of the mid-summer morning sun. Memories of her childhood were gradually revealed as if seen for the first time without the gnawing of incessant migraines. Yet the faint scent of ubiquitous trepidation and accompanying grief lingered.

Her *joie de vivre* from those childhood times had since been beset by the accumulation of hapless events that conjured a raft of unsolicited responses. Some were quiet but not quieting. All too often, she had heard it in the deafening silence and seen it in the blinding shards of muted memories.

There were nights when she did not sleep, would not allow herself to close her eyes. As long as she stayed awake thinking about her mother, she would not lose her or be left to fend for herself like a fawn that had witnessed a hunter take its mother. The law of the jungle. Rise to the circumstance or fall prey. She was her mother's daughter – *de l'audace, encore de l'audace, et toujours de l'audace* – audacity, more audacity, and always audacity.

She took a slow, deep breath to settle her uneasiness, but her doubts remained and with them, prolonged apprehension.

"The truths of those times are masked in the mists of the Moselle," her mother had said when Alexandra asked what her mother had done when she was younger. "Your roots and destiny are those of Charlemagne. In them you will discover your strengths and unearth the truths."

But at this moment, she was just thankful that the modern Eurail first class passenger cars were far more comfortable and had more amenities than the old coach cars of her childhood, a few of which were still standing on abandoned laybys. Were they purposely parked there as reminders, like poppies in Flanders Field, lest we forget those times?

Alexandra would soon realize just how prophetic and ominous her mother's words and these images were. The consequences of harrowing questions remain, decades after the event.

She had felt safe growing up in Luxembourg in the late 1950s and early '60s, living with her uncle and aunt who loved her as if she was their own daughter. But she was not. She missed her mother – her *Maman* – and yearned for the warmth of her touch during those long periods of separation. She mostly missed those tender moments when her mother would lovingly brush her hair while softly singing fairy-tale verses from her own childhood.

Her uncle and aunt had both been schoolteachers. He was proficient in maths, which ran in the family. Her mother could do mental gymnastics with numbers, as could Alexandra. Her aunt taught social sciences. Both tutored her after she returned from accompanying her mother on what were described as business trips.

Their home was situated in a middle-class district of

Luxembourg City on rue Michel Welter. The neighbourhood was south of the colossal fortification of the old city with its commanding cathedral adorned with knobby spires and turreted towers, sentinels which cast furtive shadows over the city.

During the Second World War, the old city had not suffered the level of devastation at the hands of the Nazi invaders that had befallen areas of Holland, Belgium and France. Her mother explained that the Nazis had spared Luxembourg because they believed it was part of the old pre-Westphalia Prussia and the inhabitants were closer Germanic cousins.

Alexandra knew that although Germany had been defeated, the Nazi Party had not. She had recently been involved in the investigation of a murder perpetrated by Fourth Reich neo-Nazis with links to the United States. This nefarious organization was well funded by anonymous sources with roots back to the Third Reich. Interpol had been involved in the homicide case spearheaded by the CIA because of a possible al-Qaeda terrorist connection to the Middle East. The case had become high profile since the 9/11 attacks on the World Trade Center and the Pentagon. MI6 was also tracking neo-Nazi activities.

She would later reflect on just how eerily predictive these events would be as her world became entwined in the habitual intrigue of global intelligence – espionage, and counterintelligence or spy-on-spy espionage. The latter was renowned for its frequently lethal consequences parlayed by agents of the CIA and MI6, and by her mother who had worked in French counterintelligence. These relationships would lure Alexandra and others into this deadly sphere like moths to a flame.

"Run! Run! That was the impossible shot. You saved my life." Her mother's words and images of her bloodied face filled Alexandra's memory with persistent flashbacks and haunting nightmares.

"Ticket, madame," the conductor asked. His demanding tone and looming presence amplified Alexandra's apprehension and made her heart pound. She stared at the imposing, bespectacled man who stood beside her. She squeezed an imaginary pistol grip as she gasped for breath.

"I'm sorry to have startled you, madame. Are you all right?" the conductor asked.

"Yes, I'm fine. Here it is."

The conductor could not help but note the alarm in her response. He forced a reassuring smile as he returned her Eurail pass.

Some memories are like arctic wolves, she thought. *You can lock them up but you can't silence their howls.*

⁂

HE GLARED INTO THE MIRROR, SPEAKING ALOUD although alone.

"I will wear the cherry red lipstick with my blonde wig. That is what I always wear when I enter because it makes me feel strong. I will do the same tomorrow. No one will recognize me but I will be able to identify Maria's daughter, Alexandra, and those last people on my list, Maria's friends from the *Maquis*."

He paused in gratified reflection.

"It was much easier to put them out of their misery when I was younger because I could do it all – the planning, the execution and the silent, disguised escape. But now I have to rely on a select few of my subordinates to hunt them down. Yet I can still complete the final solution. I have done it so many times over the years. I am a faithful Nazi, dedicated to the Fourth Reich that I have inherited. It is my sworn duty to put the others out of their misery, like all the female cats in the barn who lapped at my special milk. They were all weak but I am strong."

CHAPTER 2

The region defined much of who Alexandra was. Her mother often spoke of the hardships of the pre-war years and particularly of the Depression that she had experienced as a child. In contrast, Alexandra had grown up in what had been described as the golden fifty years of the latter part of the century. The standard of living in Western Europe had been on a steadily upward trajectory since the end of the war. American and Canadian military occupation forces and their families who lived in northeastern France close to the German border had provided a much-needed monetary boost to the economy or at least until President de Gaulle had, on very short notice, ordered the NATO occupation forces out of France in the mid '60s.

Her mother had been employed in some capacity with these Allies, although Alexandra never really knew what she did until later in life. They had money and Alexandra couldn't remember wanting for anything materially. Life with her mother was just transient and incomplete. Perhaps that was why she didn't mind continually moving in her own career as a forensic psychologist to Paris, Lyon, Bordeaux and, most recently, Amsterdam.

She enjoyed travelling to international conferences, particularly those in the United States. There she established a network of professional affiliations. She seized opportunities to broaden her experience which, in retrospect, had helped advance her career. But they had taken a toll on her marriage.

Work had become her partner, filling the void left by the absence of her husband. In the last several years, their relationship had deteriorated exponentially. It could best be described as turbulent and tempestuous. The echo of those routine quarrels persisted like a virulent infection.

When asked about her family, Alexandra responded, "Oh, the kids are doing fine. Collette, my daughter, is attending the Université de Paris pursuing a graduate degree in psychology. My son, Marc, is working in the aerospace industry."

And then she would pause momentarily before mentioning that her husband, André, was enjoying retirement after a career as a pathologist. She had realized that enjoying retirement was a safe response because there would be no follow-up enquiries but just smiles and perhaps a comment on how fortunate she was to have had such a wonderful, successful family life and how proud she must be of their accomplishments.

"Thank you," she would reply. "I am really quite blessed."

The conversation would move on. Few would detect the distance in her demeanour and the detached tone in her voice.

Ah, you are not perceptive, she would mutter to herself, *because if you were, you would know the bitter reality of my life.*

Sometimes the truth is best left unspoken.

Alexandra had a closeness with Collette beyond the maternal, something absent in her relationship with Marc. Like her mother had recognized in Alexandra that ancient gift of intuition, Alexandra knew that Collette had the aptitude to recognize the implicit.

While studying for an undergraduate degree in psychology, Collette posed questions to her mother that demonstrated the depth of her enquiry into the realm of the spiritual, often mystical. They had frequent debates on the merits of Freudian psychoanalysis and Jungian personality archetypes. More often, on the heels of these academic excursions into human behaviour, Collette would pause, occasionally in mid-sentence, and go down the White Rabbit's tunnel in search of the unknown.

Alexandra recognized these explorations because they had been part of her own escapism as a young girl. As she matured in her own career as a forensic psychologist, she had transformed these metaphysical abilities into the semi-structured discipline of investigative enquiry.

Like mother, like daughter, she ruminated. *Collette has inherited the gift.*

Pondering her immediate circumstances, she concluded that the retirement literature was accurate. We reflect on life as we approach the end of our working career, meandering from the present to the past and back again, and into the future. *Yes, some memories, like arctic wolves, do need to remain caged and silenced.*

But what would she do in retirement? Alexandra was certain she would not retire to muse like a monk or a nun. The thought of moving out of André's house in Paris and into a home of her own had crossed her mind on more than one occasion, and even more so recently.

She could move to the south of France. Although she had never been to Carcassonne in the shadow of the Pyrénées, her mother had told her stories about her grand-maman who had lived in that region during the war.

"In those times, your grand-maman travelled many nights between Narbonne and Carcassonne," her mother explained.

Alexandra had learned only recently that during the latter years of the war, her mother had worked alongside her grand-maman with the French Resistance, the *Maquis*, smuggling downed Allied pilots and air crew who were on the run from the Nazi SS across the Pyrénées to Spain. Sometime in 1943, her mother had moved to Courseulles-sur-Mer on the Normandy coast because her identity might have been compromised and revealed to the Gestapo by a collaborator. There, her mother stayed with a lady who was referred to as her aunt.

Meanwhile her grand-maman had moved to Ver-sur-Mer in Normandy half an hour west of Alexandra's maman. They felt that it was best to be detached in the event either identity had been revealed. The anxiety of separation had begun. They could still visit as circumstances allowed but it wasn't the same.

In Normandy her mother had established contact with an American agent of the Office of Strategic Services and other Allied military agents who were working with the French Underground to prepare for the Allied invasion the following year. In the latter months of the war, her mother had continued to work with the OSS and thereafter the CIA. These liaisons would start to affect Alexandra's life now in ways she could never have imagined.

Stories circulated about *le fantôme*, the ghost. Before her death, her grand-maman had briefly spoken to Alexandra about this elusive member of the *Maquis*, and of a police detective who had previously been part of the French Underground. After the war, *le fantôme* had possibly lived in Alsace-Lorraine close to the border with Germany and Switzerland.

Alexandra felt there might have been a post-war connection between *le fantôme* and this detective capitaine. Was it just a rumour? She never discovered the whole story.

Now that would be a great retirement challenge, she mused – *finding the truth, finding le fantôme.*

A shiver ran down her spine.

"You don't talk about what went on during those times."

The words of her mother and grand-maman resonated in her mind, once again reminding her of the need for uncompromising caution and attention to consequences.

⁂

"Bonjour" – *Hello.*

"J'écoute" – *I'm listening.*

"Я буду на связи - YA byl v kontakte." – *I have been in contact.*

"Да. Принято - Da. Priznannyy" – *Yes. Acknowledged.*

CHAPTER 3

On one occasion only, on the 50th anniversary of the beginning of the end of the war in Europe, did her mother allude to anything concrete about those times. It was 1994 and they were in Normandy attending the D-Day celebrations. Alexandra surmised that the sights and sounds of the celebrations had brought back some distant memories of those times that perhaps her mother had forgotten or had purposely stored in the deep recesses of her mind.

"A penny for your thoughts?" Alexandra recalled asking.

"Thoughts are precious and not for sale," her mother had replied.

Alexandra was content with the subtle message. Her mother had great wisdom and would spend many hours explaining why it was best to be more curious and less certain, to be more pensive and less provocative, and to pause and quietly reflect.

There were others who attended the 50th anniversary celebrations who appeared to have had similar experiences to her mother. Alexandra's inquisitive, intuitive mind had been working overtime on that day of celebration.

Had they known each other or worked together during the war? If these associations existed, they did not acknowledge them. Or was it their training to purposefully ignore?

They made subtle nods or fleeting eye contact. Alexandra had learned in her training as a psychologist to recognize such elusive but nonetheless telling behaviour.

These observations and brief remarks from her mother jogged other memories for Alexandra, alluding to some less explicit and more disquieting details of the past.

Her mother never spoke much about her father, only that he

might also have been with the *Maquis*. When Alexandra was in her early teens, her mother mentioned that she had inherited her sixth sense from her own father. It was what her mother called "a sensation of the mind."

Her mother had been correct. Alexandra had advanced quickly in her career as a psychologist and police profiler because she always listened to her intuition or her *shrew* as she called it. Coupled with her audacity, she had solved numerous cold cases, much to the chagrin of many of her male counterparts who could not fathom her uncanny skill in police investigations.

In their ossified, testosterone-laden minds there was no room for what they saw as whimsical, irrational girlish pursuits. Their discipline was objective. Their training was research-based in applied forensic science.

On those occasions when Alexandra was experiencing one of her sensations of the mind, a male colleague often quoted Joe Friday, the lead character in the American TV police detective series, *Dragnet* – "Give me the facts, ma'am, just the facts."

Alexandra knew that facts were essential and were derived from the science, but how you got the facts was a combination of the science and the sensations of the mind that she knew was wisdom older than consciousness itself. She would not attempt to defend her actions to her male colleagues. Instead, she would smile confidently, knowing that the combination of the two would enable her to identify the requisite knowledge. With this skill, she was able to engage in the conversations that mattered most to her superiors.

Thinking back, she realized she was the only woman in her training cohort but she didn't mind that. Because most criminals were male, she learned more about male motivation from her meandering in the recesses of the male mind. That exposure provided her with greater knowledge than anything she might have learned from becoming mired in the minutia of cleavage cackling, which tended to be the nattering pastime of narcissistic junior females. This self-assurance contributed to the determination she depended on at times like this.

With the thought of her pending retirement in the forefront of her mind, these recollections of happier times helped to soften the foreboding obligations that had consumed her since receiving the news of her mother's death. Until the conductor announced her destination, she would enjoy her memories in solitude.

The reality of the funeral and her duties as the executor of her mother's estate would impose themselves on her soon enough. More pressing was what she would say in the eulogy about her mother, Maria, a member of the secretive *Maquis*. After nearly sixty years, would it be permissible to talk about those times or were some things best left to subtle nods and glances?

"Luxembourg City!"

The conductor's sharp announcement jolted Alexandra out of the tranquility of her all-too-short trip down memory lane.

As the train came to a stop under the canopy, she gazed out of the window across the cavernous, abandoned roundhouse where old steam engines had been maintained from when travel was more leisurely and life was simpler. She saw the broken windows and faded smoke-stained red letters "Luxembourg" painted on a white background, now faded yellow, on the curving brick wall that had greeted passengers decades before.

Now a new roundhouse, set back from the tracks, had no welcoming message. Instead, a standard aluminum Eurail blue sign with white letters on the modern station platform announced the location.

New is good, she supposed, with some reservation.

There was a timelessness in the grandeur and elegance of the station's traditional Moselle neo-baroque revival architecture, with its high vaulted ceilings and a monolithic clock tower. A certain unspoken yet recognized sophistication and charm in what the French might describe as a *je ne sais quoi* was revealed in the refined traditional craftsmanship.

Practical affairs brusquely confronted her as she walked through the station's cathedral doors onto the bustling pedestrian-filled sidewalk adjoining the multi-traffic lanes of Place de la Gare.

It would have been comforting to have had some support at this time, she thought.

But André was unable to or simply chose not to accompany her for his own reasons. He had commented many times over the years that his mother-in-law was an interfering nuisance.

The reality was that Alexandra preferred to be far removed from the distraction of his presence. Privately, she referred to him as the emotional vampire. She was tired enough without having to attend to the droning of her husband's constant demands on her time and energy.

Collette and Marc would arrive in time for the funeral.

Her intuition told her that she would find strength elsewhere.

CHAPTER 4

Alexandra checked into the Hôtel Novotel on rue du Laboratoire, a short walk from the station. It was quieter because it was off the main thoroughfare and only a ten-minute walk to her appointment with Father Luke at l'Église du Sacré Coeur.

She stopped momentarily in front of the open doors of the cathedral. *The contradiction of faith,* she ruminated – to listen to her *shrew* or to the voice of her Catholic faith, her God.

Just inside the entrance were the familiar marble holy water fonts. She dipped her fingers in and crossed herself. Father Luke stood on her right.

"Come in, my child," Father Luke greeted her. "It has been too long since you have entered this house of God and received his blessing."

"Yes, Father, it has been a long time and I miss the peace which those benedictions had given me and my family. This House of God was a sanctuary for us in those challenging times."

"Then enter, my child, and you will find peace once again at this time of grief. Jesus brings comfort to those who suffer."

Out of habit, Alexandra walked to the pew where she had sat so many Sundays ago. She knelt and prayed briefly as Father Luke looked over her as a shepherd watches over his sheep. The familiarity and support brought her a deeper level of inner peace.

"Let us proceed to my office in the rectory."

Father Luke led the way to the front of the church, through the side entrance, into the courtyard that connected the church to the priest's house, and to the front door of the rectory.

Alexandra felt a little uneasy. Parishioners would only enter the priest's house via the back door where the housekeeper met them. The front door was reserved solely for high-level religious officials such as the bishop or other important community members including the mayor. Recognizing her uneasiness, Father Luke gave Alexandra a reassuring smile and motioned her to step inside.

They entered his office to the right of the vestibule. The walls were covered with photographs of Father Luke's predecessors. As she scanned the stoic poses, Father Luke commented that they reminded him of a rogue's gallery. Alexandra thought that they bordered the office like a priest's pantheon. She was drawn to the second to last photograph. The facial features and expression were similar to Father Luke's. But perception was just that, an individual interpretation.

The housekeeper entered with a tray of refreshments as they settled themselves around an antique mahogany table that showed the wear of many visitors. Father Luke described the service and asked whether she had any special requests for hymns or prayers that her mother particularly liked.

"Not really," she replied.

Alexandra hadn't given that aspect of the service much thought. Instead, she was hoping that it would be structured in such a way that she would only have to follow the order of service. Other funeral services she had attended appeared to be similar in format.

Father Luke mentioned he had received many inquiries about the date and time of the service. If that was any indication, he calculated that the service would be well attended with parishioners and friends locally and from other places where her mother had worked and established a network of contacts. These included the Normandy coast, the Moselle Valley, the Pyrénées region, the lowlands of Holland and Belgium, and Paris, in addition to England and the United States.

From the tone of his voice and from what he described,

Alexandra deduced that some attendees would be old associates from those earlier times in her mother's life.

Alexandra again pondered what she should say in the eulogy. Should she mention the *Maquis* or leave the past to the historians?

On the horns of this dilemma, she recalled her mother once saying, "There is more truth in stories than detail in facts." If she simply told a story about her mother, others could fill in the gaps in the facts as they wished.

As she left the rectory, she sensed that God and not her intuition, her *shrew,* had spoken. Her dilemma was resolved. The foreboding weight had been lifted. She would not mention the *Maquis* in her eulogy. She would, instead, leave history to the historians.

CHAPTER 5

"The funeral service was wonderful and the story you told about your mother was the most compelling eulogy I have ever heard," a rotund grey-haired gentleman commented to Alexandra at the reception. He then nervously extended his stubby hand to her.

"You may not remember me but I was your neighbour at 45, rue Michel Welter. I remember your aunt and uncle, your mother and you. Your mother was a kind, giving person, but a bit of a mystery, if I might say. Please do not hesitate to contact me if I can be of assistance to you during these trying times," he added.

She detected a slight disquiet in his voice. His eyes appeared to be searching for something she did not know.

"Ah, yes, I do remember you, monsieur. Thank you for your gracious words."

As she spoke, the image of an enigmatic, curious, almost comedic character from a Greek tragedy entered her mind.

Weird, she thought, *where did that come from? Perhaps from the stress of the day.*

"And your children, I briefly spoke with your son. You must be so proud of him as I am sure your mother would have been. I saw your daughter but have not yet had the opportunity to pass along my condolences. And your husband, I did not see him. But there are over one hundred who have come to pay their respects. It is understandable that I have missed him."

"Yes," Alexandra replied, "I have been blessed with my children."

As she paused to formulate a polite reason for André's absence, she was rescued by one of her close friends from Amsterdam who, seeing the awkwardness of the moment, imposed herself in the conversation.

"Alexandra, how are you? Oh, am I interrupting your conversation with this gentleman? I am sorry. Please forgive me. Perhaps we can chat later."

She gently squeezed Alexandra's hand as if to say, "Don't worry. I am here to protect you from prying questions."

Father Luke approached calmly yet deliberately.

"Excuse me, Alexandra, there is someone you must speak with in private," he said quietly.

Alexandra excused herself and followed Father Luke to a side office, as a sheep would follow the shepherd.

"May I introduce you to Madame Deschaume? She is an old acquaintance of your mother. It is important that you listen to what she has to say. I will leave you."

Father Luke's reserved demeanour in the short introduction left Alexandra with an ominous feeling. This time, it was her *shrew* and not her God speaking to her.

"Please call me Simone," Madame Deschaume said in a soft voice that had a mysterious inflection.

"I am old – almost 78 – and my doctor tells me I do not have many more seasons on this Earth. That is why I must tell you of the days when I first met your mother in Carcassonne. You must realize we were very young then. I was just fifteen and your mother could not have been any older. Being so young, the Nazis were less likely to suspect we were part of the French Resistance. Did your mother mention it is still not wise to talk of those times?"

"Yes, she did, many times," Alexandra responded.

"You must be very careful with what I am about to tell you. Do you understand?"

"Yes, I do. Please carry on."

"Let me take you back to 1943. It was the way we were in those times. We did not tell each other who we were or where we lived. We often used a *nom de guerre*, a war name, so if one of us was captured and tortured by the Gestapo, we could not divulge the identity of others in the Resistance, the *Maquis*. Then came a time when many of us were being captured and executed by the Nazi SS. Someone had betrayed us. We never knew for sure, not even if it was a man or a woman. A downed RAF pilot was in our protection at the time. Your mother and I helped him cross the Pyrénées to Andorra. From there, others guided him into Spain, Basque Land and eventually back to England. He named the mysterious collaborator *Thon*. He said in English the word 'thon' was an abbreviation for 'that one.' Thereafter, we just used the expression, Thon, when referring to this betraying collaborator."

"Was Thon from the south of France, the Midi-Pyrénées region?" Alexandra asked.

"We never really knew but some suspected that Thon might have been from Alsace-Lorraine, close to the border with Germany. I later heard that Thon might have had family in southern Germany around Baden-Baden, or possibly Metz. You may recall from your history lessons in school that during the period of the Franco-Prussian War in 1870, family alliances changed as the borders moved. Even today, those deeply held beliefs influence behaviours and guide the unspoken word."

Alexandra's face confirmed her understanding and appreciation of the gravity of what Madame Deschaume had just revealed to her.

Simone continued, "Did your mother mention *le fantôme*?"

"Yes, she did, and so did my grand-maman, but only briefly."

"None of us ever met *le fantôme* but we were told by others that *le fantôme* did not believe that Thon was from Midi-Pyrénées because his accent was too harsh, perhaps Prussian or Swiss-German. But I never knew for sure. It was very confusing and during uncertain times that was dangerous, not knowing or knowing too much.

It was just before the Gestapo raids that a few of us became aware of the danger. We all moved away quickly, your mother to the Normandy region. I never knew where your grand-maman went. I only knew about your mother because I also left Carcassonne for the Normandy coast, to Le Havre. Your mother and I had some communication when preparing for the Allied invasion that took place in June 1944."

"I heard there was an American who parachuted into Normandy," Alexandra queried.

"Yes, you heard correctly. This American was an OSS officer. The OSS was the Office of Strategic Services which, after the war, became the American CIA. Those were dark, menacing times."

"*Le fantôme*. Do you know what happened to him? And Thon...?"

"I have no hard proof but was told that *le fantôme* was in the Alsace-Lorraine region still looking for Thon, as were others, but that was a long time ago when you were a baby. I also heard that Thon was stalking female members of the *Maquis* and murdering them. That is why we were always careful not to talk of those times. And you, Alexandra, must also be very wary for your own safety and for the sake of your family. We believe that Thon may be still alive. Thon would be closer to my age and, if he's alive, he's still dangerous. That is why I am telling you this."

"I didn't understand the magnitude of the threat," Alexandra reflected. "My mother just warned me not to talk of those times."

"You may hear about a member of the *Maquis* who became a policeman after the war. I heard he became a very good investigator, but alcohol became his nemesis and ultimately sabotaged his early career. His nightmares of those times during the war may have haunted him too often. He solved many cases because he had a special knack for finding criminals. He may have crossed paths with other former members of the *Maquis* but I cannot confirm this."

"Do you know if my mother knew him?"

"She may have, perhaps well. Your mother became a French Intelligence operator after the war and worked with the Allies, mostly Americans, Canadians and British, initially hunting Nazi war criminals. Later, she became involved in French Counterintelligence and Counter-terrorism. I believe she maintained contact and worked closely with the American OSS officer she met in Normandy in 1944 when he joined the CIA. She also worked with a British MI6 agent."

"Thank you so much for telling me this information, Madame Deschaume. I can now appreciate the need for sensitivity and caution. I never knew exactly what my mother did. All this makes sense now. It explains the reason for all the moves and the mysterious business trips to the Moselle Valley and Normandy, and the occasional trip to the south."

"I saw you and your mother in Normandy in 1994 at the 50th anniversary. Your mother and I did not speak or even acknowledge each other for fear that Thon might be there and stalking us. He may be here, today. It is bad to still live in fear after all these years. That is why we do not talk of those times and I caution you, Alexandra, to be very careful."

A cold shiver ran down Alexandra's spine at the possibility of Thon being there.

"Yes, I remember seeing you, and that my mother reminded me to be wary on our way to Normandy and again when we left."

"Your mother and I met several weeks after the anniversary celebration at her request. I promised her I would tell you the story of those times and about Thon, if she died before me. That is why we are talking now. Father Luke was to be our liaison."

Simone stood up and with a reassuring smile, extended her

gloved hand. As Alexandra felt her firm grip, she thought, *Madame Deschaume, you are a lady of elegance. You may be frail in body now but you would have been a force to be reckoned with in your youth, and even today. Thon would be wise not to tangle with you.*

Alexandra thanked her for passing along missing pieces of the puzzle from those times.

CHAPTER 6

By the time Alexandra returned to the funeral reception, some of the attendees had left. She spoke with Collette who told her that those who departed had passed along their condolences and signed the guest book with brief messages.

Alexandra paused to glance at some of the notes and gather her thoughts after the encounter with Madame Deschaume and before engaging with other guests.

"AV, how are you?"

Alexandra's heart immediately jumped as she caught her breath. There was only one person who had ever called her AV and that was when she was thirteen years old, temporarily living in Montigny-lès-Metz on one of those extended business trips she had taken with her mother. Could it be? She looked up and saw an older yet still youthful and strikingly handsome man who had been her first puppy love.

His dress and deportment were exquisite and complemented his confident six-foot muscular physique. She was struck by his clothes, a tailored Yves Saint Laurent and Pierre Bergé-designed suit, Egyptian cotton French cut white shirt complete with pearl cuff links inlaid with miniature gold Eiffel Towers and a matching gold and pearl tie tack attached to a silk tie. He might have just walked off a fashion runway in Paris, Rome, London or New York.

She recognized superior quality in men's clothing from boutiques along the Champs-Élysées whose proprietors greeted sophisticated shoppers. This level of quality was in stark contrast to André's bohemian peasant wardrobe of mismatched frayed polyester clothes purchased from aisles of on-sale racks in second-hand warehouse outlets. To even suggest that André's taste in clothing was *via media* would be a huge exaggeration. His investment in their mismatched marriage was also polyester and frayed.

"Paul," she gasped with astonishment. Her immediate urge was to hug him but she held out her hand instead.

"How are you? How did you know about the funeral? Did you travel far? Do you have time to get together before you have to leave?"

She had so many questions. The surge of adrenaline from hearing his voice and seeing him again had excited her in a way she only imagined in those fantasy-filled private moments. She felt a blush on her cheeks and neck that she had not experienced for many years.

She realized she was still holding his hand. Her palm was moist. There would have been an advantage in wearing gloves, like Madame Deschaume, to mask the emotions on such occasions, if not just to be elegant. But she had not broken eye contact either and you could not mask those emotions with a glove, well perhaps with sunglasses, but not inside a church reception hall.

Her thoughts were racing, as was her heart. She needed to regain her composure but that meant letting go of his hand. She did not want to let go.

Here she was, like an awkward teenager, not knowing how to respond maturely to strong hormonal urges.

Paul's immediate thought upon seeing her after all these years was *foxy lady!* But that would remain a thought for the moment. He too was oblivious about their extended handshake and mutual eye contact.

With an almost critical tone, Alexandra asked, "Why didn't you reply to my letters? I wrote to you several times." Her question was terse and rebuffed him in one respect but was as inclusive as an endearing hug in another.

"I did reply but only to one letter. Why didn't you answer my letters?" he asked in an equally assertive manner.

"Because I didn't receive any replies to my letters. I thought you didn't reply because you didn't care or weren't interested," she shot back. "Did you address them to our home at 47, rue Michel Welter here in Luxembourg?"

Paul acknowledged the tattered piece of paper that Alexandra had written her rue Michel Welter address on all those years ago. Its existence in his wallet had been a talisman throughout the decades that marked their separation.

"Yes, that was the address you gave me just before you and your mother left Montigny-lès-Metz. I've kept it with me after all this time, with the faint hope that we would meet again. This morning, just before the funeral, I walked by your home. It was dilapidated and the shutters were broken. It looked abandoned. I didn't know what had happened to you."

"There are other guests I must speak with, Paul. Do you have time to meet later this evening?"

"Yes, of course. Where?"

"Do you know the courtyard where the Hôtel de Ville is, in the old city centre across the Viaduct?"

"I can find it," he assured her.

"Across the courtyard, opposite the Hôtel de Ville, there is a coffee shop and restaurant, the Café Kaempff-Kohler. It is beside Café Beim Rénert. Can you meet me there for dinner?"

"Yes. What time?"

"How about 7:00 p.m.?"

"I'll be there."

Alexandra took a moment to compose herself before speaking with other guests but found herself distracted by the brief encounter with Paul and the prospect of an evening rendezvous with her first love.

"Who was that you were talking to, Maman?" Collette asked.

"An old friend, a colleague, we worked on a case together, and he was bringing me up to date on some recent facts that have come to light. We'll need to meet after the reception so I won't be able to have dinner with you and Marc at the hotel."

She was always evasive when responding to questions about her work and associates so she had no problem being elusive now with Collette.

"That's all right. We don't have to meet, Maman. Marc said he had to leave and I met a friend who has invited me out to dinner. Is that fine?"

"Yes, that's fine, dear, but be especially careful. Now go and have a wonderful time. It's been a long day for you."

Collette paused, tilted her head slightly and stared at her mother. "You have always asked me to be careful and I respect that. But rarely have you told me to be especially careful. Is there a particular reason? Is there something I should know?"

Alexandra reached out and firmly took hold of her hand. Collette recognized the gesture and the inherent message. There were other times when she had known that she needed to raise the radar higher and be more aware of her environment.

Collette never asked why but she knew caution was in order. That was part of her life, living under the same roof as a forensic psychologist who worked on gruesome criminal cases. Her mother kept most work at her office, but there were times when the cases closed in on their home like the hordes approaching the ramparts of the castle. During those times her mother would remind her that she needed SA – situational awareness.

As Collette turned to leave, she motioned to her mother.

"I almost forgot. A distinguished elderly English gentleman gave me a letter and told me to give it to you personally. He was adamant that I was not to leave it but to hand it to you. He emphasized "personally." So here it is. He said you would understand. He also wrote a condolence note in the guest book and signed it, Group Captain.... I can't remember his name. But there were some initials after his name. They may have related to the military. Thinking back now, Maman, I felt that he might have known Grand-maman, perhaps during those times. When he shook my hand, there was something there. You know, the feeling."

"Thank you, dear. Now have a good time, and...."

Collette cut her off politely. "Yes, Maman, I know. I'll be careful, extra careful."

Alexandra put the letter in her pocket. She would read it later when she was less distracted.

After the last guest departed, she gathered up the other letters and cards and the guest book and thought to herself, *Another time constraint has been lifted from my shoulders and I'm now free to meet with Paul.*

Remaining on the to-do list was a big task – dealing with the estate, but it had no looming timeline, as she was both executor of the estate and sole beneficiary. She should send thank you notes to all those who left their condolences with their addresses. But that could wait too.

She took a deep breath then noticed Father Luke silently watching her. He approached and she thanked him for all his assistance, and especially for the introduction to Madame Deschaume. She spoke no further about what Simone had told her but sensed he knew that what needed to be said had been relayed.

He gave Alexandra a final blessing before she departed and reminded her she was one of God's special children.

Did he know of her talents to differentiate the good from the bad? Was he aware of her attuned intuition, her *shrew*? Was that the reference to "special" in his blessing?

The reception had taken longer than anticipated because of her meeting with Madame Deschaume. In addition, the large number of people who wished to speak with her in person extended individual conversation times.

The setting sun was casting long shadows as Alexandra departed. She walked briskly back to her hotel to shower and change. Immediate and most important decisions had to be made. What would she wear to meet Paul? Should she wear slacks or a dress? Or should she select a skirt and blouse with a jacket? After all, she was a professional lady with a long and distinguished career. Which shoes should she wear? She had not brought many with her. What should she do with her hair? Did she have time to shampoo and curl it? There was a hairdresser just around the corner from the hotel. And what about earrings or a necklace?

She was fretting like a nervous schoolgirl about to go on her first date. She didn't have to worry about all these things living with André because he never noticed and certainly never complimented her on her appearance. His manners were like his wrinkled, frayed polyester suits.

CHAPTER 7

As Paul sat waiting for Alexandra at the Café Kaempff-Kohler, a little girl walked across the square with her parents. The image flashed before him of another little girl lying face down in a ditch, her thin arms tied behind her back with barbed wire that had ripped into her wrists, and her light blue dress stained with blood that had oozed out of a bullet hole in the back of her head. His mouth dried as his heart began to pound, battling for space with his lungs that fought back in his ever-tightening chest cavity.

Du calme, du calme, he repeated to himself as he took slow deliberate breaths in an attempt to wrestle for possession of his mind and soul. He felt light-headed. In the depth of such mental duels, he was unable to recall a solitary image of his puppy love. Yet he could describe every vivid detail of the emaciated little girl in the blood-stained light-blue dress. He searched desperately for a distraction.

There it was. Alexandra was approaching. The setting sun created a glowing halo around her chestnut hair and accentuated every contour of her supple physique. Her luminous eyes captivated him. Her natural beauty absorbed him. Her closeness excited him. Her subtle scent embraced him. He stood and kissed her cheeks as they briefly embraced. Her presence replaced the image of the little girl in the light-blue bloodstained dress. He pulled the chair out for her.

Such etiquette was unknown to André, Alexandra lamented. How long had it been since she felt cared for in any special way? How long had she yearned for such a cherished moment even if fleeting? Was it just in fairy tales? She had retreated into the security of that sanctuary of make-believe often as a child and many times as an adult. But childhood fairy tales were just that, to be replaced by reality.

"You look wonderful, AV."

"Do you remember, Paul, when you first called me AV?"

"I certainly do. When we first met in Montigny-lès-Metz all those years ago, I called you *mon petit chou-fleur* – my little cauliflower."

"You have an excellent memory. I told you in no uncertain terms that I was not yours and I was not a cauliflower."

"Yes, you certainly did. You then explained that your name was Alexandra Vanessa and that you had been named after your grand-maman. I replied that Alexandra Vanessa was a mouthful, so I would just call you AV."

"Again, I compliment you on your memory. My job would be much easier if everyone I met had such accurate recall. I liked AV because it made me feel special. After that turbulent first *rencontre*, I liked you much better. You were the only one to ever call me AV, so when you greeted me as AV at the funeral reception, I was taken aback. I hope I didn't appear impolite. If I did, I apologize."

"On the contrary," Paul replied, "you were just as I imagined after all these years, gracious, elegant, and, if I might add, most attractive. I was taken aback as much if not more than you were. You just mentioned that your job had to do with people's memories. What have you been up to?"

"Please, you start, Paul. But first, how much time do you have? I have all evening as my children told me after the funeral service they have made their own plans for this evening. My son lives a carefree Pompeii life and my daughter less so but still quite independent."

"I don't have anything on my schedule either. Shall we order dinner before we start so we won't be interrupted? Between the two of us, we have about eighty years to catch up on! Have you eaten here before and, if so, what do you recommend?"

A gentleman asking me what I recommend, she thought to herself. *This start to the evening is showing definite promise.*

"I recommend the beef bourguignon."

"One of my favourites," Paul replied. "You have excellent taste. And a wine, what is your favourite?"

"I've been exploring Burgundies, lately," Alexandra responded. "I lived in Dijon some time ago and gained an appreciation for the Pinot Noirs from the Morey St-Denis and Chambolle-Musigny districts. The Côtes du Rhône produces some superlative wines from just a few small vineyards. Well, there is some production of Pinot Noir in Alsace and the Loire Valley but they're not really comparable to those of Burgundy. What tempts your palate, Paul?"

"I'm impressed. We're too much alike. I've never lived in Dijon, but I spent several vacations touring the region from Gevrey-Chambertin south to Nuits-Saint-Georges. I've always enjoyed Pinot Noir, especially those from the higher elevations of the Côte d'Or that used to be reserved for the kings. Even Napoleon knew where the best wines from Burgundy could be found, and before him, the Cistercian and Benedictine monks knew the secrets of the calcium-rich soil. So that's settled."

"You know your wines. I've also hiked those slopes," Alexandra acknowledged with admiration in her voice.

"We can consider after-dinner drinks with our coffee and dessert. I see on the menu that they serve Rémy Martin. May I recommend this cognac if the occasion allows, perhaps with crème brûlée?"

"Absolutely."

She could not recall any time in her marriage when André had asked her what she liked. Instead, he just ordered whatever he wanted. For wine, he had a *patois* palate, always ordering a *verre de vin*, a glass of the house wine. André never knew what brandy tasted like, let alone cognac or an excellent cognac like Rémy.

He never once acknowledged her certification as a credentialed sommelier.

"Well then, let me begin, AV. The philosopher, Søren Kierkegaard, said that life must be understood backwards, but it must be lived forward. So, I'll start in Montigny-lès-Metz. You may remember that my father was a policeman in Montigny. Sometime after you and your mother left, he was promoted and we moved to Strasbourg. He did quite well there and was quickly promoted to capitaine. We then moved to Paris where he finished his career in the Criminal Investigation Division."

"How long has he been retired?" Alexandra asked.

"Let me think. Ahhh… it has been too long for me to recall exactly. Why do you ask?"

"It's nothing, sorry for interrupting," Alexandra gently replied. "Carry on."

"I attended the Université de Paris and completed an undergraduate degree in biochemistry. I liked the sciences but wanted another interest so I took courses in Latin and Greek studies. I really enjoyed reading the Greek tragedies – Homer's *The Iliad* and *The Odyssey* and so on. Learning Latin actually helped me with my French grammar that had only been fair until I entered university. But I digress."

"I'm intrigued with your love and knowledge of the ancient arts and culture," Alexandra exclaimed.

"I worked for a few years in a chemical lab before returning to university where I completed a graduate degree in biochemistry, specializing in pathogens carried in human blood. I graduated at the top of my class and was offered a job working in the police crime laboratory. I think my father may have had an influence. But I didn't mind his meddling because I was able to work in a field that I enjoyed and was good at. I ultimately completed a PhD, part-time while working. I just retired a couple of weeks ago. I'm actually on retirement leave for the next several weeks."

Not wanting to interrupt his story but seeking clarification, Alexandra asked, "Did you ever hear of *le fantôme* in the Moselle Valley or Alsace region who might have been with the French Resistance, the *Maquis*, during the war?"

"It sounds vaguely familiar. I think I might have heard rumours but never knew for sure. Although my memory is good, it's not that good. There was someone in the police station in Montigny-lès-Metz who was a bit different, according to my father. He had a special knack for solving cases and might have been working on a case involving the *Maquis*. When we were in Paris, I think my father spoke about it a few times. He might know more. Why do you ask?"

"Just an interest," Alexandra answered nonchalantly. "Where is your father now?"

"He's in Paris in a seniors' home. His health is poor after years of smoking and a diet too high in cholesterol. I'm surprised that my mother and I didn't die of lung cancer from all his second-hand smoke. He has the constitution of an old bull. Analyzing a sample of his blood would be a case and a half."

Paul paused for a sip of wine while gazing at Alexandra over the brim of his wine glass. Her beauty consumed the moment that lingered in boundless space. He had neither seriously looked at nor felt such attraction to another woman since taking his wedding vows. His thoughts at this moment were with his young love all those years ago and their first kiss. But they were just reflections of another time. He gathered his thoughts.

"I'm married with a couple of kids. My wife, Suzette, had been a lab technician but didn't work after she became pregnant. She was just content to stay at home and do nothing much except spend all my money shopping for what I don't really know."

He refilled Alexandra's goblet and then his own. *This lady is so beautiful, physically, yes, but also mentally, spiritually and emotionally beautiful,* he thought. *I won't mention that I get more satisfaction examining a sample of blood in a petri dish under a microscope than looking at Suzette.*

Noting an enquiring expression on Alexandra's face, he continued.

"To keep active, I run marathons. I got interested when I was studying Greek culture in my undergraduate days. I travelled to Athens one summer and got the bug after visiting the Acropolis and Apollo's temple."

With a chuckle he admitted, "Lately, it takes me a bit longer to get my second wind at the start of a marathon and a bit longer at the end to recover my first breath."

Alexandra found herself quietly smiling in appreciation of the moment that she wanted to extend to infinity. But she needed to remain connected to the conversation.

"I've toured Athens and Santorini myself while attending conferences," she commented. "I've often thought of returning for a more relaxed holiday. Do you still visit Greece and the Mediterranean Islands on holiday?"

"I haven't for many years. Suzette doesn't like to travel. She came with me once but spent the entire trip complaining about the food and the heat and the boredom."

"You've had a busy life," Alexandra noted, while inwardly admiring his quest for experiential knowledge, akin to her own aspirations. "I'm surprised that we haven't crossed paths in our professions or at least on the slopes of the Côtes du Rhône."

"Running marathons was actually a stress reducer. It gave me the chance to collect my thoughts. In my spare time, I also fenced. I was actually pretty good at it. For a few years, I was on the French National Fencing team. I still have my foil but I think that my eldest son lost most of my clothing including my mask. Or he pawned it off. Somewhere in the house, I have a box full of medals and trophies. I used to have them on display. Suzette complained that they just gathered dust, so they ended up in boxes in a closet."

"I'd be honoured to see them should the opportunity present itself," Alexandra commented, admiring his accomplishments.

"If I wasn't running marathons, I immersed myself in the arts. It's so much easier to appreciate music, literature and the arts when you walk the same streets as Mozart, Voltaire and Monet." He failed to mention that he submerged himself in any activity that would give him an excuse to get out of the house and away from Suzette.

"So, that's it, AV, a pretty boring life. Now on the eve of retirement, I don't know what I'll do. I don't have any outside interests or hobbies. I suppose that I could coach aspiring Olympians in the art and science of the foil."

"Hardly a boring life," she responded in astonishment. *He's cultured and charming, the complete opposite of André,* she reflected with remorse.

God, this lady is lovely, Paul pondered, as he gazed into her eyes. The evening was in its infancy, yet it seemed he had known her for eternity and beyond. She was a Greek goddess with the beauty of Helen of Troy. Homer was correct. Helen's beauty could launch a fleet of a thousand ships. AV's beauty could launch a thousand fleets, each with a thousand ships.

Paul broke the meditative richness of the moment. "To answer your question about how I knew about the funeral, it was my father who heard from his colleagues that your mother had died. He told me, well asked me, if I could attend the funeral on his behalf and extend our family's respect. When he posed the request, memories of Montigny-lès-Metz came flooding back. I jumped at the opportunity, hoping that you would be there and might still remember the good times we had. To be honest, I always carried your address in my wallet in anticipation that we would meet one day, and here we are. I've been blessed. I'll report back to my father whose memory is fading now with early dementia, but he can certainly remember the past. Ask him about a case he worked on twenty years ago or longer and he'll tell you every detail. So, AV, what have you been up to?"

⁂

"Bonjour, c'est Aulne" – *Hello, this is Aulne.*
"J'écoute" – *I'm listening.*
"Она встретила кого-то. Мужчину, которого знала в прошлом. Фотография отправлена. Мне нужна будет помощь в следовании за ним" – *She has met someone. A man she knew from her past. Photograph being transmitted. I will need assistance to follow him."*
"Да. Принято" – *Yes. Acknowledged.*

CHAPTER 8

"It's uncanny, Paul," Alexandra exclaimed. "We share more than the same tastes in superb cuisine and fine wine."

She took a moment to collect her thoughts. She had only one friend with whom she could be this honest and relaxed in conversation. Now there were two.

"Let's go back to the last time we lived in Montigny-lès-Metz, when we met," she directed. "After we left for Luxembourg, I really did write to you, Paul, several times. It's important that you know I did write. I don't know what happened." With compassion and a sense of urgency in her voice, she leaned forward and said earnestly, "It's important you believe me, Paul."

Looking into her eyes, he responded in an equally sincere tone, "I do believe you, AV. And it's important you know I wrote to you, also."

Alexandra nodded and took a deep breath before continuing. "We returned to Luxembourg where I lived with my mother's brother and his wife. With my mother, I lived in an enchanted world. But my uncle and aunt raised me as their own child ever since I was born because my mother was constantly travelling. For a long time, I never knew what my mother did for a living but I'll get to that later. The older I got, the less I accompanied her. She said I had a good head on my shoulders and could look after myself but she still phoned me when she was on her business trips."

"So, was it your uncle's house on rue Michel Welter or your mother's?" Paul asked.

"It belonged to my uncle, initially. He was a wizard with numbers. This allowed him to master the art and science of financial investments that, in turn, brought considerable return on investments into the home. My aunt had equal proficiency in the real estate market which also translated into profit, including several lucrative rental properties they held. I think their finesse at business motivated them more than their teaching. I loved the conversations around the dinner table, and they went out of their way to involve me in discussions. I learned more about life from those two than from school."

Alexandra paused and took a slow deep breath which Paul could not help but notice. He joined her in her quiet space.

Her voice broke slightly as she continued. "Shortly after I started my graduate degree, my uncle and aunt were killed in a car accident by an impaired driver. I almost lost it but somehow kept myself together. They were my guardian parents as much as my mother was my mother, if that makes any sense."

"It makes perfect sense."

After a pause, she continued.

"I gained some solace from the fact they died together. They were so much in love that I cannot imagine how one would have survived without the other. They were not two peas in the same pod but the same pea, one with the other. I thought that was what married life was supposed to be. But I was wrong. They were the rare exception."

Paul bowed in sympathy of her devastating loss.

Alexandra took a long sip of wine before continuing. "Their estate was considerable. My mother inherited the house on rue Michel Welter and I received all their rental properties and investments. About five years ago, I sold all the properties before the market took a downturn. In retrospect, it was a good business decision."

"How did the house end up in such a dilapidated condition?"

"It's an interesting story that will get even more interesting. I never knew all the details, as my mother never told me everything.

There is a mystery there because of the connection to her work. Let me continue in some sense of chronological order."

Paul nodded sagely as he refilled her glass while gazing into her hazel eyes, which triggered a warm, captivating smile.

"I completed my undergraduate degree in psychology and criminology and, like you, worked a bit to gain experience before completing a graduate degree, also in psychology. The effect of culture on psychology captivated me so I ended up branching out into the history of Mediterranean cultures. That was when I attended conferences in Athens and Santorini. I spent several months island hopping around the Aegean Sea. My first summer job was working in a community liaison role with one of the police precincts in Paris. That led to other work experience in policing which got me interested in the psychology of criminology. That, in turn, ultimately led me to a career in forensic psychology among other things."

"It's amazing that our paths never crossed," Paul interjected. "We were like ships passing in the night. If I spent summers in Greece and you were island hopping in the Aegean, we must have travelled on parallel elliptical orbits, sampling similar cuisines and wines, perhaps in the same restaurants."

Paul's assessment of their summer sojourns allowed Alexandra to prepare for a less passionate and more painful summary of her life.

"I had just started a PhD when I met my husband, André. He was twelve years older and established in his career as a pathologist. He came from a stable family and had lived all his life in one house just northeast of Paris. This ordinariness is probably what drew me to him, having lived an extraordinary life with my uncle and aunt, and my mother. Getting married to André was not one of my better decisions. I had completed all my course work and passed the comprehensives for my PhD but then I got pregnant with Marc and dropped out of the program. Collette came along two years later."

"Did you ever complete your doctorate? It would have been a shame to have gone that far without completing the final stretch."

"Yes, I did. Once the kids were in school and I had more time, I returned to my studies and finished the PhD in psychology. I completed my practicum with a psych firm in Paris. My mentor was a fellow by the name of Frederik Jorgensen who had contracts with the Préfecture de police de Paris, the Police nationale and the Gendarmerie nationale to work as a forensic profiling psychologist on some of the most bizarre criminal cases. I accompanied him on a few cases, which I found fascinating. When I graduated, Fred hired me and I continued to work on other forensic profiling cases."

"So, when you said you wished everyone had memory recall like mine, I now understand. Do you teach about the psychology of memory?"

"Yes, in a way. My second vocation was teaching psychology at different universities. I started working full-time as faculty but am now part-time by choice. I hold positions as adjunct faculty at a few institutions, including the University of Amsterdam where I currently live. In my dual careers, I moved while André stayed in Paris, so ours became a progressively more distant relationship as the years passed. My son, Marc, stayed with his father while my daughter, Collette, wanted to move with me. That just happened to work out."

"And outside interests?" Paul enquired. "Did you return to your island hopping in the Aegean?"

"From my travels I gained an appreciation of the wine from different districts. I can say with confidence that Greek wines may have been highly sought after when Socrates wandered the streets of Athens but they certainly don't rank in the top ten today! Now French wines are another matter. They tweaked my interest and increased my penchant for the fruits of the regional vines, especially Pinot Noir. I ultimately received my certification as a sommelier from the Union des Sommeliers."

"Ahhhh… a lady of exquisite elegance who can distinguish the vines of virtuous vintage from the ones with vague roots."

Paul graciously acknowledged Alexandra's endorsement of the Pinot Noir they had agreed upon to pair with the dinner.

"Now I have an apartment near the Van Gogh Museum of Amsterdam in the old part of the city on Amstel overlooking the canal. It's actually owned by a friend who had to move in with her elderly mother. It's only a fifteen-minute walk to the university where I teach two classes per week. I continue to consult with select police departments as a forensic profiling psychologist. I'm so busy that I don't have much time to return to Gagne where André lives. That's where he grew up. Are you familiar with that region of greater Paris?"

"I know where Gagne is but my travels have never taken me there. I live on the southwest side of Paris. I'm actually more familiar with the Amstel district of Amsterdam. I've stayed at the Hampshire Rembrandt Square Hotel several times because it's close to antique shops."

"To sum up this short account of my life, Paul, I'm thinking of retiring from teaching and maybe from consulting altogether. I don't have to work, as I'm financially independent. I just like keeping my mind busy. Each time I complete a consulting contract, I tell myself it will be the last case. But then I get another call and I'm off on another intriguing escapade. Or the dean calls me from a university and asks if I would teach just one more course. I attended a retirement seminar at the University of Amsterdam just before I left for the funeral. They talked about balance and I'm thinking that if I retired completely, I'd be out of balance. On the other end of the spectrum, my schedule as of late has been so hectic that events feel more like mirages than reality."

"When will you move back to Paris?"

Alexandra paused. She found herself more comfortable with Paul than she had ever been with her husband. The moment provided a sense of trust that should be nurtured.

"I'm not certain I will return to Paris permanently. Being here again in Luxembourg has brought back so many memories of my childhood that I'm actually considering living here in my mother's apartment just around the corner from this café. Or I may buy a place of my own. The lure of the old city centre is very appealing. But I'll miss being close to my Collette. We've always been very tight. Although Luxembourg isn't far from Paris, you can't just meet for an impromptu coffee."

"What will you do with the house on rue Michel Welter?"

"I'll probably sell it. That's one of the things on my to-do list I must attend to tomorrow. Let me bring you up to speed on this chapter of my life. After the deaths of my uncle and aunt, my mother rented it out. While she travelled, she felt more comfortable with someone being in the house. Her last renter was a friend from Dieppe. They met during the war. Last year, her friend died. My mother thought it was suspicious because she had been in excellent health yet her death was sudden. My mother told me she never felt comfortable after the death of her tenant so she simply lowered the shutters, locked the door and moved into an apartment above a shop close to the Palais Grand-Ducal here in the old city. There are soldiers with rifles on duty guarding the palace 24/7. Their presence made her feel safer. I dropped by the house yesterday and had an unsettling feeling about the place. Like mother, like daughter, I guess."

"You mentioned your mother travelled on business trips and that you would accompany her on occasion. What was that about?"

"I've only recently learned what she actually did, what took us to Montigny-lès-Metz all those years ago, and to the Normandy coast, to Dieppe. She worked for French Counterintelligence. In the early years, she was tracking Nazi war criminals and collaborators. She never talked about it back then and neither did my uncle or aunt who were aware but never mentioned it to me. I was just told that she worked with some interesting people doing interesting things in interesting places. Once I found out, I was cautioned not to talk about it either. So, I don't. In the fullness of time, you may gain an appreciation."

Alexandra stopped abruptly. With a curt nod and an expression of finality, she just stared at Paul.

Paul nodded in response. "More coffee?"

"Yes, please."

"I'm still dumbfounded as to why we never received each other's letters, and now, hearing of your travels, why we never bumped into each other either in the Mediterranean or in Paris," Paul stated.

Their server approached and reminded them that the café was closing. Like synchronized swimmers, they simultaneously looked around and noted that they were the last patrons and the square was all but deserted.

"Can I walk you to your hotel? Where are you staying?"

"That would be wonderful. I have a room at the Hôtel Novotel Centre on rue Du Laboratoire across the Passerelle Viaduct on the left.

Alexandra could not remember the last time a gentleman had escorted her back to any accommodation to ensure her safety.

"The Novotel is close to where I'm staying at the Mercure Grand Hotel on Place de la Gare, adjacent to the Eurail station. We can talk more as we walk. We have not yet caught up on the eighty collective years that have transpired since Montigny-lès-Metz!"

Paul contemplated the enjoyment that such future liaisons might bring over more Pinot Noir and Rémy.

After bidding Alexandra good night at the Novotel, he remembered Tolstoy saying in one of his books that "every unhappy marriage is different." Yet perhaps in the combination of his and Alexandra's different unhappy marriages there was hope for a happy one.

CHAPTER 9

Alexandra awoke early, still tired. She had not slept well but was not surprised, given the roller coaster ride of the previous day with the funeral, the meeting with Madame Deschaume, the brief encounters with other guests, and the unexpected reunion and dinner with Paul.

For some reason, the introduction by her neighbour, the rotund grey-haired gentleman, haunted her.

Today, she would start to deal with the most pressing items on her to-do list. The sale of the house would occupy a considerable amount of her time with lawyers and real estate agents. She was not particularly looking forward to the bureaucracy.

And then there was the banking and the safe deposit box. Now this task might be like Christmas morning. What gifts had Père Noël left for her under the tree, in the safe deposit box?

As time permitted, she would vet the cards and letters left at the reception along with the guest book. Oh yes, there was the letter that Collette had handed to her from the distinguished elderly English gentleman, as Collette described him.

The ringing of her cell phone disturbed her prioritizing.

"Who would be calling at this hour?" she mumbled. "Was there more than one person who had not slept well?"

"AV, it's Paul. How are you?"

She chuckled to herself. The night may have been distressing but the day was starting off well.

"How pleasant to hear your voice, Paul."

"I was thinking, AV, I have nothing pressing on my calendar. In fact, I have nothing on my calendar. I was thinking that, while I was here, I could offer my services to help you with any real estate matters. I don't wish to impose...."

Alexandra interrupted with the enthusiastic graciousness a young lady might extend to a gentleman's invitation to dance.

"That would be wonderful. I'd very much enjoy your support as I delve into the legalities of executor duties. I have a meeting with a real estate agent at the house at nine and with the assistant bank manager at ten-thirty. Can we meet for lunch at one, say at the café where we had dinner last evening?"

"That's a date! Looking forward to lunch."

The morning air was clear and crisp. People on their way to work were full of energy, smiling and greeting others as they met. She noticed a mother with two small daughters who appeared to be twins, religiously crossing themselves as they walked past the cathedral. Each looked up at their mother who smiled and nodded. Alexandra recalled her mother instructing her to acknowledge God's house in the same way and reinforcing her performance with a warm smile when she was the same age. Tradition and respect shown by placing others before self, like excellence in craftsmanship for the sake of service, were steadily being eroded and replaced by narcissistic self-indulgence with no concept of others, let alone deference. But today would not be blemished by such thoughts. With the soothing warmth of the morning sun on her face, the day could only improve.

THE REAL ESTATE AGENT WAS WAITING AT 47, rue Michel Welter by the time Alexandra arrived. After a professional introduction, they assessed the condition of the exterior of the structure.

The dingy, discoloured beige paint on the façade had peeled off most of the surface, exposing the raw stucco. The cream paint on the wooden shutters was equally in need of redoing as were several of the wooden slats on the shutters themselves. A lifeless vine hung from the frame of a second-floor window. Grey slate shingles fixed to the outer wall of the third floor showed weathering.

The disrepair from neglect of the house was in stark contrast to the manicured pastel pink and cream and the light grey and white fascia of 45 and 49, rue Michel Welter. The former was the home of the rotund grey-haired gentleman who had introduced himself to Alexandra at the funeral reception. The lives of the occupants of all three were conveyed by the fabric of the façades.

As Alexandra glanced at the neighbouring homes, she thought she noticed a lace curtain being covertly drawn on a second-floor window of the rotund gentleman's house. She sensed something that was hardly ominous but intriguing, nonetheless.

Returning to her mother's house, both she and the real estate agent agreed that improvements would have to be made before the property was listed.

They went through the wrought iron gate that posed a challenge to open because rust had consumed the paint on the latch and hinges, gluing the moving parts together. With a grunt, the agent opened the gate with a grinding shriek.

Alexandra pushed through and approached a front door that also cried out for a face-lift and considerable make-up. She inserted her key into the lock but it didn't fit. On close examination, the problem was not the corrosion which had tainted the copper to a shade of green, like the rusted gate, but the realization the key style was inconsistent with the lock. Her mother had changed the lock at some point and not notified her.

"Well, that changes the schedule," she muttered to the agent. "I'll have to rummage through my mother's possessions in her apartment and find the key before we can look at the interior. I apologize for this inconvenience."

"Understandable," the agent replied. "Please note that my

schedule is entirely full for the balance of today, and tomorrow is almost booked."

"I think it would be a better use of our time if I call you for another appointment once I have the key," Alexandra acknowledged.

"That would be best, madame. For now, we can complete the paperwork for the listing and you can sign the contract authorizing me to act as your agent. Once inside and, I suspect, after the house has been cleaned, I'll take photographs for the listing. We can then advertise the property online and in the local real estate newspaper. Houses in this neighbourhood are highly sought after because the location is so central."

Alexandra thanked him and apologized once again for the mix-up with the keys. Having learned about real estate from her aunt and having managed the rental properties bequeathed to her, she was acutely aware of property valuation. This experience gave her confidence. She knew there were many dishonest agents in this industry. Her *shrew* suggested this agent was trustworthy.

"I note that you are walking, madame. Can I drive you to your next appointment?"

"Thank you for your kind offer, monsieur, but I will decline this morning. I have ample time to walk to the bank for my next meeting now that our appointment here has been shortened. The walk will allow me to reacquaint myself with the neighbourhood and enjoy the wonderful weather. I might see another property I could purchase. I'm on the eve of retirement and consider Luxembourg a good location to settle. Perhaps you could act as my agent in such a purchase."

"I'm at your service. With your consent, I'll send you some listings you may find appealing."

"That would be useful. I like this district because it echoes the symmetry and refinement of the old city. But I'm also attracted to the old city centre. I'm most fond of the grandeur and magnificence of the Luxembourgian culture. You have my email address."

"I do, madame, and will send you a few listings shortly."

"I must now bid you *au revoir*," she closed.

As she walked in the general direction of the bank, the rays of the sun followed her, as if welcoming her home. Although always proud to have been born in Luxembourg, she felt more patriotic as she observed the red, white and blue flag flying from atop government buildings and on several stately homes, even alongside the European Union flag. Luxembourg brought proximity. The cobblestone streets reminded her of Amsterdam and Paris, each with their own art, architecture and ambience. How she loved old Europe, but with the modern amenities.

Walking by the Place des Martyrs, she could not help but notice couples, young and old, sitting and holding hands. She and André had never done that. As she observed them from a distance, she imagined what it would have been like to savour such experiences with Paul. She could certainly perceive their current relationship, brief as it was, blossoming to that level of affection. For a moment, she experienced a twinge of remorse for a life missed.

CHAPTER 10

The assistant bank manager extended his condolences as she entered his office.

"I am so sorry to hear of your mother's passing. She was such a gracious lady and, I might add, a very loyal client."

"Thank you, monsieur. Now, I would like to gain access to her safety deposit box. Here is the key and the Will appointing me as the sole executor of the estate."

"Thank you, madame. You are most efficient for without the Will, I would not be able to allow you access. Please follow me."

As they walked down the passage and into the vault, he respectfully added, "This morning, we will need to set up an estate account which will remain open until the matter of her death is finalized. I'll provide you with special cheques for this new account."

She completed the administration requirements. It took longer than she had anticipated, including signing for the contents of the safety deposit box which included a manila folder, some loose papers, sealed envelopes and a bundle of what appeared to be letters tied together with a midnight blue velvet ribbon. It was close to noon by the time she left the bank so she decided to go to the Café Kaempff-Kohler to have a coffee and sort through the papers while she waited for Paul.

Arriving at the café, she sat at the same table where she and Paul had dined last evening.

The waiter approached and quietly said, "I am honoured you have returned to our wonderful café, madame."

She looked up and recognized him from last evening and much earlier this morning when he courteously informed them the restaurant was closing. She bowed her head slightly, acknowledging his welcome.

"Thank you for your wonderful service last evening. The superior quality of the Pinot Noir was only exceeded by the excellence of the cuisine. If I omitted to do so last evening, please pass along my sincere compliments to the chef and the proprietor. I hope we did not inconvenience you with our late departure. Time slipped away from us."

"You are most gracious, madame. I will do so. No, you did not inconvenience us at all. I'm only happy you found our service and the ambience of our establishment to your liking. Will the gentleman from last evening be joining you for lunch? May I bring you a coffee?"

"Yes, he should be along shortly."

Alexandra sipped the coffee the waiter delivered. She then opened her briefcase which contained the contents of the safety deposit box. The folder holding papers looked bureaucratic as if from the kingdom of officialdom. She had had enough of that this morning, so set it aside. The bundle of letters was more intriguing. She remembered the dark midnight blue as being her favourite colour. The velvet of the ribbon brought back memories of the high school graduation dress her mother had hired a seamstress to make for her.

Her mother had kept several ribbons in a small wooden box. As a child, she thought they were empowered. She would pretend to be a princess. Each of the ribbons was magical. When she gave them to her dolls and stuffed bears, they would come alive. In her castle, in her room, in her house, she felt safe.

Remembering those times brought a warm smile to her face and made her feel at peace. It seemed appropriate to have these feelings of security as she sat at the café in the castle of the old city, waiting for her Prince Charming to arrive.

She gently pulled at the velvet ribbon to undo the bow, as she had softly pulled petals from daisies as a child, reciting, "He loves me, he loves me not." In the years following her meeting with Paul as a young teenager in Montigny-lès-Metz, she would think of him each time she quietly recited this verse. Even after her marriage to André, she would think about Paul when she saw daisies and when she taught Collette the verse as a young child.

"May I refresh your coffee, madame?" the waiter asked.

Alexandra nodded and again looked at the midnight blue ribbon as it lay by the pile of letters. The top envelope was addressed to her. Her mother had written in bold uppercase letters, "READ THIS BEFORE READING ANYTHING ELSE." Inside was a letter dated only months before:

> "My dearest daughter, Alexandra. We all have our crosses to bear. I know that you have carried the cross of André all these years for the sake of Marc and Collette. May God bless you for that noble sacrifice. I now confess two crosses to you. I know what you are about to read will cause you pain. But I am confident you will find it in your heart to understand and to forgive me. What I have done, I have done for you – to protect you and Collette.
>
> "If you are reading this letter then I will have died before Madame Deschaume. She will have explained many details of my past, including the story of Thon. As you now know, I worked with your grand-maman in the French Resistance toward the end of the war, in the south of France and later on the Normandy coast. While in Carcassonne, I fell deeply in love with one of the other resistance fighters. His name was Philip Marchand and he was several years older than me. When Thon betrayed us, I left for the Normandy coast and Courselles-sur-Mer. I never knew where Philip went or

even if he still was alive. You will hear of *le fantôme*. Philip said he was the head of the *Maquis* in our region. I believed Philip then because I was so in love with him. Today, I don't believe that *le fantôme* was real but rather just invented to have the Nazis waste resources chasing after a ghost. Of course, I might be wrong.

"After the war, I became part of the French Intelligence. Our initial task was to hunt down Nazi war criminals and collaborators, including Thon. In 1950, my work took me to Alsace, in fact to Metz, where I worked with American and Canadian Military Intelligence officers. That was where you met Paul (I will explain later in this letter). One part of the investigation required me to travel to Montigny-lès-Metz where I worked with a few police officers. One day, while in the police precinct, I saw Philip. He was a detective capitaine. Our love was instantly rekindled. I never told Philip the purpose of my duties or anything about Thon but I knew from our intelligence that Philip suspected Thon was in the region and may have been responsible for the death of a woman and her daughter. The woman had also served with the French Resistance, the *Maquis*, during the war.

"My dearest Alexandra, Philip was your father. I say *was* because he has since died and is buried in Paris. I did not tell Philip about you at the time because of the sensitivity of the case. On subsequent business trips to Montigny-lès-Metz, I didn't contact Philip for fear that Thon might connect us if he was watching. The murder of the mother and daughter was just too threatening. To have developed a relationship with Philip would have put you in imminent danger and I could not allow that to occur. I had to sacrifice my happiness with Philip for your safety. You will find a ring and a key to a safe deposit box in an envelope. It belonged to Philip. It is all I ever had to remind me of him. I do not know which lock the key will open. You needed to have lived through the constant feeling of fear as a *Maquis* fighter during and after the war to understand the depths to which fear can control your emotions and subsequent actions. That threat was as real as Madame Deschaume will have explained. I would observe Philip from shadowy recesses. I pined after him and ached for his touch. My heart was broken for not telling him about you.

"Now for the second cross that I bear. I knew that you and Paul had fallen in love. You were approximately the age I was when I met Philip and fell in love with him. Paul's father was a policeman who was working on the double murder case with Philip which we knew at that time involved Thon. So, I had to keep you and Paul apart to protect you. Enclosed in this bundle are most of the letters you wrote to Paul. Every time your uncle and aunt said they would mail them for you, they did not. Instead, they kept them. Likewise, they intercepted and kept the letters Paul mailed to you. They gave them all to me. They did this on my insistence. They did not know all the details about Thon but I did tell them about the imminent threat he posed. Intercepting the letters caused them no end of pain as it did me. As far as anyone was concerned, you were their daughter. No one else knew, or so we thought initially. But somehow, someone found out you were my daughter. We could never determine who that was. The lethal threat was and remains dangerously real.

"I hope you can forgive me. I did it for your safety. Thon is an evil psychopath and we were confident he was killing former members of the *Maquis* – women and their daughters, as we later discovered. That is why I did what I did.

"In the back of the manila folder, you will find some photographs. The ones of the German soldiers in uniform standing by the armoured vehicles were taken in the area of Carcassonne. I believe they might have been working with Thon. In fact, Thon may have been one of them or may have taken the photographs. The other photographs of men in German uniforms were taken in the Normandy region, and the ones with German soldiers and others in civilian desert attire standing by the trucks and boxes were taken in North Africa. I could never confirm their identity. I'm convinced there is a connection to Thon somehow. I kept these photographs and only shared them with a select few because collaborators and other spies, including Russians, had infiltrated our French Intelligence Services by then. I didn't trust anyone who was new to the Service.

"You must be equally cautious. The only person I trusted completely was a British Intelligence officer, Sir James Pennington, who lives in England, and an American OSS officer, Major Mike Murphy, who has since died. Major Mike had a protégé code-named 'Alder' whom he introduced to me. I trusted him because I trusted Major Mike. Sir James may contact you. We first met during the war under other circumstances and after the war as intelligence agents. You can trust him.

"There was a considerable amount of gold taken by the Nazis, stolen from French banks and other sources. It was never found after the war. I believe the Nazis in the photographs were responsible and Thon was connected. Other international sources have strong suspicions that some but not all the gold was deposited in Swiss banks and in the Vatican bank. Thon is funding his operations today from this gold. So much gold and other priceless artefacts were stolen that

Thon could live off the interest and not need to tap into the main cache of gold itself. That is why I was so concerned for our safety, for your safety. Thon was able to hire anyone. We know today the gold is financing a neo-Nazi group whose intention is to create the Fourth Reich. The gold is also connected to Russian communist spies and Middle East terrorists. They are linked to the 9/11 attack on the World Trade Center in New York. Among these photos you will find some old Germanic script. I am not sure what the connection might be but I suspect the Fourth Reich and Thon.

"By merely being my daughter, you have become involved and your safety is in jeopardy. I have been able to protect you thus far, but now you are on your own. You need to be ever so careful with whom you associate. You now have intelligence some will want and others will not want circulated. They will all kill in order to achieve their purpose.

"The photographs of the woman taken by the Luxembourg station is a mystery but may be connected to the other photo of the man on rue Michel Welter, which might be Thon or one of his close associates. In all the years after the war, I have never been able to identify Thon, and that is what's most frightening. I believe this person killed my renter, the lady from Dieppe whom I met during the war. She was not an active member of the French Resistance sabotaging Nazi installations and communication systems. She was working as a courier on the periphery. I locked up the house and never returned after her death. My heart became weary and I succumbed to the years of work that took me on all those business trips.

"The task of re-entering our home, I leave to you. I can only caution you and encourage you to be the excellent investigator you are in conducting forensic psychological profiles. Evidence of Thon is still in the house for you to find and identify.

"So, my dear Alexandra, I pass the torch to you. Know that a mother could not be prouder of her daughter than I am of you. No more so than on that fateful day when I instructed you to run. But you stayed instead.

"I have only one final request – that you forgive me for my two crosses. I am certain you will appreciate how heavy they have been all these years. Perhaps you and Paul will meet again and you can explain my motivation for intercepting your love letters.

"— Your adoring mother."

Alexandra was numbed by the letter. She felt she had re-entered the museum of her life with a tour guide who pointed out artefacts she hadn't imagined. The explosion of her senses left her numb.

She then started to read the letters from Paul who professed his youthful love for her, and her letters to him also confessing her innocent love. Both explained how they felt jilted by the other because they had not received a reply. She could not read further because her eyes welled up with tears and she could not focus.

She found herself grasping for breath as her chest tightened from the grip of emotion. Grief distorts reality. The death of her mother was bad enough. The realization of a lost love was unbearable. At this moment she could not come to grips with the fact that love and loss are unavoidable parts of the human condition.

CHAPTER 11

"Hi, AV, you beat me to the café this time!"

She looked up at Paul who instantly saw the tears streaming down her cheeks.

"What? What happened? What's wrong?"

She stood up and wrapped her arms tightly around his neck while kissing him on the cheek. Holding on to him as if he was a life preserver thrown to a drowning soul in a tempest, she wept inconsolably, her entire body racked with emotion. With his arms enveloping her, he waited for her sobbing to subside. He then gently lowered her into her chair and sat down beside her. Looking into her swollen eyes, he asked his questions again. She pushed the pile of letters toward him and mumbled in a broken voice, "Read."

She then slumped back in the chair, lowered her face into her clenched fingers which held the letter from her mother, and cried softly.

Paul studied every word, phrase and sentence of the letters she had written to him and those he had written to her all those years ago. He gasped as he read the youthful proclamation of adoration in each letter. A loud silence followed. All other sounds were muted. His mind spun. The letters mirrored what might have been the tragic communication between Romeo and Juliet who were the same age when they declared their love for each other.

Paul looked up at Alexandra who realized that he was as emotionally distraught as she was. They gazed blankly at each other through swollen, tearful eyes, feeling as if they were moving sluggishly underwater against a powerful current. They sat attempting to gather what remained of their shattered emotions, neither making an effort to speak. Instead, they held each other's hand, quiet. It was an impossible moment.

After several minutes they relaxed. They gently massaged each other's stiff fingers.

Their waiter, recognizing the importance of the meeting, kept vigil from a distance. Recalling their taste for cognac, he delicately and imperceptibly placed two snifters of Rémy on their table and resumed his protective post. The sentiment was contagious.

Paul broke the silence.

"I am so deeply, deeply sorry, AV, for accusing you at the funeral yesterday of not writing to me all those years ago. I felt you rebuffed me after I had poured my heart out to you."

"Oh no, I must apologize to you for challenging you and asking why you hadn't replied to my letters. I am so deeply sorry for my behaviour yesterday. Can you find it in your heart to forgive me, Paul? Hearing your voice and seeing you at the reception threw me completely off-balance. I felt elated and devastated at the same time."

"Let's go for a walk, a long walk, and try to put this into context."

Paul approached their waiter who waved him away with an understanding bow, acknowledging their emotions. Paul returned to the table and left a correspondingly generous gratuity.

He helped Alexandra gather up the letters. They walked into the centre of the old city wending their way along the cobblestone lanes and through silent arches. They sometimes held hands or just walked, occasionally touching arms and shoulders.

It was dusk by the time they returned to the Café Kaempff-Kohler where they ordered dinner. The Pinot Noir complemented the exceptional cuisine once again but the atmosphere was more relaxed. Spirits that had plummeted at noon rose as the sunset and the evening drew in around them. The revelation of their emotions had thawed any lingering inhibitions.

Their first rendezvous the previous evening had united them in exhilaration. Their second at noon today had united them in despondency. This evening would be a celebration of certainty. For the first time, they were aware of each other's genuine feelings.

Decisions made after their Montigny-lès-Metz parting so long ago had been dogged by the absence of the truth. All decisions made henceforth would be premised on the truth. Pinot Noir and Rémy would proclaim this *fête nouvelle* – celebration of newness.

The day ended, as it had started, exhausting but promising. Their spirits had been revived. Yesterday was punctuated by the twisted emotions of yet another rollercoaster ride. As on the previous evening, Paul escorted Alexandra to her hotel but unlike last evening, they gently kissed, oblivious of their surroundings. For both, the kiss made peace with the past. In the present, it acknowledged the affirmation of the future, whatever that might be.

Sometimes, silent actions speak more loudly than words can ever do. This was one of those times.

Paul then returned to his hotel.

CHAPTER 12

Alexandra awoke at the ring of her cell phone. The number displayed didn't register in her mental Rolodex. As she was about to cancel the call, she recognized the initials FL. It was Father Luke.

"Hello, Father."

"Do you have time to meet? It is most urgent."

"Yes, of course. I can meet you in about forty-five minutes at your office, if that is convenient."

"Please come to the back door of the priest's house."

Curiosity motivated her to arrive early. She knocked on the back door, hoping he would hear her. The door opened and the housekeeper whisked her in and escorted her down the hall. Father Luke's dark figure was silhouetted against a shaft of sunlight entering from the window by the front door.

"Come in, my child. I have troubling news."

Nothing could be more troubling than reading the letters from her mother, she reflected. But Father Luke's frown and the lines on his forehead suggested otherwise.

"It is Madame Simone Deschaume. She is dead."

"How? Where? What happened?"

"I received a call this morning. I don't have all the details but it appears she fell to her death from one of the old German gun emplacements on the beach at Dieppe. I was aware that her health was declining and she was frail. That is what causes me to question the accident. She could not have climbed up onto a concrete bunker on her own – not that she ever would go there.

My parishioner, if I may use that term, expressed grave concern for your safety and that of your daughter. We both have the protection of God, but I have the added protection of the bastions of l'Église du Sacré-Coeur, whereas you do not. My parishioner emphasized the need for you to be extra cautious at this time."

Alexandra had not fully recovered her energy from the news in her mother's letter. Nonetheless, adrenaline started flowing: safety would have to be a high priority for her and especially Collette. In times of threat, her *modus operandi* was always to be on the offensive after gathering the relevant information. She had never been intimidated. She needed to go to Dieppe to assess the threat and confirm the facts. From this moment on, it would be, *de l'audace, encore de l'audace, et toujours de l'audace.*

She would have to warn Collette. Whether God was speaking to her or her *shrew*, she had a strong feeling that Collette was in danger. Like a lioness with her young, she would defend her daughter at all costs.

With a protective blessing from Father Luke, Alexandra crossed herself with the holy water and departed the same way she had entered. Her step and bearing were now purposeful, reflecting a resolution on this maternal protective mission.

From her experience and training in profiling criminals as a forensic psychologist, she knew there would be a proclivity for the person behind these threats to try to terrify. If this was indeed the legendary Thon resurrected after a span of decades, simply killing would not be enough for this demented mind; he (or she) would be obsessed with creating panic and dread in the intended victims. Alexandra would find out. The other items on her to-do list would have to be postponed. Even getting to know Paul better would have to wait.

She called Paul and asked him to meet her in her hotel room. She would catch the Eurail to Brussels, rent a car and drive to Dieppe. She then called Collette but there was no answer so she left a guarded message to be *especially wary*. She would call later to confirm receipt of the message and emphasize the need to raise her radar. That was her code for maximum vigilance, even to consider restricting all movements outside the home.

Although the walk to her hotel was relatively short, it provided ample time to organize her thoughts. As she entered her room, she called the forensic pathologist in Dieppe. He was a colleague of André's and she had worked with him on a few cases.

"Jacques, this is Alexandra. Do you have a moment?"

"I always have a moment for you. How can I assist you?"

"Do you have a Madame Simone Deschaume in your morgue?"

"News travels fast. Yes, I do."

"Can you tell me how she died?"

"She appears to have slipped and fallen from a bunker onto the beach below. It is a great height, as you know. She suffered multiple contusions and fractures including a fractured skull. Her death would have been instantaneous."

"Will you be conducting an autopsy?"

"I reviewed her doctor's report which informed me she was frail and suffered from some ailments consistent with old age. So, given these facts, no, probably not. Why do you ask?"

"Could you do an autopsy and take an additional blood sample for me and a sample of the content of her stomach?"

"Conducting an autopsy and taking a blood sample in addition to a sample of the content of her stomach would not be out of order. I have no one else on my table so I have the time. But why two samples?"

Alexandra murmured. "Ahhhhhh…."

"I recognize the Alexandra pause. Am I correct in concluding that this could be one of those *special* cases, perhaps?"

"You are correct, my friend. This is one of those special cases."

"The second sample is contrary to policy, but policy is just that, policy to be interpreted."

"I'll be leaving for Dieppe soon," she announced, "and should be there sometime tonight. I'll call you when I arrive, or in the morning if I arrive too late."

"Shall we meet at our usual café?"

"Perhaps elsewhere, Jacques. I'll fill you in when I call. Oh, can you make a reservation for me at the Hôtel Mercure Dieppe de Présidence?"

"Consider it done."

No sooner had she hung up than Paul knocked on her hotel door. She let him in but not before checking the hallway to confirm he was alone.

"What's going on, AV? Why are you packing?"

"I need to go to Dieppe."

"Okay, I'll go with you."

"No, Paul, I need to go alone."

He sensed the alarm and urgency in her voice and the change in her demeanour. "What do you mean 'go alone?' After forty years of being apart and after what we have just been through together in the past forty-eight hours, do you really believe that I'm going to let you walk out of my life?"

"It's complicated and dangerous. It relates to my mother's work."

Paul stared at her with one of his notorious no-way responses that colleagues in his office had come to recognize and Alexandra was about to learn. Charming he was, but determined and, at times, bloody-minded.

"It's complicated," she repeated.

"Well then, explain it to me on the way to Dieppe," he replied in a controlled, calm tone.

Alexandra knew she had met her match. Paul could punch at his own weight which was a lean fit physique. She wasn't accustomed to having a strong supportive partner, but she was learning.

"All right," she said reluctantly, "but you do as I say if the world gets interesting."

Did she really think he would stand by and do nothing if push came to shove? Besides, she would very much enjoy his company and the trip would give them time to catch up on the years apart.

After stopping at Paul's hotel, they arrived at the Luxembourg Eurail station with time to spare. This translated into a treat, a latté and a decadent chocolate éclair. While standing at a table next to the coffee kiosk, they observed police sniffer dogs searching random passengers and luggage for drugs or other contraband. Their masters were appropriately armed with automatic weapons hung over their shoulders and barrette pistols in holsters on their hips. It was post-9/11, a sign of the times.

Paul gently leaned over and nudged Alexandra's shoulder to get her attention. "I get the feeling you feel safe in their presence."

Her relaxed smile confirmed his observation yet she remained vigilant, scanning like ground radar the movements of others in the station for any irregularities which would be a cause for concern.

After a career of seeking subtle nuances, she was able to detect telling variances in behaviour. Tired travellers tended to wander, looking but not seeing or just sitting with repeated glances at clocks, wishing spells onto the minutes of the display to advance more quickly. Energetic travellers examined over-priced merchandise displayed in brightly-lit display windows or paid attention to newly-purchased trinkets. The veteran traveller was well organized, sitting and reading their favourite book or current edition of a newspaper. The professional security agent had a polished, confident method of observation, often over the top of a newspaper or other aids to their surveillance vocation. Then there was the criminal opportunist who, if working solo, would stalk their prey for a fast grab-and-run, noting the most direct escape route. If in partnership, they would move in predetermined patterns in tandem, one to distract like a jackal culling a weaker stray from the herd while the other engaged in the predatory manoeuvre.

Alexandra noted all these patterns in the station.

Finally, there was the sociopath, or worse the psychopath, whose behavioural patterns were too erratic to be predictable. Their obsession with detail, however obscure, was their dogma and their downfall to the trained investigator. Her eyes locked on to one such target, tracking the neurotic movements out of habit. All the while, she remained aware of the comforting nearness of Paul.

The garbled announcement of their train's arrival was barely discernible. Holding their bags in one hand and their Eurail passes in the other, they joined the parade of passengers travelling to Brussels and other destinations along the route. Younger travellers and backpackers tended to enter coaches at the rear. Those like Paul and Alexandra, who years ago had concluded life was too short to travel in less comfort, or others whose arthritis reminded them of their mortality, boarded the first-class cars at the front.

Alexandra had a structured routine that included putting her Eurail pass back into the zippered side pocket of her purse. She had tucked the letter from her mother in this most secure recess.

Now may be the best time to allow Paul to read the letter, she considered. After all, if he was going to accompany her, then he had better know what he was getting himself into, for his safety and hers.

"Can we switch seats, Paul? I like to sit by the aisle."

It would be best if he sat by the window and she were away from prying eyes with more access to the aisle.

Paul looked at her with an amused glance.

"Sure."

He was beginning to understand some of her nuances and they intrigued him all the more. He also found himself arrested by the singularity of her mannerisms. They were most alluring.

Resettled, she whispered, "Remember what I said to you in the hotel room just before I agreed to have you join me."

"Yes, and...."

Slowly, so as not to draw attention, she looked over each shoulder to ensure that passengers in the seat behind them and across the aisle would not have a clear line of sight or sound. Not noting any curious surveillance, she quietly murmured to Paul, "Read this." She reached over and gently pressed her mother's letter against Paul's chest. He placed his hand over hers and held it there.

"We can talk more once we are enroute on the next leg of our journey. The contents will provide an explanation about our letters to each other and a little about my motivation for saying what I said. After you have read it, ponder the prospects. You will understand better."

Only at that point did Alexandra withdraw her hand from his gentle grasp. She had savoured the closeness and the opportunity to monitor his heartbeat, which was slightly elevated. His breathing was slow and deep. The tactile contact also allowed her to become more aware of his muscular physique.

Holding the letter close to his chest, away from the view of others, Paul read it once, and then several times more. After each re-read, he took a deep breath and looked up at the ceiling to reflect. The reasoning and consequences of her mother's actions overwhelmed him.

With limited success, he attempted to put the depth and severity of the communiqué into the context of his world, which was based on the requirement for factual evidence in an objective judicial context. His reality was in complete contrast to the reality of Alexandra's mother's world of treachery and deceit that had drawn her daughter into the consuming deadly vortex of espionage and duplicity. He only knew about this kind of intrigue from the periphery.

Retirement was supposed to be a time when all the worries of his career could be replaced with uncomplicated choices of: What should I do today… play a round of golf or not play a round of golf?

Was Alexandra being naïvely glib with him when she mentioned that he should just ponder the content of the letter for now and talk later when in the privacy of the car as they drove to Dieppe? At this moment, he couldn't conceptualize let alone compose a coherent assessment if he tried, and he was trying.

Alexandra was in imminent danger and she knew it! Yet she was advancing against an unknown adversary who had killed in the past and was more than likely bent on killing her and possibly Collette. This was courage he had never experienced, only read about in stories of war heroes who advanced against the hail of bullets from enemy machine guns on the hallowed ground of the Ardennes over which their train was currently travelling.

Paul found his mind swirling with the emotionally laden images he had experienced at the Café Kaempff-Kohler when he read their youthful Romeo and Juliet proclamations of adoration. His response was in full stress mode from the perceived threats to his Juliet. Taking a deep, slow breath, he looked straight ahead, eyes blank, and lowered the letter to his lap.

Alexandra picked up on his response. She was, once again, experiencing a similar emotion. She softly placed her hand on his.

After a few moments, he relaxed his clenched grip. This allowed her to slowly withdraw the letter from his hands and place it back into the secure pocket in her purse. Returning her hand to his, they sat silently. She followed his gaze out of the window at the world passing by, bringing them ever closer to a destiny burdened with the unknown unknowns they would soon confront together.

CHAPTER 13

Paul stirred from his trance when the conductor announced their approach to Brussels. The digital sign over the car door displayed: Bestemming Brussel-Zuid. "Our stop is coming up shortly, AV."

They glanced at each other, smiled and gently squeezed hands, which they had been holding since Alexandra replaced the letter in her purse.

There was something calming about her touch like the salve of a South Sea breeze. He had attended a conference in Bali years before and recalled how soothing the light evening winds off the ocean felt, like a balm. On the return flight to Paris, he realized he would probably never again know such tropical tranquility. Yet now, on this train, he was experiencing the salve of a South Sea breeze with her touch.

Their Eurail station was underground, below the Brussels International Airport. There they would rent a car and drive west to Dieppe. Paul took care of the rental, a Cadillac, and registered them both as drivers in case the need arose. They would take the E40 to the Channel, the A16 to Abbeville, and finally the D925 to Dieppe.

"I like your choice in cars," Alexandra exclaimed, bowing slightly to acknowledge his selection. His choice in cars equated to his choice in attire – quality, bar none.

"We might as well drive a chariot rather than an ox cart. It comes with a GPS just in case we need to do some route research on our own."

They took the elevator down to the parking lot and located their chariot of fire. Paul loaded their luggage into the trunk and opened the door for Alexandra.

"*Avec plaisir, madame.*"

Alexandra was taken aback. For a moment, she stood stationary. His gentlemanly etiquette once again astounded her. He didn't open the door for her in comic jest but with sincerity and respect for a lady. *Such propriety, such sensitivity,* she thought.

Out of habit, Alexandra scanned the parking lot as she was getting into the car. She noticed someone opening the door of a late model black Mercedes parked a few rows to her left. This circumstance caught her eye because of the tinted windows. A blond man turned away and bent down out of sight when she looked at him. Her *shrew* became acute, alerting her to the avoidance behaviour.

Observing the immediate change in her demeanour, Paul quietly muttered, "What's up?"

"Not sure."

Paul noted a cryptic inflection in her voice that caused him consternation. He followed her stare, keeping a sniper's eye out for anything out of the normal. Glancing in Alexandra's direction, he became painfully conscious of her amplified apprehension. A security guard poked his head around the corner and asked them, "Everything satisfactory with the car, folks?"

"Yes, thanks," Paul replied.

"Very well, have a pleasant trip," the guard replied as he continued his patrol in the direction of the black Mercedes and the man Alexandra had observed. They did not hear his voice again.

"Perhaps it was nothing," she murmured after one last scan of the parking lot.

Paul followed her reconnaissance.

"Let's be on our way. Can you drive?" Alexandra asked. "I have a couple of calls to make once we are out of the parking lot and I have a stronger signal."

As they pulled out, Paul noticed her glancing in the rear-view mirror on the passenger's side. He followed suit but saw nothing that caused him concern.

Out of the garage, Paul immediately became preoccupied with the heavy traffic. He turned on the GPS and punched in a reverse-route request, hoping the previous driver had entered a route of the surrounding network of roads. No luck. The GPS did not provide any route information.

"I've got a pretty good idea which way we need to go. Just to be sure, can you check for a map?"

Alexandra searched the glove compartment, the side pockets in the passenger door and the seat but without success.

"No luck. Let me enter the route into the GPS."

Within moments, a confident female e-voice was providing directions. Paul settled into pilot mode. Alexandra had taken care of the co-pilot navigator duties. She could now attend to a few communication priorities.

Her first call was to Collette. Again, there was no answer, so she left another coded message. Her second call was to the Hôtel Mercure Dieppe la Présidence for an additional reservation. A third call was to a friend, Josephine, who was a librarian and the best database researcher she knew. There was no answer to her call to her friend so she sent a text message with an "URGENT" tag.

"Jo – need you to search for refs to '*le fantôme*' and '*Maquis*.' Maman's funeral was exhausting but doing okay. Enroute from Brussels to Dieppe so may not have consistent comms, Alex. PS – let's ride soon."

Within a minute, a text marked URGENT flashed back.

"What do you mean your mother's funeral???? I didn't know. Why didn't you tell me? I would have come. Dieppe???"

Alexandra replied:

"OMG so sorry. Life has been a blur since finding out myself.

Funeral was in Lux. Still buzzing. I feel so bad for not letting you know. Will explain later Dieppe ref."

Jo sent an immediate response.

"Will research and inform soonest. Still mad at you. Yes, let's ride. We need f2f girl time. When meet?"

"Is everything all right?" Paul asked.

"Just texted a librarian friend to do a search on *le fantôme* and *Maquis*."

"What are you hoping to find?"

"I don't know, but I have to find all the information I can. Just before you came up to me at the reception following the funeral, do you recall seeing me with an elderly lady? She left just before I scanned the guest book."

"Yes… vaguely."

"That was Madame Simone Deschaume. Father Luke introduced me to her. She gave me information about my mother and their relationship with the French Resistance. Father Luke called me this morning about half an hour before I called you. She's dead. She supposedly fell from a German bunker emplacement onto the beach in Dieppe where she lives… lived. That's why we are going to Dieppe. When we spoke at the funeral reception, she mentioned *le fantôme*."

"Dead! Your mother alluded to that ghost also, in her letter. I'm a novice at this game, but am starting to connect the dots or at least the fog banks."

"That's why I asked my friend to search those names. If I'm going to complete a psych profile of *le fantôme* and Thon, I need every bit of information I can find."

It had been about an hour since they left Brussels. Paul had become aware of Alexandra's frequent monitoring of the rear view from the vanity mirror she had lowered and left down. As they approached a rest stop, she asked him to pull in.

"Just pull into the far end of the parking lot by the restaurant," she directed. She did not get out. Instead, she continued to monitor movement in the vanity mirror, pausing only to gaze over her shoulder a couple of times. Paul sat patiently, occasionally looking in his rear-view mirrors – for what, he wasn't sure.

"Okay, let's go," Alexandra instructed.

After another hour marked by constant monitoring of her mirror, she again directed him to pull into an approaching rest stop.

He checked the fuel gauge. It read about three-quarters full. They didn't need gas but could top up. He found himself scanning the vehicles at other gas pumps and others waiting in line. Nothing seemed to be out of the ordinary. Back in the car, he looked at Alexandra and pointedly asked, "What's going on? You've been glued to the vanity mirror since we left Brussels. I'm uncomfortable just watching your discomfort. Talk to me."

"I just have a funny feeling about the black Mercedes in the parking lot at the airport. I get these feelings every so often. When I was a little girl, my mother told me that I should always listen to my intuition. She explained that our intuition is never wrong. It's just our misinterpretation of our intuition which gets us into trouble."

"I can accept that. But what is your intuition telling you?"

"I don't know right now, only that I need to have my radar up."

"So, how can I help you?"

"Just work with me, Paul, just work with me on this."

Her unambiguous emotionally-laden appeal for support touched a chord with him. Tilting his head and viewing her from a slant, he smiled reassuringly. He reached over and took her hand. There was no mistaking her cool apprehension. He thought, *Work with her, support her, reassure her.*

The balance of the trip to Dieppe was punctuated with several more stops. She did not have to ask him to pull over. Instead, he pulled off when he sensed her gaze into the vanity mirror was increasing in frequency and duration. He perceived the subtle relief in her face each time he put on the turn signal. When they did step out of the car for a stretch and refreshments, Alexandra could not help but notice that he hovered close and constantly scanned for any unusual activity.

With all the surveillance stops, they arrived at the Hôtel Mercure Dieppe la Présidence later than initially planned, tired but feeling more assured. Morning would come early enough. They retired to their respective rooms, each conscious of what the other was contemplating.

CHAPTER 14

Alexandra was on her second cup of coffee by the time Paul came down to breakfast.

"How did you sleep?"

"Not well," he replied. "It took me a while to drop off and then I woke up several times. My mind was struggling to process the events from yesterday."

"I tossed and turned most of the night too, thinking about what needed to be done and just other stuff."

Each knew what the "other stuff" thoughts were. Like couples who had grown to be the best of friends over years of mutual experience, in just a few days they had developed an understanding of what the other was thinking and sensing, without having to search for an explanation. Gestures and gazes were quickly becoming natural.

In this space of serene silence, they both realized, with regret, they had never achieved this level of emotional calmness and comfort with their own spouse. They were both thinking: *so this is what an idyllic, blissful and supportive relationship is supposed to be like!*

"I called a friend of mine, Jacques Moreau, who is the pathologist here in Dieppe and made arrangements to meet him this morning around ten on the quai du Hâble just where the boulevard de Verdun intersects. We spoke yesterday. He assured me he would fill me in on the results of the autopsy, blood work and stomach-content analysis. First, I... *we* need to go to the old German bunker fortifications on the beach where Madame Deschaume supposedly fell to her death. If I remember correctly, it would take an agile person to climb up onto the bunker. That's what bothers me, Paul. She was frail, far from fit."

They finished their breakfast, checked out of the hotel, and headed for the beach and the bunker. Once there, it did not take either of them long to conclude that even a person as fit as Paul would be challenged by such a climb. In addition, anyone with a speck of common sense would not attempt such a feat. The drive to the quai du Hâble rendezvous was short and they arrived early, ahead of Jacques.

"I think I'll walk along the water, Paul. If you don't mind, I'd like to be alone to think. I love your distraction, but I need some space to organize my thoughts."

"That's fine."

He watched her walk toward the water in awe of the serenity of her presence. The tranquility was abruptly interrupted by the laughter of children playing on the beach. *Du calme, du calme*, he repeated to himself. His heart began to race as images of mortars raining down on children playing in a courtyard flooded his thoughts. The image of the little girl lying face down in the ditch with her arms tied behind her back with barbed wire which had ripped her wrists, and her light blue dress stained with blood that had oozed from a bullet hole in the back of her head took front stage, as it always did. He took slow deep breaths. He knew that the sound of young voices was one of the triggers. He knew he needed a distraction.

Looking at Alexandra, he saw a Kodak moment. He reached for his camera in the back seat. The telephoto lens made it awkward to remove from the case but the camera was soon in operation.

A lingering soft morning mist breathed over the beach. As Alexandra stood gazing into the distance, her chestnut hair framing her cheeks, Paul found her profile compelling. He kept moving the frame to keep her as the sole focus, away from any background distractions.

"Damn," he muttered, "how dare that car disturb my perfect frame."

A late-model black Mercedes had slowly crept into view. It came to a stop at such an angle the driver could view Alexandra's movements while minimizing any clear observation of the interior of the car. Paul adjusted the focus to gain a better perspective.

"What the hell?" he muttered under his breath.

As the driver lowered the tinted window slightly, Paul quickly adjusted the ISO and f-stop to maximize detail of exposure in the late-morning diffused light and braced himself and the camera against the car to compensate for the slower shutter speed. The softness of the mist that had complemented Alexandra's beauty was now making it difficult to achieve the optimum detail to identify the intruder in his frame. The camera captured frames in rapid succession with the shutter on repeat mode. This was one of those times when the technology of digital photographs had a distinct advantage over film.

Through the telephoto lens, he could only confirm the driver had light hair. He wasn't sure of other facial features because the driver had withdrawn into the darker nucleus of his vehicle, possibly in a conscious effort to obscure his identity.

Paul found himself becoming exceedingly anxious as it became apparent the driver was also photographing Alexandra. The vehicle and driver were beyond the range of Alexandra's peripheral vision because she had turned slightly away from the Mercedes. Paul's assessment of the driver's actions was that this was clandestine professional surveillance. He recalled Alexandra's description of sociopathic behaviour as they stood at the kiosk at the train station in Luxembourg. The behavioural pattern of the driver was too erratic. The threat was imminent, real and present.

The Mercedes suddenly drove off at speed in the opposite direction. A newer model red Peugeot had pulled up a short distance ahead of Alexandra. Noticing it pull up, Alexandra walked toward the car with a deliberate stride. A tall wiry man got out and moved to the rear of his vehicle. Looking at Paul, she motioned for him to remain where he was beside their car. Alexandra and the driver shook hands.

"I won't ask, Alexandra," Jacques commented with indifference in his voice as he handed her a container.

"Just as well, *mon ami*. In the fullness of time, I will let you know as much as I can."

"From the autopsy, I can confirm that Madame Deschaume died as a result of injuries sustained in the fall, particularly the fractured skull and neck. That is as much as I can tell you right now. I sent the blood and stomach content samples off to our local lab for a level one analysis. I'll call you when I receive the results. Do not hesitate to contact me, Alexandra, if there is anything else I can assist you with."

She thanked Jacques, turned and walked toward Paul.

"That was Jacques Moreau," she explained as they got in their car.

"I thought as much."

Paul had immediately recognized the container as an insulated carrying case for vials of blood or other perishable fluids. He had handled too many in his career to mistake it for anything else. As he glanced at the container, Alexandra looked at him with another of her quirky wide-eyed, I'll-explain-later expressions that he was beginning to realize was an endearing albeit at times frustrating aspect of her personality.

How undeniably elegant yet remotely mysterious she was. Her intrigue energized him, as he had never experienced before with anyone else. Perhaps it was the menace of the moment, but danger be damned. She radiated such beauty, yes physical, but also mental, spiritual, emotional and intellectual.

"You hadn't mentioned that you were a photographer, and a serious one by the look of your camera," Alexandra commented.

"I've been dabbling in photography for a long time. I used to do landscapes but now my passion is portraits. I hope you don't mind but I took a few of you standing by the water."

As he spoke, he scanned the images of the black Mercedes on the camera's display. Some shots of the driver showed higher resolution and excellent detail. He should be able to enhance them with the digital software on his desktop at home. Although he much preferred to have his finger on the shutter behind the camera than on a keyboard in front of a monitor, he appreciated the need to be proficient at both.

CHAPTER 15

As he put his camera away, he contemplated whether or not he should tell Alexandra now or later about the black Mercedes and the driver. *Would it upset her and cause her more grief?* He concluded she had to know now, given the level of demonstrated threat.

"In the airport parking lot in Brussels, do you recall any distinct features about the man who was standing by the black Mercedes?" he asked in as calm a tone as possible.

"Not much, I think he was average height and build with light hair, light sandy brown or blond possibly. I only had a brief glimpse before he disappeared. Why do you ask?"

"While you were standing by the water, I'm not sure if you noticed a C300 Class black Mercedes with an unusual tint on the windows stop ahead of us. The driver opened the window just slightly and appeared to be looking in your direction."

"My intuition was yelling at me to be careful," Alexandra interjected, "but I chose to ignore it because I just wanted to clear my head, not clutter it with more input. Damn."

"I took some shots. That's when it helps to have a high-quality telephoto lens. I could barely make out his appearance. I'm certain that he had light brown or blond hair. He drove away quickly when Jacques pulled up. And, AV, he was taking pictures of you."

Alexandra's face became pale as she stared at Paul, frowning. The contemplative silence that followed was broken only by their mutual acknowledgment of the threat of the circumstance. Taking deep breaths was becoming an all-too-common behaviour for them both, yet here they were again breathing in unison like synchronized swimmers.

"Thanks for sharing that with me. You would think that after all these years of listening to my intuition, what I call my *shrew*, I'd disregard my denial and instead pay attention. Damn, damn, damn! I've always listened to my sixth sense when working on other cases. It's just that with this case, where I'm so involved, I was challenged to interpret the signals so I decided to disregard them. That was a bad move on my part."

"Don't beat yourself up. You've been through an emotional maelstrom this past week and stuff is still coming your way from left field. It's my fault for not protecting your flank."

He reached over and rested his hand reassuringly on her shoulder. The reason for her distress was uncomplicated.

The undeniable truth flooded his mind. *I failed to protect her. I didn't do what I should have. But why?* He knew he had to do better next time and for all time. But what if there wasn't a next time?

Alexandra looked at him with renewed conviction. Her feelings for him and her confidence in his ability to protect her had not been dislodged by these circumstances. His hand on her shoulder encouraged her to reciprocate. In a gesture of deepening affection that she had not clearly conveyed previously, and in gratitude for the strength of his compassion, she leaned over and gently kissed him on the cheek.

Paul paused in an effort to prolong the moment. Her expression of fondness had thawed any lingering inhibitions.

"So, what's in the vial case?" he coolly asked.

"Ahhhh…" Alexandra muttered. It just dawned on her he would have recognized the carrier. No doubt he had handled several hundred, perhaps thousands, during his career.

"I asked Jacques for a sample of Madame Deschaume's blood and contents of her stomach. Let's go back to Brussels. I'll fill you in along the way."

No sooner had they departed Dieppe, than her phone rang.

"Hello, Jacques, what's up?"

"Two items, Alexandra. First, due to financial cutbacks, my request for the blood and stomach analyses was denied because the police report indicated her death was not suspicious. She died from natural causes, the police investigator concluded in the report."

Jacques sighed in dumbfounded resignation.

"A frail elderly person scaling a bunker and falling to the beach below is a new interpretation of natural causes," Alexandra responded.

"The bean counters in the local police precinct and in our own coroner's office are looking to save money everywhere they can and the senior administrators are allowing them to call the shots so they can look good in the eyes of their bosses. Welcome to the world of cutbacks. So, your vial of blood and sample of the stomach contents are it."

"Thank you, Jacques, I suspected that might happen. I've been experiencing the same financial squeeze. So you can understand why I requested the second samples. You mentioned another item."

"Yes, I received a very strange phone call from a man who would not identify himself by name, just that he was a friend of Madame Deschaume. He wanted to know if anyone had claimed the body. The vagueness in his voice was suspicious. It sounded German. It just didn't sit well with me. *C'est tout*, that's all I have."

"Thank you very much for calling, Jacques. I'll keep in contact."

Alexandra relayed Jacques's two points to Paul.

"So, you were wondering why I asked Jacques for the second vial of blood and sample of the stomach content. I suspected his request for the analyses would be denied because of government-wide cuts to all budgets. This is where I really need your help, Paul. I don't believe that Madame Deschaume died from natural causes. My *shrew* tells me there were other intervening variables. A full spectrum analysis of her blood and contents of her stomach might provide a clue. As I mentioned before, I need all the information I can get in order for me to complete a psych profile on whoever is behind this. I just know from my experience of conducting profile analyses that you throw your net as far as possible and as wide as possible. Invariably, you find a little minnow of a clue in the fabric of the netting."

"I think I know where you're coming from. You want me to conduct the full analysis of both samples. Is that correct?"

"You've got it, my friend. I appreciate you are on retirement leave and have probably left the building, like Elvis. But can you get back into your lab just this once?"

"Oh, yes," he replied confidently. "I still have my keys and technically I'm still on the payroll. If I get caught, what are they going to do, fire me?"

Before he re-met Alexandra, he would have adopted the official denial response to her request. Today was different.

The drive back to Brussels was marked by similar monitoring of rear-view mirrors but without the anxiety that had accompanied the scrutiny enroute to Dieppe. Almost without conscious effort, Paul pulled into several rest stops just to affirm their situational awareness.

Given the circumstances, they agreed without any debate to take the Eurail from Brussels to Paris where Paul would conduct the analyses. He had insisted that she not proceed to Amsterdam alone as previously planned. Until they became aware of the intervening variables, as she put it, he would be her bodyguard. Together, they would go to Amsterdam after Paris to collect her clothes from the apartment. Thereafter, they would proceed to Luxembourg where she would attend to the sale of the house on rue Michel Welter and other items on her to-do list.

No sooner had they discussed the sale of the house than her phone rang. The real estate agent had forwarded her an email with listings for her to review. She responded, acknowledging receipt of the listings and stated that her plans had changed slightly. It would be a few days before she could make any decisions. It would be best if he held off with further emails until she was back in Luxembourg.

Being more relaxed on this leg of the journey, they took the opportunity to catch up on the years that had passed under the bridge since Montigny-lès-Metz.

After pulling into the airport parking lot, Alexandra deleted their route from the GPS. A quick assessment of the parking lot and a check-in with her *shrew* resulted in no concerns. They then returned their chariot of fire to the car rental agency and went to the underground Eurail station.

CHAPTER 16

On the Eurail ride to Paris, Alexandra took the opportunity to vet the balance of the contents of her mother's safety deposit box.

"Not much here of pressing urgency," she mumbled.

Paul turned and smiled in support. He disliked matters of administration and bureaucracy as much as she did.

One of the dividers in the manila folder contained a torn, stained envelope. Inside were the old black and white photographs her mother had referred to in her letter. Some were dog-eared while others were marked with water stains. Everything had a faint yeasty smell from the dampness.

As she reviewed them, her curiosity was overshadowed by caution. Most depicted men in Nazi uniforms either relaxing around World War II Nazi armoured vehicles or standing in front of bombed-out brick buildings. Other photos were taken in a desert and showed men in military versions of the attire archaeologists might wear in that climate. They were standing by trucks and tarp-covered boxes. Someone had written on the back of one of the photographs – *Boche*. She recognized the word. It was a derogatory term for German. What caused her most concern were two pictures, one depicting a woman dressed in an out-of-fashion dress and the second of a man in slacks and a shirt. She recognized the scenes to be in Luxembourg, the first in front of the train station and the other on rue Michel Welter. One had been annotated on the back, *'fm?' What was the relevance of this inscription?*

Paul watched as she repeatedly shuffled through them. After a moment of hesitation, she gave him a searching look and passed the photographs over. Paul examined them in equal detail. He was also drawn to the ones of the woman and the man in Luxembourg. They were both wearing distinctive owlish horn-rimmed glasses accentuating the dark pockets beneath their eyes. Pointing to these two photos, he whispered, "They are in an uneven frame and the resolution is grainy. There is subtle distortion around the edges. So, I would say they appear to have been taken at a distance with a telephoto lens mounted on a camera of moderate quality. Not a typical friends and family set-up."

He searched Alexandra's face for an indication of emotion but her expression remained neutral. Neither made an effort to speak in the silence that followed. Instead, Paul concentrated on Alexandra as she looked at the photos. Finally, relief was obvious in her expression. A smile quickly returned to his face in response to her re-engagement.

"So, what other surprises has your mother left for you to find in this mysterious Easter egg hunt?" Paul asked.

Comedy and tragedy are dependent upon one another. The moment called for the former.

Alexandra chuckled and delved further into the bag. It held other goodies of unknown consequence.

Not included in the manila folder was a separate envelope. Inside the second envelope she retrieved an adhesive note that was attached to a claim tag. Her mother had written on the note: "Bring this with you when you come to my apartment and present it to the proprietor of the jewellery store." The claim tag described the item being stored or repaired as a *"replica Lady Diana ring."*

As in *Alice's Adventure in Wonderland*, this Easter egg hunt into the contents of the safe deposit box was becoming curiouser and curiouser.

The final Easter egg was a key threaded with a small chain that held a tag for *47, rue Michel Welter*. With an exasperated breath, she uttered softly, "Eureka, I've found it!"

"You've found what?" Paul asked with an inquisitive smile.

"The key to our house on rue Michel Welter. When I met the real estate agent at the house before we left for Brussels, the key I had didn't fit. I figured my mother had changed the lock but hadn't sent me a new key. Now, I can contact the real estate agent. But first, I'd better try it out to make sure it works."

She exclaimed gleefully, "I can now almost strike one more thing off my list. Almost counts, doesn't it?"

Paul's grin of admiration for her depth of deductive reasoning and whimsical response supported her supposition.

"Absolutely, AV, it almost counts."

⁂

THE CONDUCTOR WALKED DOWN THE AISLE AND announced their approaching destination as the digital sign above the door confirmed Paris Gare Du Nord.

Alexandra made two calls as the train pulled up to the platform, one to Collette and one to her librarian friend, Jo. She asked Collette to meet her for dinner at the Novotel Paris Les Halles. Her friend did not answer so she left a text message advising that she was back in Paris. They would confirm a time to meet later for some face-to-face girl talk and ride time.

Paul was puzzled that she wanted to meet Collette for dinner at the Novotel because it was in the core of the city at least a two- if not three-hour drive from her home in Gagne. Those time estimates were in normal rather than the rush hour traffic that was threatening to grip Paris in 24/7 gridlock.

Once inside the station, they coordinated their calendars. Paul would go to his office to conduct the analyses of the blood and stomach contents. He would pick her up at the Novotel at 8 a.m. tomorrow. They would then go to the seniors' home where his father was lodged and ask him what he knew about *le fantôme*.

Thereafter, they would return to the Novotel for lunch and a critical review of any facts they had gained. It was a plan.

Their lingering adieu at the station was punctuated not by shaking hands but by holding hands to prolong the moment of separation. It hadn't yet been ninety-six hours since Paul greeted her with, "AV, how are you?" The emotional rollercoaster ride that followed their meeting after forty years had been stirring.

Parting now, if only until the morning, was not sweet sorrow as suggested by Shakespeare in Romeo and Juliet, *but painful*, he pondered.

Alexandra thought to herself: *Being separated from hearth and home in Gagne no longer has any meaning because I never did have a home, instead just a house occupied by my husband. It contains unfortunate memories and constant tension.* The shared mortgage was one source of her torment. She hated the house that retained her anguish and anger. In contrast, the reality of being separated from Paul until the morning was now causing her trepidation. *He is my bodyguard, my knight, my prince. What if I need him immediately?* With this thought, she began to experience some anxiety.

Paul became acutely aware that her hand had become markedly cold and tense. In concern and perhaps in an effort to lengthen their conversation and palpable connection, he looked at her affectionately and asked, "Are you okay?"

The ambient noise created by the commerce of the station muffled his voice but she recognized what he had asked and, most importantly, knew what he meant.

She told him she was fine and he told himself she was fine.

Yet they both knew the emotions of the moment could not lie. Their holding hands transformed into a final handshake. This gesture closed their proximity to each other. Paul leaned forward, tilted his head slightly toward her, and said softly into her ear,

"À demain."

She mimicked his posture and whispered softly into his ear.

"À *demain*."

He paused for one last fleeting glance and a heartfelt smile before turning and walking toward the exit doors. He felt anguished. At least this time it wouldn't be for forty years.

He hadn't noticed Alexandra was standing motionless, consumed by her feelings. She stared after him as he strode away. Even if she called out to him over the clamour, he wouldn't hear her.

But, she resolved, *at least this time it won't be for forty years.*

CHAPTER 17

Paul arrived at the Novotel Paris Les Halles about half an hour early. Perhaps Alexandra might be ready and they could have a coffee before heading to the seniors' home to talk with his father.

He walked into the lounge. She was seated, staring at the entrance. Their eyes met.

Thank you, Apollo, I owe you one, he thought.

She stood up as he approached, radiating a smile that warmed the room like rays of the early morning sun.

"I was hoping you might arrive early so we could confirm our day or at least sketch out some contingencies."

"But of course," he said heartily. "When I plan, I am always reminded of the old Yiddish expression, *'Man plans and God laughs.'* That has certainly proven to be accurate when I consider my retirement plans of late."

They agreed on the schedule as if it needed to be agreed to at all.

"Let's take the Metro as the traffic is more congested than I can ever remember, and parking is terrible," Paul suggested. "Our stop is just a short walk to the seniors' home."

Alexandra agreed and they walked to the Metro station. The seniors' home was just four stops away. As they were leaving the Metro, a passenger by the door stood and bowed in respect.

"Monsieur le Colonel, bonjour."

Paul nodded in response as the other passengers pushed them out of the door and onto the platform before he could reply. As he looked back at the man, his heart rate increased, his chest tightened, and his breathing became more laborious. He knew the reaction and the required response, to breathe slowly with deliberate deep breaths. He knew he could control his physiological response if he intervened early through the strength of his intellect and the endurance of his character. It was mind over matter of the mind.

"That man just called you *colonel*. What was that about?" Alexandra asked. *Where do I know him? Where have we met before?* she asked herself.

Paul paused before responding, "I was in the army reserve and retired as a colonel. He and I met in Sarajevo when I served with the United Nations Protection Force mission in 1992 to 1993. His name is Marcel Cousteau and he was my driver."

Alexandra looked astonished. "You served with the UN in Sarajevo, when the war was on, when bullets were flying and snipers were killing innocent civilians running like frightened mice in the maze of streets?"

"It wasn't that bad," he suggested nonchalantly. "As long as you knew when it was safe and when not to poke your head up, it was okay."

It dawned on him that if Alexandra was aware of the pounding in his chest she would conclude otherwise.

"Are you kidding me? Snipers? Bombs? What were you doing in Sarajevo at the height of the war?"

"We were working in what was colloquially named Tito's Palace, with other international United Nations Protection Force headquarters staff. The interior of Tito's residence was opulent although without the excesses of Versailles. It was breathtaking nonetheless. The three centuries of art that adorned the walls reminded me of the Louvre. What was most startling was the row of chandeliers. They hung over the dining room table that could seat a platoon of generals, which it almost did on occasion. It really was a memorable experience, and safe from the destructive forces which had devastated the city. All the warring factions respected Tito as the leader of the Yugoslavian partisans during the Second World

War and later as prime minister. So, in deference, they tended not to shoot at his palace."

Paul held the door to the seniors' home open for Alexandra to enter. They checked in at the reception counter and then walked toward the elevator that welcomed them with open doors. His deep breathing had mitigated the tension and slowed his heart rate.

As the doors closed, Alexandra turned and faced Paul and said in a quiet voice. "You never mentioned that you worked with the UN. You never cease to amaze me."

"It was no big deal. You did what you had to do to help bring about peace. When the bugle calls, you do what you must do. That's what blue beret peacekeeping is all about."

Alexandra leaned forward until the tip of her nose touched his.

"You are incredible," she whispered.

The bell announcing their floor did not resonate in their minds. When the doors opened, a cleaner who was waiting to enter with her cart paused in polite respect as she observed the closeness of the moment of the two occupants. She then purposely cleared her throat in a not-so-subtle communication. Paul and Alexandra broke eye contact and walked out to the room where Paul's father was resting in bed.

"Papa, how are you? How are they treating you?"

"Terribly, Paul, they won't let me smoke. They don't accept my assessment that smoking helps me to stop wheezing."

"Papa, this is Alexandra. She is Maria's daughter."

"You have grown since last I saw you, Alexandra. If I might add, you have become a beautiful, elegant lady. I sincerely hope my son is treating you with the respect due to a most gracious princess."

"He has been a prince, and thank you for the compliment. It is not often that a maturing woman is noticed amongst the youthful."

"Wisdom of age and the lure of enduring beauty will always triumph over misspent youth and misguided vigour," he added.

Alexandra and Paul glanced at each other, smiling, and then bowed cordially to acknowledge his astute humour.

"I am pleased the dementia has not diminished your wittiness, Papa."

"I was so sorry to hear of your mother's passing, Alexandra. Paul may have mentioned that we worked together briefly on a case in Montigny-lès-Metz that stumped us both and the other investigators. I have often thought about that case, more so lately as I lay here reflecting on the skeletons in my life's closet. Mine, I fear, is a double walk-in closet!"

"Papa, what can you remember about that case? Alexandra is interested in learning more about what her mother did back then."

"*Ma chérie*, if I may call you that, I suffer from the ills of dementia. It causes my mind to wander, so please forgive the ramblings of an old man. However, my recall of events long ago remains crystal clear, fortunately. The lead investigator was Philip Marchand. If anyone could solve a case, it was Philip with his dogged determination, excellent investigative skills and sixth sense. But this case was the exception. Philip and I crossed paths here in Paris a few times after he retired and our conversations would invariably end up discussing this case. I know it bothered him until the day he died because the murderer was still out there stalking more victims, women. They died not knowing who had killed them or the reason why they had been targeted. I can't remember where Philip is buried, but others will. The devil of dementia has stolen that detail from my memory. I have lost my train of thought. I am sorry if I have repeated myself. Remind me of your question, Paul."

"I asked what you remembered about Maria's involvement in the case and you said what a skilful investigator Philip was."

"Yes, thank you. There were some details that I know Philip did not record in the file. We knew there were two victims in our case, a mother and her daughter, and we suspected that both might have succumbed to poison of some sort, although I don't believe Philip recorded our suspicions in the file. A witness, a neighbour, described them as appearing disoriented and dazed just before they died. Philip had a hunch these deaths were related to other deaths outside the jurisdiction of our precinct. I recall Philip going to Lyon and Carcassonne, and perhaps elsewhere. What he may have found out he never recorded in the file. Each time he returned from one of these trips he would be withdrawn and pensive for several days. There was something about this case that Philip took personally. It really haunted him. He was never like that with other cases."

"Did he ever talk to you about those details he didn't record, Papa, or anything else to do with the case that could help Alexandra determine Maria's involvement?"

"Yes and no. I listened closely when he mused and muttered under his breath. I would often just watch him. What he didn't say would often hold more details. There were times when Philip acted differently, out of character. He was always very careful, but he was extra cautious at times when working on this case as if he had a premonition of imminent danger. Criminals involved in some other cases could be dangerous, but this case was different, almost as if it had a satanic, sinister element. What bothered Philip most was that all the victims were women. In addition to our case, in at least one other I became aware of, a mother and daughter were poisoned. There may have been others. He did mention once he wasn't certain whether the murderer was male or female. Philip wasn't a particularly religious man but he would sit in the cathedral and meditate as if ritually praying. Being in God's house must have given him a sense of solace and security, and perhaps some guidance."

"And Alexandra's mother, did she work with Philip just on this case or were there other cases? How close were you and Philip and Maria?"

"You must remember I was a just a patrol officer back then and Philip was a senior investigator. So, under normal conditions, we would not have had much contact beyond the professional pleasantries. I do recall Maria and Philip talking at length in his office on at least one occasion, but that's all I knew. As far as my closeness to Philip, I was deeply honoured when he chose me to be one of his protégés. We just got along. No doubt my career advanced quickly as a result of what he taught me. One of his lessons was that there were two types of knowledge: *sophia* and *phronesis*. He would say, 'I can teach you about sophia, but you must learn about phronesis on your own. I cannot teach you that. He was correct and I would mention that to others I was assigned to train or mentor in later years."

"One last question, Papa. Did Philip ever mention *le fantôme* either when discussing this case or at another time?"

"I remember hearing Philip mutter the name but that's all. If I remember correctly, he mentioned something about *le fantôme* after he returned from one of his trips to Lyon or Carcassonne. I had no hard evidence. I just had a feeling Philip might have known *le fantôme* during the war and may have met him again while working as a detective. I could be wrong. I was never part of the conversations he had with Maria and he never mentioned anything to me about what they had discussed. Thinking back now, I always had the impression that Maria and Philip knew each other before this case. I don't know why and maybe it was nothing, but it has been a long time. I will think about it more now that you have asked, and let you know if I remember anything when you next come to visit."

"Thank you, Papa. You are looking a little tired. We can come back later, just to visit, and play some chess as long as you let me win at least one game."

"*Au revoir, ma chérie*. Please grace me with your beautiful presence as often as possible. You have an aura that brightens my day. And you can accompany Alexandra if you wish, Paul!"

"I would be honoured and thank you for your compliments. I will visit with Paul and watch you beat him at chess."

"Alexandra, would you excuse us just for a moment, please? Paul, one personal item."

As Alexandra left the room, Paul paused for additional deep slow breaths. "Yes, Papa?"

"Just an observation, mon fils. Your life with your wife, whatever her name is… I can't remember…."

"Suzette, Papa, her name is Suzette."

"Whatever, Paul. She has been a millstone around your neck all these years. Some people have crutches while others have crosses to bear. Your wife has been a millstone, the manifestation of her own self-indulging misery, and a cross for you to bear. I have not seen you truly happy with her, not before you got married and certainly not after."

"Yes, I'm aware of that, Papa. I've been reflecting on my life these past few days, particularly because of my impending retirement. I've come to the same realization. I really haven't been very happy. It's been a tough pill to swallow."

"Hear me out, mon fils. In the last several minutes, I've never seen you happier and more content and it is due to the company you presently keep with Alexandra. You know I have always read your aura and let you know what I see. Right now, your aura is more relaxed and warmer than ever before, and I mean ever. I see the same warmth and compassion in Alexandra's aura, together with you. The two of you are like dancing otters gleefully swirling in each other's presence. I see in the two of you together the harmony of the spirit your mother and I cherished all those years, and so wanted you to experience. You and Alexandra seem to be at each other's centre but apart."

"I know what you are saying. I've always admired what you and Maman had and wondered what went wrong with my marriage. I know it takes two to tango and I had the wrong dance partner. I take responsibility for that bad choice."

"Your mother and I brought you up in the Catholic Church. It taught you to honour the sanctity of marriage, and you have lived your life honouring those precepts. I never thought the day would arrive when I said this but, mon fils, divorce your wife and enjoy what your mother and I had, before it's too late. Don't find yourself on your deathbed regretting decisions which are in your power to change. The Pope is not always right!"

"You are correct once again, Papa. But…."

"But nothing, Paul. Alexandra is meant for you and you for her. Your mother and I saw this ordained destiny when you were together all those years ago in Montigny-lès-Metz. Fate separated the two of you then, but now the serendipitous circumstance of her mother's death has brought you together. Alexandra was always meant to be your soul mate. One of my deep regrets is that I could have intervened to influence fate back then but chose not to. That is one of the skeletons in my closet that I will carry to my grave. For whatever cause or reason, it is of no consequence now. I thank God that Providence has now intervened."

Paul sighed, acknowledging the truth of what his father had said. Affairs of the heart can become *la dance savage*. The reality was that he was so traumatized by his perceived rejection by Alexandra when they were young that he became insecure in other relationships, including his marriage. With his father's blessing to move on in pursuit of happiness, he would ponder the options and their consequences.

Paul sensed Alexandra's presence at this moment. It made him feel fulfilled. His father's analogy of the otters dancing as soul mates in unison rang true with his feeling towards her.

He reached forward and grasped his father's hand. It was weaker than normal. He whispered, "Thank you, Papa, know that I love you, more so now with this blessing and concern for my happiness than ever before."

Holding his hand, he paused as his father drifted off to sleep. His pale complexion resembled the steel-grey clouds gathering on the Parisian skyline.

Alexandra was waiting for him as he quietly slipped out of the room and closed the door. Noting a distance in his demeanour, she leant forward and gently grasped his forearm.

"Everything all right?"

"Yes, fine," he replied.

His heart was calm with a regular beat and a reassuring wholeness.

"Let's go back to the Novotel for an early lunch, review our plans and adjust as needed."

The metro was packed with busy people consumed with their own lives. With no available adjacent seats, they chose to stand close together, holding on to the railings and straps. As the train swayed on the tracks, sometimes causing passengers to lurch back and forth, he held on to her waist and she to his. They were, once again, swirling and dancing in unison like playful otters in a watery recital of a performance unfolding without a scripted finale.

CHAPTER 18

Back at the hotel, they reviewed the facts in sequential order as best they could. There were more questions than answers, more unknowns than knowns. What was of greatest concern were the unknown unknowns and the consequences of such uncertainties. Their immediate calculation led both to the same conclusion. They needed more facts.

"This is frustrating, Paul."

"Yes, but there is a Zen proverb that suggests sometimes the obstacle *is* the path. So, let's focus on the obstacles while maintaining a strategic perspective of paths."

The next step was to analyse the samples. Yesterday, the lab was too busy with priority cases. Paul would have this completed by late afternoon.

"Can we meet this evening after I get the results?"

"Collette is driving me to Gagne this afternoon. Last evening at dinner, she mentioned her father was away doing something or other, so it would be a good time to get some laundry done and to attend to a few other domestic duties without other distractions. Could we meet tomorrow morning, say ten-ish, in the parking lot of Gregorim Distribution on the rue de Paris in Les Lilas?"

"Ten-ish is good as I need to drop off my car at the dealership first thing in the morning for scheduled maintenance."

Alexandra sensed the time was right to delve into aspects of his life he had only alluded to.

"You mentioned you have two sons. Where are they and what are they doing?"

Paul paused for a sip of coffee and to gather his thoughts.

"My elder son, Yvon, can best be described as a disaster. He has been walking a tightrope with the law since he was very young. In school, he was caught cheating repeatedly. His mother defended him to the hilt, blaming the other students, the teachers and the school. He was caught plagiarizing papers at college and at the second incident was suspended. He never returned. He has always sought the easy way. In college, he picked courses where group work was involved because he saw these collective activities as his key to graduation where others would do the work and carry him. Last I heard, he was a dead-beat dad on the run from responsibility."

"I'm surprised, given your philosophy and accomplishments," Alexandra commented. "But people chart their own course, especially some young people who want to shrug off the influence of their parents. My Marc was like that when he was a teenager. Yet Collette followed closely in my path."

Paul continued, "To be honest, Yvon takes after his aunt. Suzette has a twin sister whose life has been a debacle, one disaster after another. She has affairs with guys she scarcely knows. She is currently in Argentina working on her fifth husband. Her first husband was a drug addict she met on the streets when she was dealing. He OD'ed. Her second was a dealer who had profited from the proceeds of his illicit trade but was murdered by a rival drug dealer. She lost most of the money he had left her in nightclubs and bars while supposedly mourning his death. That's when she met hubby number three who blew the balance of her bank account on great investments which would make them wealthy. He left her when the money ran out. Number four was from Argentina. She followed him to Buenos Aires where they got married, only to find out that he was already married. Last we heard, she was hooked up with number five but was crying in her soup because he was in jail and she had to work for a living. Word on the street is that Yvon took off to Argentina to be with her."

His eyes had fallen away from Alexandra as he replenished their cups from the carafe. She smiled softly and patiently waited for him to continue.

"My younger son, Jean, is the complete opposite. He excelled academically and in sports, track and field while at school. My father introduced him to the game of chess at a very young age, like me. Jean became fascinated with the game and learned the art and science of strategy under the rigorous tutelage of his grand-papa. My papa was very good, but Jean surpassed him in a few years, much to the chagrin and pride of his Master Yoda. You could say that the sorcerer became the sorcerer's apprentice. Jean went on to become a master chess player, winning numerous awards and trophies. Like my trophies in fencing, his mother would not allow him to display them even in his bedroom because she said they just collected dust, not that she ever dusted."

"You mentioned to your father that the two of you should play. Do you often play chess with him or your son?"

"Papa is still a pretty good player but has difficulty concentrating. I play with Jean only when I want to eat a large piece of humble pie! I believe he respects his father so he beats me in fifteen moves as opposed to ten. That way, I don't feel so inferior."

Alexandra chuckled in response. "I get the feeling you do not feel inferior. My uncle and aunt taught me to play chess but not at the level of you, Jean and your father. Perhaps we could play sometime and you could help me improve my game. It's been many years since I've played so I'm a bit rusty."

"I'd enjoy that very much. I'll tell Papa next time we visit I've met another worthy opponent. But be prepared. He'll probably challenge you to a friendly game."

Alexandra noticed the veil over his distant smile and a slight withdrawal in Paul's demeanour as they spoke. Something suggested he might not wish to reveal anything further. Now was not the occasion to proceed down the White Rabbit's tunnel. In the fullness of time and in a space of greater trust, these secrets of the soul might surface. For now, she was learning about what motivated him and the less explicit details of his life.

"Back to Jean. He always strove for gold. He would work with others on projects in school but only if the others set gold as the goal. Jean was not willing to settle for average. He described compromise as the best of the worst and the worst of the best, the cream of the crap."

"That sounds like his father and grand-papa," Alexandra commented.

"Jean completed a master's degree in computer science with a double major in linguistics. He felt languages have a common foundation, both spoken languages and computer languages. He is currently working as an analyst with the Préfecture de police de Paris in their newly formed Forensic Digital Investigation Unit. He is perfectly tri-lingual in French, German and English, and has a working knowledge of Italian and Spanish. As he advanced through his career, he completed courses at the Police Academy, the Maisons Alfort in Paris, and the Gendarmerie School in Brussels. You would know from your experience that it is the biggest and best in Belgium. Jean is on the fast track and unless he shoots himself in the foot, which I doubt he will because he is too intuitive, he should advance well in his career. On a personal level, he has been in a long-term relationship but recently it seems to have dissolved. Like his papa, he works long hours. More than likely, that routine affected the relationship."

As he described his two sons, Alexandra could not help but notice the disappointment in his voice when he talked about Yvon and the pride as he described Jean's accomplishments. *I wonder if he sees the same emotions in me when I spoke of Marc and Collette?* she wondered.

Working long hours certainly had an adverse impact on her marriage with André. Thinking back, she concluded there wasn't anything there to hold it together in the first place. She had married André for all the wrong reasons.

Collette now arrived to take her mother to Gagne. Alexandra introduced Paul as a colleague. She explained they were working on one last case together before she formally retired. She added that Paul was also on the eve of retirement.

"I recognize you from the funeral reception, Dr. Bernard. Thank you for attending."

"I am honoured to meet you, Collette, and please call me Paul. My father and your grand-maman also worked together on a case many years ago. Your mother has told me a great deal about you. How are your studies at university?"

"I very much enjoy the discipline of psychology and really like statistics and quantitative research. I'm actually tutoring some friends who are amazed at how I can complete mental calculations faster than they can do them electronically. One day, I hope to be as successful in a career that provides rewards, just like my mother."

"Being your mother's daughter, I'm confident you will. I hope we meet again soon and you can tell me more of your plans but for now, I must be off. I'll call you this evening, AV."

He held back the urge to reach out and hug her, forever. The more he was with her the less he wanted to leave her. Instead, he just extended his hand.

He sensed that Alexandra was experiencing similar feelings about his departure.

Collette looked at her mother and asked, "Who's AV and what's that about?"

"It's just casual protocol, dear. Sometimes it's easier to use a person's initials in an informal or relaxed working environment. Let's go to Gagne before the traffic gets any worse."

The women quickly walked to the door of the hotel. Alexandra was hoping to get a last glimpse of Paul but to no avail. Her heart sank slightly as she experienced the emotions of her first love. Tomorrow would bring a reunion and, in the interim, she would be busy organizing her separation from Gagne. It wasn't a question of *if*; it was a matter of *when*, and that would be soon.

CHAPTER 19

The next morning, Paul arrived at the parking lot of Gregorim Distribution in Les Lilas before Alexandra. As he stepped out of the car, he was distracted by a loud motorcycle approaching the parking lot.

There should be a noise by-law to deal with these intrusions into the peace and quiet of law-abiding citizens of the community, he thought.

The increasing intensity of muffler rumble suggested the bike was getting closer. He looked up to see a late model Harley-Davidson pulling into the parking stall beside him. The body-tight leather jacket and chaps worn by the rider left little to the imagination. Even before he noticed the long chestnut hair tied in a leather-bound ponytail extending below the helmet, it was obvious the rider was female.

He reconciled his initial assessment of the ruckus. The disturbance of the loud muffler had its redeeming qualities. He relaxed and took in the aesthetics of the moment as the rider got off the bike and removed her helmet.

"AV, is that you?!" he exclaimed.

"Yes, why wouldn't it be me?" she replied. "We did agree to meet here."

"You ride a Harley-Davidson?"

"Did you think that only *les gars* rode hogs? That's a male chauvinist attitude, don't you think?"

"Ahhhhhh... No! I just...."

"You just what, Paul?" she laughed. "Don't you ride?"

Alexandra caught the terseness of her response and immediately regretted it. Before she could apologize, Paul replied, "I've never ridden a serious bike like a Harley. I had a Solex as a kid and then traded up to a Moped. I had a Vespa after that when I was in the last year at the Lycée Louis-le-Grand. It was grey like thousands of others back then, but it was my pride and joy. Someone stole it and I was heartbroken. I never got another one after that. My younger son, Jean, had a Moped I would ride but when he got a Ducati, I was only allowed to take it out on the rare occasion when he wasn't using it and only with his permission."

"You attended the Lycée Louis-le-Grand? I'm impressed. That's one of the most prestigious secondary schools in France."

"I guess so but there weren't any elective courses in riding Harleys. So, how long have you been riding?"

"I got my first Harley, a used Sportster, when I was completing my undergraduate degree. I wanted to make a fashion statement. It was cheap transportation, and I was a starving student… well, not exactly starving."

"I don't know my bikes as well as I know Greek Mythology, but this one is a classic. What year is it and where did you get it?"

"Here in Paris at the Harley dealership. It has a captivating history."

Paul thought to himself that everything about her was classic and captivating, especially this Harlista persona. It was a side of Alexandra he admired. *Candens es – you are hot,* he thought. *Candens es* had become his favourite Latin reflection for her.

"Are you listening to me, Paul? The story behind the bike? I was about to tell you."

"I'm with you," he replied.

"When you buy a Harley, the dealer is required to provide you with a background as best they know it. It's part of the purchase agreement. This bike is a 1972 Electra Glide 1200 and was initially used by the California Highway Patrol. An American military officer got it when it was auctioned by the State. He brought it with him when he was transferred to Germany, I think to the American base in Frankfurt. At some point, he ended up in Paris on some hush-hush assignment. There, he traded it in for a new Street Glide because he was riding a lot and the newer model suited his needs. I walked into the dealership as the deal was being closed and immediately fell in love with it. I had to have it. End of story."

Paul was a bit perplexed, so she elaborated.

"At the time, I had been riding another Harley, what they called a Dyna. It was a hard, fast ride. It would start every time I turned the key and didn't require much maintenance. It was just there when I wanted it, for any short rides. Now this classic provides me with everything the Dyna did but with cruiser comforts. She has a saddle that wraps itself around me and provides me with the support I need. The chassis is designed for handling at both slow and fast speeds. Although she has some kilometres on her, she's just broken in. Rev up her RPM's and she will purr like a kitten. I call her Sophia and she takes care of my every need. It's all about the ride and the comfort of the saddle, Paul. The journey, not so much the destination, and the company you keep and the people you meet along the way."

Paul pondered whether Alexandra was talking just about the bike or was insinuating a more sensual relationship.

"Harley has a saying: Live to Ride and Ride to Live. I do some of my best thinking when I ride. The experience is Zen-like."

Has God punished me with Suzette, only to reward me with this Greek goddess in black leather? The name "Sophia" is Greek for "knowledge." Sophia was the goddess of wisdom in Greek mythology. Was there some hidden knowledge or wisdom here somewhere?

"Wanna ride with me, Paul?"

Ohhhhhhh...what a loaded question that was, he thought. *A hot lady in body-tight leather, what could be more blissful than that?*

He had driven behind female bikers and the perspective from that southern vantage point was most pleasing to sore eyes. Riding behind Alexandra might be more of a distraction than he could handle. His contemplation would keep a confessional priest busy and blushing.

"Yes! I would absolutely accept your invitation to ride with you. But I don't have a motorcycle, certainly not a Harley."

"That's a simple fix. We'll buy one at the Harley-Davidson dealership here in Paris. They usually have a full fleet in their showroom."

What a wonderful retirement activity that would be, and in the company of AV, he reckoned. *It would get me out of the house for long periods of time, perhaps days or even weeks for longer trips. Sophia, you have educated me, provided me with knowledge I have been seeking,* he concluded. *Retirement was already looking much more promising.*

Alexandra interrupted his train of thought and with a mischievous smile posed a spirited proposition. "I can hone your riding skills in the saddle. Are you up to it?"

Here in the parking lot they were dancing like playful otters once again. Nothing else mattered in the swirling space that had been created by the conversation. A silence surrounded them. He found himself standing close to her as she sat on the side of Sophia's saddle.

She found herself looking up into his brown eyes. He was off in Neverland with Peter Pan and Tinkerbell once again. That didn't bother her now. She just wanted to fuse the magic of the moment on the monitor of her mind.

This guy is incredible, she thought. *He is bright and intelligent and sensitive and charming and respectful and cultured and engaging and fun, and very handsome.*

Paul broke the silence. "Penny for your thoughts?"

Alexandra found herself replying, “Thoughts are precious and not for sale.”

But that was her mother’s response. What had just transpired between them?

“So, what did the analysis of the blood and stomach contents show?”

“Very interesting. In addition to a blood analysis, I also conducted a mass spectrometry scan. It’s an analytical technique that helps identify the amount and type of chemicals such as peptides and other similar compounds present in a sample by measuring the mass-to-charge ratio and abundance of gas-phase ions. Finally, I conducted a molecular analysis. Here, let me show you.”

Paul laid out a computer printout of the full spectrum analysis on the dented dirty hood of his ailing Renault.

“Sorry for the condition of this four-wheeled display table. This is my wife’s car. She doesn’t take any pride in it and gets really annoyed if I suggest that she wash it once in a while,” he explained apologetically. “Mine is in the garage for a tune-up. I’ll pick it up later today.”

“Not a problem,” Alexandra replied, as she relished yet another opportunity to move alongside him.

“See these four plots, graphs. They show that Madame Deschaume was taking Fenofibrate. This drug is mainly used to reduce cholesterol levels in people at risk of cardiovascular disease. A common drug name you may recognize is Lipidil. I would not be surprised if she had a prescription bottle of that in her purse. This second plot indicates the presence of acetylsalicylic acid commonly found in aspirin. She was probably taking this for arthritis. The third plot is Metformin, a medication that people take for diabetes, common for those who have late-onset Type 2 diabetes.”

“Would any of these meds or a combination cause her to feel faint or dizzy enough to fall off the gun emplacement?”

"Nothing would be surprising, given her age. Yet lots of people take these drugs in combination and do not experience any complications. Low blood pressure could cause fainting but there is no indication she suffered from that. But look at this plot. It is highly irregular. *It's cyanide!* This dosage would cause a person to feel dizzy and become confused or disoriented. In a weakened state, a person could die within several minutes, certainly within an hour. You can't get this cyanide across the counter at a drug store. I have seen it in other cases I've worked on. All the cases involved purposeful poisoning.

"Cyanide was certainly more common in the economy forty, sixty years ago," Paul continued, "but less so today. During the war, spies kept cyanide capsules and would take them if captured. Death would have been instantaneous because the dosage would have been high. Cyanide is still used today in some industries. Until not very long ago, it was used in photography for developing film. Jewellers also used it for cleaning tarnished jewellery, though they may be using less toxic alternatives these days."

CHAPTER 20

They looked at each other inquiringly, then broke eye contact as a motorcycle roared up beside them. "Hi, Alex," the rider yelled out. "Who's the adorable guy?"

Alexandra looked over her shoulder. It was Jo, her librarian friend. In the distraction of talking with Paul, she had temporarily forgotten they had made arrangements to ride today and to chat.

"I've got the information you were asking about, gal," Jo blurted out. She switched off the engine, took off her helmet and walked over to where Paul and Alexandra were standing.

"Jo, I'd like you to meet my friend, Paul. Paul, this is Josephine. We have been riding together forever. She is a librarian by profession but she doesn't meet the traditional profile of a demure, reserved, introverted bookworm."

Paul put out his hand.

"Very nice to meet you, Josephine. I see that you also ride a Harley. How's your saddle?"

Jo cocked her head slightly and glanced over at Alexandra who smiled with one of her quirky wide-eyed I'll-explain-later expressions. Jo's gaze returned to Paul as she shook his hand.

"Very nice to meet you too, Paul. Just call me Jo."

She immediately picked up on the vibes dancing around like freshly fallen leaves skittering along the Champs-Elysées energized by a brisk late-September breeze. Still holding Paul's hand, she glanced back at Alexandra with her eyes wide open as if to say, *What's with the hot dude, girl?*

Alexandra winked back in a semaphore code that communicated, yes, we'll definitely talk later.

"So, what got you into a career of being a librarian, Jo?" Paul asked.

"Not sure, exactly. I was a bookish girl. My first job was in a bookstore, stocking shelves with new inventory. The owner had a second store where she sold used books and some quite valuable rare editions. I think exposure to the classics tweaked my interest. Since working in the bookstores, I've developed a symbiotic relationship with books. I wonder about who reads books and what motivated the authors to write them, especially fiction. Now I find myself more interested in why people read and write in a certain genre."

"And where did you and AV first meet?" Paul followed up.

"I'm a bit of an amateur philosopher and psychologist in that way. That's where we first crossed paths. We were in some of the same classes at university, and we both rode Harleys back then. In the Sorbonne's Grand Amphitheatre, we sat in the front row because that was where the studious students congregated. The serious but less organized sat in the middle rows and the students who didn't know why they were there sat in the back where you couldn't hear anything anyway. I could tell you about some of the exploits that Alexandra and I did back then."

Alexandra immediately interrupted her before Jo could say more. Some of those stories she would rather Paul not know about, at least not now.

"I know that you have things to do, Paul. Jo and I need to ride before the weather turns bad. We can talk later."

"I look forward to hearing those stories of you and AV back then, Jo," Paul replied with a grin.

Alexandra was still very much of an enigma and he wanted to learn everything he could. Jo would be a good source.

"I'll call you this evening, AV. Take very good care of yourself, and Sophia."

As Paul drove off, Jo turned to Alexandra and said, "What's with the vibes, girl, and what's *AV* all about? The sparks are flying between the two of you, and I mean flying. Venus is aligned with Mars. I've never seen you so strong and beautiful. Talk to me, girl. You are just glowing!"

"I don't know what to say, Jo. I'm trying to make sense of it myself."

"What's his background? Where and when did you meet?"

"It's an interesting story, Jo. I'll tell you later but first, what did you find out?"

"Well, you asked me to search through the library database for the ghost and *le fantôme*. Under ghost, there are thousands of entries as you might expect, certainly too many to look at, a lot related to spirits and other such phenomenon. But under *le fantôme* and any cross-reference to the *Maquis*, now that was interesting. I came across one reference I thought you might be fascinated by. *Le fantôme* is mentioned in a murder mystery entitled, *'Until Death Do Us Part.'* The plot is set in the Vosgues Mountains around Saint-Avold, back in the '60s. In the story, the hero was with the *Maquis* during the war. The author is a Joan Cardiff who wrote dozens of novels, all set in the region. The lead investigator in the book is a detective who has the ability to solve tough cases because he doesn't always follow the rules and has a bit of a sixth sense, like you, Alex."

"Sorry to interrupt, Jo, but you mentioned the *Maquis*. What was that reference?"

"Something about the Midi-Pyrénées region in the south of France and smuggling downed Allied airmen to Spain, if I remember correctly."

Alexandra's heart started to beat faster. *That is a possible lead,* she thought. *Perhaps le fantôme isn't a mythical character and the connection might be real. If so, what's the relationship between the myth and circumstance?*

Jo continued, "I researched the author. All I can say for sure is she appears to be British and may have vacationed in northeast France and the Saar region of southern Germany at one point. From the date of publication and her apparent age from a photograph on the cover of the book, I estimate she would be about the same age as our parents or perhaps a little older. That's all I have thus far. I can send you the URL link if you want. Is that any help?"

"That's a great help, Jo. I owe you one."

"You mean you owe me one more. I'll add it to the collection of IOUs that I have on file under *Alexandra owes me one.*"

They both chuckled. It was true that Jo had so many of Alexandra's IOUs that one more simply made them laugh. Perhaps in her retirement, she could start paying Jo back.

"Now your turn. Tell me about Paul."

Alexandra briefly related the story of how they met as teenagers, how Paul came up with his nickname for her, and how they met again at the reception after her mother's funeral. She found herself talking to Jo about the depths of her emotions at dinner with Paul at the Café Kaempff-Kohler that evening, and how they talked into the wee hours of the night, until the proprietor politely reminded them the café was closed. It was a cliché, but time did seem to stand still as they were living in the moment.

At the end of the explanation, and for the first time she could remember, Jo did not respond immediately. Jo had a quick wit and would invariably return the volley in any discussion with her, but not on this occasion. She knew the emotional revelation was very special. Only when Collette was born did Alexandra ever express a similar depth of emotion.

After a long time, Jo just quietly whispered, "Wow!"

"It's weird, Jo. You know me better than anyone else. I'm

always in control of my feelings and emotions. Now, I'm not so sure. Yet, I think I'm okay with being less in control. I actually feel more in control, more alive, if that makes any sense."

"It sort of makes sense. But I'm not the one to judge, never having been able to maintain a long-term relationship with any guy."

After a pause, Alexandra looked at Jo, took a deep breath and gave the command.

"Saddle up, Jo. Let's ride!"

While on the ride, she asked Jo if she could leave Sophia in her garage and stay with her for a few days. She just could not face the prospect of staying in André's house even if he wasn't there. She felt ill at the thought. It would be one more IOU!

Jo welcomed her request. She had lots of room in her new place and would enjoy the company. After all, it would allow them more face-to-face girl time.

When Alexandra returned from her ride, she checked her voice mail. Paul had called and asked if they could meet tomorrow morning. He had developed and printed the digital images of the black Mercedes he had taken in Dieppe but had forgotten to show them to her.

She texted back to confirm the time and location. She then called Collette who was still in Gagne. She would ride back to André's, pack and load her suitcases into Collette's car. They would then travel to Jo's where she would move in. She explained to Collette she and Paul needed to be in close proximity as they worked on the case.

⁂

The next morning, she met Paul as planned.

"When we spoke yesterday about the analyses," Paul explained, "I got distracted by Jo's arrival and forgot to show you these photos I had taken of the black Mercedes in Dieppe. They exposed at a higher resolution than I had expected. You can make out some facial features of the driver quite well despite the fact he had withdrawn into the car. Take a look."

Alexandra scanned the photos examining one showing clearly the light-brown-blond hair of the driver and his face. She couldn't remember seeing him before or recognizing him from any previous encounters through her work. Putting on her forensic psych-profiling hat, she deduced he had an air of hubris, of indifference, as if he believed he was superior and held the upper hand. In all the photos, he was holding his head high, almost daring anyone to challenge him.

"AV, I've just had an idea – maybe a bit wacky though. We can compare these photos with the ones your mother left in the safe deposit box. My son, Jean, has shown me some of the cutting-edge digital imagery comparison work he has been developing. He can do some pretty incredible facial feature recognition and analyses. Of course, I'd be surprised if he could determine, see any direct matches to the Nazis standing by the armoured vehicles or the ones taken in Luxembourg and in the desert because this blond fellow doesn't look to be in his 70s or 80s as those soldiers would now be. But it's not impossible there's a connection. I could ask Jean to take a look if you can give them to me. Who knows what clues might emerge – he's a very clever fellow and loves to solve puzzles."

"Okay, I'll bring the photos with me next time we meet."

"I mentioned I took other photos of you, if you would like to take a look at some prints. You can keep any you like. I can enlarge or shrink them."

Alexandra shuffled through several photos, pausing on all but stopping on one.

"These are excellent, Paul, just excellent. I really like this one."

"It's my favourite, too. I like the way your ponytail flows over the nape of your neck and onto your shoulder. It really accentuates your profile."

"I'm usually not very photogenic. Cameras don't like me and I tend to shy away, especially if I know someone is taking my picture. But you are a really talented photographer! As a retirement hobby or even as a second career, you could hang out your shingle and be as busy as you wanted to be. I'd be a model for you any day."

If AV was my model, I wouldn't get any other work done, he mused. *I'd be pushing the limit of available digital frames on the memory card and spending the rest of my time in front of my monitor enhancing the images. I couldn't improve on her beauty, only on my ability to allow the beauty to be set free.*

"Could you take some of Sophia?" she asked.

"I'd be honoured to shoot Sophia and you in your leathers. Just name the time and place, and I'll be there."

"We could take some of you on your inaugural ride on your new Harley. So, when do we visit the Harley-Davidson dealership to get you back in the saddle?"

"I haven't set a date yet. I was hoping that you could advise me on which models I should take for a test ride."

"I'll add it to my list as number one priority. Well, number two. Number one is going through the cards and letters left at the funeral reception. I have to respond before any more time passes.

"And," she added, "we'll need to make a plan to follow up on Madame Deschaume's murder, now we know the cause was cyanide poisoning."

CHAPTER 21

Alexandra stayed up late replying to the many cards and letters left at the funeral and reviewing the names and messages in the guest book. Close to one hundred people had attended the funeral from the Benelux region, France, Germany, England, and surprisingly, from the United States. She had not realized just how many people her mother had met in her career. And then there were the associates from those times like Madame Deschaume. Alexandra had intended to read the letter from the distinguished elderly English gentleman Collette had handed her but her eyes were too tired from burning the midnight oil.

She recalled one of the points listed in the retirement literature – you are not as young as you once were so be kind to yourself and don't try to work at the same speed and level of endurance as you did when you were twenty-one.

Paul awoke tired and restless. His mind just would not relax as he continued to process events from when he and AV met all those years ago, his tumultuous marriage with Suzette, his perceived failure as a father to Yvon yet success with Jean, his accomplishments in his civilian career and perceived inability to deal with the stress as a UN Peacekeeper and International Criminal Court investigator, his father's impending death and permission to divorce his wife, and his recent reunion with AV, his puppy love.

This would be a full-pot-of-coffee morning. He was on his second cup when his cell phone danced across the tabletop with the vibration of an incoming call. He grabbed it before it boogied onto the floor.

"Paul, can we meet this morning?" Alexandra asked.

"Yes, of course," he said, his voice tender. "I'm at your beck and call. How can I help?"

"I was up most of the night trying to organize my life. I thought retirement was supposed to be relaxing. I've got so many things on the go I almost wish I was back at work. Most pressing are a few estate items creeping up the priority ladder."

"Do you have a top three on your priority list?"

"My top priority wasn't on my previous list. I tracked down where my father is buried and I'd like to visit his grave first. I need to start to make peace with that missing part of my life. This morning, I received an email from the real estate agent in Luxembourg with some listings. That has now been bumped down the list."

"I may not be much help as I haven't slept very well myself and I'm somewhat dazed. Where do you want to meet, and what real estate listings? I thought you were selling your house, not buying. I don't want to impose on you but I am a pretty good listener if you want to talk about your father. I can only imagine what you are trying to deal with."

"I'll explain about the listings when we meet. Can you come to Jo's place in Garches? I'm staying with her for a while, as it is too long a drive from Gagne. There is a coffee shop just around the corner. Sophia is parked in her carport. Perhaps we can look at some Harleys for you as I need a distraction from my life."

"Sure, I'll meet you there. I shouldn't be much more than forty minutes as I live in Meudon."

He noted her address, finished his breakfast and a third cup of coffee for the morning, and went out. Suzette wasn't up yet so there was no need for an explanation, not that he would reveal the details of his mission this morning even if she asked. With the self-prescribed cocktail of pills she was taking on a regular basis, Suzette rarely got up before late morning, and when she did, she was in a stupor.

Garches and Meudon, on the southwest side of Paris, had once been small separate communities with town squares and a town hall on the commons much like the old city centre of Luxembourg. With the expansion of Paris, these quaint communities had been subsumed in the modern Parisian architecture, a mixture of traditional and contemporary under the guise of the *proche banlieue…* the nearby suburbs.

Traffic was light so he was knocking on the door of Jo's house in a half hour.

"Nice place Jo has, spacious for just one person. Wow, she certainly has a lot of books. It reminds me of a small community library. And she is quite the green thumb."

"Jo likes to spread out with her books. She has relatives in Brest and Bordeaux who come to visit on a regular basis so this space is convenient for entertaining guests. She used to live in an apartment in the Latin Quarter where she was close to her library and copious bookstores. After a while, she found the hustle and bustle of the city was just too much so she moved out into the suburbs. She calls it the 'burbs or the 'hood. She was never much of a green thumb when we went to university together."

"I sense that has changed," Paul commented.

"It certainly has. She finds it peaceful just to putter in her garden and, as you can see, she has dozens of indoor plants. Watering day takes a fair amount of time because she talks to each one individually. They all have names."

"Let's go for java," Paul suggested, feeling the need for another caffeine fix.

"We can walk as it's just around the corner."

"Okay, let me lock my car."

"You can park in her driveway if you like. It'll be more secure. Just give me a moment to put the dishes in the washer. Jo is fastidious about tidiness."

"Great, I'll meet you out front."

As Alexandra was securing the door, she noticed Paul locking his car.

"You drive a Jaguar!" she exclaimed.

Paul paused then stared at her, grinning. "Yes, doesn't everyone?"

"Touché, monsieur le colonel!" Alexandra recalled that she had replied to him with the same jovial good-humoured response when she arrived in the parking lot in Les Lilas on Sophia and he had exclaimed, "You ride a Harley."

They both laughed. Alexandra walked around the Jag, seductively drawing her index finger smoothly along the curves of the hood.

"Very nice wheels, guy. Ooowwww, I very much like," she softly purred. "What's her name?"

"I don't have a name for her."

"You don't have a name for her? A chariot as exquisite as this must have a name. I have a Scandinavian friend who uses the term *svelte* when she wants to describe something that is sleek and elegant. So, why don't we call her Svelte?"

"Svelte," he murmured. "Svelte is most appropriate. She would be honoured to have this title bestowed upon her by a princess. From this day forward, I... *we* shall refer to her as Svelte," he exclaimed with a tone of regal authority.

He then thought to himself. *AV is svelte if ever there was a svelte, sleek, elegant and an absolutely beautiful creation with all the lines and curves. She is a Jaguar in every respect.*

They laughed and playfully jostled as they walked to the coffee shop. Banter came easily and was natural to old-new friends.

As they stood in line for coffee, Paul leaned over taking the opportunity to slide his cheek against hers and become enveloped in the scent of her hair flowing over her shoulder.

"I have some interesting news," he announced. "I just received a letter from the Office of the President advising I am to be inducted into *la Légion d'honneur* supposedly for '*extraordinarily meritorious career service* to France and the international community.' The letter cites my 'meticulous effort and resolute determination solving cold cases.' The ceremony will take place in the Élysée Palace next month. I am to be inducted as *un commandeur de la Légion d'Honneur*, a rank higher than chavalier or officier."

"You are to join la Légion d'honneur! That's incredible, Paul," Alexandra exclaimed. "Do you realize what an honour it is to receive this award?"

Her excitement caught the attention of others in line, some of whom extended congratulations and handshakes.

With a reserved smile, Paul acknowledged the tributes. Feeling a little embarrassed by the unsolicited attention, he sheepishly replied to Alexandra.

"I guess so. It really hasn't sunk in. I just received the letter yesterday. I mentioned it to Suzette who simply shrugged it off. I think she was hoping it wouldn't be another trophy to gather dust."

Alexandra leaned over and gave him a laudatory peck on the cheek.

"I applaud you, mon colonel. You are remarkable."

She then snuggled against him and whispered as quietly as she could, "Sorry about my outburst. I sense it embarrassed you a bit. I just couldn't control my excitement for you. But what exactly did you do? People don't receive this award for just working hard."

She couldn't remember being this proud of anything André had done. In fact, to her knowledge, André had never done anything which would be considered out of the ordinary, let alone exceptional or meritorious. André may have had friends who received awards but the absence of visitors to their house, his house, or invitations to other gatherings for any celebratory occasion suggested otherwise.

Once they had picked up their coffee and croissants and sat at a corner table away from listeners, Paul quietly elaborated.

"I think it may have more to do with a couple of the cases, well, several cases, involving war crimes against humanity involving some international affairs France had co-sponsored with some of its NATO partners. Interpol was involved as a facilitating agency. On those occasions, I had been whisked away to work with some interesting people doing interesting things in interesting places as you would say, perhaps like your mother. We were gathering forensic evidence at crime scenes. On a couple of cases, our force protection team was taking and returning fire while we worked feverishly to gather the evidence before it could be destroyed. Later, I gave evidence at the International Criminal Court in The Hague. The experience certainly expanded my perspective on the intricacies of intrigue in international détente. Because of the terrorist connection, American CIA and British MI6 and a few other players were monitoring the activities while we worked. I still can't talk about the details."

The enormity of the danger on the missions he glazed over but the threat to his life overwhelmed Alexandra to the point she was speechless. Paul had more surprises than she could ever have imagined. Added to her list of adjectives she had told Jo in their conversation would be mysterious, enigmatic, courageous, dauntless and daring.

Sensing her perplexed state of mind, Paul broke the silence. "So, what's on your to-do list and what's overflowing that needs to be attended to? How can I help you with your priorities? Remember, I am on retirement leave, so haven't yet mastered the art of organizing relaxation time."

"Wonderful, we have the blind leading the blind," she retorted with a giggle.

Teasing and joking was just so relaxed. God, how she missed this aspect in a relationship. She had friends, good friends like Jo, with whom she could share good times and face-to-face girl talk, but no deep relationship with a male partner. Realizing what she had been missing, she pined for such a partnership.

After they had organized her list and worked out what she needed to do and what Paul could do to take a few metaphorical strands of spaghetti off her plate, they left the coffee shop to go back to Jo's place.

"My day is looking more relaxed now," she concluded. "Why don't we go into Paris and look at some Harleys. You asked for recommendations. I would suggest you check out a Road King. It's built for highway cruising but still retains the biker image."

"That's a plan. Do you mind if we don't drive? I would prefer to take the Metro as it's tough finding a parking space anywhere near the downtown core."

"I agree. We can leave your car at Jo's. I'll send her an email letting her know. I'm sure she will be equally impressed having a Jaguar in her driveway. She will brag to her neighbours she has a friend who drives in luxury. A Jag in the driveway and two Harleys in the carport, life could be worse!"

CHAPTER 22

On the Metro, they continued to laugh like kids on the way to meet Père Noël and present him with a wish list. They were oblivious of other passengers, most of whom were sombrely focused on their own affairs. Together, today, they were teenagers experiencing what had been denied them by their years of separation. Prior conversations over Pinot Noir and cognac had provided details of those years, but conversations were no substitute for holding hands. They could not make up for lost time. But the truth as revealed in their love of so long ago and only just realized, provided them with a point of embarkation for a future, whatever that might be. Memories would be made of this.

As they approached the Harley dealership, Paul stopped and looked at 43 and 49 boulevard Beaumarchais just around the corner from Place de la Bastille. One location was dedicated to bikes while the other sold parts, accessories and clothing. In between the two was a Triumph dealership.

"Interesting. Is Triumph being aggressive with its marketing, driving a wedge between Harley's storefront locations? Or is Harley situating itself to squeeze out the competition?"

Alexandra paused and scanned the stores.

"I never really noticed the Triumph dealership. You're once again more perceptive than I am. Is that your penchant for detail or my weakness due to familiarity and being too close? I'm usually the one who scans for the maximum detail and then conducts the critical analysis. I got the sense your strengths were in the macro strategic perspective. We make a good team, mon colonel."

"I don't think it's a weakness. When you focus on the details, I scan the big picture and vice versa. You're right – we make a good team. Perhaps we should consider a partnership in a retirement business."

Reflecting on what might have been but never was, they looked at each other inquiringly. Deep down, each pondered the possibility of a life partnership. They would ride together. That was a given. They could work together. That was an option. They should be together. That was becoming readily apparent.

After examining the different bikes and models, and sitting in the saddle of those on the short-list, Paul decided on the Road King, primarily because Alexandra had recommended it. She was a sommelier and an expert on Pinot Noir, a connoisseur of motorcycles and an aficionado of Harleys.

The dealership did not have one of this year's models in stock because it was later in the season. They could not locate one in the inventory in the immediate area. Accordingly, Paul ordered a new model. It would be delivered within a few weeks. He purchased boots, chaps, gloves, a jacket and helmet. They took them with them.

As they were leaving the Harley shop, Alexandra called out, "Now I remember where I met that man on the Metro before, the one who called you *monsieur le colonel*."

"Marcel Cousteau?"

"Yes, he is a road captain in the Harley riding group."

"What's a road captain?"

"When you ride as a group, one person is designated as the leader of the group, the road captain, to coordinate and lead the ride."

Not very different from the military in some respects, Paul thought, with the corporal leading the colonel, once again!

On the return Metro trip to Jo's place, Alexandra explained the quality features of the helmet, and the body armour in the back, shoulders and elbows of the jacket. These features reminded Paul of the body armour and flack vest he had worn when deployed with the UN Mission in Bosnia and the other forensic-evidence-gathering missions.

As she spoke, he felt a rising level of tenseness at the recollection of those times. His chest tightened and his breathing became laboured. His mouth stiffened and his vision blurred. The all-too-familiar grip of the ice-cold mail gauntlet clutched his head. In response, he rubbed his temples in an effort to mitigate the throbbing pain.

Sensing Alexandra had become aware of his disquiet, he explained his reaction. Although there were exciting times in Sarajevo and on those other mysterious ICC missions, they were also stressful times, especially when they left the security of the fortified compounds and came under fire.

She smiled calmly and held his arm. This unconscious expression of closeness and trust had become natural for her since Luxembourg. Their growing support for one another was like musical harmony. Every look, every word, every thought blended to create a harmony in the notes of their mutual adoration. Support him she could and support him she would.

"You just recalled where you had known Marcel Cousteau before."

"Yes. When we first met Marcel, I think I mentioned he was my driver in Sarajevo. On one sortie, we came under fire and he was shot. I took over driving and zigzagged our way to one of our UN hospital units. His body armour saved his life. Although the bullet penetrated the armour, it was slowed enough that it didn't enter his chest too deeply. So when I see the body armour in this jacket, I am reminded."

Alexandra continued to hold on to his arm gently. From her training, she was acutely aware of what stress can do to the body.

She too had experienced tension headaches when at work but more so in recent years when with André.

"Come to think of it, you are the first person I've ever told this to," Paul acknowledged.

The rest of the Metro ride was spent in quiet reflection. Paul massaged his temples and drifted into Neverland as Peter Pan. AV would be Wendy by his side.

CHAPTER 23

It was late in the afternoon by the time they got back to Jo's place. While loading the Harley riding gear into the truck of his car, Alexandra purred as she admired the quality and skill that went into the design and manufacture of the Jaguar. It reminded her of the pride and proficiency of the masons who built the Luxembourg train station, who accepted only the highest standard. Like other major buildings of that era, it had stood the test of time.

Throughout their careers, both she and Paul had worked to that standard of excellence and found no excuse for anything less. She had received numerous accolades and awards for her persistence in solving cold cases instead of quitting when faced with adversity. Paul was being honoured for his adherence to excellence above and beyond with his induction into the Légion d'honneur. She concluded that was one of the fundamental reasons why they got along so well, why she and André had constantly been in conflict throughout their marriage, and why Paul and Suzette had little in common.

Agreement on cultural canons of integrity was the foundation of any sustainable relationship be it professional or personal, and certainly intimate.

Paul's cell buzzed. Looking down, he noticed the code name *'CHESS'* illuminated. "Excuse me, it's from Jean."

"Papa, I just left Grand-papa's room. I'm worried about his memory. We tried to play a game of chess but he couldn't concentrate. He could talk about games we had played when I was a kid but couldn't focus on one move for more than a few seconds. He wanted me to pass on a couple of names to you about a case he had worked on in Montigny-lès-Metz. He just couldn't remember why he needed to pass them along. One was a Sergeant Joseph Lortie and the other was Sergeant Etienne Beauregard. I'm not sure if it makes any sense to you or if he was just rambling through old memories."

"Thanks for the update, Jean. I'll drop in and see him tomorrow. And, yes, the names do mean something. He wasn't rambling. When Alexandra and I visited him after we returned from Dieppe, he said he would try and remember some more details of a case he had worked on in Montigny-lès-Metz. Thanks for passing this along. Take care, mon fils. I love you."

Paul nodded to Alexandra. "More facts, partner. Jean had just come from a visit with his grand-papa who gave him a couple of names of old colleagues who might have worked on the Thon case. We'll need to follow up soonest. I'd be available to drive to Montigny-lès-Metz tomorrow if your calendar is open but I want to see my father before we go. Jean mentioned he was experiencing more memory loss than usual. If you want, we could drive to Amsterdam to retrieve your clothes and then bring them to Luxembourg afterwards. I'm getting used to my retirement schedule void of appointments."

"We could probably do that tomorrow but I need to coordinate with Collette on a few things first. Let's talk."

Jo arrived home just as they started up the walkway. Looking at Paul, she exclaimed enthusiastically, "Alex sent me a message letting me know my neighbours would be impressed with a Jag in my driveway. Hot wheels, guy! You can visit as often and as long as you like."

Transferring her gaze to Alexandra, she winked with one of those mischievous girl-to-girl expressions.

"So what trouble have the two of you been up to in my absence?"

Alexandra smiled impishly, tilted her head slightly and returned the non-verbal with her own wide-eyed we'll-talk-later communiqué.

"We've just returned from the Harley-Davidson dealership

where Paul bought a Road King. It should be delivered in a few weeks. He also got all the riding gear, so we are all set for some enjoyable time in the saddle."

Realizing the connotation of what she had just said and what Jo immediately picked up, a blush suffused her face.

Jo chuckled under her breath, and then smoothed the awkwardness of the moment with an invitation for both to stay for dinner.

"What do you think, Paul? Are you up to dining with two biker ladies?" Alexandra enquired without looking directly at him in the hope he wouldn't notice her reddish complexion.

On any other occasion, he would have respectfully declined the offer with an equally eloquent response. Today was different. Without looking at his watch and without hesitation, he accepted the invitation. The evening would provide a relaxed atmosphere to confirm the details of their upcoming trip to Montigny-lès-Metz to gather information, to travel to Amsterdam to retrieve Alexandra's possessions, and to Luxembourg to deal with the outstanding real estate matters, including the house on rue Michel Welter and Maria's apartment.

Out of habit, he called Suzette to tell her he wouldn't be home for dinner. There was no answer. He left no message.

"I'll start dinner if you pour the wine, Alex. Pasta okay, Paul?"

"Got the wine on the go."

"Pasta would be wonderful, Jo."

"What's her name?" Jo asked.

Alexandra replied excitedly, "We decided on Svelte, a Jag named Svelte because she is so sleek and elegant."

"No, I mean the Road King. What have you decided to name your Road King, Paul?"

"Ahhh... we haven't got around to naming it yet."

He was rapidly learning from two classification specialists about the importance of Harley names. Clearly, his youthful teachers and mentors had been remiss in their duty to advance his education in this regard.

"Well, that's number one priority before dinner," declared Jo. "Pour the Pinot, Alex, and let's put our collective heads together."

Alexandra mentioned the colour of the Road King – dark pearl blue. They should consider that in the mix.

By the time dinner was ready, they had run the gamut of names like expectant parents. 'Charles de Gaulle' had somehow got on the short list but they unanimously agreed it was too stuffy and too much of a mouthful. Further, President de Gaulle was an old stick in the mud. 'Charles' was all right but still not in the Harley Road King genre. They needed a rocker name for a retired professional who would be riding alongside a classy chic Lady of Harley on a Hog named Sophia.

As Jo served the pasta, they agreed on 'Chuck.' Paul felt there was a stalwart, down-to-earth *je ne sais quoi* mystique about that name.

In honour of the christening, Jo volunteered to have a brass name plate made which would be affixed to the covered parking stall where Chuck would spend his non-mobile times. Jo reminded him that, unlike lesser brands of bikes, Harleys needed their own parking space.

Alexandra had hired an airbrush painter to inscribe 'Sophia' on the side of the gas tank of her Electra Glide and offered to commission him to do the same for Chuck. Feeling outnumbered, Paul graciously agreed to both baptismal gifts.

While Jo was clearing away the dishes and preparing coffee, Alexandra quietly asked Paul if she could announce to Jo that he would be made a commandeur de la Légion d'honneur at the Élysée Palace next month. She was acutely aware that in her excitement at hearing the news in the café she had embarrassed him by expressing her excitement. She now wanted to ask his permission. With some reservation, he agreed.

On hearing the news, Jo exclaimed how honoured she was to be in the company of a commandeur and suggested she host a congratulatory get-together at her place.

Sensing Paul's sensitivity and reticence to participate in such a social event, Alexandra suggested to Jo they could talk later. Jo picked up on the hesitancy in her voice and immediately backed off.

To move the conversation away from the award, Alexandra advised Jo that she and Paul would be driving to Montigny-lès-Metz to follow up on a conversation they'd had with Paul's father about an old case. They would then drive to Amsterdam where she would pick up her stuff because she had decided to retire in Luxembourg.

"Are you going to retire completely and do nothing? If you are then we are going to have to schedule into our calendar set times for some serious riding and girl talk. You had better get a place with at least two bedrooms and a double carport in order to accommodate two Harleys, and maybe more."

Alexandra gave her a return volley of her quirky we'll-talk-later look.

Jo had become aware of the increasing vibes maturing between Alexandra and Paul.

"Jo, I don't think I'll retire completely but I'm certainly going to cut back on my nomadic shorter-term travels. I've decided that Luxembourg will be my permanent home. I was born there and I want to spend more time there before I die, if that makes any sense. I'll probably get a place of my own in the old city. The house on rue Michel Welter was where I grew up, but it will always be my uncle's home and later my mother's, but not mine. I need a place where I can create my own nest."

"What about the house in Gagne?" Jo asked.

"That house was always André's. It never truly felt like it was my home. I have realized I travelled throughout my working career just to get away, stay away from that house," she paused, "and from André. Now I just want to retire to my own home."

She recalled that was one of the points the people who put on the retirement seminar emphasized, the difference between a house and a home. A house is a place with walls, doors and a roof and little more. A home is where you need to be emotionally, psychologically and spiritually, where the hearth is, and the heart.

"My mother's death and all the stuff I have been dealing with since then have opened my eyes to that stark realization. I need a home and not a house."

"Good for you, girl!" Jo exclaimed with excitement in her voice that Alexandra had not noticed before.

Alexandra smiled in complete contentment.

"One day you may find you have a new neighbour who once was a librarian. We've ridden most of the routes around Paris over the years. We can explore a new network of back roads in the Benelux region."

"Jo, this isn't a vague melancholy notion, a product of Pinot Noir. After my uncle and aunt died, I often thought forty-two would have been a good age to retire. I could have done so with my inheritance, but life was far too interesting back then to disengage altogether. My uncle and aunt had a beautiful life together, so sadly cut short. Knowing more about my mother, I'm sure she had a good life. But I need to slow down."

Her unfulfilled teenage dream had been occupying more of her thoughts since reading her mother's letter. It was a fantasy now within reach.

CHAPTER 24

In the excitement of the moment, Alexandra realized Paul had been excluded from their conversation, as did Jo.

"Help me in the kitchen, Alex. Would you excuse us for a moment, Paul?"

"Only if you leave the wine and you allow me to change the music to a Strauss waltz. I promise not to play any Wagner."

Jo nodded as she and Alexandra moved into the quasi-seclusion of the kitchen where Jo turned on the tap to mask their murmurs.

"Girl-talk time. What's going on with the two of you? I get the sense it's becoming more serious or you would like it to move in that direction."

Alexandra looked at Jo and confirmed her suspicions.

"Being with Paul has renewed my faith in the possibility of true happiness. Before I took the teaching position at the University in Amsterdam, in my own mind I knew I would never retire to Gagne but I hadn't scripted an exit strategy. I knew André would not be in my future but I didn't know who would be, besides you and Collette."

"All right, so what are the options?"

"Now there is Paul but I don't know how that will unfold. I know he isn't happy in his marriage but he's fiercely loyal to the sanctity of his marriage vows. I know, I just need to be patient. I can't pull him away and he can't perceive me as pulling him away from that relationship if we are going to be happy and I'm confident in that possibility."

"I agree, Alex. He can't see you as the cause of the breakup of his marriage."

"I'm pretty sure it has already dissolved but I can't interfere. It has to be his decision. To be completely honest with you, I yearn for him as much today as I did when my mother took me away all those years ago."

"I'm picking that up, Alexandra."

"Someday, I'll tell you about the letter my mother left me. I can tell you now Paul and I both know the love we had and shared for each other when we were teenagers is as strong today as it was back then. But we both need to deal with all the stuff in our lives. He's dealing with his retirement issues, as am I. Although he is honoured to be inducted as a commandeur de la Légion d'honneur, it is yet another stressor for him. I have learned he is a very humble, private person who doesn't like attention, so please don't host any social event."

"Ya, sorry about that. I'm learning about him, like you. If I look as though I'm stepping out of bounds, just shoot me one of your infamous back-off signals. *Damn*, I've overflowed the sink!"

Jo shut off the tap and they mopped up the water which had flooded the counter and the floor. They then returned to the living room where they found Paul leant back on the sofa with his eyes closed. Alexandra snuggled up beside him and whispered into his ear.

"Anyone for coffee?"

Without opening his eyes, he responded with a warm smile and agreed coffee would be an excellent idea. He would need a few cups before heading back to Meudon. At the moment, though, his house and Suzette were the last things on his mind. In his dream he was dancing with Alexandra to a Strauss waltz in the grand ballroom at Versailles. He didn't want to return to the reality of retirement strategies. That would have to be the product of sobering thoughts. He reached for her hand to continue the dance. Jo retired to the kitchen to prepare a fresh pot of coffee.

By the time Jo had returned, Paul had stirred and was discussing plans with Alexandra to drive to Montigny-lès-Metz, Amsterdam and Luxembourg.

"I'd like to see my father tomorrow as Jean felt his condition was deteriorating. We could leave the day after tomorrow. What are your thoughts?"

"I still have some cards from the funeral I need to answer. I'd like to visit my father's grave tomorrow. I thought it a bit strange the person I was speaking with yesterday about the location of his grave asked if I was related to him and when I would be visiting the grave site. Weird. Could you come with me, for moral support if I need it?"

Paul immediately sat up and gave Alexandra a cautious glance. "Certainly. I can go with you. I could pick you up around nine and then we could visit with my father around noon if you like. But first explain to me what your senses were telling you with that call? Why did you feel it was weird? Is this like the solo beach walk you had before Jacques pulled up, when you chose to disregard your sensations in favour of decompressing? Would you say it was time to raise the radar if this was Collette?"

Jo and Paul watched her eyes dart back and forth as she replayed the phone call and the tone and motivation of the enquiry.

"You're right. I would tell Collette to raise the radar. Good question. Why would anyone ask about my relationship to a grave?"

"So, what do you want to do?"

"I didn't divulge what my relationship was or when I might visit the grave. I still want to visit the grave soon. Nine would be good but I'll pass on visiting your father with you as my mental state will not be at its best and I wouldn't want your father to be upset. He's a pretty intuitive man and I don't know that I would be able to mask my emotions. More importantly, you should have some one-on-one time for your assessment. I can call you early afternoon after your visit with him."

"Okay. I'll pick you up at nine. It would be best if I called you late afternoon. We could meet for coffee if you are caught up. I can come here if Jo doesn't mind or we can meet here and walk to the coffee shop around the corner."

Jo chimed in, "I have my monthly librarian meeting tomorrow evening so won't be here. But the two of you are welcome to kick back and make yourselves at home."

"Thanks, Jo. Perhaps you can meet me here, Paul, and we can play it by ear. I need to get these last cards answered so I can clear that item off my list or else it will be another week or so before we get back from Luxembourg. I want to hear how your father is doing. First thing after we return I'd like to see him. Would that be okay?"

"I'm good with that," Paul confirmed, still expressing cautious optimism. Looking at Alexandra he mused playing it by ear with her ear would be absolutely wonderful.

"We walk to the coffee shop tomorrow evening," Alexandra suggested.

"Do you think Collette would like to join us? I don't want to play matchmaker but I could ask Jean if he wanted to join us also. Thoughts?"

"That would be a great idea. I'll speak with Collette."

"Before I forget, do you have the names of the two sergeants from Montigny-lès-Metz and would you mind if Jo researched anything on them so we could be better prepared?"

"Excellent idea." Paul wrote down the names and gave them to Alexandra.

"Jo," Alexandra asked in an I'll-owe-you-another-one tone of voice, "would you have time tomorrow to do a bit of research on these two names? They're retired police sergeants from Montigny-lès-Metz who may be associated with a file. It would be great if we had the info before we left."

"Sure, I can do that. I could email you the results before you and Paul meet tomorrow evening."

Paul finished his second cup of coffee. It woke him up and would probably keep him awake for a few more hours – better that than fall asleep on the way home. He bid his Ladies of Harley a good night and pointed Svelte in the direction of Meudon. He couldn't remember the last time he had enjoyed such a relaxed day in the company of others.

Jean was up watching TV when he got home. Suzette was asleep. He briefed Jean on his pending trip to Montigny-lès-Metz, Amsterdam and Luxembourg. He then asked if he wanted to join him tomorrow evening for coffee with Alexandra and Collette. He described Collette in such a way Jean could not refuse. Jean was single and on the prowl for a partner now that his previous relationship was officially over.

CHAPTER 25

Paul was up early. Again, he hadn't slept well because he was bothered by Alexandra's call regarding Philip's gravesite. Something wasn't right. He asked Jean at breakfast if he had ever called and enquired about a grave location.

"Don't think so, Papa. Why do you ask?"

"It's nothing. Have a good day at work. I'll see you tonight and remember we are going out for coffee with AV and Collette."

Alexandra was ready when he arrived to pick her up. He found his eyes on the rear-view mirrors more frequently than usual as they drove to the cemetery and followed Alexandra's directions once they passed through the gates.

"I spoke with Jean last evening and again this morning and he's eager to meet Collette."

"I spoke with Collette and she is looking forward to meeting Jean. Good. We're confirmed for this evening. The turn-off to the grave should be just up here on the right."

Paul stopped short of her directions and turned off the car.

"Let's just sit here a while. We have some time."

"All right but I'm picking up some tension, mon colonel. Your turn to talk to me."

"I didn't sleep well last night because I was mulling over your explanation about the phone call regarding your father's grave. It isn't sitting well with me for some reason. I'd be much happier if we just sat here and watched for a while. Consider this a rest stop surveillance."

"I didn't sleep very well either. I chalked it up to anticipating my visit to his grave. My emotions have been all over the map and I know that. I'll need to defer to you. If you say that caution and surveillance are in order then I'll follow your lead on this one."

Paul reached in the back seat and pulled out his camera. He had fitted it with a 600mm telephoto lens. He passed Alexandra his binoculars. He scanned the left and right arcs of the gravesite and asked her to do the same. "I'm not sure how busy cemeteries are supposed to be but this one is active this morning. I have an interment off to my left with a dozen or so people in attendance. What do you see?"

"I have a young couple standing by a grave and another older couple sitting on a bench. There is one guy on the other side of the knoll to my right just standing by a tree carrying something but I can't make out what it is."

Paul traversed his view to the man. He then extended his surveillance past the tree before returning his focus on the man.

"He has a camera like mine with a telephoto lens. This isn't unusual if he is looking at birds but he doesn't appear to be. I'll just focus on him if you can continue to scan left and right. Tell me if you see anything different."

"Nothing, mon colonel."

"He's lifted up his camera and is aiming it at us! Slide low on the seat to keep out of sight. He looks like the guy in the black Mercedes, tall and blond. I'll bet that's the same man and he's now pissing me off, excuse my language. *En garde*, you SOB. The best defence is a good offence and he's about to experience the full vector thrust of my offence. I've got him eyes on, locked on."

"Do you have a plan?"

"I'm going to step out of the car and snap some fast photos so the resolution won't be impaired by my tinted windshield. As soon as I step out, you slide over into the driver's seat and I'll pass you my camera. You immediately put it on the passenger's seat and start the car. I'm going to challenge him to a marathon. As soon as I take off running after him, you start the car and lock the doors.

If anyone approaches you, drive away fast and head for the coffee shop by Jo's. I'll meet you there. On my count... *Move NOW!"*

After snapping the shots and passing his camera to Alex, Paul sprinted towards the tall blond man. His target lowered his camera as he realized the swiftness of the attack. Paul had reduced the distance to his target to less than half by the time he topped the knoll only to see the man running toward a black Mercedes and jumping in. As he started to speed away, Paul picked up a rock and threw it with full force at the Mercedes now less than a car length away. The impact broke the right rear taillight with an audible crash. The driver must have heard and felt the impact. The car immediately swung right, preventing Paul from seeing the licence plate, and drove off.

After catching his breath, Paul walked back up to the knoll and looked at Alexandra who was seated in the Jag. He subtly signalled her to remain where she was while he patrolled the knoll in plain sight. Not seeing any danger, he approached and she opened the door.

"It's all safe now for you to go to Philip's grave. I'll walk with you just to the top of the knoll."

Alexandra scanned the headstones until she saw the name of her father, Philip Joseph Marchand. The inscription underneath read, "In Loving Memory of My One and Only and Father of Our Daughter." Two small letters followed – MB for Maria Belliveau. Alexandra bent down and delicately drew her fingers across her father's name and her mother's initials. The inscriptions were warm and alive to her touch in contrast to the polished surface of the cold granite slab mirroring her presence. She felt overwhelming sadness for what she had been denied. She lowered her head as tears flowed down her cheeks. She held out her hand to Paul who came to her side and knelt down beside her.

"Run, run... that was the impossible shot... you saved my life, daughter." Her mother's bloodied face filled her memory. Again, her mother's voice rang like cathedral bells. "You saved my life. It was not your fight. But because you were my daughter, you were drawn into my world of espionage and counterintelligence at far too tender an age. Ironically the age when I entered the *Maquis* vortex that defined my future, our future."

⁂

She and Paul simply drove around for the rest of the morning. Nothing was said. Nothing needed to be said. She accompanied Paul to the seniors' home but did not enter his father's room. Paul didn't stay long because his father was sleeping. The attending nurse informed him he was sleeping more than normal and when awake appeared to be distant but content in his own world.

Jo had emailed Alexandra. An obituary listed Étienne Beauregard as deceased but nothing recent on Joseph Lortie. There was just one older newspaper listing that announced his retirement.

By the time all four met for coffee, Alexandra's spirits had lifted although the conversation was subdued. Collette and Jean hit it off although some sparks flew. They walked together in front of their parents on their way back to Jo's. Alexandra took the opportunity to whisper.

"Kids just don't get along these days."

Paul reminded her they hadn't got along the first time they met, at least until he called her AV. Before departing for Meudon, they confirmed he would pick her up at Jo's at 8 a.m.

After Jo returned home, Alexandra brought her up to date on what had transpired at the cemetery and asked if Collette could move into her room while she and Paul were away because of the heightened need for security. Jo agreed. Alexandra then called Collette and explained why she needed to temporarily move in with Jo without mentioning the incident at Philip's grave or about Philip's identity. She would tell Collette about her grand-papa in the fullness of time. Collette was a bit surprised but agreed to move in tomorrow.

CHAPTER 26

Paul arrived at Jo's as planned. Collette was to email her itinerary and whereabouts every four hours or immediately if she deviated from her scheduled activities. This was not a new routine for Collette. There had been other times when her mother was working on certain high-profile cases which posed an elevated risk level. Radar had to be up on these occasions. It was just part of being her mother's daughter. The intrigue was exciting but it had its constraints, which Collette accepted.

"How was your night or is the question rhetorical, given yesterday's events?" Paul asked.

"Probably as restless as yours. Your intuition certainly came through in spades and saved the day where my sensations were blinded by the emotions of dealing with the grave. It's going to take me a long time, perhaps a lifetime, to put the whole thing in context. Seeing his name on the headstone with the inscription my mother had left and her initials hit me to my core."

"I understand that. It will take a long time. From your mother's letter, I got the feeling she and Philip were very much in love."

"My mother's remains were cremated at her request and the ashes are at the crematorium in Luxembourg. That's another thing on my to-do list. I'm thinking I may have them interred beside Philip after Thon has been captured or killed, preferably the latter. I'll talk with Father Luke at some point."

Alexandra reached over and put her hand on Paul's.

"Words cannot describe how much I appreciate you being there, yes to chase away whoever it was taking pictures, but taking care of me, supporting me. I don't know how I will ever be able to repay you."

Paul held her hand firmly. "No need to create an IOU list like you have with Jo," he chuckled. "That's just what friends are for. I've got forty years to make up to you, so I need to do double duty."

Paul thought to himself that SOB taking photos will know better next time to take on a marathon-running commandeur de la Légion d'honneur – if there is a next time. *He just needs to know there isn't a rock on Planet Earth he can crawl under and hide where I won't find him, drag him out and ensure that justice is served.*

They took the E5 east, exited onto the A4 and headed for Reims where they stopped for coffee. They followed the same disciplined procedures they had developed on the Dieppe trip, checking rear-view mirrors for any unusual vehicles following and periodically pulling into rest stops where they would park for several minutes and conduct a three-sixty scan. It became a routine and they used the time to hone their skills further to work as partners. It came naturally. Each would adopt a one-eighty-degree scan. Alexandra chuckled as she assumed the subordinate role to the colonel's military lingo of left and right arcs of fire.

"Confirmed, sir," she acknowledged.

It was a game with serious undertones but a game nonetheless which they played lightly. On occasion, Alexandra would beat Paul in identifying the points for the left and right arcs of fire. Neither noticed a black Mercedes or other suspicious vehicles. Thus, they determined there was no portent of misfortune.

Both shared with the other they had never experienced this kind of amusement with their respective spouses and, for that reason, had not vacationed together for many years. Holidays were meant to be occasions when stress was to be reduced, not accentuated.

"So how was Jean after last evening's meeting with Collette?" Alexandra enquired.

"I was about to ask you the same about Collette."

"I asked you first. But in deference to your senior age by a couple of weeks, if I remember correctly, I will start off."

"I had forgotten all about that but now you mention it, I expect you to respect your seniors in the future," Paul hooted back.

After telling tales out of school, they surmised Collette and Jean might develop a relationship, albeit one with some initial head butting between two strong-willed young people.

Alexandra commented that Collette went on at length about how bright and intelligent and courteous Jean was before ending each complimentary comment with a 'but' which was followed by a series of qualifiers. He was bright but a bit conceited. He was intelligent but could be overbearing.

Paul explained Jean had described Collette in much the same way. Jean was captivated by the freshness of her personality and her physical attractiveness. He had also ended each admiring narrative of Collette with a qualifier. Collette was very cute with her luminous eyes but perhaps too focused on her good looks. She was motivated but a bit of a Type A personality.

Laughing as they spoke, they concluded they had never been like that when they met and even if they had stayed together would not have criticized the other in the same way. In the final analysis, they agreed Collette and Jean should meet again. It was simply the duty of parents to intervene to keep the relationship alive.

Love was on loan like a library book which could be recalled. There would be an ebb and flow and they would need to know that love doesn't grow at a steady rate. It can decline towards the end of its existence at which time, a recall notice is issued for the library book.

After a few more rest stops, they approached the turn off to the N3. It would take them to Metz and Montigny-lès-Metz. They reviewed their strategy.

"We should find a place to eat before we visit the police station and enquire as to the whereabouts of Sergeant Joseph Lortie. If located, we will arrange to meet. Regardless of how long the meeting lasts, we will spend the night at the Hôtel Novotel Metz Centre."

"I know it well," Alexandra said. "There are some great out-of-the-way restaurants within a ten-minute walk."

It had been years since Paul had been to his old stomping ground but he started to recognize landmarks as they approached Sainte Ruffine. A lunch break to address their hunger pangs and a fuel stop to replenish Svelte's empty gas tank was in order.

Alexandra suggested they look for a restaurant frequented by truck drivers and the police because she recalled from her travels that truckers always knew where the best food was served and police knew where the cheapest meals could be found. If you located a truck stop with police cars then you could rest assured the food would be good and cheap. They spotted a restaurant where several trucks were parked. "That's a good indication of the quality, at least."

As they entered the restaurant, Paul remarked, "Funky place. I like the seventeenth century ambience and décor complete with a portcullis entranceway." The servers were dressed as wenches in medieval garb and the walls were decorated with crested shields and crossed swords. The hostess pointed to the only table available by a wall. It had crossed foils hung adjacent to their seats.

"They're real, not replicas," Paul noted with a curious glance. "Hopefully the cuisine is authentic medieval as well but not to the extent we need to eat with our hands and throw the bones in the direction of the twenty-first century electric fireplace!"

"Can I bring you something to drink before you order?" the server asked.

As Paul and Alexandra were about to respond, they were interrupted by a loud voice from the bar.

"Hey, who's the hot chick?"

"Ignore him," the server said. "He's drunk and the owner has already called the police to have him removed."

"Hey, I said, who's the hot chick?"

Paul looked up to see the drunk shove the server aside and move towards Alexandra.

"I suggest you go back to the bar," Paul said calmly.

"I wasn't talking to you, *idiot.* I was talking to *la pépée* who obviously doesn't know how to pick up a real man."

"I suggest that you go back to the bar," Paul responded again.

As he did so, the drunk reached for Alexandra who pulled back. Paul stood up and forcefully ordered the intruder to back off.

The drunk swung at him and missed his face. Instead his fist hit the wall as he tumbled forward. Seeing the fencing foils through his impaired eyes, he grabbed one and lunged at Paul but again lost his balance.

Paul grasped the second foil and stepped away from the table and Alexandra and from the drunk who was stumbling back to his feet. Having previously noted the foils were real, he knew a strike could easily cause injury. His intent was to draw the drunk away from the patrons, many of whom had stood up and moved to avoid the drunk flaying his arms and the foil around.

"Put the sword down," Paul said in a commanding yet calm voice.

"You're in for it now, *connard.*"

The drunk swung at Paul who deflected the amateurish clumsy manoeuvre with a swift parry.

"Put the sword down," Paul said again in a calm, firm voice as the drunk started to regain his balance and focus.

Lunging at Paul straight on, he fell to the ground after Paul again deftly deflected the attack with a parry and followed with a riposte.

From his vulnerable position on the floor, the drunk looked up to see the tip of Paul's foil an inch from his face and felt his foot firmly pressing down on his crotch. He recoiled while yelling in pain.

"I strongly recommend you apologize to the patrons in this restaurant and to the lady, and then leave immediately."

As the drunk began to continue his verbal abuse, Paul stepped a little more firmly on his groin. That resulted in a louder groan of objection.

The door opened wide as two patrol officers entered. An elderly man they recognized who had been standing by the door throughout the commotion met them immediately. After a brief verbal exchange, the officers cuffed the drunk and removed him from the premises.

The patrons broke into applause and commended Paul for his astute actions, as did the owner of the restaurant who deeply apologized for the disturbance and indicated that his lunch and that of Alexandra would be complimentary.

CHAPTER 27

The man at the door approached Paul and introduced himself as Joseph Lortie, a retired sergeant with the Montigny-lès-Metz precinct. He said he had relayed to the patrol officers what had transpired and he would provide a complete statement. The police knew the drunk who had a long record of causing disturbance, assault and resisting arrest. There would be no need to interview Paul. All they would need would be his name and address. Sergeant Lortie had assured the arresting officers he would record Paul and Alexandra's names and pass those details on to them. The proprietor had already preferred charges.

Some patrons left after the police intervention. This exodus allowed the owner to set up the best table for Paul, Alexandra and Sergeant Lortie.

"Sergeant Joseph Lortie, I am very pleased to meet you." Paul welcomed his intervention and introduction. "It is remarkably serendipitous that we meet, monsieur, as the purpose of our trip was to find you and to speak with you about a case you may be aware of."

After introducing himself and Alexandra, and providing background information about his father and the case, Sergeant Lortie acknowledged he knew of Paul's father and was aware of the case.

"I was a junior patrol officer who started working at the precinct sometime after your father was transferred. As the junior man, I had been directed to destroy old files relating to cold cases. Too many unsolved cases looked bad for the precinct commandeur so he ordered one or two files shredded each month. It was all about statistics, cases reported and cases cleared off the books. Wanting to learn my profession better, I took the time to review all files but read others in depth before condemning them to the jaws of the paper shredder."

"What happened to the files?" Alexandra enquired with a sense of urgency in her voice.

"That's an intriguing question. Let me explain. There was another officer working on the case by the name of Philip Marchand. He was a particularly good investigator so I wanted to read every file he had been involved in to learn as much as I could about his investigative techniques. I was captivated by one file of an unsolved suspicious death of a woman and her daughter that your father and Philip Marchand had worked on. Surreptitiously, I squirrelled the file away in a remote filing drawer because there was something about the case that fascinated me. I tell you in confidence, when that hideaway became apparent to the bureaucratic auditors whose mantra was less is best, I slid it into my patrol satchel and took it home. I subsequently reported it as *cleared otherwise*. That meant I had shredded it, but I never did. I knew if my efforts to hide the file were discovered, I could have been charged and my career prospects would have been jeopardized. But I had a feeling that, in the fullness of time, it would be reclassified from cold case to solved case, and I would be vindicated. But alas, I retired before the case could be solved," he said, then smiled. "What can they do to me now, fire me?"

Alexandra and Paul exchanged glances signalling they felt Sergeant Lortie was an honest person who could be trusted.

"I can't tell you how much this information means to us," Alexandra said appreciatively. "We are attempting to piece together a number of details about this case and several others involving the deaths of women, some with their daughters."

"Would you like to read the file and go to the house where the bodies were found, where the murders took place? Although never proven, I remain convinced they were murdered. I still refer to it as an unsolved murder. The house is vacant now and has been for several years. A few people lived there after the murders but moved away relatively quickly. The word was the house still holds the ghosts of the mother and her daughter. I don't believe in ghosts but I do respect the spirit world. I was a *flic* long enough to realize there is hard evidence and intelligence from other sources which could lead to evidence. Although there was nothing written in the file, I got the feeling Philip Marchand respected the spirit world. I believe that was how he solved so many cases."

"We would very much like to review the file and visit the crime scene if it's not too much trouble," Paul replied.

"No trouble at all, and after dealing so adeptly with that obnoxious drunk, I owe you a favour. I will call the property management agent who is looking after the house and tell him I have a possible buyer or tenant. That will get his attention to see it right away."

"Thank you, monsieur! We can't tell you how much we appreciate your kind offer to help."

"I am honoured to have the opportunity to meet the son of Jean-Paul Bernard. Perhaps this cold case will be solved after all and the ghosts put to rest."

As they followed Sergeant Lortie's car to his home to review the file, Alexandra commented,

"You are most skilful with the foil, mon colonel. Although startled by the drunk, I immediately felt safe with you *en garde*."

"He was no match *pour le bout* or *en garde* as some would say. I think I mentioned to you the first evening we had dinner in Luxembourg I was a fencing champion in my youth and then a member of the French Fencing Team. My concern was for any injury he might inflict on you or any other patron because the foils were real and had not been buttoned to make them less lethal. In competition, foils have a small ball affixed to the tip called a button to prevent it from penetrating the body armour or the skin of the opponent."

Sergeant Lortie gingerly pulled the file out of an old patrol satchel. He had repeated this retrieval behaviour so many times over the years that the edges had become tattered and soiled with stains from thumbing, as was the spine of the folder. He had frequently taped it, to preserve it longer. Paul noted in the photographs there were two cups lying on the floor with what appeared to be a wet stain on the carpet.

"Joseph, do you remember whether there was any physical evidence seized at the scene? Were the cups held in evidence or an analysis of the liquid conducted?"

"I don't remember if there was. I have read and re-read this file so many times I would have remembered any physical evidence. I did notice the cups in the photos and maybe that was one of the oddities which tweaked my interest in this case."

"Do you recall anyone mentioning a faint smell at the crime scene? I didn't notice anything in the file but do you remember anyone saying anything?"

"I don't. I wasn't working at the time of the incident but just read the file after your father left for Strasbourg. I asked myself what I would have done differently in this investigation if I had been on the case. The thought crossed my mind on several occasions over the years that I should have contacted your father or Philip Marchand and posed these questions to them. But your father was senior to me and in Paris by then, and I didn't know where Philip Marchand was. I felt humbled and a bit intimidated by their reputation as investigators, so I never pursued it. You mentioned that your father is still alive. Perhaps you could ask him if he remembers anything and let me know as a professional courtesy to a retired *flic*."

CHAPTER 28

From Sergeant Lortie's home, they drove to the scene of the crime where the property management agent met them.

"These are the people who expressed an interest in the house," Sergeant Lortie explained. He chuckled to himself knowing what he said was the truth but in a very different context.

Paul could not help but notice in the first few moments of the introduction that the agent spent more time admiring Paul's Jaguar than watching his clients. The sight of Svelte heightened the agent's interest.

"May we enter the house and look around?"

"Most certainly. Once you have viewed the house, I would be pleased to provide you with any background information. I'm sure Monsieur Lortie has filled you in on some of the details but I would like to add that it's a charming, quaint home which the two of you would find very comfortable."

His eyes darted back and forth between Paul and Alexandra, attempting to read their neutral body language.

"Thank you," said Paul. "Perhaps you could check around the yard to ensure it is safe for inspection. I notice it is overgrown from lack of maintenance."

Once the agent had gone outside, Joseph explained the crime scene as best he could.

Paul was drawn to Alexandra's stillness and sensed she needed to be alone in the kitchen.

"Shall we take a look outside?" Paul asked.

"Yes. Let's chat with the agent and hear what he has to say about the maintenance of the yard. He looked a little stunned by your comment. I assume you asked him that to get him out of the house while we discussed the scene. Well done. I commend you on your professional staging."

They looked around the yard methodically, keeping the agent with them until Alexandra joined them.

"The house shows definite promise," Alexandra said to Paul loudly enough for the agent to hear. "Let's reconsider our options."

Alexandra looked straight at the agent, maintaining a neutral expression.

"May we get back to you in the next few days? We will be visiting other properties suitable for retirement."

Passing Alexandra and Paul his business card, the agent responded with a hopeful smile.

"By all means. Please contact me day or night if you have any questions. There are other properties we manage in which you might be interested. Perhaps I could email information to you."

"Not for now," Alexandra replied, "but thank you for the offer."

After thanking Sergeant Lortie and assuring him they would keep him informed on any developments in the case, they departed for Metz central and their hotel.

"Let me call Jean and ask him to visit Papa to find out if he remembers any particular smell at the crime scene. I think if it was a poison by cyanide there would have been a faint odour of bitter almonds from the liquid on the floor or a residue in the cup. If that was the cause of death, it would provide a lead. We could tie that into the cyanide detected in the sample analysis from Madame Deschaume. Cyanide is highly soluble in water so it could be easily put into a cup of any fluid such as water or juice or coffee. Not everybody can smell it. I won't be surprised if Papa recalls it one way or the other. His long-term memory has been excellent when we have been able to tap into it. That has become more of a challenge lately as his dementia gets worse. What were your senses of the mind, your *shrew* telling you, AV?"

"Before I get into that, let me call Jacques Moreau in Dieppe and find out if there was any evidence that Madame Deschaume drank anything at the scene. He might have included it in his pathologist report but not mentioned it to me at our meeting. It's a long shot but we have everything to gain from the call."

Alexandra called Jacques and left a message to call her back. She then took a long breath and paused before responding to Paul.

"The spirit of the mother communicated with me in the same rather muffled way other spirits connect with me at other crime scenes. Her daughter was less forthcoming and perhaps more fragile and fearful. The mother received a call from a woman who spoke of her time in the *Maquis*. The woman then appeared at her home. There was something about drinking and feeling dizzy and confused. The visitor changed her appearance in some way and then there was black. The mother described eyeglasses and something about dark sinister eyes. The mother is unsettled and remains in the house with her daughter who expresses vestiges of fearfulness of people entering the house or even being on the property. They were less perturbed with just me although not completely open and did not want anyone else in their home. I am convinced it was Thon who killed them. We just have to find the hard evidence that can help us track him down."

"You're looking washed out and your breathing is shallow. I've never seen you like this. How are you feeling?" Paul said.

"Don't worry. I get this way after these experiences. I just need time. Can we eat later? I'd like to take a shower, change and go for a walk. I'm feeling quite drained on this one."

"Yes, we can eat later for sure. Call me in my room when you're ready and we can walk around. Is there anything I can do to help right now?"

"No, not really. Just be there when I call. I've been through several of these episodes over the years and it just takes time to rebalance. The experiences are always rewarding and I gain such insight into the cases but they can be completely exhausting or disorienting, particularly when the spirits are unsettled."

Their evening was quieter than normal as was dinner followed by a long walk along rue des Allemands to the German Gates. Somehow the 13th-century architecture of the Porte des Allemands and the old railway station brought feelings of peace and comfort. They reflected the strength of the edifices and the endurance of the French and German cultures intertwined throughout their history. Surprisingly, there were enclaves of peace to be found in such monuments to respective triumphs.

Alexandra took that to mean she would also find peace in the resolution of this menacing murderous bender.

CHAPTER 29

The next morning they were up early. Jean had returned Paul's call. It had a high priority. His grand-papa did remember conversations he'd had with Philip who commented several times at the scene that the smell reminded him of the cyanide he had experienced during the war. Why it wasn't included in the report, he didn't know. It was just one of those things Philip kept to himself for some mysterious reason. When they did talk about the case, Philip became more cautious and withdrawn as if it was an omen from the past, his past. Perhaps the investigation might have had calamitous consequences if mishandled.

Paul shared the information with Alexandra over their continental breakfast. Just before leaving the hotel, they made reservations at the Novotel Luxembourg Centre where Alexandra had stayed for the funeral. They were on the A31 enroute to Luxembourg within the hour.

Once back in surveillance routine, they re-evaluated the information they had gleaned from their time with Sergeant Lortie. Of particular interest were the review of the file and their visit to the house where the mother and daughter had been murdered. Plus there was the apparent confirmation of cyanide smell from Jean's visit with his grand-papa.

"I think we should contact one of our colleagues at the Police Nationale and have them open a file," Paul suggested, feeling concerned. "The risk level of threat has risen to the point the police need to be informed. Your father took to his grave facts that could have helped in the case. We have facts that need to be analyzed or at least recorded. God forbid something should happen to us. If it did, it would be tough if not impossible for others to pick up the case where we left off."

"I agree but where's the evidence? What hard facts do we have to take to the police? There is my *shrew*, my sensations of the mind, but not hard facts. There is the information your father passed on to us about my father's involvement yet my father did not record it in the file and instead took it to his grave, again not hard facts. There are your father's memories, but probably not considered hard facts because of his dementia. There are the warnings from Father Luke that he heard from his parishioner, but once again not hard facts. There is the analysis from the blood and stomach sample Jacques took and gave to me, contrary to his policy. Yes, hard evidence, but the source would be indisputably harmed at this juncture. In addition, the police in Dieppe classified her death as an accident. What do we have to refute that supposed fact and in doing so embarrass the department and the senior bureaucrats in addition to the bean counters? There is the file that Sergeant Lortie hid and subsequently took off-site to his home because he had a hunch there might be something that has never been proven. His actions are in complete violation of police policy, apart from disobeying an order from his superior to destroy it, and then lying to his superiors that he had destroyed it. He would be hung out to dry if this source was revealed. There is my mother's letter which is personal and is couched cautiously, signalling me to be wary of just about everyone. And then there are the unidentified photographs which could be the most damning evidence if whoever was in them knew of their existence. I suspect they may be aware of their existence because they knew they were being photographed. So, what's the evidence and where are the hard facts?"

Paul slowly shook his head. "You make a strong argument, and you are absolutely correct. I agree with your analysis and support you fully, but I just don't like it."

"I agree with you, Paul, one hundred percent. We need to involve the police or someone in authority for all the reasons you mention. Skirting on the edges of this case with Thon, who has been described by everyone we meet as an extremely dangerous person and more than likely a psychotic serial killer, is not the best-case scenario."

"Do we involve Fred or Jean?" Paul asked.

"They would be in a position to take the intelligence forward should something happen to us. I use the term "intelligence" because it isn't necessarily evidence. But should we put their lives in danger by passing along this information? Our least-worst option would be to contact some of my mother's colleagues with French Intelligence but who do we trust with all the warnings which shroud her communications? That might be our death knell if we speak with the wrong person. That person needn't be a Nazi sympathizer to be dangerous to us; it could be someone corrupted by lust for Nazi gold."

"All right, but I'm feeling vulnerable for you and that is causing me considerable anxiety," Paul responded. "If something were to happen to you and Collette, I wouldn't be able to forgive myself. But if we revealed what we have to the wrong person and something happened, I wouldn't be able to live with myself for that either."

There was a period of silence as they considered their options.

"So, what do we do? How do we leave a trail of breadcrumbs?" Paul queried.

"Speaking with Fred and/or Jean might be our best option. Alternately, we could record all the facts and intuitive messages and leave them in my safety deposit box for Collette or Fred. Or your safety deposit box for Jean who you say is very intuitive and has a wise head on his shoulders."

Alexandra thought to herself, *Even when we disagree, Paul is on my side, unlike André who always had to win every damn argument and then constantly remind me that I was wrong.*

Her cell phone interrupted her thoughts. It was Jacques. The police had made no notation of finding a water bottle on the old gun emplacement. Nor did the police make a note of any fluid container as being evidence. Discourteous tourists were prone to discarding bottles on the beach and around the bunkers, so possibly no notice had been taken.

"Okay, so we need to update our strategy," Paul muttered in frustration. "Where do we get the hard facts that we can take to the police? And perhaps more importantly, who can we trust?"

"Isn't this ironic," Alexandra concluded after a pensive pause. "I've spent a career working in the world of forensic psychology in a policing environment with police officers who are perceived by a declining number of citizens as stalwart and there to protect the public interest. You have done the same, yet neither of us really knows anyone we trust."

"Yes, a sad condemnation," Paul replied.

"Perhaps worse, the police have become instigators and products of their own waning trustworthiness as they have withdrawn from public view to hide behind their computer monitors to supposedly improve efficiency but not effectiveness. They are proxies of a system that they trust only minimally and which trusts them even less."

Paul hesitated, at odds with his critical-thinking process. His thoughts were thumping round his head like an unbalanced load of laundry on spin dry.

"What does that say about the state of affairs? Is there more honour among thieves?"

"Perhaps there is," Alexandra acknowledged.

"In the old cowboy movies I watched as a kid, the good guys always wore white hats and were visible signs of law and order. The bad guys always wore black hats and stayed in the shadows. Life was simple. Now, the good guys such as Jacques Moreau, Sergeant Lortie, Father Luke and his parishioner, and you and I, have been relegated to the dark shadows. Are the bad guys purposefully more visible, like wolves dressed in sheep's clothing as a cunning strategy? Do we need to adjust our stratagem also?"

CHAPTER 30

"You are brilliant, mon colonel! You have just identified a viable strategy for us to adopt. I remember watching a cowboy movie probably twenty years ago about how the bad guys in the black hats couldn't defeat the good guys in the white hats. So, the bad guys got one of their own to dress up in a white hat and outfit. The hero in the white hat couldn't shoot that particular bad guy because he was wearing a white hat, despite the fact that the hero knew that he was bad. Everybody became confused. It could be that Thon is out there masquerading as a white-hatted good guy but all along he is a psychotic serial killer. So, what if we played the same game but reversed the role and wore black hats?"

"You're the psychologist. Explain your thinking to a humble scientist who spent his career looking through microscopes at blood samples in petri dishes and then as a senior administrator pushing reams of redundant paper. A while back, you suggested that in retirement we should go into business together, perhaps with Collette, to solve unsolved crimes. Is this what you are proposing?"

"I wasn't really thinking about a partnership in retirement immediately but now that you mention it, what do you think, *partner*?"

"I do like the idea of a possible partnership but let's put it on the back burner for now. We can explore those options over a Burgundy this evening. Now, about the immediate threat, do you suggest we wear black hats to defeat Thon?"

"That's what I was thinking about," Alexandra confirmed.

"Okay, let me put this in a related context," said Paul. "When I worked with those interesting people doing those unspeakable interesting things in those interesting places, our evidence group and force protection team often adopted a deceptive strategy in order to access the forensic evidence and quickly withdraw. We exploited the weakness of the perpetrators of the war crimes and used them to our advantage while working to ensure they could not do the same to us."

"Yes, that's the concept," said Alexandra. "The bad guys, the black hats, have correctly identified the weakness of the current criminal justice system which has been infiltrated by bleeding heart liberals and seedy lawyers who are bottom feeders because they can't make a decent living practicing ethical law. We exploit *their* weakness. If you want to catch a crazy fox by luring it into your trap then you need to think and act like a crazy fox."

"I'm with you so far," Paul responded curiously.

Alexandra continued, "We have every reason to believe Thon is a psychopath or at least he has been exhibiting symptoms of psychopathy. He has been able to exploit the consistency in the character of his victims. So first, we would use multiple identities, each with their own psychological profiles some of the time but not all of the time. Second, we need to be inconsistently inconsistent so any one inconsistency does not become a consistent pattern. This is where the multiple identities come into play. We flip back and forth between identities. We morph into another psychological profile each time we return to a previous identity. Finally, we use the inconsistencies in the law and forensics as quantum nebulae in which to hide as black hatters and search the myriad labyrinths of the White Rabbit's tunnel like the Mad Hatter in Alice's Wonderland."

"I like your style of thinking, partner, very much. Morphing is how the most virulent bacteria and viruses not only survive but also propagate. Each time they are hit with an antibiotic, they evolve to counter the threat posed by the antibiotic. By the time we humans have created another antibiotic, the bacteria and viruses have morphed again, now into superbugs for which there is no antibiotic strong enough to kill them. In the world of pathogens, we supposedly smart humans attack with one of two strategies. We surround the bacteria and viruses and starve them, or, we enter them and attack from within, starting at their core. My concern is that Thon may be more like a virus than a bacterium. Antibiotics have no detrimental effects on viruses. As a strategy to take on the Thon bacteria, we could surround and starve or attack from within, but as a Thon virus, we need an alternate strategy."

"Right," Alexandra acknowledged. "I think I follow this pathology analogy. We need to identify and take advantage of his weaknesses. Do you remember the Scarlet Pimpernel in the book by Baroness Orczy, set in the time of the French Revolution? The lead character, Sir Percy Blakeney, adopted the character of a wealthy fop, pleasant but harmless. Meanwhile, he was a formidable guardian of the good, fighting with his foil against evil, although no one suspected him, including his wife. He was a white-hatted good guy who used his shrewdness and black-hat alter ego to gain access to the core of the bad guys and then defeat them. There are numerous examples of the white-hat good guys disguising their identity in order to get the job done, like Don Diego de la Vega, who became Zorro. John Reid became the Lone Ranger with his Indian partner, Tonto, and Bruce Wayne became Batman along with his trusty partner, Robin. And not to be gender-biased, there was Kathy Kane who became the super-heroine Batwoman. We can switch roles as circumstances dictate."

"The good guys wear black hats and the bad guys wear white hats. I like it," Paul responded mischievously. "Six months ago, when I considered retirement, I really didn't know what I would do or what I wanted to do. I'm now as motivated about the prospects of a second career as when I first started working in the lab as a junior technician."

"Me too," Alexandra giggled.

"I think my covert black hat should be something that virtually no one could connect with me but something I really enjoy. After I showed you the photos I took in Dieppe, you said I had talent that I could turn into a retirement activity. What do you think of the idea of me hanging out my shingle as a professional photographer? I could actually do some portraits to demonstrate that it would be a revenue-generating enterprise. It could be ambiguous whether I was somewhat of a black-hat who also took risqué images. Then when I was off working with you on cases, I could hang out another shingle that would read, 'Away on Assignment.' Who would ever know otherwise? Photographers are often out of their studio on randomly-scheduled assignments."

"Now that would be a great covert black hat, mon colonel."

Alexandra paused in reflection.

"Not to break away from that discussion, but are you all right with me calling you *mon colonel*? Back when we first met, you called me AV and I liked it because it made me feel special. Lately, I have been calling you mon colonel. May I do so?"

Paul thought for a moment. "Yes, because it is you. Marcel calls me that because it had been our working relationship in Sarajevo. As much as 'AV' signalled the beginning of our relationship when we were younger, 'mon colonel' can be the other bookend now we are back together again. I actually like that and I feel good about the partner relationship. Regardless of hat colour."

"Thanks. Marcel uses the expression out of respect for you and what the two of you went through. I can never replace that and nor would I ever want to. I call you mon colonel out of respect for your accomplishments and as an expression of flattery as a business partner."

Paul reached over and held Alexandra's hand in affirmation of their developing relationship.

"There's the traffic sign announcing that we have just left France and entered Luxembourg. Remember when this was a formal border with customs officers? The adoption of the EU changed all that and the way business is conducted. Your photography business would fall within the EU business and trade regulations, so you'll be able to work as a photographer in any EU member state where our cases take us. You can just be an amateur photographer if we travel outside the EU."

"So, I have my black hat," Paul confirmed happily. "Now what about you? What could you do that would provide you with some clandestine cover no one would suspect and you would enjoy."

"I think I already have it," mused Alexandra. "Sometimes the best cover is being completely obvious. Being an adjunct university faculty member who is teaching psychology is just that. Or I could hang out my shingle as a career or retirement counsellor. As adjunct faculty with so many universities, I could work part-time. A few deans have already asked me if I would consider conducting Socratic seminars with a select few graduate students. I could engage the students as protégés of forensic psychology by presenting the facts of the cold cases we would be working on and asking them to profile the black-hatted bad guys. Many minds are greater than one. But we need to be aware of the inherent danger in any stealth strategy."

"I like your cover. Hiding in the open. Yes, I agree with the need for caution about the inherent dangers. As an aside, have you ever thought of writing novels, murder mysteries with characters who reflect some of the criminal minds you've analyzed? Now that would be a natural black hat-white hat for you."

"Interesting you ask. The thought had crossed my mind. I could use it as a cover, telling people that I'm researching for a book. Perhaps we could co-author under one *nom de plume*. So, what say you, partner? Should we shake on it?" Alexandra asked as she held out her hand.

Paul held it as if they were life partners rather than novice contractual business associates.

"Okay, partner, now navigator." Paul requested, "Punch the coordinates of the Novotel Centre into the GPS or guide me there."

Alexandra didn't need a GPS. She knew the route to rue Michel Welter better than the contours on the back of her hand and she knew the Hôtel Novotel Centre equally well.

Within the hour, they were at their destination. The hotel valet offered to park their svelte chariot of fire.

CHAPTER 31

The receptionist greeted Alexandra with a sincere smile as they entered the foyer.

"Welcome to the Hôtel Novotel Luxembourg Centre. We are most pleased to greet you as one of our respected elite members and again, since your recent visit with us. We have your rooms ready which we hope will have everything you need."

"Thank you. It's good to be back. Novotel is like a home away from home."

The receptionist whispered to Alexandra, "In confidence, madame, I wish to inform you that someone enquired about you."

"Oh?" Alexandra replied.

"Yes, a person called enquiring if you were registered or had been in the recent past. The person wished to leave condolences. The caller had a southern German or northern Swiss accent that sounded female at times but strangely changed to a deeper tone. I recognized the accent because I had worked in Zürich for a few years before coming to Luxembourg."

The receptionist assured Alexandra that she had not provided any information to the caller one way or the other. She then mentioned that her sister who works at the Novotel Kirchberg in Luxembourg received a similar enquiry and had also not revealed any details.

On hearing this information, Alexandra and Paul immediately decided to adopt alternative identities and change to black hats. Instead of staying at the Novotel in Amsterdam, as was their initial plan, they made reservations at the Hampshire Rembrandt Square Hotel where Paul had stayed on his visits. It was close to the apartment on Amstel where Alexandra was living. Parking was relatively convenient which would make it easier to pack and load her suitcases.

Paul had a business American Express card. He would order a replacement card once he had his photography business registered.

Alexandra would register as his sister using her grand-maman's first name, Vanessa, and her papa's last name, Marchand. Both rooms would be paid for with his credit card. They agreed that they would not stay in any more Novotel hotels until Thon was caught or confirmed dead, preferably the latter. Alexandra then called Jo and Collette, updated them on their plans, directing them to continue their watchfulness and to advise if anything appeared odd.

⁂

ONCE CHECKED INTO THEIR ROOMS, ALEXANDRA CALLED the real estate agent and made arrangements to meet at the house the following afternoon. She also asked if he could email her recommendations for reputable tradespeople who could upgrade both the exterior and interior on rue Michel Welter.

She still wasn't certain if she should keep the house and live there or sell it and start afresh in her own home. Regardless, it desperately needed repairs. She would have a better idea about the house after she and Paul inspected it in the morning.

But first, they would go to her mother's apartment in the old part of the city to determine how much space there was for moving in items for storage including the possessions they would bring back from Amsterdam. She had not yet seen her mother's apartment.

"I'll make reservations for dinner at the Café Kaempff-Kohler? We could sit inside, out of sight," Paul suggested.

"From the map, it looked like my mother's apartment is just around the corner. Mind you, everything in the old city is just around the corner."

Before leaving the hotel, Alexandra asked the receptionist if the parking valet could keep a watchful eye on their car. Looking in the direction of the valet, the receptionist brought their attention to a middle-aged gentleman in a blue pinstriped suit standing by the front door. "He is the head of the hotel security and is aware of the circumstances," the receptionist murmured.

As they approached the entrance, the gentleman held the door open and gave them a reassuring nod and smile.

"Do you remember when we were in the Luxembourg station waiting for the train to Brussels and I pointed out the profile of the Eurail security person sitting and pretending to read a paper as he scanned everyone over the paper?"

"You said those types of security guards are obvious by trying not to be obvious."

"Really professional security people are not obvious by their behaviour. The head of security at the hotel here is not obvious. I would not have recognized him as such had the receptionist not pointed him out to us. Why would a professional of that calibre be a hotel security person, even the head of hotel security? My *shrew* isn't signalling me to be wary. It is beckoning me to be aware. This is weird."

"I was picking up your concern you were somehow especially aware of him."

"Paul, our intuition is never wrong. It is only our misinterpretation of our intuition that gets us into trouble. So, what is your intuition telling you? Is it caution or curiosity?"

"It was just odd, curious but no need for caution." The feeling was not like the call to action to avoid danger that he had experienced in Sarajevo or on those other missions collecting forensic evidence. "I need to hang out with you more often, AV, to learn about the senses of the mind so we can be better partners as diamond duo crime fighters. Yes, weird. Describe what you sense and how you interpret your peripheral subsidiary experiences. And read my reactions and responses as you lead me down the myriad White Rabbit tunnels."

They felt comfortable and confident as they approached the far end of the viaduct and entered the old city through the archway. Within minutes, they were standing on the cobblestone lane outside her mother's apartment yet they could not identify a dedicated entrance. There was just a door into the jewellery store. Her mother had described this in her letter and the address on the claim for the Lady Diana replica ring. Alexandra was to present the claim to the proprietor in the store.

As they entered, they were greeted by an elderly lady.

"May I be of assistance?" the lady asked.

Alexandra showed her the claim.

The propriétaire replied forthrightly, "Yes, we have such a ring."

"I believe that my mother lived in an apartment at this address," Alexandra said quietly.

The propriétaire looked at Alexandra and Paul, and briefly glanced at a man standing in a shadowed recess by the window before returning her focus to Alexandra.

"You must be Alexandra. I recognize you from your mother's description and a photograph she showed me. I am most honoured to meet you after all these years. I pass along my condolences. Your mother was a distinguished lady in the truest sense of the word. Her apartment can only be accessed through this business entrance. It used to be the residence of the previous proprietor. Please follow me."

Staring at the man standing by the window, she asked him to watch the store. Alexandra and Paul followed her gaze and recognized him as the waiter from the Café Kaempff-Kohler.

"You are the waiter from the Café Kaempff-Kohler," Paul said as if searching for affirmation of his identity and the reason for the clerk's familiarity.

"Yes, you are correct. Will you require a reservation this evening for two at your usual table? If so, I would be pleased to take care of that for you after I pick up a watch. The jeweller here is the only one who can repair old pocket watches with such precision that the original watchmaker would have been proud to employ him."

"We would appreciate a reservation for seven thirty but at an inside private table away from the window. Thank you for your kind offer."

Paul looked at Alexandra who angled her head slightly and gave him her we-need-to-talk-later communiqué. It was the same look she had given Jo in the parking lot. Paul confirmed her subtle signal with a slight nod of his own.

"Follow me," the propriétaire beckoned.

She led them up a winding narrow staircase that opened to a landing with one door directly ahead and a second to the right.

"This door leads into her apartment while the other is a washroom. Both doors are open and neither requires a key to access. I will leave you to look around. I'll be downstairs in the shop if you need anything."

When her steps faded, Alexandra and Paul entered the apartment and did a cursory scan of the bland orderly living space. A small bedroom was to the right and an even smaller kitchen to the left. All overlooked the cobblestoned lane below. They had a clear view through windows covered in sheer material. Dark outer curtains had been drawn open which would have obscured all light when closed. On either side of the doorway into the apartment were narrow closets only large enough to store possessions for single short-term occupancy.

There was something foreign and impersonal about the decor. Alexandra could not recognize any furnishings or personal possessions that belonged to her mother with the exception of one photograph of her with her uncle and aunt. Her mother had taken it at her school graduation when she was wearing the midnight blue velvet dress. Some clothes in the closet seemed familiar and faintly exuded the recognizable scent of her mother's Chanel No. 5 perfume.

Paul stepped aside so as not to interfere with Alexandra's efforts to become reacquainted with her mother's things.

Silently inhaling the fragrance and holding the photograph tightly to her chest, Alexandra momentarily withdrew into the memories of her childhood, to Montigny-lès-Metz, to Paul, to their letters, to the business trips with her mother, and to her surrogate parents, her uncle and aunt.

He observed her eyes closing over the tears that began to slip down her cheeks as her breathing became tranquil and quiet.

Alexandra had not cried at the funeral or even when she received the notice of her mother's death. The reality of her loss was now unambiguous in this impersonal space.

"Is this what it comes down to for Maria, the mysterious member of the *Maquis* and counterintelligence agent?" she murmured.

Unaware of what she did, Alexandra leaned into Paul's encircling embrace. She had always yearned for this closeness since that day long ago when he first called her AV. This intimacy now provided her with all the safety and comfort she would ever need.

⁂

"Bonjour" – *Hello.*

"J'écoute" – *I'm listening.*

"Они в квартире матери. Это подает большие надежды." – *They are in her mother's apartment. This is promising.*

"Да. Принято" – *Yes. Acknowledged.*

CHAPTER 32

The creaking of the worn stairs announced their descent into the jewellery shop vacant of any patrons, including the waiter.

"Can you tell me about the apartment?" Alexandra enquired.

"What would you like to know?"

"Some of my mother's clothes and a few of her possessions are here but I don't understand. She lived here but I don't get the feeling that she lived here. This doesn't feel like her home."

"This was a safe place for your mother, my dear Alexandra. Your mother came here to live after the death of her friend in the house on rue Michel Welter. She didn't feel comfortable in the house after that suspicious incident, the death. This apartment was a place for your mother to regain her sense of security. Her health was rapidly failing and we knew she just needed a place to live out her remaining days in peace. We provided that sanctuary and service."

Alexandra gazed at Paul as if seeking confirmation of the description of the living arrangements. He smiled and nodded, providing her with a sense of comfort.

"By now you are aware of what business your mother was in and the nature of her work. It can best be described as singular for those who follow that path. She was a remarkable lady and was able to accomplish great things because of her special talents and her ability to work in solitude much of the time. You must understand there were only a small number of colleagues with whom she could communicate in complete confidence. Again, that is the nature of espionage work. In order to survive and succeed, such people who choose this profession need at least one place where they can find safety."

"Thank you for providing that security. I will always be indebted to you."

"You are welcome, Alexandra. Please understand that your mother never spoke about her exploits and I never asked. On those occasions when we shared a cup of tea, your mother talked about you and how much she loved you and how proud she was of you. She had two items with her that she always cherished. The first was the photo of you with your aunt and uncle. The second was a small wooden box containing ribbons that you used to play with as a child. Both are upstairs. She wanted me to tell you this. She also left with me a box of rare antique books. I will give them to you when you are settled."

Alexandra's face lit up on hearing the news of the wooden box. Some of her fondest memories were associated with the ribbons.

"Your mother did not want you to worry, so she never told you of her ailing health. I can say that she never suffered. Her heart was tired and she just died in her sleep."

"Thank you for your kind words, madame, and thank you once again for keeping her safe. I am only now starting to understand the gravity and extent of her work. May I ask you for one last favour?"

"Certainly. How may I help you?"

"May I keep her clothes here for a few more weeks? I will be moving my own possessions from Amsterdam, where I have been living for the past year, to Luxembourg. I would like to store them here until I find a place of my own. I appreciate this apartment really isn't my mother's but if I could impose on you, I would be forever grateful."

"Yes, you may. There is no rush. There are other such apartments available and there are no immediate requests that I have been made aware of for new tenants to take up residency here. We cannot provide you with a key to the front door for obvious reasons but here is my card with my telephone number. I live just around the corner and can let you in after normal business hours."

"Thank you so much. I'll be back in a couple of days and will call to let you know the time. I doubt I'll need to enter after hours. I will be meeting a real estate agent tomorrow and hope to have a place of my own very soon."

Alexandra gave her a warm hug, which was reciprocated in kind.

As they left the jewellery shop, Alexandra put her arm around Paul.

"Thank you for just being here. You may never know how much it has meant to me. Now, are you up for a walk, to work up an appetite before dinner? I promise not to keep you up past your bed-time. I'm aware that those who are older than me need extra beauty sleep."

Paul put his arm around her shoulder and looked at her with a wry expression acknowledging her as the senior partner in the relationship.

"Be careful what you ask for, youngster. I haven't seen you running marathons lately with seniors."

They chatted about nothing important as they walked. Alexandra commented that the old city felt like home. Tomorrow she would as-sess the house on rue Michel Welter as a residence but she just had a feeling the old city would be her new retirement neighbourhood.

Dinner provided further relaxation and the opportunity to de-brief events of the day. Their server was an enigma, much like the head of security at the hotel. They concluded that he displayed more of a collegial relationship with the jewellery shop propriétaire than that of a customer. Neither he nor the head of hotel security appeared to pose a threat. On the contrary, they had a fraternal relationship with an element of secrecy for whatever purpose. Regardless, they appeared to be professionals.

After dinner, they walked across the viaduct to their hotel where they were met by the head of security and the receptionist who assured them that all was in order.

CHAPTER 32

After breakfast, their top priority was the house on rue Michel Welter. It was a pleasant stroll in the morning sun.

The tired façade suggested what they would face once Alexandra unlocked the door. Inside, the air was musty. Raising the shutters, drawing the curtains and opening the windows revealed an interior that desperately needed the full range of repairs, maintenance and cleaning. Nothing had been done since her mother lowered the shutters, locked the door and walked away.

Their assessment was interrupted by a knock on the door. Alexandra checked her watch. It was far too early for the real estate agent unless he just happened to be in the neighbourhood and noticed the shutters had been raised. Opening the door, she was greeted by the rotund grey-haired neighbour.

"Good morning, madame, I introduced myself to you at your mother's funeral. I am your neighbour next door at 45, rue Michel Welter. My name is Gilbert Roger d'Estaine. Please call me Roger. I saw you arrive and I wanted to re-introduce myself."

"Yes, thank you for reminding me, Roger. I can invite you in but the house has not been attended to since the death of my mother's tenant and it's in terrible disrepair and very dirty."

"No problem, madame. It is I who owe you the apology. This is the first time I've been in the house since she was found dead, since I found her dead. I deeply regret my inaction on that day."

His voice became raspy and dry, and trembled as his face reddened. His eyes welled up.

"Are you all right, Roger?"

"Yes, madame. This is just very emotional for me."

"Can I get you anything? Can I help you home where perhaps I could get you some water? I dare not give you anything from this house as it's so filthy dirty."

"Just give me a moment to catch my breath. I suffer from anxiety disorder and re-entering this house has triggered an episode. It's what happened to me on the day she died, I mean when that horrid individual killed her, murdered her. I'm so sorry."

Alexandra and Paul looked at each other in astonishment before returning their attention to Roger who was regaining his composure but was still trembling. Paul helped him into the sitting room and sat him down. Alexandra and Paul joined him in a huddle on two similar brocade armchairs. His face showed emotions of sorrow and guilt. His manner was apologetic. There were more emotions lying in wait.

"You said she was killed, murdered, Roger. I wasn't aware of that. I had heard that she died from unknown causes perhaps related to her advanced age."

"That is not so, madame. I promised your mother that I would watch over the house and assist her tenant with any needs. I'm so sorry that I failed in my commitment to her. The day she was killed, I heard someone speaking with her in a muffled voice at the door. I was sitting in my living room reading with my back to the window. The person entered as I turned, so I only got a side and back glimpse. It was a woman but there was something odd about her blonde hair."

"Did she see you, Roger?" Alexandra asked.

"No, she wouldn't have been able to see me through the sheer curtains. I always keep the curtains drawn as it helps me to control my anxiety if I know others on the street cannot see me."

"So, why did you feel suspicious? What tweaked your curiosity?"

"Your mother's tenant never had guests so I was immediately suspicious. I wanted to go next door to check on her. I knew it was my duty to intervene but my fear overtook me. I froze in the clutches of a paralyzing anxiety attack. After several minutes, I heard the door open and saw a man leave the house. It was the same person with the same horn-rimmed glasses but in different clothes, as I remember, and different hair. It was shorter, like a man's. It must have been a wig that I first saw. I had a camera and secretly took a photograph of him as he was leaving. I have always been an amateur photographer, you see. I ran next door once he was out of sight. She was lying on the floor in the kitchen gasping for breath. I immediately called the police but by the time the ambulance arrived she was dead. I felt so guilty for not acting sooner. I froze. The ambulance attendant helped me."

"Did you tell the police?"

"No. I was too afraid, too embarrassed, too consumed with guilt for not being able to help in any way. I thought they would accuse me of being complicit in her death."

"Do you still have the photo?" Alexandra enquired, hoping that Roger would be able to provide some hard evidence.

"Yes, I do. I gave one copy to your mother when she locked up the house."

He reached into his breast pocket with shaking hands and pulled out an envelope.

"Here is another copy. The image is not very clear because I took it through my window with a telephoto lens so it appears to be grainy. He walked away quickly but turned around and that was when I took this photo. I explained to your mother what had happened and begged her forgiveness for not doing what I promised her I would do, to protect the house and her tenant. Your mother said it wasn't my fault. She was so gracious and kind, but it was my fault, all my fault. I knew that I was obliged to tell you at the funeral but could not muster the courage to do so. You see, madame, I'm a coward. I'm so sorry."

"I am a psychologist, Roger, and I can tell you with the utmost assurance that you are not a coward. You are a very brave man and courageous for taking the photograph. There is a very good chance you would have been killed had you tried to intervene and so would not be here today to tell us this news."

Reaching over and touching his taut fingers splayed over his face, Alexandra assured him he had done the right thing.

Paul placed his hand on Roger's shoulder as Alexandra asked the man to take his hands from his face and look at her. Looking into his eyes, she spoke with sincere compassion.

"Trust me, Roger, you are a brave man. You have nothing to be sorry for."

"Thank you, madame," he replied faintly, still gripped by anxiety. "You are as kind and forgiving as your mother. I am indebted to you for allowing me to tell you these details. It has been a curse to me since that day. I feel a bit lighter now that my actions and inactions have been atoned in this small way."

Roger's demeanour fluctuated from abject one moment to over-emphatic the next as he told the story.

"Like you, Roger, I am a photographer," said Paul. "Your ability to take this photograph demonstrates great skill and perception to catch his face as he turned. The clarity is remarkably good, given the circumstances under which you were operating. I commend you on your proficiency with the shutter."

"You too are gracious with your compliments, monsieur. I did my best. I saw you at the funeral but was not aware that you were madame's husband. I would have introduced myself had I known. I did speak with your son and daughter."

Paul smiled, contemplating the different circumstances had he been Alexandra's husband.

"There is one last observation I must bring to your attention," Roger said, his voice barely above a whisper. "At the funeral and reception, I thought I saw him, the man in the picture. But it wasn't a man. It was a woman with blonde hair. I am certain it was a wig. I distinctly remember the bright red lipstick because it was more obvious than the lipstick worn by all the other ladies. She was standing in the background, just staring. She left hurriedly when she noticed me looking at her or at least that's the impression I got. I couldn't remember where I had seen the face before. That was why I kept staring but as she was leaving the reception, she turned and I remembered. I recognized the profile from the picture, especially her owlish glasses. I remember them distinctly and the dark bags under her eyes. I'm not absolutely sure but it is my best guess."

On hearing this news, Alexandra and Paul instantly looked at each and then returned their attention to Roger.

"Thank you for listening to me but I must go home and rest. Please knock on my door if I can assist you in any way. I will not shy away with anxiety now that I have met you both. I remain indebted to you. Because of the vagaries of memory, I may have merged a few facts from different moments on that day and the funeral reception but I remain confident about what I saw. It is just that anxiety can fog the mind with false chronologies, which happens to me on occasion."

CHAPTER 34

Watching him ascend the moss-stained steps and go through the rusted wrought iron gate to the sidewalk, Alexandra burst out, "I wasn't expecting that, especially the description of the woman at the reception. I have no doubt he mulled that over and over again. When people try to remember too hard, the facts become more and more confused until fact and fiction become so intertwined they cannot be unravelled. That's not to say we shouldn't place some weight on his recollection about the reception. As he admits, anxiety can fog the mind with false recollections."

"I tend to believe him because he was so sincere," Paul commented.

Alexandra paused to think about Paul's observation.

"It's a possibility but we need to keep it in context. In contrast, there is nothing foggy about the photograph or the details of her death. When he first introduced himself to me at the funeral, I just thought he was an inquisitive sort of character. I sensed there was more to him than just being a good neighbour but there was nothing threatening. The poor soul. I can only imagine what he must have gone through since that day. The constant image of this house and the memory of that event would have been a festering wound repeatedly triggering his anxiety."

"I'm a bit stunned too," said Paul. "The photograph is clear enough to see the face despite being grainy. I have no doubt he has been trying to recollect the details. From the photo, you can clearly distinguish the round eyeglasses. This is hard evidence we can take to the police."

"I agree. Finally, we have one up for the good guys in white hats. We're making progress."

"I'll give this photo and the others you have to Jean when we get back to Paris and ask him to conduct a digital analysis, as that is his speciality. I may have mentioned to you that Jean showed me some of the work he does and it's incredible. He has developed his own software for digital imagery comparison not just facial but also skeletal that is a significant improvement over the program his department uses. I'm pretty sure he'll be able to tell us something one way or the other."

As he spoke, Paul noticed Alexandra looking at him but becoming increasingly distant as she shifted her focus away from their discussion and into her sensations. He watched with admiration as she slowed her breathing to two or three breaths per minute and became immersed in her intuitive peripheral world. Taking the opportunity to reflect, he again mused over Roger's misinterpretation of their marital status. *How different life would have been had I been AV's husband. But past what-ifs are mere flirtations of the mind.*

Alexandra's focus returned to him in the present after several minutes. Her complexion was radiant with its usual glow. Her breathing was once again strong and regular. This was in complete contrast to her experience in Montigny-lès-Metz in the house where the mother and daughter had been the victims.

"And?" Paul murmured softly as he smiled at her.

"Very interesting. The tenant is feeling more peaceful now that these facts have been revealed to us. She has great compassion for Roger and is glad the weight of these events is now lifted from his shoulders. She will bring calmness to his anguished soul. She is able to move on in peace. I don't know if you can sense it but the air in the house feels lighter, cooler now."

"Come to think of it, it does feel lighter."

"I'm now confident about selling this house and moving on myself. I wasn't sure before if I should move in here or find a place of my own. Now I know. I'll ask the real estate agent for the utmost confidentiality concerning the sale of the house and equal secrecy in finding a new place for me in the old city as close to the Palais Grand-Ducal as possible."

Paul gently wrapped his arm around her shoulder and gave her a comforting hug. Alexandra reciprocated.

"I'm convinced the tenant will become a guardian angel for me," she said. "I'm more convinced, if I wasn't before, that Thon is behind this and is evil to his core. And I will gladly accept all the help I can muster from the spirit world and the mortal world to rid this planet of his wickedness."

"You have my vote."

"By the way, thanks for being intuitive enough to accompany me as I moved into my sensations of the mind and not interrupt with commentary."

"I'm learning and I have the best partner to teach me. How about we assess the house, go for Java and a bite to eat and then return to meet the real estate agent?"

"Good plan. We've been hanging out together enough that you can readily read my senses of the spiritual and my earthly requirements for the sustenance of the body," she said with a smile. "I'll treat you to a croissant or a chocolate éclair."

"It's a date but I had better check my geriatric dietary chart and my glucose scale to confirm that I can have a treat. After all, I am your senior!"

"I think I'll regret the day I reminded you of your seniority. You're going to play this card for all its worth."

Paul merely acknowledged her junior status with a gleeful grin.

"Lead on, young madame. I will follow you anywhere!"

"Ya, ya. Okay, back to work. After meeting with the real estate agent, I'd like to check with the local police to ascertain whether they noted any spilt fluids at the scene. I still have a good relationship with them from a cold case I helped them solve a few years ago."

"They could have taken photos of the scene as part of a routine investigation. Perhaps you can ask if we might be able to examine them."

"Good plan," Alexandra confirmed. "Ideally, there would have been an autopsy. But they might not have done one if they concluded the cause of death was due to natural causes, like Madame Deschaume. Excuse the sarcasm in my voice! It's no wonder some people can get away with murder. There have been many a day I just shook my head at the ineptness of the local constabulary, our fathers being the exception. I fear their kind are a dying breed, literally. Nonetheless, it's worth a trip to the precinct to collect more hard facts if they are there."

CHAPTER 35

The meeting with the real estate agent concluded without interruptions or obstacles. They had agreed on the maintenance schedule for both the interior repairs and the exterior face lift.

The agent was convinced all repairs, maintenance and cleaning could be completed in a month. He agreed to a confidential listing as requested but reminded Alexandra that by law he would have to disclose the fact there had been a death by natural causes in the house.

Alexandra acknowledged the need for this disclosure. She figured if the police report concluded death by natural causes, who was she to suggest otherwise to the agent or to a prospective buyer. A technicality was a fact until proven otherwise. The black hats used technicalities in the bureaucratic process to their advantage, so the white hats could follow suit.

Alexandra gave the front door key to the agent who promised to make a copy and personally leave the original for her at the Hotel Novotel. Given the heightened level of security, she called the hotel and informed the receptionist.

On their way to the police precinct, Alexandra and Paul passed l'Église du Sacré-Cœur.

"I'd like to pay a social call on Father Luke if you don't mind. I want to let him know about my plans to move back to the city and become an active member of the parish once again. There's something comforting about returning to the flock."

"Of course. Father Luke introduced himself to me at the funeral reception and made me feel most welcome. I was left with the feeling that he is a kind and caring person who has the best interests of his parishioners at heart, although there was something enigmatic about him. Perhaps it was the occasion and my anticipation of meeting you that left me with that impression. I find my church in Meudon to be distant and the priest somewhat austere. He's a nice enough person but certainly not as warm and welcoming as Father Luke."

"If he's in and he invites us into his office, take a look at the photos of the previous parish priests hanging on the walls. Take particular notice of the picture of the last priests and then Father Luke. We can talk about what you might notice after we leave."

"What do you want me to look at?"

"I don't want to say anything more now that might influence your perception one way or the other. Just take note."

Paul nodded with a smile.

"Orders understood, madame."

The housekeeper greeted them at the back door of the priest's house. She summoned Father Luke who welcomed them with open arms.

"Come into my office, my children."

Glancing at the housekeeper, he asked her to bring coffee and biscuits to his study.

"Thank you, Father. Do you remember Paul Bernard? He was at the reception. We are working on a case together."

"Yes, I do remember. And how are you, Dr. Bernard?"

"Please call me Paul. I am well, thank you. I was just commenting to Alexandra how welcome you made me feel when we met."

"Thank you for your kind words. God's house is home to all. And what brings you back to our parish, my child? Good news, I hope."

"Yes, very good news, Father. I have decided to retire here in Luxembourg. I will sell the house on rue Michel Welter and buy a place of my own in the old city. That means I will be an active member of the church community once again."

"I'm so pleased to hear this news and, if I might add, you seem very relaxed and confident with your decision."

Father Luke and Alexandra continued their conversation as Paul quietly scanned the photographs adorning the walls of the study. Their conversation was interrupted briefly as the housekeeper entered and served coffee.

"That's quite a distinguished display of past parish priests," Paul commented. "I'm a photographer. The photographers have captured the essence of the spirit of those who have worked in the service of God. I used the term 'spirit' in the most honourable way as one cannot help but feel the sense of service which they portray."

"They are indeed and each time I look at them I am reminded of the honoured role that our parish has played in the history of this community. Our bishops have been strategic in their recommendations to the cardinals. I'm deeply honoured to have been chosen to serve. I'm sure Alexandra has told you about her mother and her family."

Interrupted by the housekeeper who had quietly appeared at the door, Father Luke apologized for having to cut their meeting short. He had an appointment with another parishioner who had just arrived.

"Thank you for making time to see me, Father. I just wanted to take the opportunity to bring you up to date on my plans. We have business to attend to regarding the estate so must be off. Thank you again."

"Know that you will always be welcome, my child. May God's blessing be with you both."

CHAPTER 36

As they left the priest's house, Alexandra looked at Paul. "Your thoughts on the photo, partner?"

"I can now understand why you asked me to scan the photo of the previous priests. I'm leaning toward a resemblance."

"Curiouser and curiouser, and down the White Rabbit's tunnel we go again, mon colonel. I think Lewis Carroll might have been a closet detective when he wrote about *Alice's Adventures in Wonderland*. The resemblance of Father Luke to the second to last photograph was my initial reaction also."

Alexandra tilted her head as she raised her eyebrows.

"Father Luke spoke about an unnamed parishioner who would bring him intelligence and information about Thon and imminent threats. Something to ponder for sure. I'd like to talk with Father Luke about that parishioner when the time is right but the time is not right. I don't mind that because I'm confident he has our back, so to speak. But I can't help but suspect there is much more to Father Luke than meets the eye."

⁂

THE DESK SERGEANT AT THE POLICE PRECINCT remembered Alexandra and summoned his capitaine who also recalled her involvement in the cold case she helped to solve. With a relationship re-established, the capitaine granted Alexandra permission to review the file on the death of the tenant. No autopsy had been conducted as the investigators concluded she had died from natural causes. Photographs of the kitchen where the body was found had been taken. They showed a broken cup and saucer on the floor along with a creamer, sugar bowl and plastic vials containing medication.

A chair was overturned. She appeared to be clutching a tablecloth. The investigator concluded that this reinforced his belief she had experienced a seizure of some sort or a heart attack. There was no sign of forced entry or theft to suggest foul play of any kind was involved.

Alexandra concluded the deduction was plausible in the absence of other evidence. Even Roger's statement, which could be assessed as less than reliable, would be insufficient evidence to substantiate a request to reopen the case.

No facts on this lead. Score one more for the bad guy in the black hat and one less for the good guys in the white hats.

Both Alexandra and Paul were gaining a better appreciation for the frustration which some police investigators experience on a daily basis, while others just glaze over possible evidence. It was much less frustrating for the others in their supportive professions just to present evidence and walk away feeling they had done their bit for justice.

"We have some time before dinner so do you mind if we check out a few properties around the Palais Grand-Ducal? It would be nice if I was closer to finding my own place. I don't mind storing stuff at my mother's apartment but it's clearly temporary and I'd like to have a better appreciation of what is available."

"Sure, we can do that," Paul responded with a supportive nod.

"In my previous moves, I've always had a permanent place to move into so would like to have that sense of comfort on this final retirement move. I'm actually looking forward to my own place, a real home where I can nest, after all these years of living out of a suitcase, as visiting faculty and working on cold cases across the country."

"I'm at your service, madame. *Après vous*. Although I don't know how much assistance I can provide – I have virtually no experience of moving. I always had our house to return to as I travelled around with work."

"Thanks," Alexandra replied. "If we called it an early night, we could be up early and checked into the hotel in Amsterdam by late afternoon. That could put us back in Lux by late afternoon the day after tomorrow."

"I agree. Again, being inconsistently inconsistent, we should make reservations at another hotel here, perhaps the Grand Hôtel where I stayed when I came for the funeral. You could ask the real estate agent to line up some properties. Thoughts?"

"Sounds like a plan. I'll confirm with the agent, while you can make the reservations at the Grand. I'm feeling good about the prospects."

"Are you all right with being my sister, Vanessa Marchand, for the Grand reservations?

"Absolutely, brother. I'm getting into her character."

She had so longed for the depth of a supportive relationship. If she wanted to go swimming in the Arctic Ocean, Paul would support her and be holding a heated towel for her when she ran out of the frigid water. She needed to have a girl-talk with Jo who may never have had a lengthy relationship with a man but strangely was the best person to talk to about relationships. She'd bent Jo's ear many times about how she hated her marriage to André.

In the morning, as they checked out of the Novotel, the receptionist asked if she could make further reservations for them. Alexandra declined with an appreciative gesture. That seemed normal in the context of customer service. The head of hotel security was in the lobby when they departed and wished them a safe journey.

The drive to Amsterdam was uneventful from a security perspective. The driving routine came naturally, as did their mutual surveillance tactics.

⁂

THE APARTMENT WHERE ALEXANDRA HAD BEEN STAYING in Amsterdam was spacious and modern. Paul was surprised at how little Alexandra had to move apart from clothes. One box accommodated all the possessions from her office at the university.

In contrast, when Suzette travelled she brought everything with her just in case she might need it. It took hours of packing, unpacking and repacking and even then, she complained she had forgotten something.

They were back in Luxembourg by late afternoon the following day and Alexandra's possessions were carried into her mother's apartment.

The real estate agent had emailed Alexandra some listings in the old city and confirmed appointments to view the properties. Surprisingly, one of the properties on offer was a rental unit that Alexandra had inherited from her uncle and aunt and was available for immediate possession as it was empty. She counter-offered and purchased for a slightly lower price than she had sold it for several years before. She had learned well the art and science of real estate from her aunt.

By the end of the week, Alexandra was a property owner once again and had moved everything from her mother's apartment to her new abode just around the corner from the Palais Grand-Ducal with its 24/7 armed guards.

CHAPTER 37

Darkening clouds accompanied them back to Paris in more ways than one. The weather had changed and rain poured down in torrents. All traffic was slower as wipers were barely able to clear the windshields.

Surveillance was impaired because the relentless spray obscured their vision. They didn't take as many rest stops as usual because they didn't have much depth of vision. On a positive note, they agreed that if they couldn't see any other vehicles clearly, others couldn't keep them in sight either. The line between objective caution and subjective paranoia was blurred. The deluge actually provided a break from the stress of constant surveillance that had overshadowed their travels since Dieppe.

"Can you check this, please? I need both hands on the wheel and my full attention in this traffic."

Paul handed Alexandra his cell phone. It was buzzing with an incoming call.

"It's from Bastille Harley-Davidson. Shall I answer it?"

"Yes, please."

Alexandra took the call.

"One moment. I'll confirm with Dr. Bernard."

She put the phone on mute.

"Your Road King is in and has been serviced. They want to know when you can pick it up."

"Tell them I'll drop by tomorrow morning to complete the paperwork. Ask them if they can deliver it to my house tomorrow afternoon. With this weather, I don't want to risk an accident on my inaugural ride."

Alexandra relayed the instructions less the risk analysis and hung up, all the while reflecting on his choice of words. Had he used the term house instead of home purposely or was it a Freudian slip?

"So, when can we ride?" Paul inquired.

"I need to spend some time with Collette to let her know about my place in Lux and my plan to retire there. I suspect she knows I won't be moving back to André's house but I'll confirm that. I should also talk with Jo over dinner tomorrow evening. So, how about we ride the day after tomorrow?"

"Yes, absolutely. I don't think I need a reminder in my calendar."

"We can do what I call the Versailles loop, staying off the main highways. We'll ride the secondary roads instead through Le Chesnay, Versailles and back via Virofay. Can you meet me at Jo's around nine?"

"I certainly can and will, madame."

"Most of the commuters will be in Paris by then so traffic should be lighter. We'll be riding away from the morning rush hour. Before I forget, remember to bring your camera for photos of you and Chuck, and Sophia. You promised that you'd take some portraits of Sophia and me."

"I rarely go anywhere without it. Before I forget, can you dig out the photographs that your mother had in her safety deposit box? I'll hand them over to Jean along with the one from Roger."

"I'll give them to you when you drop me off."

Alexandra took the time to cross off a few more items from her to-do list but one more was added. She had just finished reading the letter from the distinguished elderly English gentleman who had given it to Collette at the funeral reception. The letterhead read *Sir James Pennington, KCB, DSO, DFC*. It was apparent she would need to travel to Dover on the south coast of England to speak with him. She felt annoyed for not having read it sooner because the urgency to meet in person seemed to be as important as her private discussion with Madame Deschaume at the funeral reception. After briefing Paul on the content of the letter, he agreed that they should reserve seats on the Eurostar after their inaugural ride. They needed some down time just to relax.

⇹

AFTER DROPPING ALEXANDRA OFF AT JO'S AND picking up the photos, Paul called Jean and asked him to meet after dinner.

"Sure, Papa. I know this tone. It spells quiet urgency. What's up?"

This wasn't the first time his father had asked him to discretely research what he called "stuff." Like Alexandra, who didn't know all the details of what her mother did, Jean knew that his father occasionally travelled abroad on business trips but wasn't aware of the exact itinerary. In fact, he knew more about his father than his mother did because her self-medicated stupor left her numb to the world.

"I'll explain when we meet and, yes, there is a need to be sensitive."

After dinner, they met behind the closed door of their study, not that Suzette would have known anything different.

"Like the other times, Jean, we need great discretion about what I would like you to do. The other requests I asked of you were more at arm's length but this one is here and now and has an added element of immediate danger to people near and dear to us. By involving you, I'll be putting you in danger. That concerns me, of course, but the need outranks the risk. The work you do on a daily basis puts you at risk anyway and, as a result, requires a heightened level of secrecy. What I am about to tell you raises that risk several notches."

Jean was used to this type of request and the level of security that came with it. Leaning forward, he prepared to concentrate on his father's words.

"There is a distinct possibility it may raise flags with your superiors somewhere in the security and intelligence system. So, if asked, disclose the source of the request but not the details before first checking with me. You can use the authority of the memorandum of understanding that provided the blanket requests for my international work. I'm not officially retired yet so technically that MOU is still valid. If anyone asks for more particulars, simply refer them to me. Are you all right with this?"

"I'm in, Papa. How can I help?"

Paul gave him the photos of the Germans standing by the armoured vehicles and others by the vehicles in the desert, the two of the people dressed in more contemporary attire in Luxembourg, in addition to the photos he'd taken of the man seated in the black Mercedes in Dieppe. He added the photo Roger has taken to the pile. He instructed Jean not to show the photos to anyone. He took time to explain the background and the threat to Alexandra and Collette, and himself through association.

"Even being in possession of the photos puts you at risk of falling in the cross-hairs of Thon. It's a bit of a long shot, Jean, but I thought you might be the best person to do it."

"The older photos are not the greatest quality, Papa. Obviously, your digital photos will be much easier to work with. Do you have the digital images with you on your camera? If so, can you send them to me?"

"I thought you might ask so I transferred them to this memory stick."

"Right. I'll get to them as soon as I can. I have one high-priority case I need to do first and another one in the mill. I should be able to get to these by the end of the week, if not sooner. In the interim, I can run them on my own profile software. It's at the beta developmental phase. But I won't be able to access the main database of criminal profiles on the mainframe. I'll let you know if I get any hits."

"Thanks, Jean. I was pretty sure you'd be keen."

"These images will actually provide me with a great pilot run for my program. If they work then I'll be ready to market with greater confidence. The timing of your request couldn't be better, Papa."

"I can't emphasize enough the need for caution, Jean. If you become suspicious of anything untoward or anyone, call me immediately. We live in interesting times but interesting has its hazards and hidden landmines."

"That's for sure, Papa."

"On a lighter note, I won't be bugging you to lend me your Ducati anymore. I've bought a Harley-Davidson, a Road King. It'll be delivered tomorrow afternoon. I'll be taking it out for my first ride with Alexandra for what she calls the Versailles loop."

"Outstanding, Papa! Perhaps you can lower your Harley standards and allow a mere Ducati to tag along some day. I promise to keep my distance so as not to embarrass you."

"I get the jab, Jean. AV explained to me that all you Harley wannabes say the same thing. We'll have to plan our weekends for saddle time. I'm sure AV and her friend Jo, who also rides a Harley, would enjoy your company. And maybe we can lure Collette along somehow," he added with a smile.

CHAPTER 38

As planned, Paul met Alexandra at 9 a.m. for the inaugural ride. With Alexandra in the lead, they took the secondary road south to Le Chesnay, past the Palace of Versailles. Their itinerary would continue south to the Lycée de Notre Dame before turning east to Viroflay and north back to Garches and Jo's. But first, close to Versailles, Alexandra pulled into the parking lot of a warehouse where they stopped.

"Photos," she called out as she dismounted. "Where do you want Sophia and Chuck for the best backdrop?"

Paul scanned the lot and directed Alexandra to park Sophia by a wooded area and moved Chuck over there. Frames flashed as he repeatedly pressed the shutter. He then set the camera on the tripod for the foursome. They found themselves lost in the moment as they giggled and laughed, posing and mugging like kids on a holiday outing.

"You know, Paul, if I was Thon, there would be two places in France that would really be a bur in my saddle – if I was a vengeful German unable to let go of history after decades. One place would be here in Versailles because it was here in the Hall of Mirrors that Germany was forced to sign the ill-considered peace treaty on the 28th June 1919, five years to the day after Archduke Ferdinand's murder in Sarajevo, which triggered the Great War. Some of the Versailles artifacts are stored in this warehouse. The second place would be in Compiègne in the forest where Germany was forced to sign the armistice on the morning of the 11th November 1918 in Marshal Ferdinand Foch's railway car. Hitler got his revenge for that humiliating moment in June 1940 when he forced Marshal Foch to surrender France in the same railway car."

"You have a point there. They'd be festering wounds with me if I was Thon or one of his compatriots. I'm surprised they haven't been targeted already by the Fourth Reich neo-Nazis."

"We can plan a full day's ride to Compiègne for another trip. I've been there a couple of times and really enjoyed the ride. Once we are north of Paris, we can take the back roads. There's a really nice out-of-the-way restaurant just outside Compiègne that caters to bikers. Hopefully, there won't be any obnoxious drunks who want to take on a couple of Harlistas."

Paul chuckled. "I think our new black hat covers will incorporate time in the saddle. What a great thought, bikers as cold-case sleuths. Now that's an inconsistency that even Thon wouldn't consider."

Or would he? Alexandra thought. *He hasn't survived this long by being naïve.*

Paul reached into his pocket and pulled out an official envelope with the Élysée Palace seal embossed on the front.

"Before I forget, madame, I was sent invitations for the awards ceremony. As Yvon isn't here, would you like to attend? There are two tickets for you and Collette."

Alexandra paused in astonishment before replying. She was deeply honoured by the personal invitation but anxious about what could be a delicate situation with Suzette and Jean also in attendance.

"I'd be pleased to attend as your guest, but are you sure?"

"Yes, I'm sure, completely sure. I want you there," he replied in a reassuring voice as if there was no other option.

"Then Collette and I will be there. Thank you so much. I can't say how honoured I feel. Jo will be so envious."

Alexandra didn't want to overanalyze what might be a simple situation but couldn't help but consider the underlying implications. Paul was retiring. The awards ceremony was a symbolic event marking the transition and celebration of retirement. But was his invitation an equally symbolic indicator of his unspoken decision to leave Suzette and start a new life perhaps with her as a partner in more ways than one, and perhaps in Luxembourg?

"I'll print the photos when I get home and email the best to you this evening. I can put them all on a memory stick and give them to you tomorrow before we catch the Eurostar if you like. That way I won't clog up your server, even as compressed files."

"That would be great."

Before departing, they confirmed the schedule for their trip to Dover to meet Sir James Pennington.

⁂

PAUL SPENT THE EVENING EXAMINING THE DIGITAL photos of the inaugural ride and reminiscing over the day's events as he scanned the images. He was pleased with their quality even without any Photoshop adjustments, but for whatever reason he felt he was missing something. He knew enough about perfection not to brush off these feelings. If there was something missing, then there was something missing. He would return to them later and search with fresh eyes.

Looking at the photos reminded him that retirement involved a transition period. He didn't need to attend a retirement seminar to figure that out. Before Maria's funeral, he didn't know what the future would hold. The fog of uncertainty had now cleared and the prospect of a future with Alexandra as a crime-fighting sleuth and riding partner was reassuring.

She had been open with him about her move to Luxembourg and imminent separation from André. He needed to make peace with his God and reciprocate the honesty.

His father's words resonated in his mind: *The Pope is not always right.*

CHAPTER 39

Alexandra and Paul boarded the Eurostar for London at the Paris Gare du Nord. Most Eurail routes on the continent were efficient but this route was both fast and efficient, at least for the French section of the track between Paris and Coquelles at the Pas de Calais. These tracks were straight for long stretches, allowing the train to get up to maximum speed in excess of 300 kph for longer periods.

"Vive la France," he murmured proudly.

Speed was better for business, Paul reflected, as he observed the multi-tasking, mid-management minions in the first-class coach. They were like drones talking quietly on their cell phones, spreading documents on their mini-tables, and feverishly entering data on their laptops. The two-hour fifteen-minute trip was undisturbed time. He had dutifully fallen into lockstep with these bulldogs of the corporate world far too often in his career.

Now on the eve of retirement and with a blank calendar, he could contemplate deadlines without any guilt. He had never succumbed to the pressures of a type A personality. Instead, he had learned to work alongside those who had that affliction, if not at their frenzied pace.

On this, his first quasi-retirement mission abroad, he was pleased just to ponder a future with Alexandra as a provisional business partner on this rather worrying caper. At this juncture the parameters of another, perhaps more intimate, relationship was a distinct possibility that tangoed with his emotions.

He looked over at Alexandra who was lost in the rolling countryside punctuated by silent steeples marking distant villages.

Smiling affectionately, he quietly whispered, "Penny for your thoughts."

He wanted to learn more about her perceptual wanderings and feelings, and how they were manifested in facial expressions and body language, and in excursions and wanderings down White Rabbit tunnel labyrinths. Who and what were her nemeses, her Mad Hatters? In her meditative moments, she could be so attractive and so mysterious. In the few weeks since the funeral, he had got to know some of her subtleties better than he knew or ever cared to know of Suzette's.

When he had posed this question before, Alexandra had responded as her mother had always responded – that thoughts were precious and not for sale. They were still precious but now she wanted to share them with him.

Not since her mother was alive had she felt such a strong attachment to anyone, certainly not André, and as close as she was to Collette, not her daughter, not this uniquely private world of thoughts, emotions and feelings. A mother-daughter relationship was special, but it was a different kind of trust than a true friend or intimate partner would share – *to be one with* – as the Buddha had described it. She needed a platonic relationship, yes, but she needed a deep relationship that involved an intimate connection.

It could only arise from a gradual process of building trust. In retrospect, it dawned on her that trust, the basis of all relationships, had been absent in her marriage. She never did trust André. She didn't believe he had defiled their marriage with a sexual affair, no matter how easy it would have been for a French man of his generation to rationalize. He was far too lifeless and apathetic to even stroll down that crooked path.

With a tranquil smile, she gazed at Paul with a sincerity she had never felt before.

"I was thinking that, on the one hand, I have never been so

content, so completely content, as I have been since we met at the funeral reception, never mind the revelations from our letters. On the other hand, I am so sad we were robbed of the past forty years. My life has been full of wonderful experiences with Collette and other friends such as Jo, both of whom continue to bring absolute joy to my heart. But at the same time, it has been a *Paradise Lost* as only John Milton could describe it in his poetry. I purposely re-read excerpts from Milton's poem last night and strongly identified with it. I then re-read some parts of *Paradise Regained* and thought about the blank verse. I've had blank verses, too many blank verses that did not need to be but were, nonetheless. Since reading my mother's letter, I've been consumed by emotional upheaval when I think of what my mother did to keep us apart. And although I understand her motivation to protect me, as I protect Collette, I'm devastated by what has been taken from me, from us. Could it be that in retirement, I – *we* – can experience *Paradise Found*?"

Paul found himself without words in the face of the depth of her honesty. It mirrored his thoughts perfectly. He took a slow breath but could not speak. How could he respond with equal honesty? He was not used to such emotions. He had no recent experience in his relationship with Suzette in envisioning and expressing such words. Emotional openness had been there in his youth with his mother and father but that was so far in the past that he was no longer capable. The depth of his response to Alexandra's openness could only be echoed in the adoration which he now felt. Even the first words of love written all those years ago were inadequate at this moment.

He reached for her hand and by this simple expression, revealed himself in a way that surpassed any *Paradise Lost*.

CHAPTER 40

They followed directions in Sir James' letter that led them to a quaint cottage on the Dover coast with an unobstructed view of the English Channel. A middle-aged gentleman answered the door. He was dressed as every quintessential English butler should be down to the polished black shoes, pressed dark-grey striped trousers, white shirt with gold cufflinks, Windsor-knotted regimental tie, and dark-blue starched apron.

"May I be of service?" he asked.

"I am Alexandra. Sir James Pennington is expecting us."

"Yes. Please follow me to the sunroom."

As they followed the butler, they noted there wasn't a crease or wrinkle on the back of his shirt or trousers and not a hair out of place which, like his dress and deportment, was regimented to the standard of a sergeant-major on dress parade.

"Good afternoon, Alexandra. Please come in. I have been looking forward to meeting you for many years. Your mother told me about you, and I have been following your career with keen interest. And you have brought Dr. Bernard with you."

Turning to Paul, he bowed his head slightly and extended his hand.

"I am deeply honoured to meet you. Although retired, I still follow international activities with interest."

He spoke with an eloquence and accent known only to Oxford scholars.

"I admire you for your forensic work and your involvement in some of the more recent cases brought before the International Criminal Court in The Hague. You have a sterling reputation for courage under fire and professionalism on the witness stand. I understand that you are to be inducted into la Légion d'honneur as a commandeur, an award much overdue."

"You are well informed, Sir James," Paul replied. "I am at a distinct disadvantage not knowing all your accomplishments but I understand you have several distinguished awards. I am likewise deeply honoured to be in the presence of a Knight Commander of the Order of the Bath."

After pausing and bowing, Paul continued. "Alexandra has told me about the contents of the letter which you left for her at the funeral reception. I am indebted to you, sir, for watching over her. She is very special to me. We have known each other for a long time."

Turning to the butler, Sir James quietly asked if he could serve the tea. The butler nodded courteously and took his leave.

"Afternoon tea is a custom in traditional English homes but I fear that tradition has been eroded by modern ways. I continue to believe that much can be resolved in a face-to-face conversation over a cup of tea."

"We agree, Sir James," Alexandra replied. "I too believe in tradition. It holds a culture together like a common pledge of allegiance. Individuals bond to and identify with tradition because it creates our culture, and our culture provides the foundation for our identity. Today, we have too much fragmentation, manifested in narcissism. It is quickly deflating the world you so gallantly defended as an RAF fighter pilot during the war. But I'm preaching to the converted."

"Perhaps I am just a doddering old man clinging to the past as I gaze out over the Channel reminiscing about those days when I flew missions deep into the heart of Nazi incursions across Europe and later in North Africa. But, they were good times. It was noble work."

As Sir James stared out of the window, for a few moments he

was flying another mission in his Mosquito in defence of his island and its people. Alexandra and Paul followed his gaze and joined him in remembrance and reflection.

Breaking away from his memory, he motioned to them.

"Please, have a seat. It has been a long time since I have had the pleasure of entertaining such distinguished guests and talking about matters close to my heart. I expect we have much to share. Certainly, I have information which will make your travels more enjoyable if not easier and more productive."

Alexandra and Paul waited for Sir James to sit down and gesture to soft armchairs that welcomed them as old friends.

"Thank you for the thoughtful letter which you left with my daughter, Collette. I was warmed by your kind expressions of the work my mother was involved in, and your personal relationship. In another letter to me, she mentioned a downed RAF pilot whom she helped escape to Spain but that was all I knew of your initial encounter, and nothing more of any later contact."

"Allow me to fill in some details of those times, Alexandra. It was 1943 and I was flying Mosquitos out of Luqa on Malta with the 23 Squadron Red Eagles. The battle for Malta had just ended and the Allies were now on the offensive. Among other missions in North Africa and Sicily, we were dispatched to strafe and destroy enemy supply shipping in the Mediterranean, mostly by moonlight. If we could not find our designated targets, we were free to attack what were called targets of opportunity. One night, I was undertaking a low-level attack on a target of opportunity, a German patrol boat. I took some cannon fire that disabled my rudder. I climbed to evade further enemy fire and put some distance between myself and the patrol boat, but I was forced to make a water landing. Fortunately, a French fisherman rescued me. He hid me under a tarp that was under his fishing nets. Still today, when I smell fish, I am reminded of that harrowing escape."

"What happened to your other crew member?" Paul asked.

Tragically, he was killed by the patrol boat's shells. I learned that his body had been spotted by one of our Blenheim Air Sea Rescue crews and subsequently taken back to Malta. In my case, in the wee small hours of the morning, I was smuggled ashore, picked up by the French Underground and taken to Carcassonne. That was where I met your mother, Alexandra. Her group was under duress because a collaborator had infiltrated them. So, she and another girl quickly whisked me away into the mountains."

He continued after a pause, "I gather you were aware that this other brave girl was at the funeral. Her name was Simone Deschaume."

"Father Luke introduced us," Alexandra replied. "She filled me in on some of details of my mother's work. She was killed shortly after we met. I… we believe it was Thon and one of his neo-Nazi compatriots who pushed her to her death from an old German gun emplacement in Dieppe."

"I am so sorry to hear this news. I tell you I was so impressed by the bravery and stealth of your mother and her friend, Simone, that when I returned to England I applied for a transfer to Military Intelligence."

Alexandra saw the chance to interject. "I concluded from our conversation at the reception that people did not acknowledge acquaintances from back then, especially with Thon still active."

Sir James nodded. "That would probably explain why. We wouldn't have recognized each other anyway. To continue, I lost track of Maria. I thought she might have been captured by the SS and executed. After the war, I transferred to British Intelligence, what you know as MI6. It was then that Maria and I were reacquainted as she was working with French Counterintelligence, la Direction générale des études et recherches, and later la Direction générale de la Sécurité extérieure. Maria and a few of her colleagues were tracking Nazi war criminals and others who had collaborated with the Nazis and committed terrible war crimes."

"That is what Simone confirmed but she was very cautious and warned me to guard what I said."

"You would be wise to remember her words. You must understand that there were two groups in the Intelligence world back then. There were those of us who had fought together during the war and knew each other as devoted patriots, and those who came after who could not be trusted to that same level of commitment. Your mother and I tended not to completely trust those who came after because we knew some collaborators had infiltrated our intelligence services and were engaged in the same double agent manoeuvres as during the war. At the end of the war, there were too many loose ends spawning subsequent global conflicts. By the early 1950s, the Cold War was raging and Russian spies, among others, had penetrated the bastions of western intelligence services. The most pernicious of the Russian spies were those who had survived the Stalinist purges of the late 1930s.The Cambridge Five in England were the most notorious. Kim Philby was the most infamous."

"Do you know anything about an OSS officer mentioned in my mother's letter? I think his name was Major Mike Murphy. How is he connected to all of this?" Alexandra enquired.

"Major Mike Murphy was OSS. He had been parachuted into Normandy in February 1944 because he spoke fluent French and German. His primary mission was to establish a liaison with the French Underground and to create a strategic deception prior to the Allied invasion in June. It was there he met Maria."

"What was his background?" asked Alexandra. "Again, when Simone was talking about their relationship, I noted extreme caution, even fear, as she spoke."

"I subsequently learned Major Mike Murphy's father had been

an American journalist covering the Great War and later the Paris Peace talks in 1919. He married a French schoolteacher. Major Mike was schooled in Paris before returning to the US in the mid-1930s. He graduated from West Point and was one of the original members of Office of Strategic Services, the OSS, who in late 1942 were sent to England for training by MI5 and MI6. Ironically, Kim Philby, the Russian spy who had infiltrated British Intelligence as one of the Cambridge Five, was one of their trainers. From the onset, Major Mike did not trust Philby and his suspicions proved accurate."

"The Philby connection would explain Simone's grave concern," Alexandra commented.

"After the Normandy invasion," Sir James continued, "Major Mike worked in advance of General Patton's Third Army on the trail of Nazi gold. Some of the gold had been moved from the Reichsbank in Berlin to an abandoned potassium mine in Merkers in the Thuringian Plain after the bank had been bombed in February 1945. Other gold had been shipped by the Nazis to other underground mines."

"So, this is a link to my mother's work. The hunt for Nazi gold."

"Yes, that's right," Sir James acknowledged. "Major Mike also worked with an American intelligence team whose responsibility it was to hand out what were referred to as 'purple primers' to German enemy agents who stayed behind after the Nazis retreated to Berlin. These agents were offered one of two choices: either imprisonment and possible execution, or cooperation."

"Did you or my mother or Major Mike trust these agents or did they become double or even triple agents, making the best of a bad thing just to survive?

"Nobody fully trusted them, neither your mother, Major Mike nor me. You need to know that it wasn't just the Americans who were involved in the purple primer project. British intelligence folks also handed out purple primers. But it was really helpful to know who they were. All agencies operated on the premise that it was essential to have levels of secrecy, and secrecy within secrecy. But all these levels caused constipation in the systems. The trusted relationship of Maria, Major Mike and I tended to mitigate this negative impact."

"What happened after the war? You transferred to MI6. My mother joined French Counterintelligence. But what about Major Murphy? You obviously stayed connected."

"After the war," Sir James replied, "Major Mike joined the CIA and returned to Europe. He maintained contact with Maria and through her, he introduced us to his protégé, code-named 'Alder.' At that meeting, he told Alder we were the only two people he should trust. If Alder needed anything, he was to contact either Maria or me. Maria, Mike and I became tight and worked together on a number of cases of interest to our respective employers. Finding the hidden Nazi gold remained our number one priority. Major Mike has since died but Alder may contact you. He would be approximately your age."

Noticing the butler approaching the sunroom, Sir James stopped talking. The butler placed the tray on the wicker table and withdrew, taking a moment to close the French doors that provided privacy.

CHAPTER 41

"Let me back up a bit in the story," Sir James continued after serving tea. "The Russian advance toward Berlin in 1945 was in large part motivated by the race for the Nazi gold, some of which had been moved into underground mines along with stolen art and other treasures. Some of the gold went to Switzerland, Spain, Portugal and Turkey where it was reinvested, and to South America, primarily Argentina, for easier access by the ex-Nazi SS such as Adolf Eichmann. But the Russians did not stop in Berlin. Communist agents moved into all crevices and cracks of Western Europe and North America as spies, some into the intelligence services in France, England and the United States. Russia wanted the gold to fund the expansion of communism. Today, we believe that some gold found by the advancing Russian Army funded the Muslim Brotherhood. That led to the ousting of British Forces from the Suez region. It was all part of the Russian grand strategy as an instrument of aggression against the West, particularly the U.S. and Britain.

Alexandra paused and took a breath before posing a nagging question.

"How much gold are we talking about?"

"It's hard to say," Sir James acknowledged. "The exact amount of gold, artwork and precious stones stolen from conquered countries and from Jewish victims and enterprises is not known. Are we talking pre- or post-Brenton Woods Conference value of 1944? In war years' value, approximately 2.6 million U.S. dollars was stolen from the Czech Reserve Bank, 32 million from the Hungarian National Bank, 200 million from France, part of which was Belgian, which had been moved to France as the Germans were on the eve of their western advance. Another 100 million was Italian. A conservative estimate was 500 million in equivalent U.S. dollars based on war value – some hundreds of billions in today's valuations."

"That's unbelievable," she gasped. "No wonder the CIA, MI6 and my mother were hot on the trail."

"You need to know that not all stolen gold was moved to the Reichsbank in Berlin. Some was held at special storage points. There were also special Nazi SS bank accounts that had been used to run the concentration camps."

"What?" Alexandra exclaimed.

"Much of the gold taken from concentration camp victims in jewellery and melted down gold from tooth fillings we suspect was subsequently transferred to Swiss banks and the Vatican Bank. We knew the Swiss Security Service, the Bundespolizei, was aware but we weren't certain what their intelligence strategies were."

"Where have I been all my life?" Alexandra cried in astonishment. "I have above average education and experience but now hearing this I can only conclude that I know virtually nothing about what is really going on around me. Why is it that more people don't know about this? Is it so complex it's inexplicable to a layperson?"

"Don't feel badly, Alexandra. Most people have no idea about the inner workings of the world in which we live, and perhaps it is better that way," Sir James replied. "Even now I find myself shaking my head in amazement when I hear of such events."

Paul nodded. "It may be best if people don't know. As I mentioned to you, AV, in the past ten years or so I have been gathering evidence on war crimes in interesting places. Before each mission abroad, I received a detailed briefing and, like Sir James, I constantly shook my head in amazement at what is not known to the general public. The scale of evilness is appalling."

"Back to your mother's work," Sir James interjected. "Your

mother was a brilliant cryptographer. She could break and make codes like no one I had ever known. She made Alan Turing and the folks at Bletchley Park and the American cryptanalyst Meredith Gardner look like amateurs. This was even more surprising given the fact that Maria had no formal university training in maths. I think her success was due to her photographic memory and being an absolute whiz with mathematics and advanced calculus. Because we worked together so well – a large part due to our mutual admiration and trust that was born out of our first contact back in 1943 – she created a code that we could use to communicate informally. We included Major Mike because of the bond forged among us. This was highly irregular because MI6, CIA and DPSD did not share their codes with one another for some obvious and some less obvious security reasons. It was just easier for the three of us that way. Her – *our* – code was simple but as unbreakable as any code could be because the cryptonym was so vague in its simplicity."

Sir James pulled out a file folder and showed Alexandra and Paul how it worked and explained that if they ever needed to communicate any sensitive information to him, they could use it.

After a brief review of the code protocol, they looked at each other in awe.

"I didn't know my mother had this talent. In school and at university I was, as you described my mother, a whiz when it came to numbers and calculations. Interestingly, Collette, my daughter, has the same knack for maths. I loved quantitative research methodologies and got straight A's in all these courses. I just thought I did well because my uncle had tutored me all my school life. I have no doubt that helped, plus the fact that I had an uncanny ability to remember things. But I see now it runs in the family. Thank you so much for showing me this. It's obvious that I knew my mother all my life, but I really didn't know her. Now it all makes sense. How I wish I had known this when she was alive."

Sir James quizzed Alexandra and Paul to confirm they knew the code protocols and reminded them they could communicate with him using the code if circumstances dictated a need for secrecy.

"I thought people needed to study codes for a long time in order to work with them," Alexandra commented. "I'm certainly not an expert on codes but I do know about the inter-relationship of numbers like the Fibonacci Sequence and the Golden Ratio. I can only say that this is absolutely elegant. It's so simple in its complexity. I can imagine code breakers going berserk trying to solve it. This is so much my mother, so mysterious yet so beautifully simple."

Sir James chuckled at Alexandra's reaction.

"Maria told me about the roots of your relationship when the two of you were just teenagers," Sir James continued as he poured more tea for his guests. "On many occasions, she regretted her decision but believed in her heart that it was necessary for your safety. When we last spoke several months ago, her health was poor. The years of stalwart work and her broken heart over the decisions to protect your best interests had taken their toll. She knew she did not have long to live. She did tell me she would leave you a detailed letter explaining her motivation. I presume you have read her correspondence. She also knew the two of you would meet at the funeral. She asked me to contact friends of your father, Paul, and ask them to tell you of her death. Keeping the two of you apart caused her terrible grief and so did not telling your father Philip of your existence."

Alexandra nodded.

"Yes, with mixed emotion I read her letter. She mentioned that I needed to be very wary because there were wolves in sheep's clothing everywhere. There were only a very few people in whom

I could confide. You, Sir James, were one of them." She paused before asking bluntly, "What can you tell me about Thon?"

"We did find many Nazis, Gestapo SS, and they were held to account for their perfidious behaviour." Looking at Alexandra and Paul over the top of his glasses, he said, "Accountability comes in many forms which are not all publicly advertised. There is justice and there is justice. But Thon was one we could not bring to account. He was as elusive as a ghost."

"Simone said that fear of Thon's murderous rampage caused her to be very cautious after the war. At the funeral reception, she expressed this fear in her voice and body language."

"She was wise. Maria, Major Mike and I and others agreed that Thon was a psychopath. We also agreed that Thon was somehow connected to the Nazi gold. The details regarding the gruesome murders of those he left in his wake strongly suggest he could not distinguish right from wrong. There was just his interpretation of right. As far as we could determine, he only murdered previous female members of the French Resistance and their daughters. His MO was always poisoning. In one case, we were able to learn from one of his victims before she died that he had called her to tell her he was a former member of the *Maquis* and needed to speak with her. We believed that was how he gained entry into her home. We just could not understand why daughters and not sons or spouses were targeted."

"Do you believe there is just one Thon out there or are there several murderers obeying his orders, or copycat killers?" Alexandra asked.

"I've often wondered whether there were many Thons. I'm now convinced there is just one and he is still out there. That disturbs me greatly. That is why, Alexandra, you must be so careful. Thon is fastidious in his attention to detail in all his murders. Once he has eyes-on and is locked-on to his target, he executes his strategy meticulously. Then, like a ghost, he just evaporates into seclusion where he plans, stalks and executes his next murder. There could be a month or perhaps a few years, before he strikes again. He has two lives. In one, he may be your neighbour and in the other he is a psychotic murderer. He is not invincible. He is just a master at the assassin's game. Indeed I believe it is like a game in his warped mind."

During the revelation, Alexandra and Paul concentrated on the information provided and on occasion looked at each other to confirm their dedication to defeat this threat. Alexandra sat low in her chair drumming her fingers methodically on the padded arms. She pondered the details, formulating a more precise psychological profile with each added tidbit of information. Paul sat upright with his chin resting on the steepled index fingers of his clasped hands. He weighed the facts and formulated a strategy to counter the threat by examining the broader implications of the renewed risk assessment and threat analysis.

CHAPTER 42

"I often find I can analyze better if I walk." Sir James suggested, "Would you like to join me as I stretch my arthritic knees in the garden?"

"Excellent idea," Paul replied.

"This chair is so comfortable, I may just sit and reflect," Alexandra replied.

Leaving Alexandra to the relaxed cosiness of the sunroom, Sir James and Paul went out into the garden and slowly but systematically wended their way along the scrubbed curved stone path bordered with bellflowers, giant daisies, columbines, coralbells and delphiniums, all skirted by red, pink and yellow roses.

"Your garden is beautiful, Sir James. An English garden is called *un jardin anglais* in French. In both languages and cultures, it is most welcoming."

"That it is and I do enjoy the fragrance." Pointing to a purple hand-shaped flower with a grove of steeples in the centre, Sir James stated it is called a monkshood, wolf's bane or devil's helmet – and was highly poisonous. Just behind it was a small shrub with shiny black berries which he explained have been known to cause delirium and hallucinations, as well as the occasional death. The yew tree, he pointed out at the far edge of the garden, bears berries that can bring on convulsions and cardiac arrest.

"I keep them in the garden as a constant reminder that in what might seem a tranquil, friendly place, there lurks evil with poisonous intent."

"I take your caution to heart, Sir James. We both agree that Alexandra is a most beautiful flower who needs to be protected against the threats that abound. We need to join forces, you and I, to protect her at all costs."

Motioning to a wooden bench in the garden, Sir James said, "Sit with me, Paul. I am old but my life is not yet complete. I firmly believe we all have a purpose in this life. I was meant to meet Maria in the war and I was meant to be in MI6, and we were meant to meet, you and I and Alexandra. You are a strategist, Paul, and that is good. You complement Alexandra in many ways. Maria said she believed the two of you were destined to be together. In the fullness of time, fate would intervene. The time has arrived for the two of you to fulfil your destiny together."

"You are very perceptive, Sir James. I have come to the same conclusion since meeting Alexandra at her mother's funeral, but life seems to have an agenda of its own."

Glancing toward the sunroom, they saw Alexandra resting with eyes closed and head gently supported by the chair back. Sir James put his hand into his blazer pocket and pulled out a small box. He gave it to Paul. With an inquisitive smile, Paul removed the lid and observed white tissue paper. Looking at Sir James, he tilted his head with a silent question. Unfolding the white tissue, he noticed an Ab amulet in the form of a winged bird on a cross with a blue stone in the centre glistening in the sunlight. A gold chain was threaded through an eyelet attaching a wreath-shaped ring suspended from the pendant. Puzzled, he looked back at Sir James.

"Yes, I will explain, Paul. Over the years, my belief in faith has morphed from my being a devoted member of the Anglican Church and one God, to a firm believer in the faith of our spiritual world, as held by Druids and resurrected by the Wiccans. I am convinced that forces in our environment are interconnected and control our lives. There are those who might refer to it as string theory in quantum mechanics but I just call it the spirit world. This amulet is empowered for the protection of the receiver and not the giver. The giver is also empowered, but to protect the receiver. You need to give this to Alexandra for her protection and for you as protector. It is meant to be, it is deemed to be so."

Paul thought about what Sir James had said. *Had this moment been preordained somehow? Was it meant to be?*

Looking directly at Paul, Sir James stressed, "Alexandra needs your protection now. This amulet will shield her in her quest which will be life threatening. It is imperative that you give it to her, not me. You are her protector. On those occasions when she is not in your immediate sphere, she must wear this at all times."

Paul sensed the deep sincerity with which the gift was being given to him on Alexandra's behalf and the magnitude of the concern. There were objective threat assessments deduced from the analysis of facts, and then there were threat assessments acquired through the senses. He carefully re-wrapped the amulet in the white tissue paper, firmly replaced the lid and put it in his pocket.

Sir James took out another box, opened it and unfolded the white tissue. Taking Paul's left hand, he placed a silver ring with a blue stone on his index finger.

"This ring will protect the protector. Wear it at all times as you and Alexandra navigate this journey fraught with danger. There are forces of good and forces of evil. You have fought gallantly against the latter and, like all of us who have been called upon to fight against evil, you have suffered the stresses of the slings and arrows, and the wounds of battle. This ring will renew your strength over time."

Holding Paul's hands between his, he said, "Have faith in my words, Paul. Have faith in my words."

He then recited a blessing only the last few words of which Paul could discern as Sir James repeated them three times, "…in the power of the lady, by the power of the lady, through the power of the lady… so be it."

Paul paused in reverence, processing his heightened emotions. His faith was in his God and the Pope, but he sensed there was another conviction in an earthly spirit which apparently did not conflict with his Church but rather complemented it.

He looked away from Sir James to the sunroom and as he observed Alexandra sleeping in the chair, warmed by the sun, he reaffirmed his devotion. Alexandra had become his *raison d'être* and the focus of his being. Her health and safety were his mission and he would do whatever was necessary to protect her, even to calling on all spirits, all energies and forces, earthly and heavenly, to assure the success of that mission. He heard his father's words again: *The Pope is not always right.*

Paul and Sir James returned to the sunroom, and as they lifted the latch on the wooden door and entered, Alexandra slowly opened her eyes and greeted them with a serene smile.

"I drifted off a bit and had the strangest dream about a mysterious mist going before and after a shaft of sunlight. It reminded me a bit of my Eurail trip from Amsterdam to Luxembourg the day before the funeral when the ground mist was vaporized by the sun. I felt the mist in this dream was my mother. It was mystical but consoling."

After a moment's reflection, she asked, "And what were you two gentlemen conspiring about in my absence?"

"Just admiring the wonderful garden," Paul replied as he glanced over at Sir James with an expression that conveyed his sincere gratitude.

"I wish I could bring this chair with me, Sir James. It has become a dear friend, but we must be off if we are to catch the Eurostar back to Paris."

"You remind me of your mother. When she came to visit, she always sat in this chair and drummed her fingers on the padded arms just as you did. After our talks, she would tell me how relaxed she felt. She called the chair her cocoon. After a sleep, she would awaken rested. You are certainly your mother's daughter, Alexandra. So, the chair is yours anytime you wish to grace my humble abode."

"I am deeply honoured, Sir James. I do feel my mother's presence."

"You and Paul will always be welcome. I have no family of my own so, with your permission, I would like to adopt you as my honorary daughter and son. Please come and visit frequently and plan to stay much longer."

"I – *we* – promise to return," Alexandra confirmed.

As Sir James shook hands, he bid them farewell with instructions cloaked in caution. "Be safe in your journey together and above all be very careful. Thon is evil but there are others who have less than honourable intentions too. They are the wolves in sheep's clothing."

CHAPTER 43

As the Eurostar left St. Pancras Station, Alexandra and Paul re-evaluated the evidence and discussed Thon's character. They then re-assessed who they could trust and with what information. They were sympathetic to the aims of some at the Préfecture de police de Paris, the Police nationale and the Gendarmerie nationale where they both had established professional networks. They were also wary of the motivation and suspicious intent of others, as Alexandra's perceptions called for caution.

"You mentioned you work with your psychologist friend, Frederik. What's your trust level with him?" Paul asked.

"Fred is Swedish from Uppsala just north of Stockholm. His mother, now deceased, was a school counsellor. His father was a general in the Swedish army. The father is alive but, like your father, he is in a seniors' home. The family worked with the Swedish Underground during the war and even today they despise the Germans with a passion. Fred completed his graduate degree in psychology at Stockholm's Universitet and his doctorate at the Université de Paris. After graduation, he worked for the psych firm where I completed my practicum. He now owns this organization and, as I mentioned, has worked as a forensic profiler for the Préfecture de police de Paris, the Police nationale and the Gendarmerie nationale. He is married and has three grown children, all professionals in their own way. Through a friend, I gained access to his file and the background checks confirm his credibility and credentials. I work with him the most and am completely comfortable. There's nothing political about him and he calls it how he sees it. I respect that. We have worked on a few big cases and I like his style. Bottom line, I trust him."

"Others, police officers you work with. What are your thoughts?" Paul asked.

"When I arrived at the Gendarmerie nationale, I worked with Commandant Benoit Parent. He was a straight shooter and a salt-of-the-earth fellow who would do anything to help you. He often removed what appeared to be insurmountable barriers to our search for information. He did such an excellent job, he was promoted to head the new Anti-terrorist Unit."

"Right, two good white hat guys on our side. That makes me feel a bit better. And others?"

"His replacement, Capitaine Dominique Roland, came from the Préfecture, highly recommended."

"I sense some reservation in your voice," Paul noted.

"You're correct. I like her and we get along well but there is something about her that causes me concern at times. No major red flags go up. Instead, just caution on occasion as if something or someone else is controlling her strings. Her file is as good as they come. I've been completely honest with her on most cases, but not all. My senses tell me to be careful with her because she has a shadowy side.

"There are others I just do not trust," she continued. "They hang around like vultures and give me the creeps. Fred doesn't trust them either. We've had this who-do-we-trust conversation several times. Fortunately, I haven't had to work with these other officers. I've done some work with the Préfecture and the Police nationale and – like the Gendarmerie nationale – there are some I trust and others I do not."

Paul pondered for a few moments, humming under his breath, before nodding slowly in silent acceptance of Alexandra's objective and intuitive assessment of her immediate colleagues.

What a true professional she is, he reflected. *What an honour it is to work alongside her.*

He found himself slightly jealous of Fred and their close collegial relationship.

"Paul, you asked about my *sensations of the mind* as my mother described them. Let me tell you about that so you can understand better."

Paul had quickly learned to defer to her sensation, her *shrew* as she called it. He might not have understood her uncanny ability to interpret the intuitive but he had complete confidence in her judgement to weigh the facts against the instinctual. Although his intuition was not as visceral, he had, since Sarajevo, come to rely on what his feelings told him about which direction he ought to go. He recalled that when Marcel had been wounded and he had taken the wheel, he drove to the nearest UN medical unit more by instinct than by map, along unknown and unmarked roads and through intersections with no signs. While under fire, he didn't have the luxury of time to conduct a map recce.

He listened closely to Alexandra's explanation of the sensations of her mind.

"My mother told me I was born with it, I had inherited it from my father. As best I can explain it, my *shrew* is a perception, an integration of all my body's inputs including the tactile feelings from my skin, and smell, taste and hearing. My perception is always open-ended, so I'm constantly re-evaluating what these inputs are telling me individually but, more importantly, collectively."

"Are they with you all the time?"

"It takes a great deal of concentration sometimes to disassociate from the noise of the immediate world and maintain concentration. It's weird, my eyes may be open but I'm not looking outward. Instead, I'm fixated on the monitor of my mind. You might recognize it as a blank stare. Trust me when I say it really is much easier to break free of the phenomenon than to maintain the deep concentration. For me, it becomes an exercise in the intertwining and fusion of all these senses. Only then can I hear the delicate muffled whispering. It's like seeing sounds on the fringe of my awareness that speak to me. When I'm completely focused, I can hear the colours and see the tastes. Does this make any sense to you, Paul?" she enquired with genuine concern about his unconditional understanding and validation of her *shrew*.

Paul nodded. "Yes, it makes total sense. I've read about this phenomenon, the ability of some to connect with the energy around us. Once when I was off working with interesting people doing interesting things in interesting places, a feeling consumed me and told me to get away as fast as I possibly could. I did so and within seconds, mortars rained down on that position destroying everything, including some evidence. I would not be here with you today had I not paid attention to what the feelings told me."

"That would be it, or part of it," Alexandra confirmed. "I think the rhythms and patterns of inanimate objects and the natural elements like wood and water or what I call the artefacts in the archives of life which have co-evolved, have their own uncanny language, inviting us to engage in conversations that matter. And it is an invitation. If we don't respond to this invitation, we remain blind and deaf to the knowledge of these whispers which are older than time itself."

At this juncture in the conversation, Paul felt that the time was right. Reaching into his pocket, he took out the box Sir James had given him. As he took off the lid and reverently unfolded the white tissue paper, he explained Sir James's directions regarding the amulet and his ring.

Awestruck by the explanation of its source and perceived power of protection for the receiver and the obligation of the giver, Alexandra stared at the amulet. She was drawn to the blue stone, glistening with hidden depths. Her skin tingled all over as she looked at Paul. Her eyes glowed with the same allure as the stone.

Paul took the amulet out of the box, unfastened the clasp then refastened it around Alexandra's neck. Its darkened golden tint melded with her tanned skin and chestnut hair. He then murmured the words that Sir James had spoken.

"In the power of the lady, by the power of the lady, through the power of the lady… so be it."

Alexandra took Paul's left hand and ran her finger over his ring and the stone as if reading a braille message written within. With her other hand, she reached up and stroked the amulet, implicitly engaging in a conversation with it. She followed the intricate design of the winged cross and the blue stone inlaid below the wreath. Words were inappropriate for there was no mortal language in this medium.

The Eurostar entered the Channel Tunnel and for the next fifty kilometres, they reaffirmed their coalition, their commitment.

⁂

RE-EMERGING ON THE FRENCH SIDE OF THE tunnel brought with it an increase in activity as cell phones signalled the reconnection with the commerce community and the re-establishment of bondage to the e-world. Those who had spent the channel time in slumber, stirred and stretched. The aroma of freshly brewed coffee announced the arrival of the culinary servers who refilled the cups of those seeking the added boost of caffeine to re-engage with the world.

Alexandra's aura mirrored the pure pleasure of her peaceful state of mind. She could not remember being this relaxed and reassured for a long time, not even with her mother. The prospects of retirement were looking better with every passing second she spent with Paul. Somehow, they would come together. She just knew it would be because it was meant to be.

If she had not realized it before, this moment reinforced her decision not to return to Paris, André and the escalation of negative energy in his house. There was nothing in that house she wanted or needed because there was nothing in the house that was hers. Sophia was in Jo's carport and any personal items she treasured she had brought with her as she moved in her career. There was no reason to return to André's house. The house, property and possessions would be his. She would not contest the separation and ultimate divorce.

In the present, the hunt for Thon would occupy her mind and facilitate the psychological transition from being married to André but not living together to being separated and divorced. She would retire in Luxembourg and it would be a home and not a house. Collette would just be a phone call away or a planned coffee meeting with a half-day interval. If she called in the morning, they could meet at lunch.

CHAPTER 44

About an hour out of Paris, Alexandra's phone rang. She didn't recognize the caller ID but had an immediate sense of foreboding that prompted her to reach for the amulet as she answered.

"Hello."

"Alexandra, I am pleased to be talking with you after such a long time. We will meet in person soon."

"Who is this?"

"Oh, you should know who this is. Your mother will have told you about me, but now she is dead and her death has robbed me of my obligation to rid the world of suffering and misery for all those sorrowful mother cats and their kittens. Their sanctuary was the barn that was also the source of their pain and suffering. That was where discipline had to be administered. You are like all the rest who are suffering but the end is near for you and your kitten. She is suffering also but I will help as I did with your mother's associates. They shouldn't have done what they did."

Alexandra did not recognize the voice, which changed from moderate to effeminate and child-like. The speaker started rambling. Curiously, the tone seemed to come from a delicate person with an accent from the Alsace region. She felt shocked as she realized the possible ID of the caller.

She released the amulet long enough to motion to Paul to give her a pen and paper. "THON" she wrote followed by a series of exclamation marks. She stared at Paul with a calculated yet excited expression. She looked up at the ceiling of the rail car as she started to organize her questions for this impromptu interview based on the profile which she and Paul had just sketched out.

"Well, I am pleased to be speaking with you, too," she responded.

"You sound like a man of conviction who would like to be addressed as an equal. Would it be appropriate to introduce yourself to me as one professional to another?"

"Ah, you will learn my name soon enough for I am always polite. My father insisted that I be manly when speaking, even with inferiors… females, despite the fact they all suffer as he so many times reminded me. He instilled that in me with his strictness. Discipline is essential as I'm sure you know. Most do not have the ability to correct themselves but I learned that from him."

Alexandra noted a continuing fluctuation in the tone of his voice as the conversation wavered between her and her "kitten" Collette, and back to references to his father.

"You mentioned your father. It sounds as though your father taught you to be disciplined and you believe that discipline is very important to you." Alexandra paused.

"I don't want to talk about my father!" Thon abruptly barked in a deeper, more aggressive voice.

Alexandra wanted to keep control and direct the conversation without offending Thon. She didn't want to isolate him. She needed to maintain communication in order to learn as much as possible about his background and his modus operandi. A comprehensive understanding of his MO would be key to his capture. The two modulating voice tones had different sets of traits.

"I apologize for upsetting you, but I heard you say that he disciplined you and you felt you learned from that. Am I correct in saying there were times when you appreciated his discipline and times when you did not?"

"I told you I do not want to talk about that! I'm calling you to tell you I will soon be putting you and your kitten out of your misery."

Alexandra interjected brusquely in order to regain control of the conversation.

"I very much appreciate your concern for my suffering. You sound like a compassionate person who cares about suffering in this world. To help me understand more, can you tell me about the kittens? You have mentioned them a few times and I sense you have great compassion for mother cats and their kittens. I get the feeling you had cats when you were younger, and you noticed them suffering and wanted to help them."

Alexandra was searching for triggers. Thon's father appeared to be a hot button and the kittens might be another. She sensed there was conflict, perhaps abuse because of his emphasis on discipline, which he projected onto the kittens.

"You are correct. From when I was young, I saw the cats suffering in the barn and I knew I could help by putting them out of their misery. I would milk the cow and put down my special formula for them and they would go to sleep. But the other cats kept having kittens so I had to give them the special milk I had prepared. I had to stop the mother cats and their kittens. I tried to keep the male kittens alive because they would kill the rats in the barn that got into the grain. We need strong pure males for the Thousand-Year Reich. My father said so and I wanted to please my father so he wouldn't take me aside in the barn and discipline me in private. I joined the Nazi Youth to show him I could be strong to kill all the rats. He didn't discipline me when I was a strong soldier of the Reich. He wasn't accepted as a soldier but I was."

The more Thon rambled, the more Alexandra was able to distinguish his expressions and categorize them into two voices. For whatever reason, the reference to the female cat and her kittens, especially the female kittens, was a door to his personality. Abusers are often victims of abuse. From Thon's terse description of his father and the discipline, she concluded he had been abused, perhaps sexually, with the reference to the private discipline in the barn. The reference to the killing of *Maquis* females and their daughters was starting to make sense. She didn't want to be patronizing him but wanted to explore other triggers.

"Thank you for sharing this with me. I have a better sense of why you have compassion for those who are suffering. I commend you for helping those many female cats and their kittens, and for keeping the male cats alive to get rid of the rats which would eat the grain of those who needed it to become strong. Was your mother suffering, and were your sisters suffering, also?"

Alexandra was searching for other triggers.

"Yes, they suffered but they don't anymore, and my father doesn't discipline me anymore."

Thon's voice immediately became more agitated and louder.

"But why are you asking me all this? I don't want to talk about that. The farm was a bad place. You are bad and suffering and I have a duty, an obligation to stop you from suffering. You have tricked me. I know women like you always try to trick strong men. I'm a strong Nazi soldier of the Fourth Reich and we will rule as we were destined to. Hitler was weak and suffering and needed to be put out of his misery. But I'm strong and will lead. I'm disciplined. I'm not weak as my father said. That's the only way you weak women work. You trick the strong. Your mother was weak. She robbed me of my duty to rid the farm of suffering cats and their kittens. Now, you and your kitten must be put out of your misery. There are too many like you."

Alexandra's phone sounded a dial tone indicating that the caller had disconnected.

Throughout the phone call, she and Paul had been looking at each other, Alexandra searching for a strategy to keep Thon talking and revealing details of his personality and motivation. All the while, Paul attempted to follow her conversation and support her in whatever way he could. She closed her phone and held up her hand indicating don't interrupt my train of thought for a moment.

"I need to make notes on the call."

She recorded a first draft of the sequence of events, Thon's initial words, her response, his verbal and emotional responses, and the changes in the tone of his voice as he responded to her queries either submissively or aggressively. She reviewed her marginal notes with addenda and re-reviewed to assure accuracy. Every detail would be critical in the subsequent analysis. Finally, she closed her eyes and visualized the conversation, passing the emotions through the filter of her *shrew*. With final cyphers recorded, she concluded that Thon's disciplined behavioural patterns were erratically predictable as they reflected his disturbed state of mind. She let out a deep breath and turned to Paul.

"Thank you for your patience. Give me another moment. I need to call Fred and set up a meeting to review and reconstruct Thon's profile."

Paul nodded in approval as she dialled.

"Fred, drop everything. We need to meet immediately. I just received a very disturbing call and we need to talk now. I'll tell you everything when we meet. I'll be arriving in Paris shortly."

Feeling the urgency in her voice, Fred acknowledged her request. "Fine. I'll call you back with a time. I just need to clear a few appointments from my calendar."

She and Paul looked at each other as they monitored their own responses and queried the other. Paul noticed Alexandra rubbing the amulet with deliberate circling of the stone. He then realized he was doing the same with his ring. Both were experiencing quasi-controlled yet cautious excitement at the exposure to the immediate threat and possible capture of Thon.

"Are you okay?" he asked.

"I think so. Reverting to an interview mode with a structured, albeit reactive focus, sure helped me get through this one. I think I can best sum up the call as a narcotic-like rush. How many times does anyone, a forensic psychologist, get the opportunity to engage with a psychotic murderer so directly? I've interviewed psychopaths and sociopaths before but was always prepared. My training and all those previous experiences certainly helped me put this one together on the fly. Give me another moment, I need to make a few more follow-up notes."

She knew the importance of not eliminating what, on the surface, might appear to be innocuous details. At the beginning of many cases, it was a matter of connecting the fog banks, but as details emerged, investigators were able to connect the dots. That meant identifying and giving equal weight to all the variables that comprised the dots. It was often the afterthoughts that provided the indispensable details that broke the case – a pause, a word, an expression, a breath of anticipation, an inflection. Visuals of a face-to-face interview were invaluable but they could also obscure the richness of the words and jargon. Her years of experience examining the context of a case with input from her *shrew* had honed her skills to differentiate between interference and the valuable nuances that surfaced.

Give me the facts, ma'am, only the facts, she recalled one of her male colleagues from her training days saying. How many cases went unsolved with just that limited adage as a mantra?

The best way Paul figured he could help at this juncture was to say nothing but just be there in the moment with her. Her professionalism, especially under such duress, amazed him. It was one thing to remain composed in the presence of notorious criminals who did not pose an immediate threat, but it was astonishing to demonstrate such presence of mind, objective command and control, and complete composure when under personal threat. *AV should be the one receiving the appointment of commandeur de la Légion d'honneur, not me.*

As the train pulled into the station, Alexandra's phone rang again. This time, she recognized the caller. It was Fred. He had cleared his calendar and they confirmed the meeting. She recognized the anticipation in his voice. They had both experienced this excitement in other cases when new information was revealed that could break the case wide open.

How her mother would have liked to be present at this meeting of the minds as they closed the net on Thon. At the appropriate time, she would call Sir James and update him, and Father Luke, and Paul's father.

For now, though, she would collect her thoughts and amend her notes in preparation for her meeting with Fred who was an expert in forensic hypnosis. They shared a mutual confidence. He would hypnotize her and they would record that meeting and compare the transcript with the accuracy of her notes. Improving the accuracy of memory recall was an area of research she and Fred shared.

They were working on a joint paper that they planned to present at the European Federation of Psychologists' Association and publish in the EFPA journal. Data acquisition as hot as this phone call was rare, and even rarer, the validity and reliability of the data. A warm self-assured smile came over her face.

"What a way to retire," she mused. But then again, maybe she wouldn't retire, not completely at any rate. She did enjoy the narcotic-like rush. She had a rendezvous with destiny; the fate of surviving *Maquis* cats and kittens depended on her.

CHAPTER 45

"I'd feel more comfortable if I could at least accompany you to Fred's," Paul suggested, "given the increased proximity of Thon. I'd also like to meet Fred."

"That's probably a good idea now that Thon has closed in and made his intentions known. I'll ask Fred whether he minds if you sit in on the session. I'd be comfortable if it's all right with him. You'd be able to fill in any details I might have missed from just watching me while I was speaking with, well, interviewing Thon."

"Thanks. I'd very much like to observe the session. Learning from two pros would be an honour."

Alexandra closed her eyes and collected her thoughts. Her cell phone buzzed with an incoming email. The subject line read: HOG Ride. "I almost forgot, Paul. Are you up to participating in a group ride this Saturday with members of the local Harley Owners Group?"

"Sure am! When and where?"

"We'll be meeting at 9:00 on Saturday morning in the parking lot of the Hotel Ibis Versailles Château on the avenue du Général de Gaulle. Jo will probably join us. So why don't we meet at the hotel parking lot? Marcel will be the road captain. I'll email him to let him know the colonel will be joining us Ladies of Harley."

"That's a date!"

⁂

THEY TOOK A TAXI TO FRED'S OFFICE while maintaining surveillance and chatting about inconsequential matters. After Alexandra's introduction, Fred agreed to allow Paul to observe the session as long as he sat behind Alexandra so as not to become a visual distraction.

After she awakened from the hypotonic session, the three compared notes. They concluded that Thon's announcement of his intent to target Alexandra and Collette was a significant deviation in his profile. This could be his Achilles' heel because he had broken a pattern of anonymity which had been flawless to date, allowing him to elude capture by the police since the war. Thon's banter duel with Alexandra was a win for the white hats due to Alexandra's professionalism and her mental prowess. He was no longer invincible – but also may be becoming even more mentally disturbed with age.

"I'm confident we can add a number of crucial characteristics to his profile," Fred concluded. "There is a high probability that Thon was sexually abused by his father in the barn and this abuse would have thrown him off his normal developmental trajectory. It may have resulted in him being partially impotent. This will have made him uncomfortable as a boy and later as a teen and a man. Today, he may have a spouse. If so, more than likely she will be weak. He will use the marriage as part of his cover. He may have had several partners before whom he would have blamed for anything he was not able to complete. There is a possibility he may have an illegitimate child, perhaps born to one of the French Resistance women he had intended to kill but in a moment of weakness and uncharacteristic kindness, perhaps instilled by his loving but hapless and weak mother, spared her life and actually created a child. He would have killed her after the child was born. He would have killed the child if it was female but saved and raised it in his own warped depraved image if it was male. This would mirror his killing of the female cats and keeping the male cats alive."

"I agree," Alexandra interjected. "More than likely, he suffers from Obsessive Compulsive Disorder. His voice was more feminine with increasing falsetto when he was raving about how mother cats and their kittens must be killed because they were disadvantaged or somehow not pure, this being the obsession. The mother cats and their female kittens must be taken out of their miserable lives, this being the compulsion. He sees himself as well-meaning and wholly justified, which suggests certain sociopathic and some psychopathic symptomology. I'm convinced there is a female and a male side to him and he uses both to his advantage whether or not each personality is conscious of the other."

"You're on target with this analysis, Alexandra," Fred confirmed. "Thon may be a transgender male who would focus on the obvious symbols of femininity in his disguise such as large fake breasts, a blonde wig and bright red lipstick. His pathology would dictate that he presents himself identically each time he slips into this female persona. Persons with such pathology are exceptionally good at hiding and covering their issues and will make every effort to catch and correct themselves if they feel their pseudo identity might be threatened. The pathology will eventually and profoundly drive his ultimate response. With rapid downward momentum once it starts, he will become fully unglued despite his best efforts to keep it together. This is the nature of such pathology, as you know."

"He mentioned that his father was increasingly critical of his effeminate tendencies," Alexandra added. "If his father was the original sexual predator, despite his father's outer tough presentation, this will have left Thon conflicted which, in turn, would have confused him developmentally."

"That fits in perfectly. With the right trigger, his whole façade will begin to unravel. That's his Achilles' heel. If he confronts you, Alexandra, you need to somehow identify the trigger that will probably be associated with the barn – I'm thinking the mother cats and their kittens."

"Would you be open to an observation from a layperson?" Paul asked.

"Certainly, I welcome your input. Often, we supposed professionals find ourselves too close to the obvious and, as a result, miss some details," Fred replied.

"Maria's neighbour on rue Michel Welter told us he thought he saw a female with blonde hair entering the tenant's house but a male leaving. The neighbour also mentioned that he saw a female with blonde hair and bright red lipstick at Maria's funeral reception. He thought he recognized her as being the female who had entered the tenant's house. There are other suggestions that Thon may be both male and female. Fred, you suggested that Thon may be a transgender male who uses the disguise of a blonde wig and bright red lipstick. This fits these descriptions perfectly."

Alexandra acknowledged his perceptive observations with a sense of gratitude.

"You should be the forensic psychologist, Paul. That observation never crossed my mind. You're correct. When Roger mentioned that to us, I didn't dismiss it altogether but downplayed it. I felt his overwhelming feeling of guilt and resulting stress and his need to be forgiven had fogged his recollection. You're good, partner! We need to figure out the age discrepancy – Roger's photo shows someone apparently too young to be the original Thon, unless it is a superb makeup job – but this definitely is tied in somehow."

CHAPTER 46

Jean conducted the digital comparison of the photos his father had given him and, surprisingly, received a high-probability result. It suggested that one of the Nazis standing beside the armoured vehicle was similar to the man in the black Mercedes. The man in the black Mercedes might be the second generation, perhaps a son or grandson.

Jean had written an algorithm to enhance such comparisons on his own laptop. The program's logic had similarities to algorithms that analyze DNA for matches but instead uses profiling that includes facial image analysis and any other available data including posture and gestures, clothing and lifestyle choices, location and limitless other factors. There were strict security protocols that prohibited uploading any unauthorized software onto the police department mainframe. Each time he had used his enhanced program in the past, he always received a higher probability, and this was no exception. He received an .83 probability of a match on this occasion.

Jean called his father and passed along the preliminary findings. He would run them against images in his own database when he had a moment.

"I knew if anyone could do it, Jean, you could. Let me know if you get anything further."

Jean then ran the image against the police database and with some surprise, received a "Denied Access" message on his monitor. He knew this meant there was a match but that the database file had a higher security level than the one he held.

"Now this is interesting," he mused. He had only bumped up against this denial response in a couple of other cases, both related

to national security. Protocol required that when this occurred, he was to report to his director. To reconfirm his accuracy, he ran the comparison again which took enough time for him to finish his cup of freshly brewed coffee.

"Need to see the director on a case," he mentioned to his immediate supervisor. "You know the drill."

As Jean was about to enter the director's office, he saw he was on the phone, so he stood just outside the door. Seeing Jean, the director waved him in and pointed to a chair. Jean sat down.

"You just submitted a search request, Jean. What's the case? That was the Police nationale on the phone. They are on their way over and want to talk to you… to us."

"That was fast," Jean replied. He then explained what he had done and how he had enhanced the results with his own algorithm. He assured the director he had not violated the software security protocol by uploading to the mainframe but had completed the second analysis on his laptop.

"Right, Jean. We need to talk to our techies and do whatever we have to do to upload your algorithm. There are too many damn silos with prima donnas in this organization who think only they know what's best in their arenas of expertise. The chief can give all his glowing accolades about how well his departments work together, but *'it ain't necessarily so,'* as George Gershwin would say."

"Yes, sir."

"Don't go anywhere until they arrive. I sensed from the urgency in the voice of the capitaine I was speaking to that you tripped a very big case. Best to recheck your analysis to ensure we are on solid ground."

"Will do, Director."

"By the way, Jean, Well done. I like it when the Police nationale have to come to us," the director chuckled. "I'll brief the boys and girls upstairs that they are paying a visit. This will bring a smile to the chief's face. He likes to talk about inter-agency cooperation. It is always useful to make the boss look good."

Jean returned to his desk and double-checked his analysis. The results were solid. He then called his father and left a message.

Perhaps now I might get the opportunity to integrate my algorithm, he reflected.

The Director's secretary called on the intercom. "Sir, Commandant Benoit Parent and Capitaine Dominique Roland from the Police nationale are here to see you."

"Thank you, please show them in. Also, call Jean Bernard and ask him to join us in my office."

Director Doucet greeted the two agents as they entered the office. With a quiet smile he said, "Commandant Parent, it is always good to see you, especially when we can assist the Police nationale." Slight good-humoured smugness was acceptable on such occasions.

Parent replied, "Claude, may I introduce Capitaine Dominique Roland. She is replacing me as I have accepted a position in our new Counter-terrorist Unit. Dominique will take the lead role in this matter and I'll assist her with any historical data which may be useful. Dominique is exceptionally well qualified. Prior to joining us, she was a lead investigator with CID in Paris, as you may recall."

With an equally cordial chuckle, he added, "And, yes, Claude, we at the Police nationale always look forward to working with your colleagues and very much appreciate your assistance."

"Please call me Dominique, Director. I sense we will be working closely together on this case and, I suspect, on other cases. I understand your people have assisted us on a few occasions, especially your digital analysts."

"And you may call me, Claude, Dominique."

At that moment, Jean entered the office.

"Speaking of our people," Director Doucet interjected, "may I introduce you to our senior digital analyst. Jean Bernard, you know Commandant Parent. This is Capitaine Dominique Roland. Dominique is replacing him because he has been transferred to the Counter-terrorist Unit."

"Please call me Dominique, Jean."

With the standard protocol of shaking hands and exchanging business cards complete, Director Doucet pointed to an oval table and invited everyone to have a seat.

"As a summary of why we are here, as I understand it, Jean was working on a profile. He attempted to conduct a database search based on a profile and received a message on his monitor, 'Access Denied.' Shortly thereafter, Capitaine Roland contacted me, per our inter-agency memorandum of understanding, and requested a meeting. Am I correct, Dominique?"

"That's correct. I will add that our trail at the Police nationale went cold on this case several years ago. With Jean's profile query, the file immediately went live."

"The meeting is yours, Dominique."

"Jean, please bring us all up to date on this file," Dominique requested.

"I spoke with my father, Dr. Paul Bernard. Actually, my father approached me and asked if I could conduct a digital facial analysis on a few photos. He has been working with Dr. Belliveau."

"Excuse me, Jean," Dominique interrupted. "Is your father the director of the forensic lab here in Paris?"

"Yes, he is."

"And this is Dr. Alexandra Belliveau who works as a consultant with the Police nationale in addition to other police agencies conducting forensic profiles?"

"Yes, I think so, although both are close to retirement."

Commandant Parent interjected. "Alexandra has been working with us as a forensic psychologist for many years but I wasn't aware she was involved in this case. However, nothing surprises me about Alexandra, she's that good. Just to fill in one last factor, and this is for your ears only and does not leave this room, Alexandra's mother, Maria, was employed with French Counterintelligence and had been working for decades on cases involving Nazi war criminals and collaborators. We believe the cases are connected."

"Thank you, Benoit, I wasn't aware of that," Dominique responded. "As an added note, I know Jean's father well. We worked together on many cold cases involving blood analysis. So, your grandfather would be retired Capitaine Jean-Paul Bernard."

"Yes, that's correct. Both my father and I are named after him."

"I worked with your grandfather several years ago when he was at CID. He mentored me and ultimately recommended me for promotion. Sorry for interrupting, Jean. I just wanted to confirm the relationship and the source of the request for you to conduct the digital facial analysis. Again, I'm impressed. Please continue. How did you conduct the analysis, Jean?"

"It's my own software I developed. It's not loaded on the mainframe."

Director Doucet explained the protocol and commented that he was working to get Jean's software installed.

"It's all in the game of chess," Jean continued. "When I was very small, my grand-papa taught me how to play chess. In no time I was beating him because I understood how the game is played and what strategies and probabilities opponents use and what strategies I could use. I quickly became a master chess player winning trophies at every tournament I entered. One of my heroes was Graham Mitchell who was ranked in the top ten in the world. He was with British Intelligence. I believe he headed D Branch for

Counterintelligence before becoming the Deputy Director General of MI6."

"—Am I hearing you correctly, Jean," Dominique interrupted, that you developed this algorithm from your knowledge of the game of chess and only that?"

"That's correct. I wrote the algorithm based on probabilities of plays on the chessboard. You see, all chess pieces have profiles – the king, queen, bishops, castles and knights, even the pawns. And pawns on the left flank and the right flank and those in the centre all have slightly different personalities, different traits like people and, hence, different profiles. Based on the profiles of the pieces, I was able to increase the probabilities of digital image profiling. In some cases, I was able to double the probability. In this case I was able to increase that probability from 0.34 to 0.83. That is amazing given the quality of the photos. Language is language whether it's spoken language such as French, Russian, Coptic or Arabic, or programming languages like BASIC, Cobol or Fortran."

Dominique looked at Director Doucet and Commandant Parent in astonishment, then turned back to Jean. "That is remarkable, Jean."

"The best strategy in chess is not to always go after the king or even the queen. Instead, watch events as they unfold, as they will invariably identify the patterns and underlying structures. The profiles of the two knights and the two bishops have similar and different profiles, just like identical twins. It's important to understand that different players with different profiles are motivated by different underlying structures. From my perspective, digital profiling and analysis is just one big game of chess."

CHAPTER 47

Dominique leaned over to Commandant Parent and whispered, "How do we get Jean on our team?"

Benoit faintly smiled and nodded. "Director Doucet, if I may be so bold as to ask—."

"All right, Benoit, I think I know what you are about to ask. Each time one of our people helps you with your cases, you pose the same question. Am I correct this time?"

Benoit smiled, bowed in acknowledgement of the director's perceptive observation, and repeated, "Director, may I be so bold as to ask if Jean could be seconded to the Police nationale, with his software, to work on this case and other cold cases? His compensation package would reflect his talent."

All three looked at Jean. With eyes wide open and a look of astonishment on his face, Jean turned to his director who smiled back, shrugging his shoulders in resigned support.

"This is an opportunity that doesn't come along every day, Jean," the director explained. "Should you wish to accept this invitation, I would certainly support the request and I'm confident that the chief would do the same. The chief is all about inter-agency support. When he attends the next conference, he'll take every opportunity to remind his colleagues just how many of his people are working with the Police nationale. This would be another feather in his cap."

The director then looked at Dominique and Benoit. "There would be one proviso, Benoit, and that is we get to share Jean's expertise and software when we need it."

"Agreed, Claude." Turning to Jean, Commandant Parent enquired, "Well, Jean, may I conclude that with the director's agreement you would welcome a secondment to our team at the Police nationale, given that you would be able to respond to his requests should the occasions arise?"

Jean immediately answered, "I would be deeply honoured to be seconded to your team. Although my grand-papa suffers from dementia, I'm sure he would be very happy for me, and to know that I'll be working with Capitaine Dominique Roland will make him very proud."

"I'll submit the request today before anyone changes their mind," Benoit concluded.

"Just as a follow-up, Director," Dominique interjected, "why did your IT department not incorporate Jean's innovation? Are we dealing with any software infringement or copyright issues?"

"I think like most organizations, there are silos, and silos within silos. If you are not from one department, in one silo, you are reluctant to seek help elsewhere because you know more. I find that those who reside in these silos will comment that to the unbiased person, they are always correct. That's the best explanation I have as to why our organization has not picked up on this innovation."

"I'll eat some humble pie on this one, Claude. There are silos in the Police nationale but I can assure you we will move heaven and earth to have Jean's software integrated into our mainframe program."

Turning to Jean, Dominique asked, "Do you have any suggestions or questions of us?"

A less confident person would have responded to new employers tentatively. But Jean was very confident about his program and in his ability to lead, even those in superior positions but not those with superior knowledge.

He had learned in his youth playing chess with his grand-papa that knowledge was processed information, facts. He spent many hours pondering the strategies of chess, processing all the information associated with any one move by individual chess pieces, except they were not just chess pieces. Instead, they were the traits of the personalities as animated as the people seated opposite him in each chess match. Thus, each chess piece integrated all the intervening variables operating in the environment. With each win and loss, Jean became humbler and only then did he start to win more and lose less and understand why the balance had nudged in his favour. Knowledge, the manifestation of cognitive processing, was the key to adjusting the fulcrum.

Jean was deeply indebted to both his grand-papa and his father for teaching him not just strategy but the strategy of strategy. They were both the reigning masters and he their grateful protégé. Today, his father was his peer but he would forever regard him as his master. Only by doing so, he was convinced, would he remain in learning mode.

There was a fine line between confidence and arrogance. Humility was the light that shone on the demarcation. Each new programming skill he learned brought with it additional revelations and satisfaction, which led to the next skill and an ever-broadening knowledge base.

"Yes, just one question, well, request," he replied to Capitaine Roland in a self-assured tone. "I'm confident I can improve the probability of the program if I could spend time talking with Dr. Alexandra Belliveau before she retires. As a guiding principle in any software that is employed for analysis, you always want to assure the simplicity of sureness gathered from individuals and not from other systems or big data. If you don't, you lose the ability to synthesize the intelligence. You might find it strange coming from a computer programmer but there is such a thing as too much technical data which leads to misleading information. That, in turn, becomes disguised as knowledge when it's not. Digital imaging profiling is a depiction of the psychological profile, itself a manifestation of the character and the traits that make up the personality. I can write an algorithm for that if I can access the source, Dr. Belliveau."

"I'm confident we can arrange those meetings before she retires, but if not, we'll extend Alexandra a personal services contract for the duration of the upgrade project. In addition, the Police nationale employs another psychologist, Doctor Frederik Jorgensen. I'm confident he would relish the opportunity to ply his trade to improve a program that would make his job easier. In the interim, you seem to have already established a relationship with Dr. Belliveau. On an informal basis, Jean, please take every opportunity to speak with her."

Looking at Commandant Parent, Dominique commented, "Given the nature of this case, we need to hold a meeting with Alexandra, Paul, Jean and probably Frederik as quickly as possible. I'll arrange it for tomorrow afternoon because it is imperative we get this case back on line."

"I would like to attend that meeting if you don't mind, Dominique," Commandant Parent asked. "Having recently reviewed several files from the Counter-terrorist Unit, I've a feeling there may be connections."

"You'll be on the distribution list, Benoit. And thank you again, Jean, for your initiative and hard work. I look forward to working with you. And, Claude, we will be in contact."

"We are always pleased to assist the Police nationale," Claude concluded with a wide smile for both Dominique and Benoit.

CHAPTER 48

Dominique called to order a meeting of the minds at precisely 1 p.m. Alexandra gazed around the room at those who were assembled and sighed wistfully. "Oh, how I dislike bureaucratic assemblies," she mumbled under her breath. Sitting next to her, Paul responded with a grin.

"Thank you all for coming," Dominique greeted everyone at the table. "I'm very keen to be this close to cracking this case after decades of effort by so many people at all levels of intelligence and policing. Allow me to introduce a few folks who may not be known to all. I have asked Commandant Benoit Parent from the Counter-terrorist Unit to join us because he has history with this case and there might be a terrorist link. I have also asked Dr. Paul Bernard to join us. He is the Director of the Crime Lab, at least for the next few weeks, pending his retirement. Although he is not part of our team at the Police nationale, he is intimately involved in this case through his association with Dr. Alexandra Belliveau. In addition, he will bring his vast experience to contribute to the discussion. Dr. Frederik Jorgensen is a forensic profiling psychologist who has been on contract with us and other departments. Frederik and Alexandra have worked together over the years on many cases that involve psychological profiling. I can assure you that two minds are exponentially greater than one when these two focus their collective talents. Jean Bernard is a member of the new digital profiling team at the Préfecture de police de Paris and recently seconded to our department. Jean wrote a software program that has increased our ability to digitally analyze facial features. Jean, you and Frederik should talk after this meeting."

"I am pleased to meet you, Frederik. Alexandra has mentioned your name. I would very much like to talk with you about profiling so I can improve my program."

"I understand that it is already far superior to any other program the Police nationale has. If I can assist you to improve the results, I'd be delighted to chat."

Dominique interjected, "The final introductions are Francine Myette and Tom Hunt. Francine is from French Counterintelligence. She is here because Alexandra's late mother, Maria, had been with DPSD and worked on this case. Maria was one of the early agents with Service de documentation extérieure et de contre-espionnage which was created in 1945. The predecessor of SDECE was the Bureau of Anti-National Activities whose mission was to track German collaborators, among other activities. Tom Hunt is an American deputy chief of police from the Los Angeles PD attached to Interpol."

They exchanged greetings and the customary business cards, which had become a platonic professional mating ritual at the start of such gatherings.

"From the players in this room, it is safe to say that Jean's enquiry triggered a number of files in several jurisdictions. Any questions before we get started?"

Benoit commented, "Because of the highly sensitive nature and the imminent threat, what is said in this room remains in this room." He made eye contact with everyone confirming individual acknowledgement with a nod.

Paul noticed Alexandra withdrawing into one of her mental states. "What's up?" he whispered.

Alexandra murmured, "Tom Hunt. His business card is inscribed 'Thomas A. Hunt.' I recognize that name and his disarming smile from somewhere. I'm trying to place it. He's a white hatter but from where and when I don't know. But Francine, there is something obtuse and shadowy in her intentions. She has a wry dark expressionless presence that flashes a black hat caveat like a Las Vegas neon sign on steroids. When I look at her, I sense devious intimacy and sex, and deceit."

Paul blinked and subtly nodded in agreement.

"Thank you, Benoit," Dominique was saying. "Just so that we are all on the same page, can you bring us up to speed, Alexandra, and describe the phone call you received from an individual we are calling Thon? I understand you and Frederik have already talked at length about that communiqué, so jump in as you see fit, Frederik. I want to turn up the heat and bring this killer to justice."

Alexandra refocused and briefed everyone on how she became aware of Thon through her mother's estate but held back on the existence of a few of the photographs and other information that her mother had left in the safety deposit box. She also omitted to mention anything associated with Sir James, Father Luke, Madame Deschaume, and Sergeant Lottie and the Montigny-lès-Metz file. She shared some but not all aspects of the letter her mother had written. Her reservation about Dominique prompted her *shrew*.

Paul and Fred picked up on this omission and her motivation for not being completely forthcoming. She had discussed her reservation with them both, who supported her decision to be selective in her briefing. In the fullness of time, she might disclose the other photos and their source, but for now she was not comfortable.

Alexandra found she was also unsettled with Francine. There was just something foreign in the *froideur* – the coolness of her presence. Every element of her *shrew* mind was flashing a warning. She became conscious of her hands which she held against her chest. She had threaded her thumb in between buttons on her blouse and was rubbing the amulet deliberately.

In contrast, Tom Hunt's presence was calming but she couldn't place his name. He was a curious enigma, much like Roger, the neighbour on rue Michel Welter, who had introduced himself at her mother's funeral.

Alexandra concluded her briefing by describing the phone call with Thon and the psychological profile she had developed with Fred.

When she had finished, they paused to reflect on the facts. The silence was broken when Jean offered, "Let's play chess."

"—Excuse me, Jean," said Dominique. "Can you explain?"

"Let's play chess," Jean repeated. "What if the bishop is the castle and the castle is the bishop? What if the king is the queen and the queen is the king? What if Thon is *le fantôme* and vice versa? What if Thon is the Nazi collaborator *and* the *Maquis* member? What if Thon is one and the same, whatever the same is – male and female, or male or female? What if there is a multiple personality or one personality purposely using two roles, in this case a dual-like personality but not necessarily so?"

Jean stepped to the white board on the wall and drew two columns. On one he listed Thon, male, personality #1, and on the other column he listed Thon *le fantôme*, female, personality #2, and then drew double arrows between each pair. Under the first he listed collaborator and under the other he wrote *Maquis* member.

Everyone in the room looked at each other in astonishment.

"Alexandra," Jean continued, "you said that Thon is confusing, hard to profile. What if you divide your profile into these two columns, not one but two personalities or perhaps a third? What if Thon is an enigma of polarities, of zeros and ones, of kings and queens on the chess board?"

"Bravo, Jean!" Alexandra said, clapping her hands. "Absolutely brilliant. That's it. You've solved the dilemma that has been driving me crazy. This conundrum is what kept my mother confused and I suspect everyone else involved in this case. I've been too close to the data. I needed a fresh set of eyes from the chess master's perspective. In a letter, my mother said that initially she thought *le fantôme* existed but later she said she doubted that initial belief, that he was a ghost."

Alexandra thought to herself, *Others suggested the same thing, like Madame Deschaume. But why?* She omitted any details about her father and how her mother initially believed Philip because she was so in love with him that she would not doubt what he said.

"Good, Jean. Please continue," Alexandra requested.

"My profile of Thon is that he is a master chess player, like me. I studied other master chess players and grandmasters like Sergei Zhigalko who was ranked as one of the best in Europe. Thon is playing chess. I believe that Thon created *le fantôme* to control his Nazi friends so they would be chasing the ghost of *le fantôme* and, as a result, would consider him a loyal Nazi. His motivation in doing so was to keep the Nazis thinking that he, Thon, was crucial and an essential agent. All along, he was with the *Maquis* keeping them thinking he was crucial and essential to *their* cause. He was playing bluff as a chess move. What if Thon was a sociopathic double-agent, playing the Nazis against the *Maquis* and vice versa? All along, he was just playing chess to control both, to control the world, his world."

Before continuing and linking his strategy to his proposed plan of action, Jean confirmed that everyone in the room was following his logic. They were.

"Thon, I am convinced, is the ultimate control freak. From Thon's perspective, it's all about the narcissistic Thon, the devout Nazi who has, as his ultimate goal, complete control. Thon sees himself as the grandmaster chess player of the world. I've seen this obsession in other chess players, but it hasn't been this fanatical."

Jean again moved to the white board and under the first column he inscribed double agent #1 and under the other column he wrote double agent #2. "Thon, whoever or whatever he or she is, is a game player."

Alexandra sighed and exclaimed again, "Brilliant, Jean. You are the master!"

Paul looked up. "Following Jean's analysis, what if 'fm,' the initials on the back of the photo, stand for 'feminine or masculine?'"

"Yes," Alexandra responded enthusiastically. "That could explain it. Whoever wrote those initials had a suspicion and left it as a breadcrumb trail for us to follow."

"So, let's play chess with Thon and *le fantôme*, now that we presume that both personalities exist," Jean announced. "Alexandra and Frederik, give me the profile to enter into the algorithm."

For the next half hour, Alexandra and Frederik described personality #1 and personality #2 in structured detail, focusing on the phone conversation between Alexandra and Thon. Jean took notes for the software update.

Integral to the profile were details of the farm, the barn, the abuse at the hands of his father, the poisoning of the mother cats and their kittens, but not the male cats.

Paul described the results of the analysis of the blood and stomach contents with the detail of sources and commercial uses of cyanide.

They concluded that Thon might have murdered his father, mother and any sisters, perhaps with cyanide. Paul suggested the search should include any jewellers or photographers because people in these vocations have ready access to cyanide.

In response, Dominique directed an investigation into similar deaths in southern Germany and northern France, although it would be a long shot. She asked Tom Hunt for liaison assistance from Interpol.

It was 3 p.m. by the time the meeting wound up. They were all exhausted but highly motivated.

Benoit reminded everyone, "There is the matter of the threat to Alexandra and her daughter, Collette. Clearly, they are in imminent danger, as Thon appears to have locked onto them."

"Yes, somehow he acquired Alexandra's cell phone number," Dominique added.

"We need to organize a security detail for two reasons. First and foremost is their safety. Second, with Thon on their trail, security for them will increase the probability of capturing him. There are some jurisdictional and logistical issues here. I'll contact Claude at the Préfecture de police de Paris to coordinate. Francine, let us identify your preferred involvement after this meeting."

"I have nothing to add but can meet as you see fit," Francine limply responded.

Alexandra thought Francine's comment was sensible yet sceptical. Her *shrew* was calling out for validation and she was on full alert to the warning signals. Reassessing the sensation, she concluded the caution had substance. She also realized that she was still rubbing the amulet because it provided a feeling of protection and control.

Previously when her *shrew* was active, she was aware of the possibility of danger but felt a sense of anxiety in the wake of its trailing disturbance. Not so on this occasion. She determined that Sir James's prediction of its protection was proving to be accurate, first with the exposure to Thon via his phone call and now with Francine in this meeting room.

Dominique continued to give directives: "Alexandra, for logistics, we will need to know your schedule and Collette's in advance so we can provide security. I appreciate that it's Friday and it may take a bit of coordination, but can you provide us with your itinerary soonest? We need to know where you are staying, who you are associating with and where you will be travelling, and the same for Collette. These details may pose some constraints on you but are necessary for your protection. We know that Thon uses poison as his MO, so be extra cautious about the source of all food, especially liquid."

"I'll contact Collette as soon as I leave and will have that information for you by this evening," affirmed Alexandra.

"Excellent," Dominique replied. "We should have the security detail in place by tomorrow morning. In the interim, be extra vigilant. If you or Collette have any concerns, do not hesitate to contact me. You have my cell number. I'll notify the duty officer immediately so all shifts are alerted."

Alexandra wrote on a note pad and slid it across the table to Dominique. "This is the address and the name of the person I will be staying with this evening and for the next week at least. I've already made arrangements for Collette to stay there starting this evening, to facilitate security. For your immediate information, I'll be attending the awards ceremony at the Élysée Palace this evening."

"Yes, I almost forgot. Thank you for reminding me," Dominique apologized.

"Could I have your attention, please, for one last announcement?" Dominique called out in a commanding voice. I omitted to mention that Dr. Bernard will be inducted as a commandeur de la Légion d'honneur at the Élysée Palace this evening."

Dominique led a round of applause. Paul reluctantly acknowledged the announcement with a humble smile.

Jean was beaming with pride in his father's accomplishment. Alexandra was communicating her support by her presence. Both expressions of personal encouragement warmed Paul.

CHAPTER 49

"It's time to go, Maman. We don't want to be late. I'm not sure that we'll be invited ever again to the Élysée Palace for the induction of a commandeur de la Légion d'honneur," Collette announced in a loud voice.

"Right there, dear."

"Wow!" both Jo and Collette exclaimed in unison as Alexandra appeared in her midnight blue velvet gown with its empire waist, flowing mid-back and sweetheart neckline framing the amulet around her neck and complemented by a Moroccan silk shawl.

"You are absolutely stunning. You remind me of Natalie Wood or Grace Kelly and certainly Princess Diana. That is traditional Hollywood Vogue if I ever saw it. No actress at the Oscars could upstage you in this dress," Jo declared. "With you in attendance, no one will notice any of the recipients at the awards ceremony, let alone anyone else in the room."

Alexandra smiled calmly in response but was reassured by the compliments.

"That dress looks like a Fashion by Fleur design if I ever saw one," Collette followed up with an equally grand pronouncement.

"It is a Fashion by Fleur designer dress, dear."

"How did you get it, Maman? It takes six months or longer to get one, even if you can get an order in, and that's a feat in itself."

"I've known Fleur for many years. She was a witness in one of the first murder investigations in which I was involved. She was just starting her career in the fashion industry and I helped her deal with the stressors of the case. We've remained friends since then. She said she owed me one and promised to pay me back by making me a dress for a very special occasion. I can't think of a more special occasion than this."

"Right, let's continue the conversation in the car, ladies," Jo interrupted, "or you'll be late for sure and I don't think that our commandeur will be impressed if you upstage him with your fashionably late entrance. If you can introduce me to Fleur and have her design me a dress, I'll erase all the IOUs I hold in my Alexandra-owes-me-one file."

⇹

As Alexandra entered the Grand Salon where the awards ceremony was to take place, a hush fell as all eyes turned on her regal presence with Collette virtually in the role of lady-in-waiting. From the opposite side of the room, Paul immediately looked up as he continued his conversation with another recipient. The Zen of her presence had announced her entrance.

Without breaking eye contact with Alexandra, he wended his way through the groups of attendees toward her, drawn by the magnetism of her beauty. Jean arrived at the same moment and became equally attuned to Collette's presence.

"May I escort you to your seat, madame, and Jean, would you follow with Collette?" Paul gestured. As they strolled to the front row seats reserved for guests of the commandeurs, others stepped aside and bowed as if in the presence of royalty. Paul found himself speechless as he directed his guests to their seats. One remained conspicuously vacant.

"Can I have a word with you in private, Papa?" Jean quietly asked.

"Certainly."

As they stepped aside, Jean whispered, "Maman won't be coming because she told me she had a headache. She's actually drunk and stoned on all the pills she's been downing. With all due respect,

Papa, I've had it with her excuses and whining and complaining and blaming and just plain bullshit. Why don't you just ditch her? I'm glad that she isn't here because I'd be embarrassed to hell to have her anywhere near this ceremony."

"Thanks for the news, son. I'm really pleased *you* are here."

From the beginning, his relationship with Suzette had been skewed as a result of his searching for acceptance and Suzette's narcissistic obsession and thus, her inability to meet her own needs, let alone his. She turned to self-medication while he concentrated on work. Ironically, he was being rewarded for his dedication to excellence and she was doomed to dependence on her addictions.

The relationship was too far gone to reconcile, and he was not motivated to step backwards into history. He concluded that Suzette was a pathetic soul of her own making.

Those who mattered most to him, Jean, AV and Collette, were with him at this auspicious event, which marked the demarcation to the next phase of his life.

"Just take your seat with AV and Collette, Jean."

In the past, Suzette's absence would have left him feeling as insecure as he had been when rejected by his first puppy love. Maria's letter to Alexandra had resolved those mistaken beliefs.

This evening, for the first time, confirmed the transformation. He did not feel rejected but empowered. He did not need Suzette's validation which he had sought but never received. His sense of self-efficacy had been unshackled. He could now enter into relationships more confidently than he ever had before.

His duty to Jean as a father was to instil in him this renewed sense of self-confidence. As a young father, he had not previously known that strength in himself. Perhaps that was one reason Yvon had failed to mature. But these were individual decisions. The acceptance of consequences was also an individual responsibility. Blaming, projection and denial were manifestations of immaturity which were personality characteristics of Yvon and his mother. Jean was the opposite.

With the bestowing of the commandeur de la Légion d'honneur, he was becoming a completely confident individual.

What an absolutely wonderful way to transition into retirement, he thought as he gazed over at AV and envisioned her from a different perspective, without the rose-coloured glasses he had hidden behind all these years.

He was drawn to her hands. She was not wearing a wedding ring. *Elegance without a ring is still elegance,* he concluded as he found himself unconsciously twirling his own wedding band with his thumb.

As the script describing his feats of bravery and heroic service to France was being recited, he found his heart starting to race as memories of harrowing events flooded his mind. He took slow deep breaths as he had learned. He also found himself consciously rubbing the ring Sir James had given him in Dover and feeling more energized than he could ever remember. Both subtle yet deliberate rubbing actions seemed to mitigate the stress response and he regained his composure and control. He recalled Sir James telling him he would feel more empowered in the fullness of time as he became one with the power imbued in the ring.

On hearing the citation, Alexandra whispered to herself, *Quel courage, quelle galanterie!*

CHAPTER 50

The recipients and their guests passed on congratulations immediately after the formal award presentations as the social aspect of the evening's festivities began. The first to join Paul were Alexandra, Collette and Jean, who were getting on well.

"I extend congratulations, Dr. Bernard, from Sir James and Major Mike." Paul and Alexandra straightaway looked up at Tom Hunt as he approached them.

"Deputy Chief of the Los Angeles Police Department attached to Interpol," Alexandra countered as Tom and Paul shook hands.

"It is a small world for some and it is equally important that it be kept small and intimate as your mother and Sir James have suggested," Tom whispered. "You are friends and you have friends, and it is good to know that friends take care of friends. Sir James educated me about the acronym 'Thon' which he first mentioned to your mother back in those times. Know that we are all interested in a fruitful and informative outcome, which will benefit all but the one whom we have reason to believe may be currently taking in the Parisian sights."

Paul glanced at Alexandra with widening eyes and projected "over to you, partner." Her curiosity had been tweaked at the meeting of the minds six hours earlier when he gave her his business card. *There's probably an encrypted identity in his name,* she surmised. Somehow, she sensed it contained the vestiges of a coded name which Sir James had mentioned in Dover. She was about to test her theory. "Thomas A. Hunt. 'A' as in Alder? LAPD indeed," she probed.

Tom paused briefly. Then with a smile, he responded to her salutation. "À *votre plaisir, madame*. You are your mother's daughter.

Have you considered a career change or perhaps a lateral move in your current career? You have qualities that should not retire. I would be honoured to explore options with you should you wish to learn more."

With a chuckle, she reflected on the recent discussions she and Paul had had about joining forces in a sleuth white-hat partnership. Further deliberations and future affiliations with Tom might reveal beneficial outcomes but she would have to chat with her new partner before making any decisions one way or the other.

"And do you still ride a Harley-Davidson, perhaps a California Highway Patrol vintage?" asked Alexandra.

"Lately the CHP have been riding BMWs but I understand from reliable sources they will be back to a full fleet of Harley cruisers soon," Tom replied.

"I have a classic 1972 Electra Glide that was once ridden by the CHP, purchased by an American military officer who brought it with him to Europe and later traded it in for a Street Glide here in Paris. You might be interested in seeing it sometime."

"Oh, you have?" Tom exclaimed, astonished. "I would be most interested in seeing such a classic and perhaps taking it for a spin to reacquaint myself with the all too familiar Harley comforts, if that's possible."

"Yes, it is a small world and, yes, that would be possible. Allowing a deputy chief of the LAPD now attached to Interpol to take her for a spin would be altogether appropriate in return for services rendered, past and future. I believe you have my new coordinates so please drop by for a reunion. We might take the opportunity to chat over java."

Tom bowed to Alexandra and once again congratulated Paul before taking his leave and moving on to commend other recipients while maintaining his observation of Alexandra and Collette.

Alexandra and Paul acknowledged his scrutiny and mirrored

his surveillance with their own scanning. For whatever reason, Alexandra, Paul and Tom in addition to a few others in the Grand Hall appeared to be in a heightened state of vigilance on this auspicious occasion in what should be one of the most secure environments. Alexandra and Paul were certainly on the same frequency. This would be an ideal setting for black hats to be dressed in white hats.

Alexandra whispered to Paul, “Tom’s a white hat.”

“You are good, madame, damn good. I need to hang out with you more often in order to hone my intuition skills, in addition to my riding skills. And what’s with the reference to the California Highway Patrol Electra Glide which I presume is a direct connection to Sophia?”

“I thought I recognized him this afternoon but just couldn’t place him. There was something about his business card that tweaked my curiosity. Hopefully, curiosity won’t kill the cat! When he said that Sir James and Major Mike send their congratulations, the fog immediately cleared and the dots connected. It was then I remembered seeing him at the Harley dealership when I bought Sophia. *He* was the military officer who traded her in. He had a presence which you notice. He still reflects it.”

“You need to teach me how you do that. I thought my memory was good but yours is incredible especially when you combine it with your sensation of the mind.”

“Now Francine Myette is another matter. My *shrew* is yelling at me. She has a dark sinister side to her persona, a hidden black-hatted agenda. Sir James spoke of the latecomers to the intelligence world who might be double agents. Everything about her suggests that she is duplicitous or a collaborator of some sorts. Remember me saying that I trusted Dominique on some things but I didn’t trust her completely, that there was a shadowy side to her honesty?

Well, she seemed to be too close to Francine this afternoon. My sense is telling me that Francine has something on her."

As Alexandra was speaking, Paul noticed her rubbing the amulet as if seeking comfort or validation for her sensation and protection.

"Just before I left Jo's to come here, I sent a message to Sir James using my mother's code asking if he knew anything about Francine. Just now I received a message back but I need to decode it."

As she was explaining, Paul's cell phone alerted him to an incoming call with a muted buzz. Discretely looking at the display screen, he saw a message from Sir James. "For your gardener – in a typical *jardin anglais*, you will find a purple hand-shaped flower with a grove of steeples in the centre." The cryptic message was clear. The purple hand-shaped flower was a reference to monkshood, the poisonous flower Sir James had pointed out when they walked in his garden. It could only mean one thing. Francine was somehow foe, certainly not friend. As he guardedly showed Alexandra the text, he whispered the interpretation. Her *shrew* was accurate once again and was now silently yelling at her.

CHAPTER 51

Alexandra looked up to confirm Collette's whereabouts. Collette was standing beside a table about three metres away. Instinctively, she walked forward to close the distance between them. Once positioned protectively behind Collette, she leaned forward and whispered a reminder to keep her radar up.

Collette put her champagne flute on the table before turning her head to acknowledge the warning. Alexandra put her glass down too and with her free hand, brushed back Collette's hair in a shielding gesture.

Paul noted Alexandra's hasty advance toward Collette. Observing this protective action and recognizing her heightened state of concern, he moved in close to confirm his proximity while scanning the Grand Hall for any suspicious activity. He became acutely aware that Tom was attuned to Alexandra's defensive manoeuvring.

Jean, who had been speaking with another award recipient behind his father, also noticed the forward movement. Out of the corner of his eye, he saw a young, physically fit blond server standing on the opposite side of the table near Collette and Alexandra. His appearance caught Jean's attention because his jacket didn't fit correctly. The other servers in the room, all impeccably attired, had been floating through the Grand Hall removing empty glasses and serving full ones to the guests. But this server had been standing still for too long. The server's eyes were locked on Collette and Alexandra. With a nervous gesture, he fluttered his hands over Collette's and Alexandra's champagne flutes and sprinkled what appeared to be a powder into both, then quickly pulled back.

At that moment, Collette and Alexandra reached for their

glasses without looking. The server continued to stare intently at them, willing them to pick up the champagne flutes.

As they extended their hands, Jean lunged forward and yelled, "No! Don't drink!" He crashed into the table knocking it askew as he dove past Collette and Alexandra in an attempt to knock the glasses out of their hands and tackle the server.

Collette, Alexandra and Paul wheeled around in astonishment. Other guests followed with equally alarmed expressions.

Tom closed ranks to within an arm's length of Alexandra in the split second after Jean yelled out his warning.

"Grab the server! He put something in her glass!" Jean yelled again.

As he fell to the ground with the server under him, security guards sprang into action. After a brief struggle, the server was handcuffed and removed.

Jean looked up and noticed Collette frozen but still holding the champagne flute in her hand. Alexandra's had been knocked away as he flew by. "Don't drink that, Collette, don't drink that!" he barked. "The server put something in it. It's been poisoned."

"Let me take that from you," said a uniformed Élysée Palace security guard to Collette, who was still standing motionless.

A heavy-set man dressed in a black tuxedo and in the company of two uniformed officers identified himself as Sergeant Drapeau with the Préfecture de police de Paris. He hurriedly ushered Collette, Alexandra, Paul and Jean out of the Grand Hall and into an adjoining security room.

"Capitaine Dominique Roland of the Police nationale called our office late this afternoon and requested our surveillance at the awards ceremony. It's a good thing that she did contact us. Is everyone all right?"

All four checked themselves and each other. With the exception of bruising and grazes on Jean's hand, they reported they were safe and uninjured.

"We'll analyze the contents of the champagne glass and review the security tapes which have been constantly monitoring all movements throughout the building. The server will be taken to the precinct for questioning."

Looking at Jean, Sergeant Drapeau acknowledged him in gratitude. "Had it not been for your perceptive observation and quick action, this evening's outcome would have been very different and an embarrassment to our force and the government. And your name is?"

"I'm Jean Bernard, Dr. Bernard's son."

Reaching forward to shake his hand, he said to Jean, "Well, like father, like son. I have no doubt that you will be invited on this stage at some future date to receive an award for your bravery. I'll certainly be recommending it in my report."

"Sorry, I'll pass on the handshake if you don't mind. I'll just wrap my hand in this napkin. Thank you for the compliment but it was nothing. I participated in track and field while in school. It's good to know that I can still complete the long jump with some degree of grace, although my landing demonstrated slightly less finesse than I would have preferred."

Collette was transfixed, her eyes wide in amazement as Jean continued.

"I'd like to think that in my day I would have been able to complete that manoeuvre, grab both glasses without spilling a drop, subdue the suspect and do all this without knocking over the table and causing any disturbance. Age must be catching up with me!"

Jean's impromptu, self-deprecating humour broke the gravity of the situation. Everyone laughed including Sergeant Drapeau who was relieved to note that despite the incident they were in good spirits. He didn't mind taking statements from witnesses but did not like having to provide statements to Internal Affairs. He certainly would have been on the other side of the interrogation table but for the grace of God and Jean's incisive actions.

"Although we have the suspect in custody, it would be appropriate to have our patrol officers escort you home and provide security thereafter."

"I appreciate your efficient response to this incident and accept your offer of the police escort home," Paul replied. "But before I leave, I must pay my respects to our host this evening. If you all could wait here with the sergeant, I'll return in a moment."

As Paul was leaving, Sergeant Drapeau handed Jean one of his business cards. "We'll need to take a statement from you as soon as possible. Can you call me first thing tomorrow morning and arrange a time?"

"Certainly. I doubt I'll forget any of the details between now and then. In fact, my memory recall might be better after a good night's sleep, well, perhaps a night's rest. It will take me some time to unwind and process the evening's events. I'll probably be up during the night so I might as well make some notes."

Paul returned in a few minutes. An Élysée Palace security guard led the way out of the building through a side entrance and into the parking lot, followed by Sergeant Drapeau who directed patrol officers to ensure they got to their homes safely and to continue security until dawn.

After a brief discussion, they decided to go to Jo's place in Garches first. Paul and Jean would then drive home to Meudon once they were assured Collette and Alexandra were safe and secure.

Paul drove Alexandra in Svelte while Jean took Collette in his car.

"When I bid my adieu just before we left, the LAPD deputy chief enquired as to your state of health and that of Collette and

Jean. I assured him we were all well. He mentioned he would be in contact for a reunion with Sophia."

Paul reached over and took hold of Alexandra's hand which he held while driving.

"We need to talk. Had something happened to you this evening, I don't know what I would have done."

"But nothing did happen and I'm confident nothing will happen, so don't worry. I feel safe and protected with you and Tom and, yes, Jean by my side. Right now, I'm more concerned about Collette who is in shock."

"I know Jean and he will be debriefing her as we speak. I'll check with him once we get to Jo's place. We'll stay as long as he and you feel it's necessary."

"Thank you. You don't know how much that means to me. Collette is everything to me. I owe Jean a big, big hug."

"And by the way, you captivated everyone in the Grand Hall with your beauty. Your gown is so elegant, and you look radiant in it. Everyone stood still when you glided in with such elegance, such refinement, such *raffinata* as my Italian colleague would say. Those I spoke to before leaving enquired about you and without a doubt they were envious of me. If you hadn't noticed, I was speechless. I'm barely able to express myself at this moment. *Candens es*, madame, you are hot!"

CHAPTER 52

At Jo's, Paul and Jean escorted Alexandra and Collette into the house to ensure all was secure. Paul checked in with Jean about Collette's stress level and passed on Alexandra's concern. Jean reported that Collette was still a bit shaken up but would be all right. She was processing the events of the evening quite rationally, which was a good sign.

After briefing Jo on the evening's events and assuring her there would be a robust police presence henceforth, they bid good night but not before Jean was profusely hugged by all three women for his heroic acrobatics.

It's a good thing Collette and Jean are here, Paul thought, *because if they weren't, I'd be tempted to stay and that would be awkward.*

"Remember that we ride tomorrow morning, Commandeur. Jo and I will meet you in the parking lot of the Hotel Ibis Versailles Château on the avenue du Général de Gaulle at 9:00 a.m. Marcel will be the road captain for the ride so you might like to chat with him if you get a chance before we arrive."

"Looking forward to it, madame. This will be a first for Chuck and me, riding in a group with my two most favourite Ladies of Harley. And, yes, I'll have my camera with me, so have Sophia shined up."

Paul spoke with the patrol officers who had been waiting outside. The officers assured him they would be patrolling the immediate area and maintaining surveillance of the residence until dawn. The officers then departed. As he was unlocking the door to Svelte, he paused, relocked the door, walked back to Jo's front door and rang the bell.

Jo opened the door and looked at him. Recognizing the circumstance, she turned and walked down the hallway and into the living room.

"Alex, you are needed at the door," she quietly announced. "Collette, would you help me in the kitchen, please?"

Collette looked at Jo, understanding the request as her mother walked down the hall to the front door. The girl-talk was concise and the communiqué clear.

The silence spoke loudly as Alexandra and Paul embraced and stood motionless. Tears streamed down both of their faces. Nothing could be said that would add further clarity. *Le coup de foudre* – the love at first sight they had expressed all those years ago in the letters of adoration – was reconfirmed in the visceral force of this moment.

In their own ways they knew romantic love was predicated on obstacles to be resolved, like the patterns in a kaleidoscope. In their respective relationships with Suzette and André, the obstacles remained unresolved and had become hurdles. This renewed relationship was starting out with obstacles but the resolution was a given.

The front door closed. Paul drove back to Meudon with lucidity and focus. Alexandra walked back into the living room to Jo and Collette who welcomed her graciously. Their future seemed assured and calm, in stark contrast to the attack that had punctuated the evening's celebrations. With the culprit in custody, no one felt open to any impending threat.

⁂

AT THE POLICE PRECINCT, THE BLOND SERVER was searched and interrogated. The jacket he was wearing had an identification card for a Daniel Pierre Toupin. A query in the database revealed a person with that name and description had just been found dead in a parking lot. It appeared his neck had been broken.

Follow-up enquiries in the neighbourhood identified Toupin as a server with a catering company which had recently been awarded a contract to cater to government-sponsored social events. With the recent cutbacks in government, full-time staff at the Élysée Palace had been replaced by contract services. Palace security services had cautioned against the change but had lost the argument to the bureaucrats and bean-counters who saw savings and balanced budgets as steps to promotion. They had learned to define efficiency in the most creative ways but had not comprehended effectiveness in the same context.

An internal review of that decision would no doubt result in a strong recommendation to withdraw from contract services to prevent subsequent breaches of security at the Élysée Palace. Embarrassment to government was always a motivator for change in policy. News reporters would be hot on the trail of the politicians and bureaucrats by morning.

Media police scanners were already noticing an increase in chatter on the net. In such matters where the government and the department might come under criticism, an internal protocol required lead investigators to notify the department's media relations folks and the "boys and girls upstairs" as the rank and file referred to the senior executives on the top floor.

CHAPTER 53

Jean was up and dressed by the time Paul rose and readied his riding gear. "Good morning, Papa le commandeur," he spoke quietly.

"What are you doing up so early, mon fils galant?"

"I made arrangements with Collette to take her out for breakfast. You and Alexandra and Jo are riding and I didn't want Collette to be alone."

"Good thinking. Not everyone processes a shock in the same way. I'll be meeting AV and Jo at the Hotel Ibis Versailles Château on avenue du Général de Gaulle in an hour. This is where the ride will begin and end, so I'm told. I'm quite looking forward to a relaxed day after last evening's unplanned events. How are you feeling after your track and field performance?"

"I'm fine although I think I may have bruised a few ribs," he said quietly. "I don't know why I'm being so cautious speaking quietly. Maman is dead to the world from the pills and wine she consumed last evening. I'm really annoyed she didn't attend the award ceremony but maybe it was just as well, as she would no doubt have made a scene to embarrass us all. I don't know why you put up with her, Papa. Why don't you just leave her to her own self-inflicted misery?"

Paul didn't respond although he agreed with Jean's advice. It echoed his father's advice. The reality was that he wasn't far from moving on. Suzette's no-show last evening was the last straw. It would be an utter insult to AV to even contemplate a comparison between the two because there just wasn't one to be made. He was on the verge of making final amends with his God. Now he just had to make peace with his conscience.

Within twenty minutes, he and Jean were out of the door. As he pulled into the parking lot of the Hotel Ibis Versailles Château, he caught sight of Marcel and pulled into a parking stall beside him.

"Welcome, mon Colonel," Marcel said and greeted him with a salute.

"Glad to be on the ground, Road Captain. Alexandra suggested I come early to get a briefing from you on what to expect, as this will be my first group ride. She and Jo should be along shortly."

Marcel reviewed the procedures and route as other riders joined the growing assembly of bikers. He also introduced Paul to other ex-military riders who had served on UN missions including UNPROFOR. Paul recognized a few. They had provided security for the airport in Sarajevo. Nods were sufficient to affirm the shared experience of comrades-in-arms from those harrowing times.

⁂

As Alexandra and Jo were warming up their bikes in preparation for the ride, Jean parked adjacent to Jo's driveway.

"If you give us a minute, Jean, you can park in the driveway."

"No problem, I'm fine here."

"Collette's in the house just cleaning up. She should be ready shortly. Go on in and finish off the pot of coffee with her if you like."

As he walked up to the door, Alexandra and Jo rode off in rumbling unison. Jean thought to himself that his Ducati had a more cultured purr than any Harley but he wouldn't debate the point with these Ladies of Harley, whom he quietly admired.

Alexandra and Jo stopped at the stop sign at the end of the street just a couple of houses down from Jo's. As Alexandra pulled out, a black Mercedes entered the intersection at speed. She looked up in bewilderment as the car smashed into Sophia, sending her skidding along the pavement and onto the sidewalk.

Visions of the blond mystery man in the underground parking lot in Brussels and at the quai de Hable in Dieppe flashed across her mind. A large man jumped out of the car, struck her powerfully across her helmeted head and dragged her unconscious body into the back seat.

Jo's bike had also been struck in the collision and seemed to have spun out of control. She now lay in the intersection dazed, and partially pinned beneath her Harley. She felt locked in a trance as surreal images of the impact, Alexandra's violent abduction and the Mercedes speeding south played out.

The unmistakable sound of a crash had immediately drawn Jean's attention to the intersection. He too was stunned by the sequence of events. Also hearing the impact, Collette ran out of the house just as her mother's limp body was being heaved in the back of the car. She sprinted with Jean to the intersection. Other neighbours and witnesses converged on the scene.

Jo was trying to stand up as Jean and Collette came to a halt. Others were helping her get out from under the bike.

"Someone please call the police and an ambulance!" Collette yelled.

"Already on their way," a voice replied.

The ambulance arrived before the police whose arrival was announced by their shrill two-toned siren.

As the paramedics were attending to Jo, she shouted to Jean and Collette to call Paul and explain what happened. "Get in your car and drive to the Ibis Versailles Château on avenue du Général de Gaulle!"

Jean and Collette ran back to Jo's house where Jean retrieved his cell phone from his car. Still in shock after the sequence of events, he couldn't execute the speed dial for his father. When he finally dialled manually, he received a busy signal. After several unsuccessful attempts, he gave up and decided to drive to the Ibis Hotel instead.

Enroute to the hotel, Collette kept calling Paul on Jean's cell phone and finally got through. In her panic, she just explained that her mother and Jo had been involved in an accident and she and Jean were on their way to the Ibis Hotel. Jean would explain what happened when they arrived.

"Marcel," Paul called, "Jo and Alexandra were involved in an accident. My son is on his way here with more details."

As Marcel briefed the riders who were starting to mount up in preparation for the morning's ride, Paul repeatedly called Alexandra's cell phone to no avail. Everyone switched their engines off and waited in anticipation of the news.

Watching Paul frantically dialling, Marcel tried to assure him that his son would be arriving shortly with an update. Paul acknowledged Marcel's reassurance but repeatedly speed-dialled Alexandra until Jean pulled into the parking lot approximately fifteen minutes later.

"Papa," Jean yelled, "AV's been abducted!" He quickly described the accident and said the black Mercedes had headed south.

Paul's mind immediately went to the photos he had taken on their inaugural ride and their photo shoot at the warehouse. He recognized what had bothered him about the photos he processed on his digital software. There was the back end of a black car protruding from behind the warehouse building. He also remembered AV saying there were two locations in France that would be burrs in the saddle of any Nazi bent on revenge.

"I think I know where they have taken her! It's the museum's warehouse outside Versailles."

"I know exactly where it is," replied Marcel. "Everyone, mount up and follow me."

With the roar of engines, the bikers headed south behind their road captain who set a quick pace. Paul was second in the formation close on Marcel's heels. Jean and Collette followed the riders in the car.

⇹

WITH THEIR CAPTIVE IN THE BACK SEAT, the black Mercedes pulled in behind the warehouse. Alexandra was regaining consciousness as she was dragged out of the back seat of the car and into the warehouse where she was tied to a chair with duct-tape. As she recovered her focus, she noticed a tall blond man to her left holding a gun and another, shorter person standing in front of her.

"I told you when we spoke on the phone we would meet soon and now here we are, Alexandra," the shorter man announced arrogantly.

Alexandra quickly assessed her adversary as she prepared to engage in a psychological duel with Thon, the man who had been central to her mother's career and the efforts of Sir James, Thomas Hunt *aka* Alder and others in pursuit of Nazi collaborators. Although she could not hold the amulet with her hands tied, she gained strength from it hanging around her neck, positioned over her heart. She was confident Paul would move heaven and earth to get to her. She just had to stall Thon long enough.

"A gentleman of your calibre would normally introduce himself to a lady, don't you think?" Alexandra said pleasantly.

"My apologies for my rudeness, Alexandra, you are quite correct. I introduced myself to all the others before I put them out of their misery. I am Herr Ludwig Rudolf Heydrich. I knew your mother and all those other women who mistakenly worked with the *Maquis* during the war. They belittled me and all other loyal Nazis. But we are superior and that is why I am here standing in front of you, and you are finally submissive to us. Your mother, Maria, was the last of the abusers and she robbed me of the chance to put her out of her misery. It is only right that you and your daughter pay the final dues of atonement. What better location than Versailles among the furnishings from the Hall of Mirrors to complete this phase of the final solution. Now the Fourth Reich will rise unencumbered by the wrongdoings imposed on Germany's glorious past."

Alexandra concentrated on Thon as he introduced himself formally and droned on about how repressed he and his fellow Nazis were. To her informed eye he was a mouse of a man if she ever saw one and pitiful in his effeminate stature. He was insecure about his sexuality. That was why he needed to introduce himself ostentatiously as Herr Ludwig Rudolf Heydrich and not just Ludwig Heydrich or simply Ludwig.

She and Fred had come to this conclusion about his sexuality and possible impotence when they debriefed after Thon's call to her.

Staring directly at Thon, she concluded there was something petty about his facial features and his blond hair appeared false. He was wearing heavy makeup, no doubt attempting to mask his advancing years and deteriorating vitality. It smelt dark somehow. He was taking perverse enjoyment in taunting the latest prey caught in his snare yet he needed others to support him, to provide him with reinforcement for his pathetic deeds. The tall man with the gun standing to Alexandra's left was fulfilling that role.

She surmised that without the validation, Thon would crumple. That was his Achilles' heel and that would be her focus. This initial assessment of Ludwig Rudolf Heydrich reminded her of the lyrics of a satirical hit song from the 1960s, entitled *Small Sam*. It came out on the heels of *Big Bad John*. "He was narrow at the shoulders and broad at the hips, everyone knew that small Sam was a drip, small Sam, small Sam, wee small Sam." *Weird*, she concluded. *In times of stress, we humans search for humour to provide relief.*

It was time to be bold and to expose Thon to his more stereotypical Nazi subordinate who Alexandra assessed was not pleased with Thon's ramblings.

"So why do you see me as a threat, Ludwig, if I may call you Ludwig – after all, we are equals?"

"We are not equal!" Thon yelled in simpering defiance. "I am superior to everyone else and, no, you cannot call me by my first name. You will address me as Herr Ludwig Rudolf Heydrich!"

Alexandra purposely looked at the tall man and noticed him winch at that outburst. He controlled the gun and was her immediate threat but he was not behaving like Thon.

Oh ya, I'm on the right track, she mused as she returned her full attention to Thon in such a way that Thon had to notice.

"Absolutely, Ludwig. But you betrayed those in the *Maquis* and in the SS also. Is betrayal honourable behaviour for any soldier of the Fourth Reich? Betrayal seems to me and to your friend here to be a weakness."

"The war was a slaughterhouse of the human soul!" Thon yelled back in defence of his betrayal of his colleagues and country.

"Self-pity is pregnant with its own downfall," Alexandra snapped back.

At that moment, she saw a feral cat sneak by some crates with kittens following one behind the other.

"Look over there at that cat and her kittens, Ludwig. Behind you. Are they like the cats in your barn you had to kill because they were weak and suffering? This cat looks pretty confident, strong and well-fed to me, and certainly not in any misery. What do *you* think, Ludwig?"

Alexandra noticed the chameleon-like change in Thon's demeanour when she drew his attention to the cat and her kittens. She had pinged on his most vulnerable personality button.

Seeing the mother cat and her kittens, Thon reverted to a primal child-like state. He began speaking in an effeminate, thickly-accented infant voice, rambling on in a tirade about his theories on why cats must be killed because they are disadvantaged and weak and not pure like true Aryans. Both Alexandra and the tall gunman witnessed Thon becoming thoroughly unglued before their eyes. His true pathology of an obsessive-compulsive bisexual psychopath was shining through in Technicolour. Her preliminary assessment was one bad guy down, one to go. She now had to deal with the tall man with the gun.

The unmistakeable roar of Harley engines could be heard coming closer. *The timing could not have been better,* she concluded.

Looking at the man with the gun, she noticed him quickly glance toward the source of the rumbling sound of Harley engines. She deliberately directed her question at him. "Is this babbling sexually-inept pervert your great leader of the Fourth Reich?"

Without showing a trace of emotion, he deliberately moved the gun off Alexandra, pointed it at Thon's head and pulled the trigger.

CHAPTER 54

Paul had given the order for the bikers to move to the front of the warehouse and the empty parking lot and ride in circles as a distraction.

One biker yelled out, "Who the hell does he think he is, telling us what to do?"

Marcel immediately barked back, "He was my colonel in Sarajevo when I was shot and he saved my life, so you do exactly what he says."

"Okay, Marcel. Sorry, I didn't know."

As the bikers rode in circles revving up their engines, Paul and Jean bolted to the back of the warehouse where they saw a black Mercedes parked back in the woods.

"Jean, did you call Dominique and advise her of the situation? We need police support here *immediately*. Call her again."

"On it, Papa."

Paul examined the black Mercedes and noticed damage to the right rear taillight, possibly from the stone he threw at the car while at the cemetery. There was additional minor damage to the front right bumper and fender with cream-coloured paint the same shade as Sophia. He quickly looked into the car from the rear window and then just as hastily dropped out of sight. Not seeing anything on this initial scan, he again popped his eyes above the window for a more detailed scan of the interior. He did not see anyone but Alexandra's helmet was on the back seat.

At that moment, he heard a shot ring out from inside the warehouse, echoing against the concrete walls.

Just then, Jean observed Collette running toward them.

"You stay here, Collette," Jean bellowed as he and his father ran toward the warehouse's back door which was ajar. As they entered cautiously, they scanned the interior in the ill-lit spaces bordered by boxes piled awkwardly on top of each other.

Alexandra was tied to a chair and motionless, her back to them. A man was lying on the floor in front of her. A tall blond man was holding a gun. Seeing Paul and Jean's movement, the man pivoted, pointed the gun in their direction and fired two shots at them.

"Take cover, Jean!"

From behind a shipping container, Paul then yelled at the gunman, "Put down your gun! You are surrounded!"

Peering over the top of the shipping crate, they saw the gunman running to a side door away from Alexandra who had toppled to the floor, still tied to the chair. Paul dashed to her.

As he approached, he noticed a large pool of blood on the concrete floor oozing from the man's head. Paul lay prone, covering Alexandra's body while more shots rang out.

The fresh smell of cordite and the sound of repeated gunfire caused his heart to pound. The shrill of tinnitus echoed in his ears. His chest tightened. His breathing accelerated.

Images of Marcel being shot in Sarajevo, the little girl in the blood-stained, light blue dress, and the subsequent evidence-gathering missions under fire assaulted his mind with an exploding kaleidoscope of blinding colours. These images, flashing in rapid succession, temporarily impaired his perception of the situation he now found himself in. Although he knew the symptoms and knew what he had to do, breathing with slow, deliberate breaths was difficult. The shrilling in his ears together with his pounding heart was almost deafening.

He knew he must focus immediately on AV and he did. With shaking fingers, he started to remove the duct-tape that bound her arms and legs to the chair. She was breathing, unconscious but alive. He couldn't find an obvious wound.

In the meantime, Jean had chased the gunman toward the side entrance. At the door, Jean saw the man running into the woods by the black Mercedes, but before he disappeared, he turned one last time and fired another shot at Jean.

Collette, who had entered the warehouse from the back door, saw her mother on the floor and yelled, "Maman!" as she sprinted toward her.

Hearing Collette call out to her mother in panic, Jean bolted back to where Alexandra was lying on the floor beside a man's motionless body marked by an expanding pool of blood, and his father hovering over Alexandra.

Jean turned to Collette and yelled, "I thought I told you to stay outside!"

Collette whipped round toward him and glared with pursed lips, accentuating her tight mouth. Her face was beet red. Her fists were tight in a boxer's grip and her posture aggressive. Her motive was not complicated and there was no mistake in Jean's assessment. This was her primordial fight-flight response and he was the target of an attack. She would not choose flight from her mother.

Oops, he immediately reflected. *Bad move for improving interpersonal relations with her. Collette may be slight in stature, but she is feisty in nature.*

As that personal assessment culminated in this thought, he noticed his eyesight was becoming fuzzy and felt a searing pain in his shoulder.

"You're bleeding, Jean!" Collette exclaimed.

Jean took a weak breath and his knees buckled. He slithered to the floor as the ceiling swirled in a prismatic merry-go-round. He felt his concentration wane as sights and sounds became more distant and moved in a slow downward funnel.

"You okay, Colonel?" Marcel asked as he surveyed the rapidly unfolding situation.

Paul looked up and saw Marcel standing over him with his arms extended and his back toward him, as if protecting his commanding officer.

"We need perimeter security, Marcel. Unknown number of bad guys."

Marcel yelled out the order to other bikers who had entered the warehouse. Several, having served with him in Sarajevo, understood the situation and responded with automatic discipline.

"Perimeter secure, Colonel," Marcel bellowed back moments later.

"Jean has been wounded, Marcel. He needs immediate medical attention," Paul called out as he moved away from Alexandra and toward his son.

Marcel bent down beside Jean and, seeing bright crimson blood gushing from his shoulder, clamped both hands tight into his pectoral muscles around the open wound and wedged Jean's arm inward to maximize the pressure. Jean's face was ashen and his breathing sporadic and shallow.

"Jean!" Marcel shouted into his face. "Talk to me, Jean. Tell me what you feel. Tell me what you are thinking right now."

Jean's eyes fluttered opened slightly as his pupils dilated in an attempt to remain conscious of his environment.

"Keep your eyes open, Jean. Keep looking at me."

From his own experience of being wounded in Sarajevo and being barked at by his colonel during that ordeal, and from his combat First Aid training, he knew how important it was to keep the casualty focused, conscious and communicating.

Through the chaos of the crisis, sirens grew louder as police cars arrived on the scene. A police sergeant wearing full tactical gear and carrying an automatic weapon entered the warehouse and shouted, "Police! Everyone, hands up and don't move!"

Looking over toward Alexandra, Paul, Jean and the man lying

in a pool of blood, the sergeant recognized Marcel as a reserve police constable.

"Give me a situation report, Marcel!" the sergeant demanded as his eyes darted around in disciplined scrutiny.

"I can vouch for everyone here, Sergeant. The perimeter inside the warehouse has been secured by my riders. This young man has been wounded badly and needs an ambulance immediately. The woman needs medical assessment – unknown injuries – and an ambulance also. The man on the floor is clearly dead from a head wound."

The sergeant knelt beside Marcel. Deep shadows cast by a few solitary ceiling lights obscured specifics, but he could see Jean and the motionless man lying in the now coagulating pool of darkening blood. From this vantage point and despite the shadows, the sergeant could make out a gaping black hole in the right temple of the motionless figure, with grey brain matter oozing out. The right eye bulged from the socket, staring blankly in disbelief. The blunt face was awkwardly ajar which briefly held his attention because of its oddly perplexed state – like the broken mainspring of a cuckoo clock. His fate would have been instantaneous. The sweet pungent smell of death was unmistakeable to the sergeant's seasoned olfactory senses.

On his portable radio, he called for ambulances and urgent backup of more police officers to secure the scene and pursue the gunman. As he did so, he noticed out of the corner of his eye a spent casing on the floor approximately two feet away from a large cardboard box. He pointed it out to a patrol officer standing directly behind him and gave instructions to mark and guard it as evidence. He then returned to Jean.

Jean concentrated his blurred vision through his flickering eyes on the sergeant and with a faint raspy voice, reported that the gunman had run out the side door into a wood near where the black

Mercedes was parked. "Tall, blond-haired Caucasian male with a handgun, dressed in black."

In response, the sergeant called for a K-9 Unit and directed other officers who had arrived to secure the area around the Mercedes and the woods. Within minutes, the two-note high-low siren of ambulances could be heard over the ambient noise of the police presence. Jean and Alexandra were immediately evacuated from the scene and taken to the nearest hospital. The sergeant stood up and left the warehouse through the front door where he hurriedly established a command centre.

The crime scene had been secured by the first on-scene police while other officers had started to take names of witnesses and make arrangements for statements to be recorded.

The K-9 Unit tracked the gunman through the woods but lost his trail at a paved road that ran parallel to the warehouse. The dog master reported that either the gunman had a get-away car there or had been picked up by a passing motorist.

CIS had arrived and secured the black Mercedes. Preparations were underway to transport it to the Crime Lab garage for in-depth analysis.

A senior detective arrived and took over the investigation. Recognizing Paul as the Director of the Crime Lab, he offered him a ride to the hospital in one of the traffic patrol cars.

"Is there another rider who can take my bike, Marcel?" Paul asked. "I'm a bit shaken and I'd like to get a lift for me and Collette with one of the police cars to the hospital."

"Consider it done, Colonel. I'll have it taken to my place and secured there."

"Thanks, Marcel. I owe you one."

"You owe me nothing, sir."

CHAPTER 55

Collette and Paul were surprised to find Alexandra sitting in the emergency waiting area. She had regained consciousness during the ambulance ride, and was being released with minor contusions and abrasions. She was to self-monitor for possible concussion.

Capitaine Dominique Roland had arrived at the ER just before Paul and Collette. She briefly spoke with Alexandra as she was being treated. "We will talk again after you have been released. We need all the details of the incident to complete the file and then pursue leads this will have provided."

As Dominique was leaving, Alexandra noticed Tom Hunt standing inconspicuously in the background and then quietly approaching. "Deputy Chief Thomas Alder Hunt of the LAPD," Alexandra greeted him discretely.

"You have friends who are pleased and relieved that you are relatively unharmed, Alexandra. Sir James is looking forward to a quiet relaxing afternoon tea with you and Dr. Bernard when you are up to it. And I am looking forward to a reunion with a classic 1972 Harley-Davidson Electra Glide. Perhaps we can chat over java at your favourite coffee shop just around the corner from where you are staying. Please pass along my best regards to Dr. Bernard. I regret I cannot stay longer but duty calls so I must slip away."

Alexandra greeted Paul and Collette with news that Jean had been taken to the operating room. Preliminary reports indicated that his condition was critical. He was weak because he had lost over a litre of blood. The bullet in his shoulder had nicked an artery.

They unanimously agreed they would remain in the waiting room until Jean was out of surgery and in recovery. Paul called

Suzette but she was out or wasn't answering the phone. That was her usual behaviour, so he left a voice message. He really didn't care whether she responded or not.

As Paul sat beside Alexandra and Collette in the waiting room, he reassessed his own condition. His chest was still tight and his breathing laboured. The tinnitus in his left ear was loud but not extreme. Flashbacks of Sarajevo, the lifeless body of the little girl in the bloodstained light-blue dress and the other missions consumed his racing mind.

Noting his pale complexion and apparent stress, a nurse approached, sat beside him and asked if he was feeling all right. Paul explained what had happened and thanked her for her concern. At her request, he accompanied her to an examination room where she took his blood pressure and pulse.

"Your BP is extremely high, sir," she commented. "I'm a bit surprised as you appear to be in excellent physical condition but given the circumstances you've been through, I understand. May I recommend you just sit here and rest for a few minutes while I continue to monitor your vital signs?"

When she shone a flashlight in his eyes, he immediately squinted, turned his head away and started to massage his temples.

"I apologize," he said in a low voice. "When I have a headache, light really bothers me."

"I can get you something for your headache."

"No, that's fine. I've been prescribed medication but I don't like to take it because the pills impair my thinking and upset my stomach."

Paul thought that his father and grandfather had tolerated years of combat during the Great War and Second World War and had never succumbed to the lingering echoes of a cannonade although, in retrospect, he could identify symptoms in his father similar to what he was now experiencing. In comparison, he concluded he had no right to complain as a result of just one UN deployment and several other dangerous confidential missions. He had mustered intestinal fortitude and endurance when faced with extreme challenges in running marathons and fencing, and would tough it out and win over these emotional hurdles as he had done so many times before.

"You should call your family doctor for a follow-up," the nurse replied.

"Thank you for your concern. I experience reaction to certain stressors and I'm aware of my condition. I'll be fine."

Paul left the examination room and returned to Alexandra and Collette. As he sat down beside Alexandra, she gently took his hand. She could not help but notice the tension in his muscles and his sweaty palm.

"How are you?" she quietly enquired.

"Working through stuff."

"You're rubbing your head. Did you bang it?"

"Just another headache. They plague me on occasion, and this is one of those occasions. Ghosts from Christmas Past return to haunt me as they did Ebenezer Scrooge." He reminded himself he needed to bury those ghosts before they buried him.

Alexandra had seen this behaviour in police officers she had known and had received briefings on how to support those exhibiting signs and symptoms of post-traumatic stress disorder. On the Metro when they had talked about the body armour in his new riding jacket and when they had first met Marcel, Paul had exhibited these symptoms, rubbing his temples and forehead in an effort to mitigate the headache, nausea and blurred vision.

Turning to Collette, Alexandra quietly asked, "Can you get us some cold water, ma cherie?"

Collette understood the need for her to bring the water but, more immediately, to leave her mother alone to attend to Paul who appeared to be in a self-induced trance.

Du calme, Paul recited to himself as he rubbed the ring Sir James had given him, *du calme*.

His breathing slowed, as did his heart rate. He had re-established some control over his physiological responses to the events.

If the past twenty-four hours are any indication of "retirement" then perhaps I need to get back to work, he mused, *or at least get back into the saddle and ride away into the sunset with AV. That's how all the old black and white cowboy movies ended. The good guys in white hats win and the bad guys in black hats lose....*

"The strange man on the floor in the pool of blood with his brains pouring out is Thon, or was Thon," she whispered.

Paul glanced at her, smiled and commented nonchalantly, "It couldn't have happened to a nicer guy. Next time, he'll think twice before messing with a very hot lady who just happens to be a forensic psychologist. White hats one, black hats zero."

Alexandra returned his brave smile and continued to hold onto his hand while massaging his sweaty palm in a slow rhythmic motion. To Paul, her touch was subtle and supportive, and her hand was soft and soothing. Alexandra adjusted her breathing with his and would accompany her Peter Pan through Neverland in his unending brushes with his antagonist, Captain Hook, aboard the brig the *Jolly Roger*. She would again be his Wendy.

As she reflected, the images of him defending her against the drunk with the sword in the restaurant prompted her to conclude she had never been this close to anyone who had demonstrated such chivalry while clashing with a counterfeit of Captain Hook. She had merely read about such *galanterie* nurtured in the courts of seventeenth century novels by Madame de La Fayette and other courtiers of those romantic times. Only in France could one witness such refined etiquette, where courtesy and gallantry could not be described but had to be observed for its complexities to be appreciated.

Collette returned with three bottles of cold water and, after gauging the situation, sat down quietly beside her mother. Not knowing all the facts, her preliminary psych assessment was simple: say nothing but just be present in support. She too consciously adjusted her breathing to her mother's and Paul's.

⁂

"Bonjour" – *Hello.*
"J'écoute" – *I'm listening.*
"она жива. Он мертв. Это облегчит нашу миссию"– *She is alive. He is dead. That will make our mission easier.*
"Да. Принято" – *Yes. Acknowledged.*

CHAPTER 56

Alexandra, Paul and Collette remained at the hospital into the night. By late evening, Jean was out of the operating room and conscious but very groggy. His condition was serious but stable. He had lost a lot of blood and was weak as a result.

Paul wasn't going to leave Jean, Alexandra wasn't going to leave Paul, and Collette wasn't going to leave her mother. The prognosis had improved by the time the morning sun had eclipsed the night-lights so the three watchers decided to take taxis home for a shower and a bite to eat.

Paul returned to the hospital in a couple of hours and was heartened to find Jean conscious and talking. The patient's first question was about Alexandra and Collette. Paul assured him they were fine but concerned for his health. The shift nurse approached with a smile.

"She's kicking me out so you can get your rest, mon fils," said Paul. "I'll be back this afternoon during scheduled visiting hours. I love you."

At Jo's, he found all three ladies hovering over a pot of coffee like fortune-tellers over a crystal ball attempting to predict the foggy future.

"I'd hug you, Paul, but I ache in places I didn't know I had," smiled Alexandra. Jo performed an earnest surrogate hug. Collette appeared distressed about Jean's condition.

"How are you, Jo?" asked Paul. "When Jean briefed us in the parking lot yesterday, he said you had taken a hard fall and weren't up on your feet by the time he left with Collette to let me know about Alexandra's abduction."

"I'm okay. I was riding behind Alex when the car hit her and knocked Sophia over. It barely clipped my Harley's front wheel but I purposely put my bike on its side so as to avoid hitting her and slid to a stop. That was a first for me to engage in an unscheduled dismount but it reinforced my belief in wearing leather because I just got a few bruises, no road burn. Bikers don't say *ATGATT* – all the gear all the time – just for a lark. The ambulance arrived but I declined because I was walking without any severe pain or discomfort."

"An unscheduled dismount," Paul exclaimed. "That's a new term."

"Figuratively speaking, it hurts more if you fall off your bike as opposed to engaging in a dismount even if it is unscheduled," Jo chuckled. "I'd laugh more but it hurts."

Alexandra apologized to Paul for not mentioning earlier she had called Jo from the hospital and received an update. Jo confirmed she was on the mend but the bikes would need some TLC and a bit of touch-up paint. Jo had ridden her bike home and had taken the liberty of having Sophia transported to Bastille Harley-Davidson for an estimate on repairs. She had called ahead and left her phone number.

As Alexandra poured Paul a cup of coffee, she quietly enquired, "How's Suzette?"

"I don't know. She wasn't home all night and she still wasn't there by the time I left this morning. Her car was in the driveway and her cell phone was on the kitchen table so I don't think she's gone far. I checked her voice mail. She hadn't picked up any messages for several days, not even my call from the hospital about Jean. I'm mildly concerned only because she hasn't got this deep before but we all need to face up to our own choices. My focus and energy are with Jean, and you and Collette, and Jo."

"Jean helped save Maman's life twice and saved my life once.

How will I ever be able to repay him?" Collette asked Paul. "I'm indebted to him. Tell me, what I can do?"

"Well, I've an idea. You like crafts, especially crocheting. Your mother showed me some of your creative designs. Jean has a set of marble chess pieces he won at a national tournament when he was very young. They're his favourites but the box they came in fell apart years ago. He now carries them in a big bag but they're getting chipped. You could crochet a carrying satchel like a miniature saddlebag with a small pouch for each piece. His favourite colour is royal blue."

"I can do that," Collette replied excitedly. "I'll start now. Thank you so much. This will help me to take my mind off the horrible events from the warehouse and the awards ceremony. I mean, the award you received was wonderful. Well, you know what I mean. I need to apologize to him anyway for almost pummelling him when he barked at me for not staying outside. I feel so bad."

"I stopped in at the hospital and saw him just before I came over here. He was looking much better and was almost coherent. He asked about you and AV so I'm sure he'd be pleased if you paid him a visit. Visiting hours start at 3 p.m. Why don't you tell him just that, if you go up to see him. You could also ask him to help you create a webpage for your crafts. That will give him something to plan for when he gets out of the hospital. Right now, we should get something to eat. Why don't I take you all out for lunch?"

"There's a restaurant next to the café where we went with Jean," Collette replied. "Why don't we walk there?"

With unanimous agreement, they locked up the house and started to walk over.

Jo winked at Alexandra and announced quite loudly enough, "Collette and I will lead the way if you don't mind following."

Alexandra and Paul acknowledged what she was trying to do and had a chuckle.

The walk was at a slightly slower pace than usual as the Ladies of Harley nursed their stiff muscles. "I guess I'm not twenty-one anymore," Alexandra jokingly admitted.

"You're looking pretty good for twenty-two, madame. We should call the Harley dealership tomorrow to get a prognosis on Sophia now that Jean and the two of you are on the mend."

"I'm pretty sure the car just struck the rear fender which sent me into a tailspin, so I'd be surprised if Sophia was badly hurt. But tomorrow is soon enough. Where's Chuck?

"Marcel took the bike to his place for safekeeping. I called him this morning and asked if I could pick it up tomorrow. I'd like to drive over to the warehouse after lunch to pick up Jean's car as it's still in the parking lot. Could you drive Svelte and follow me back to Meudon?"

"Yes, I can do that. It would be good to view the warehouse in the safety of your company. That reminds me, I need to call Fred to set up a debriefing session. I'd appreciate it if you could come with me to fill in some of the details. I'd like Collette to talk to him about both Friday night and yesterday. I'm worried about her. She's talking, which means she's processing the events and that's good. But she is going around in circles rather than dealing with the events head on."

"Good idea. Of course I want to go with you. Can we set it up for late morning or early afternoon? That would give us time to check in with Jean before we go to Fred's office. We'll have to be quick because the head nurse is a tyrant when it comes to visiting hours."

"I'll call Fred after we eat and set that up. I'm pretty sure we can get priority booking with him."

⁂

AFTER THE MEAL, THEY WALKED BACK TO Jo's where Alexandra called Fred.

"I was about to call you, Alexandra, but you beat me to it," Fred replied. "I understand you've had an eventful weekend. How are you?"

"A bit worse for wear but otherwise fine. I acquired some bruises and dents to the bike's frame and a few to myself also. This will be a memorable weekend and not just for the rest and relaxation!"

"No doubt you will, *m'amie,* and that is why we should talk soonest," Fred suggested. "We need to complete the profile for Thon, and you and I need a debrief about the shooting."

"I agree. Can we meet tomorrow, say 10 a.m. at your office? I'd like you to spend some one-on-one time with Collette because she was present and is pretty shaken up. Do you mind if Paul joins me as the abduction and shooting also affected him? He was present in the warehouse. I'm not sure if you are aware of all the circumstances but Paul's son, Jean, was shot and is in hospital in a serious but stable condition. Also, I'd like to set up additional appointment for Collette to see you."

"I heard someone had been wounded but didn't know it was Paul's son. Yes, bring Paul along, if he wants to attend. And yes, I can see Collette tomorrow afternoon at 2 p.m."

"Thanks, Fred. I've already talked with Paul and Collette. They are looking forward to getting together with you. My brief encounter with Thon will provide more grist for the mill for our article. Primary research doesn't get more primary than this."

Capitaine Roland called just as Alexandra hung up, to set up a meeting for Friday. She was confident she'd be able to provide a synopsis by week's end. Dominique advised that all the players who attended last Friday's meeting of the minds would be present in addition to the CID Commandant who was spearheading the investigation. Commandant Parent from Counter-terrorist Unit would attend because of a confirmed connection between Thon and known Islamic terrorists associated with the neo-Nazis.

CID investigators had interviewed Alexandra, Paul and Collette by the time the sun had set. They had also briefly spoken with Jean before the head nurse escorted them out of his room.

On the way to pick up Jean's car at the warehouse, Alexandra expressed her concern about Francine Myette. "She makes my skin crawl. She's a black hatter if ever I saw one, but maybe not completely black. She's an enigma of sorts. We need to take Sir James's response to my query very seriously."

"We won't be revealing any information at this meeting. Instead, we'll just be briefed like everyone else. The meeting should just be about Thon and the outcome of the police investigation into his death. Why don't we observe Francine and debrief afterwards? If our LAPD deputy chief is present, you could take him up on his invitation for java to talk about Sophia's wounds and see where our fishing expedition with him goes from there. He might be in a position to affirm your sense about Francine. He seems to trust you, whether through his association with Maria or not, it doesn't matter. He might be open to your misgivings about Francine and appreciate your observations, so to speak."

"Good plan, partner."

The day ended with a sense of calmness and reassurance that the worst was behind them. Alexandra mused about the caveats her mother and grand-maman had repeated to her as she grew up. *"The truths of those times are masked in the mists of the Moselle."* She recalled that the words were oddly prophetic with ominous overtones at the time. But now, in retrospect, those sensations had been proven accurate in all respects.

Her mother's work in counterintelligence, terrorism and subversion with French Intelligence had lured Alexandra and others in her life into this deadly sphere. Whether she liked it or not, Alexandra had become entwined in the intricacies of global security and intelligence with the frequently lethal consequences as experienced by agents of the CIA and MI6, and others.

The white-hatted good guys had defeated the black-hatted bad guys this time. She and Paul agreed on a schedule. She would send a coded message to Sir James and call Jacques Moreau in Dieppe. Paul would call Sergeant Joseph Lortie in Montigny-lès-Metz. They would visit Paul's father to let him know Thon was history and Jean would soon be well enough to challenge him to a game of chess. And they would visit Father Luke on their next trip to Luxemburg. And maybe, just maybe, they could ease themselves into something akin to a peaceful retirement....

CHAPTER 57

Before formally starting the Friday afternoon meeting, Dominique privately mentioned to Paul, "You saved Alexandra's life but you pushed the safety envelope."

"What was I supposed to do?" he instantly replied. "Wait for Beau Geste and the French Foreign Legion to arrive, or John Wayne and the United States Marine Corps? I had the Harley cavalry with me and they did an excellent job of distracting the gunman according to Alexandra."

"You have a point, but please call sooner next time."

"What next time? Thon is confirmed dead. Without his apparent leadership, I doubt the gunman will be sticking around now that Alexandra has identified him and his profile has been distributed to every police officer in France and other jurisdictions through Interpol. Case closed. Retirement can't come quickly enough for me, for us."

"I've just got a feeling that you won't be retiring completely. The probability is higher that we'll be crossing paths in the future, Commandeur."

"Do you know something that I don't, Dominique? Will you be issuing me a company cell phone for 24/7 coverage with a bonus monthly pay cheque attached? I'm not aware of any mysterious mission on my radar to travel to interesting places to do interesting things with interesting people, unless you are."

"Not me specifically," she replied with a sheepish grin.

Turning to those assembled, she formally welcomed everyone who had been present the week before. She introduced Commandant Denis Richard, the lead investigator from CID.

"Let's start in chronological order first with the incident at the awards ceremony at the Élysée Palace, second with events at the warehouse in Versailles, and finally the findings of the follow-up investigation including information revealed by the interrogation of the self-declared neo-Nazi who was arrested at the awards ceremony. Commandant Richard, the floor is yours."

"Thank you, Dominique," Denis replied. After relating the events of Friday evening at the Élysée Palace and Saturday morning at the warehouse, he asked Paul and Alexandra if they had any details to add.

"You have been very thorough," Paul replied.

Alexandra nodded in concurrence with Paul.

"I'll now comment on the results of the investigation including the interrogation of the neo-Nazi. You will find this aspect of my briefing enlightening not just from the perspective of the criminal investigation into the deaths. You will also find it interesting from a strategic intelligence perspective as it links into terrorism and other broader implications on the international stage. Some details are still classified. Thus, they cannot be discussed here because they involve international security and intelligence agencies at a very high level with some of our friends from the CIA and MI6."

As planned, Alexandra and Paul watched Francine's response. They both noted a slight change in her stance when Denis mentioned CIA and MI6. Under the table, they tapped a confirmatory code on each other's hand.

"The fake server's name is Dieter Hans Ulrich. He is in custody and has been charged with murder and attempted murder. He claims to be a member of the Fourth Reich, a neo-Nazi organization with roots in the Third Reich. He has a tattoo on the lower right side of his neck with the old gothic letters 'VR', which stand for *Viertes Reich* or Fourth Reich. He stated he is a Lebensborn heir to the Thousand-Year Reich. His grandfather was supposedly a high-ranking member of the Nazi SS. He didn't mention his mother but if he was a child of the Lebensborn program then he probably wouldn't have known her identity. For those of you who don't know, the Lebensborn children were the outcome of a Nazi program established in 1935 to create a master race of pure, blond, blue-eyed Aryans. They were literally bred to be the elite of Hitler's Thousand-Year Reich. Ulrich stated that his membership of the Fourth Reich came with an initiation at the Wewelsburg Castle. This is where the Nazi SS received their training and initiation under Heinrich Himmler's control before and during the war. Ulrich went on at length about how the Fourth Reich is funded by stolen Nazi gold from the Third Reich and how their cause is linked to Muslim-grown jihadist terrorism in the Middle East. He bragged with an arrogant sneer, repeating several times: "Your enemy's enemy is your friend with reference to western democracy," specifically the United States and Western Europe being primary targets of the terrorists like the 9/11 attack on the Twin Towers in New York.

"I'd like to pause at this juncture," Dominique interjected. "Does anyone have any questions for Denis before we continue with the equally intriguing revelation of Thon's background? Note Denis cannot provide further details on some aspects because of the sensitivity re: national security."

Not seeing any questions, Dominique motioned to Denis to continue with the briefing.

"This is where the plot thickens," Denis remarked. "Thon's real name is Ludwig Rudolf Heydrich. Just as a side and with reference to Dieter Hans Ulrich, note that Ludwig also had the tattooed old Gothic initials 'VR' on the lower right side of his neck.

With Thon's identify confirmed, we were able to locate his residence, a farm just outside Saint-Avold. We unearthed the shallow grave of a female in a barn whom we believe was his wife. In the house we found newspaper clippings of the obituaries of the

Maquis victims. We also found the church program for Maria's funeral and reception; thereafter, the newspaper clippings of the obituary of Madame Deschaume, and the announcement of Dr. Bernard's award. So that's how Dieter Hans Ulrich got on the trail and ended up in the Grand Hall at the Élysée Palace. We also found documentation relating to Lieutenant Colonel Friedrich Rauch who was the head of the security police for Hitler's Reich Chancellery in 1941. You may recall that Rauch was the mastermind behind plans to transfer Nazi gold from the Reichsbank in Berlin to the supposed Alpine Fortress. Rauch had calculated the treasury of the Third Reich would fund the Fourth Reich. We need to follow up more on these documents.

"We have reason to believe Ludwig was born in Trier in the Saar region of Germany close to the French and Luxembourg borders in the mid to late 1920s. We haven't been able to confirm his exact date of birth yet. He was related to Reinhard Heydrich who created the SD, the Nazi Intelligence Agency and headed the Gestapo. Czech Resistance fighters killed Reinhard Heydrich in Prague in 1942. Ludwig idealized him and it is believed his assassination spurred Ludwig to kill members of the *Maquis*.

Ludwig joined the Hitler Youth in 1941. We suspect that he killed his parents and siblings in 1942 but that needs to be confirmed. Immediately thereafter, he moved to Lyon where he wangled his way into the French Resistance. His status with the Gestapo was elevated serendipitously when he saved the life of Klaus Barbie, the butcher of Lyon, by informing the SS of an assassination plot by the *Maquis* on Barbie's life.

"Thon idealized Barbie, who was considerably older. Their friendship grew when they discovered that their families were both from Trier. In addition, they both suffered abuse at the hands of their respective fathers who fought for Germany in the Great War and returned home as bitter, wounded veterans of the Verdun campaign. Their fathers dealt with their anger through alcohol and domestic violence. This fortuitous encounter allowed Ludwig to establish a broad network.

"With funding from Barbie, Ludwig moved to Toulouse where he started providing the SS with some true but also false intelligence about French Resistance movements. He established credibility with the French Resistance by providing them with some true but also false intelligence about German movements, all in the disguise of *le fantôme*.

"This is where the Ludwig-Barbie connection gets really interesting. According to OSS sources, Barbie was involved with the theft of French and other gold and its transportation to Bolivia among other clandestine locations. This was part of the Nazi Gold Master Plan of funding for the Thousand-Year Reich, and Ludwig was involved.

"After the war, the U.S. Army Counterintelligence Corp employed Barbie and other Nazi Party members in their counterintelligence agenda. The British also recruited him to provide information on the French Intelligence Service in the French zone of occupied Germany that they believed had been infiltrated by collaborators and communists.

Subsequently, Barbie was aided in his escape to Bolivia as an alleged CIA operative.

All along, Ludwig secretly maintained contact with Barbie. Ludwig disappeared off the radar screen around the time that Barbie moved to Bolivia.

"Marie had been working with a CIA agent and with an MI6 agent in their attempt to capture Thon, Ludwig. After he vanished, sources reported Barbie did not know what happened to Ludwig. We have reason to believe Barbie did know but was not prepared to divulge this information because Ludwig was by then the head of the clandestine Fourth Reich Party, Barbie's *alma mater*. Some loyalties do not change. Klaus Barbie took this information to his grave in 1991. We still don't know who the CIA or the MI6 agents were or even if they are still alive, which is doubtful."

Before continuing, Denis asked if there were any questions on what he had covered thus far. With no requests for clarification, he continued.

"In connection with our criminal case file, we do know Ludwig employed Fourth Reich Youth to find his victims, the female members of the *Maquis* and their daughters if they had any, as he had been trained to do as a member of the Hitler Youth. Ludwig would then personally administer the cyanide, his poison of choice. Ludwig learned about cyanide from his father who had been an amateur photographer and used cyanide in developing photographs.

"So, what can we conclude? First, the neo-Nazi movement under the banner of the Fourth Reich is alive with its Thousand-Year vision. It is active and it murders to achieve its goals.

"Second, intertwined with the Fourth Reich is a strong link to the stolen Nazi gold and other currency reserves moved after the Reichsbank was bombed in early February 1945. We have reason to believe both have links to Middle East Islamic terrorism today.

"And there you have it, ladies and gentlemen," Denis concluded.

"Thank you for that detailed briefing, Denis," Dominique responded. "It's been a long time coming but we finally have a conclusion to all those murders. Well done to everyone. As you can appreciate, the implications are far-reaching with tentacles in many regions. Although Ludwig is dead, the repercussions will keep reverberating."

As people began to leave the conference room, Alexandra asked Tom Hunt if he had time for java and a chat about Sophia.

"I certainly do and how is the 1972 classic? I understand it sustained a few dents and scratches."

"Indeed it did but it was delivered back to me this morning looking none the worse for wear."

"Well, I have some time tomorrow morning to drop by for a re-acquaintance if that's convenient."

"We should be up by 9 a.m. and prepared to receive visitors."

"What were your thoughts on the briefing?" Tom asked casually.

"It was a bit like a weather forecast – difficult to discern what is accurate," Alexandra commented.

"I concur with your astute observation! There can be diverse, perhaps conflicting perspectives. That is why your weather forecasting skills should not retire. Instead, you should consider employing your talents where they can be most effective. Major Mike and your mother found mutual benefit in their relationship. Perhaps you and I have more in common than riding classic Harleys. I believe Sir James would approve."

"A holiday on the south coast of England in the fresh sea air could well be in the cards."

"You've been quiet, Paul. What's your impression?" Tom asked.

"*Historia magistra vitae est* – history is life's mistress," he replied thoughtfully. "Cicero was correct. We have not learned from the mistress teacher; thus, war never ends. The search for the Nazi gold will keep us intertwined in the web which was woven before we set foot on this earth and may well do so for the foreseeable future and beyond."

"You're correct. The combination of your strategic wisdom and Alexandra's intuitive sensations will help to keep the wolves at bay. We three definitely need to chat," Tom concluded.

With that, each downed the remains of their coffee, and they stood up to leave.

"*À demain*, Tom," Alexandra gestured. "I look forward to seeing you in the morning, as will Sophia."

"I don't know about you, Paul, but I'm exhausted," she said as

Tom walked away. "Although I love your company, I'd appreciate it if you could just drop me off at Jo's. Can you join Tom and me in the morning? You and I should talk about how a business relationship with Tom might affect our white-hatted sleuth partnership, in addition to retirement plans."

"That's a date for tomorrow. I'm really drained too. This evening I just need to kick back and process all that information."

On his way home, Paul clearly saw he was living with someone he disliked, and not living with the person he wanted to spend the rest of his life with. He was about to make peace with his God and his Pope when his cell phone rang.

"Is this Dr. Paul Bernard?"

"Who is enquiring?"

"This is Capitaine Moreau of the Police Nationale Traffic Division."

"How can I help you, Capitaine Moreau?"

"Is your wife Suzette Bernard and does she drive a 1991 Renault?"

"Yes. What's happened?"

"I deeply regret to inform you that your wife has been killed in a single-vehicle accident. We need you to identify her body at the morgue."

CHAPTER 58

Paul texted Alexandra that he wouldn't be able to meet with her and Tom Hunt as planned. He was running late and wanted to see Jean before he came over.

He visited Jean to ensure he was doing well and then went to the morgue where he identified Suzette's body. He called her twin sister in Bolivia who said she wouldn't return for the funeral because she was working on another relationship. She had no idea where Yvon was. Paul texted Alexandra again and asked if she could meet him at the café by Jo's.

As he took in Suzette lying on the cold marble slab, he felt less than nothing. Not even numb. Nothing would mean that there once was something, numb that there once was feeling. The church vows required that he love and cherish, *until death us do part*. He questioned whether he had ever truly loved Suzette. To love and cherish were hollow words, even in death. He accepted responsibility for his decision to marry her. He concluded that Suzette eventually repulsed him. But she was the mother of his two sons. He felt less affection for Yvon as he grew more like his mother. In sharp contrast, he loved Jean fiercely. He was the son he and AV should have had, but never did and never would. Paul's country had acknowledged him for most honourable conduct. Yet honour was fleeting in his personal life.

He wondered if he could ever love and cherish AV. Was their relationship a charade? Was there only honour in walking away?

As Alexandra approached Paul in the café, she exclaimed cheerfully, "You beat me here. Sorry for being a bit late. Tom took an extra-long time getting reacquainted with Sophia. What's up?"

Paul looked up from his lukewarm coffee, his face ashen. "Suzette is dead. She was killed in a car accident yesterday."

Alexandra froze. She wanted to reach out to him, to hug him but that felt not appropriate under the circumstances. She wanted to say how sorry she was, but those words would be awkward and sound hollow. She was sorry, but Suzette's death freed him. Suzette had been an obstacle that could be overcome but for now her death was a spur in the path they had been travelling together since her mother's funeral. He would have to navigate this path without Alexandra, yet know she was there waiting for him. In the future, their paths could re-join if it was meant to be. Together with him at this moment she felt more alone than she had since receiving the news of her mother's death, and before that the news of the deaths of her uncle and aunt. Fear of abandonment momentarily occupied her mind. She hoped Paul knew how she was feeling but at the moment his need was greater than hers.

The background music in the café flowed over the quietness until Paul spoke. "I need to go and see Jean again, and this time tell him the news."

"Yes. Go to Jean. Would you like me to drive you?"

"Thanks, but no. I think I'll be all right. This has to be my journey."

"Call me."

Alexandra found herself running back to Jo's, not knowing if she was running away from a defined threat or running toward false security. Images of loneliness continued to overwhelm her. They were as vivid in this moment as when she was a child. Were her emotions prompted by the déjà vu of Montigny-lès-Metz? Was she being torn away from her puppy love a second time? Forever? The abyss of emptiness had a new depth.

"Oh my God," Jo exclaimed, "how horrible for Paul and you. I can only imagine how awful it must have been for the two of you to be together in that moment yet not be together. I can understand how awkward it must have been for you wanting to reach out to him but holding back."

Alexandra could only respond with stunned, vacant silence.

"Can I suggest I be your objective subjective intermediary? I can call Paul and be there for him on your behalf until the hyper-extreme of the circumstance calms, however long that might be. I'm sure he'll understand and not be offended."

"I'd appreciate that, Jo," Alexandra said quietly.

"Let me call him now, then."

Alexandra could only nod.

Jo made arrangements to meet Paul at the hospital. She was seated by him in the visitors' cafeteria in half an hour.

"I can't imagine how you are feeling, Paul. I can only offer my support. I think you know how awful Alexandra is feeling right now. She wants to be with you but also appreciates the awkwardness. Just know she is ready to come to you when you are ready."

"Thank you, Jo. You're a dear friend. I'll call in the fullness of time. Right now, I don't know where I am… where we are. I just need to work through all this stuff. I haven't told Jean yet and won't until I'm confident he'll be able to deal with it. He hasn't asked why his mother hasn't come to visit him. I think he knows she won't or wouldn't even if she was still alive."

"All right, I won't wait for you to call. Instead I'll call you every day until you tell me to get lost." Jo gave him a big hug and said, "This hug is from Alexandra, and also from Collette and me."

As soon as he left, she called Alexandra to say she was coming home.

"Thanks, Jo. I owe you another one."

Jo's heart sank as she reflected on Paul's words: "Right now, I just don't know where I am… where we are." He had not reciprocated when she hugged him. He had not used Alexandra's name.

Jo interpreted it to mean his relationship with Alexandra was in jeopardy.

⁂

BY THE TIME JO WALKED IN THE door, Alexandra had told Collette about the accident and said that Jean did not know yet. So, if she was going to visit, she'd have to put on a happy face.

"We need to talk about something else, dear. Life has been crazy since your grand-maman's death. I've constantly been asking you to be extra vigilant and you have been very good about keeping your radar up. I need to explain why. What I am about to tell you will be very upsetting, as it has been for me."

As she gave Collette the letter that Maria had left in the safety deposit box, she said, "Read this. Afterwards we'll go for a drive. You'll understand."

Collette read the letter and then reread it before looking up at her mother, stunned by the revelation.

Alexandra explained, "The dead man in the warehouse was Thon. He was bent on killing you and me. That was the threat and that was why I asked you to be careful. The man who tried to poison us at the awards ceremony was working for Thon. He's in jail and facing charges for murdering the person whose uniform he was wearing and attempting to murder both of us. That threat has now been neutralized. The other man in the warehouse who had the gun and shot Thon and Jean is on the run from the police. There's a warrant out for his arrest for the murder of Thon, the attempted murder of Jean and the unlawful confinement of me so the threat level from him is low."

"How did you deal with all that, Maman, and how do you hold it together? I thought it was just another one of your crazy cases. And Paul and your relationship way back then, now I understand what the two of you have been going through since the funeral. I've certainly picked up on that. And now with the death of his wife, where are the two of you?"

"Let's go for a drive, dear. I want to show you your grand-papa's grave."

At the cemetery they knelt by the headstone and read the words that Maria had had etched. Alexandra explained she was going to have her mother's ashes laid to rest beside Philip's grave now that Thon was dead.

On the way back to Jo's, Alexandra explained she had called André to let him know she would be living in Luxembourg and would be filing for divorce. He indicated he would not be contesting the divorce. Alexandra didn't tell Collette what else her father had said in response: "There wasn't anything between us anyway and there never has been. I got what I wanted, a son to carry on the family name." That caustic response was hurtful enough for Alexandra to hear, Collette didn't need to be exposed to such callousness.

"I suspected as much, Maman. To be honest, I can't remember feeling any warmth from my father, ever. In fact, I've felt a greater connection to Paul than I had with my father or Marc. I can't remember a time when the two of them have been anything but cold and distant. It's almost as if Paul was supposed to be my father all along. Now I want to develop that relationship and I want the two of you to be happy. God knows you deserve it, Maman, after what you've been through."

"Thank you, ma cherie. You don't know how much that means to me to hear that. It's pretty obvious Paul and I are very attracted to one another and have been since we first met all those years ago in Montigny-lès-Metz. Once he gets over Suzette's death, I hope we'll be together. Perhaps you should tell him you want to develop a closer relationship next time you see him – maybe say you consider him a cherished uncle. I think he'd really appreciate it, especially now."

"I'll do that, Maman. In fact, I'll send him a text message right now and ask to meet, just the two of us. I'll give him a big hug from both of us."

⁂

JEAN WAS STARTING TO EXHIBIT SYMPTOMS OF cabin fever after two weeks under the hawk-eyed supervision of the senior nurse who had clearly earned the epithet of *sergeant-major* from all the visitors. He was released with the proviso he not be left alone for an additional two weeks. Paul, Alexandra and Collette made those assurances.

On the Sunday after his release, he attended the brief private funeral service for his mother. Paul was overwhelmed by the expression of condolences extended in so many cards mailed to the church and his home from his friends and colleagues. He found it interesting that only a couple came from Suzette's side of the family. No friends or even acquaintances appeared. How different it was in comparison to Maria's funeral attended by over one hundred, some from half a world away. Both were women with similar opportunity, but they were far from equal.

The irony of grief is that it has shown me what is important in life, he thought. *I shall not assume the weight of Suzette's death.* He took a breath as he made peace with himself, the Pope and his God.

Like Alexandra, he now had the onerous task of replying to the condolences. Two cards particularly touched him. One was from Sir James who extended a personal invitation to walk in the *jardin anglais* and be cleansed by the coastal breezes. The other was from Father Luke who offered his personal blessing and invited him to join his congregation. Tom Hunt left an open invitation for lunch and conversation.

⁂

COLLETTE HAD CROCHETED THE SADDLEBAG FOR JEAN'S chess set in royal blue and now presented it to him as a welcome home gift. After playing a few games of chess with him, she proudly admitted to her mother he was a master champion. There were no qualifying 'buts' which had accompanied her first assessment of Jean after their initial meeting.

Jean tutored her as he did Alexandra in the strategy and tactics of chess on each occasion they stayed with him. He even explained to Alexandra what Paul's weaknesses were so when she played against him she would know how to counter his moves. They concluded conspiracy was necessary and appropriate under circumstances like this.

"In the age of chivalry and *courtoisie*," Jean explained to Alexandra, "men and women of nobility learned to play chess because the game gave them a venue where they could engage with their feelings through their kings and queens and castles and knights. This provided the ideal metaphor for the ritual of making love. The rules and strategies of the game were intended to ensure that etiquette protocols were followed between the sexes for courtship."

What he hadn't realized was that Alexandra was explaining the details of these private lessons in this seductive art and science of the game of chess to Collette who was a quick learner. Although Collette knew she would probably never win a game against Jean, she could certainly play the game as it should be played. Alexandra would do the same with Paul as her worthy opponent, her puppy love.

⁂

WHILE COLLETTE WAS ON ONE OF HER shifts supervising the patient and practicing her newly acquired skills in the game of chess, Paul and Alexandra took the opportunity to visit Paul's father. As they walked into his room, he perked up and posed a cheerful question, "What have the two of you been up to? It has to be good because your auras are beaming as I have never seen them before."

"The best news ever, Papa. Thon is dead and it was Alexandra who drove the wooden holly stake into his heart. She slayed the dragon, singlehandedly."

"Not quite singlehandedly," Alexandra interjected. "Our prince came to the rescue." After explaining what had happened, she lamented that her father and mother would be smiling from ear to ear had they been here.

"But they are here, *ma chérie,*" he replied. "They are here in you and I can see them in your presence. And how is my Jean?"

"He is recovering at home, Papa, and will be up to visit you soon to beat the master at a game of chess, so you'd better sharpen your skills."

At the news, Paul and Alexandra could see his spirits lift. The mischievous twinkle was back in his eye which Paul had not seen since before his mother's death. His father was giggling with excitement. His jubilant smile lightened the room. They didn't want to spoil the occasion with the news of Suzette's death but they sensed he knew. That formal pronouncement could wait for another visit.

"Will you bless an old man with a kiss, Princess Alexandra? You are a most beautiful and radiant princess!"

"I would be honoured, Sir Knight," she replied as she graciously gave him a kiss on the cheek and a little hug.

Paul followed with his own expression of love and whispered, "The Pope is not always right, Papa. All is getting better."

"I know, mon fils, I know. I told you before that the two of you were destined to be together, and together you would triumph over evil," he said. As he did, he reached for Paul's hand and whispered, "Everything all right, Paul?"

Paul replied, "It's getting better."

In a cheerful voice he ordered, "Now go and leave me to muse in gleeful exuberance on the knowledge that our princess has slain the dragon."

Observing Paul and his father at this moment caused Alexandra to reflect on the Eurail trip she had taken from Amsterdam to Luxembourg to attend her mother's funeral. She had not cried when she heard the news of her mother's death. She was numbed then. For the first time in her life, she had to face the reality of loneliness. This had been her greatest fear. She had been alone as a child, alone in her marriage and alone in her career. Now, for the first time in her life, she was not alone. With Paul, she had a partner, a soul mate. She would never again have to fight and slay the dragons by herself. Or would she? Her *shrew* paused.

Paul had called Sergeant Lortie in Montigny-lès-Metz and informed him of Thon's death. Squirrelling the file away from the malicious jaws of the bureaucratic paper shredder, as Sergeant Lortie had described his secretive conduct, had contributed to solving the case. For his efforts, he would quietly receive a well-deserved award for diligence and conduct above and beyond the call of duty. Alexandra had notified Jacques Moreau in Dieppe. He too would be acknowledged without fanfare for his contribution to the successful resolution of this case.

⇹

BY THE TIME JEAN WAS BACK TO work part-time, Paul had attended to the most pressing estate matters. Jean saw this change – and the financial boost that had come with his new position – as an opportunity to formally move out of his parent's house and purchase his own home in the suburbs. He enjoyed the Paris nightlife but felt drawn to the quietness of the country to recharge his batteries. He didn't mind joining other commuters on the Metro. If nothing else, coming this close to death made him realize he needed to bring balance to his life. His long hours of working had contributed to the breakdown of his previous relationship. If he was going to commit to a relationship with Collette, he'd need to change.

Alexandra advised him on real estate matters and by the time he was back to work full-time, he was the proud owner of a single-dwelling house not far from where he grew up in Meudon. Collette presented him with a Bichon Frise puppy. He named it MV for Maria Vanessa, Collette's grand-maman's name. Jean reckoned this was a wise relationship investment decision. His new neighbour had two Shih Tzu puppies so the three could play together while Jean was at work.

Paul was torn between staying in Paris with Jean and his papa, and moving to Luxembourg closer to his new business partner. With Jean now in his own home and able to keep vigil over his grand-papa, whose condition was inexplicably improving, Paul could join Alexandra on her trips to Paris for visits.

He and Alexandra met with Father Luke at their first opportunity and advised him Thon's murderous rampage was over. Father Luke would communicate this to his parishioner. Father Luke's gratification was expressed in a special blessing accompanied by a laying on of hands on both Alexandra and Paul. They sensed he was aware of their re-union and commitment to one another and to their new parish. They left with the impression Father Luke would not judge lest he who cast the first stone be judged.

On the advice of his personal real estate agent who had years of experience in the Luxembourg housing market, Paul purchased a storefront property in the old city. He had it renovated into a new photography studio at street level, with a spacious apartment upstairs. There was ample room for Svelte and Chuck in a garage that had been converted from an adjacent secure storage area.

At the same time as Paul was moving into his new home, Alexandra's real estate agent had called to confirm an offer made on the house on rue Michel Welter. Her counteroffer was accepted. On the closing day, she and Paul walked over for one last inspection of the repairs.

"Would you take some last photos of the place, Paul? I'd like to keep them as a memory of where my life began and where the tentacles of this caper intertwined in our lives. I can now talk about those times without fear of reprisal."

Paul registered his new business as "Black Hat Photography." This was his first official photo shoot. The frames of Alexandra standing on the front steps reminded him that beauty and passion are nature's tools for survival, because we will protect what we fall in love with.

Other photos of the house were good but pedestrians on the fringes of some frames were a distraction. One in particular showed a short middle-aged man walking by 47, rue Michel Welter and turning to look at the house. There was something ominous about his profile which showed his owlish horn-rimmed glasses accentuating what appeared to be dark bags under his eyes. Roger, the rotund grey-haired neighbour, could be seen looking with a startled expression at this man from behind the sheer curtains in his living room, echoing his observation of Thon on that murderous day.

As they walked toward the old city, Alexandra enquired, "Are we fine?"

"We're good," Paul replied as he put his arm around her shoulder. "Why do you ask?"

"You are a bit distant at times. Like Peter Pan off in Neverland."

"Still processing stuff."

⁂

"Bonjour." – *Hello.*

"J'écoute." – *I'm listening.*

"Я буду на связи. Мы установим микрофон." – *I have been in contact. We will instal a microphone.*

"Да. Принято" – *Yes. Acknowledged.*

À suivre ...

To be continued...

Manufactured by Amazon.ca
Acheson, AB